I Confess 2

Carol Ann Culbert Johnson

- Other Books –

By

Carol Ann Culbert Johnson

"I Confess"

"Rejection"

"Articles for the Soul"

"Torn Between Two Lovers"

"Best Best Friends" (coming soon)

Acknowledgments

To My Family and Friends,

To my co-workers at the Beverly Center in Chicago, Illinois,

To my co-workers in the Walk-In-Care Department of the Beverly Center, the PSR's, nurses, doctors, and radiology technicians.

To all the readers who purchased this book.

A Special thanks to my editor, Joanne Benham, who is the best editor in the world;

To my very best friend, in this entire universe, TONY, without your friendship, love and support, writing would just be a dream for me. I love you to the depths of my soul!

To the fans of *I* Confess,

who were eager for the sequel. May you enjoy it, and comments are

welcomed at greeniconfessbooks@yahoo.com

DEDICATION

To my Heavenly Father, for the Gift of writing; without

His gift, this book would not be possible!

***

To my mother, ANNIE BELL CULBERT, who encouraged me to

Pursue my writing; who gave me the courage, and the

Words of wisdom to believe in my dreams,

And never let anyone tarnish them.

I miss you mother, I love you mother, and I thank you

For your support, and your love!

Table of Contents

"I know my husband is having an affair," Ada said. "He comes dragging his sorry butt home in the early hours of the morning and tells me that he's been working all that time. But when I call his office, all I ever get is his answering machine. Oh, he's smooth; I'll give him that. When I asked him why no one answered the telephone, he said he spends a large portion of his day in conference and needs his secretary, so there's no one available to answer it."

I glanced at Ada Turner, a 45-year-old sister who was eager to save her marriage to her handsome, 45-year old attorney husband at any cost, and then looked at the floor, unsure of what to say. I knew her husband was having an affair, but I didn't know how to tell her.

"Follow him," Fallon said. "I do it all the time to my James. I think he's cheating on me, but so far I haven't caught him doing anything wrong. As much as I hate to admit it, we wives can't trust our husbands. Those are the sad facts."

Ada shook her head. "Fallon, I think its Donald's secretary. Alexis Taylor is only twenty-five years old. I can tell by the way she smiles at him that she wants him. He probably struts around like a rooster knowing this sweet young thing wants him and not giving a thought to his desperate housewife who has nothing to do all day but worry about who he's sleeping with."

"Maybe you should get a job," Fallon said. "I know you want to stay at home with your children, Ada, but all three of them are in school now and you're bored out of your mind. I don't know how you do it."

"Are you crazy?" Ada said. "I don't want to work. That's why I searched for a man who wanted a stay-at-home wife. Donald is insistent on me taking care of him and our children. I'm working a full-time job, thank you both very much. I just think there's more to me than just being a housewife."

"If you don't want a job, maybe you can go back to school on a part-time basis. I remember you mentioning that you always wanted to be a court reporter or paralegal. I think we all need something to fall back on should we ever need to support ourselves, which could happen if one of our husbands found him a young black bimbo, thank you so much."

"I have money saved in my own private bank account," Ada said. "Donald is very generous concerning money. I could easily afford my own apartment if the bastard decided to leave me for this woman. I'm going to find the bitch and she's going to wish she had never been born. There's no way I'm going to divorce my husband, and get a job. I loathe working. It's completely out of the question."

We three desperate housewives hung out when we could to discuss our lives, but mostly we talked about our men. My husband Mark was 53, ten years older than me, and seemed to have lost all interest in sex. I sometimes wondered if his age might be a factor, but when Mark and I met a few years ago, he was sexually active. Since we've married, he's been taking me for granted. I found it impossible to be faithful to him because he wasn't taking care of my needs.

And then there was Fallon, also 43. She was married to a 56 year-old real estate tycoon who already had five grown children from a previous marriage. He didn't care if he had any more children, which suited Fallon fine. She preferred to devote all her energy to her flourishing fashion designing career.

"You have to do what's right for you," I pointed out. "I love my paralegal job. I love the challenges I face every day when I go in and it's a good thing I do. It takes two of us working to pay the bills. There's no way I can quit my job. Besides, since I only work a four-day week, I have three free days to do anything I want."

The three of us lived next door to each other so there was little that happened to any of us that wasn't noted by another. The Marynook area on the south side of Chicago was very quiet and most of our neighbors in our little cul-de-sac were black. I spoke to my friends and their husbands almost every day as we each went our various ways. Today we were at Fallon's house, a beautiful five-bedroom Colonial, sitting on the screened-in back porch, sipping ice-cold lemonade and enjoying the cool breeze that wafted over us, helping to dispel the ninety-degree heat.

"I have to go home and find something to cook for dinner," Ada said. "Donald wants a home-cooked meal every day even though he's not there to eat it half the time. Well, it's too hot to cook much today. He's getting beans and hot dogs tonight."

"I hardly cook for my husband," Fallon said. "He has so many evening meetings that he winds up eating out most days. By the time he gets home, all he wants to do is make love to his gorgeous wife." She emphasized her words by standing up and twirling in a circle, showing off her truly stunning figure, before she collapsed back into her wicker chair. "My husband loves my size two body but he's told me a few times that it was all right if I gained some weight. Can you believe that man?"

"James is a trip," I said. "You're lucky to have him. Most men only want their women to be thin. Now you're telling us that James wants you to put on weight, but you better be careful. If you get too damn big he'll be divorcing your ass."

"You're right about taking care of your body," Ada said bitterly. "Look how faithful my husband is being to my size six body. When I find this sister bimbo there's going to be hell to pay. Why do they grab onto the married men? Lord knows there are enough men out there willing to take anything a woman offers. Maybe they think since a married man has already made a commitment once, she can get him to divorce his wife and make a commitment to her. That's the only explanation I've found."

I didn't say anything during Ada's diatribe. I knew I was guilty of enticing a married man, but I didn't want to break up his marriage. I just wanted more sex than my husband could provide. After all, we women have needs, just like men. Once again, I wished Mark appreciated me more. I was a plus size sister and proud of it, and Mark told me that he wanted a woman who had some ass and breasts on her. Why didn't he love me enough to realize I had needs too? "Men are going to cheat," I reasoned. "I think we just need to ignore their infidelity."

"I agree on that one," Fallon said. "I'm going to let you two in on a little secret of mine. I've got two men on the side. The old hubby just can't keep me happy in bed and I love the variety. I'm getting all my dreams and fantasies fulfilled."

I was stunned. It was like Fallon had read my mind. I had no idea that she and James had been having trouble in the bedroom. They always seemed so focused on each other when our families got together. Ada was peering at her and shaking her head. "Women like you cause women like me to commit murder. We do everything we can for our men, and this is the thanks we get. Why are you really cheating on James? Don't give me that bullshit that he can't take care of your needs. I've listened to you bragging too many times to buy that story."

"Because its fun and men do it," Fallon laughed. "I guess it's the thrill of doing something so bad and not getting caught. Do you think I believe that James is out there working all the time? No way. Sometimes he comes home and I can just smell another woman on him. But I can't really complain because screwing another woman seems to be foreplay for him. When he comes to me from another woman's bed, it's like he's taken a few of the little blue pills, He just wears me out, especially if I've just left his buddy George, who is really kinky in bed. You two should try it sometime. No reason for the men to have all the fun. Why not play the men's games and beat them at it? Let them find out that we're capable of playing their little games too."

"I don't agree," Ada snapped. "I love Donald, and wouldn't dream of cheating on him. Why can't women and men be faithful to one another? I just don't understand why there is a need for games. If Donald wants to be free then he needs to ask me for a divorce? In fact, I may try and see if we can talk it out tonight."

Fallon shook her head. "You can talk all you want sister, but he's just going to deny it. You need to catch his ass."

"Why don't we just change the subject?" I asked. "I'm sure we can discuss other things besides our husbands."

"What else is there to talk about," Ada said. "The children are fighting all the time and they're getting on my nerves. Saturdays are hell on wheels. The fifteen-year-old thinks she's grown and can talk to me any way she wants. I caught her going out of the house wearing the shortest skirt you've ever seen. When she argued about changing it, I slapped her face and she had the audacity to pull her hand back like she was going to slap me back."

"I'd have kicked her ass into next week," Fallon snapped. "Let a child of mine try to hit me. That's just another confirmation that I made the right decision when I elected not to have children. My sister's sixteen-year-old told her mother the other day that she was responsible for bringing her into the world and it was her job to take care of her until she was grown up."

"I'm glad my daughter is grown now," I said. "She was truly a pain in my ass growing up, and she still gets on my nerves. Legally I don't have to worry about her any more, but she still calls me about all her problems and expects me to take care of them for her."

"What time is it?" Ada asked. "I don't want Donald actually coming home on time tonight and then bitching because the dinner isn't on the table at six o'clock. If his dinner is even five minutes late, he makes the whole evening miserable for everyone. I don't know why I love that man."

"You don't love him Ada. You're just afraid to face life on your own, without a man to back you up," Fallon said. "You don't have enough faith in yourself to believe that you can take care of yourself and your children. We women need to realize that we don't need a man to make our lives worthwhile. We sound like three desperate house-wives sometimes."

"Then why in the hell did you get married, Fallon?" Ada asked. "Your business is a great success and, by your own admission, you've got three men on your string. You could be free doing what you want to do, not being accountable to anyone. I don't get it. Why marry in the first place and then stay married for ten years if you don't want to be tied down?"

Fallon frowned. "The idea of marriage is a fairy tale for women," she said thoughtfully. "We dream of walking down the aisle of love and spending the rest of our lives with a man because we've been taught that every woman needs a man. We're afraid that if we don't find him, we'll wind up old and lonely. When we reach our thirties and still haven't found that perfect someone, we get desperate, thinking that no man is going to want us and our far-from- perfect bodies. We need to break out of that mold. Look at the three of us. We're all different sizes, but each of us has a body to take pride in. But we still moan and groan and worry that our man is going to find someone smaller and better looking than us.   My friend Janey is another very successful designer, but she can't find love. She feels she has to settle for an old man because he's the only one that will talk to her. How sad is that?"

"I agree," I said. "If I hadn't found Mark, I'd be a lonely woman, and not even a housewife. We lived together for two years, and even though we broke up, we kept in touch. When he told me that he couldn't live without me, I told him to prove it, and we got married three years ago."

"Are you cheating on him?" Ada asked. "Or is he down in the bedroom? You know age doesn't mean a damn thing when you have it going on. I dated a man ten years older than me, and he was wilder in bed than I was."

I frowned. "Mark has been ill a lot lately, but he gives me all the loving I need and then some." Why was I lying to her? I can't remember the last time my husband made love to me. Mark's daily routine was go to work, come home, fix dinner and fall asleep in front of the television. I'm lucky if he even knows I'm in the house.

"Are we three happy desperate housewives or what?" Fallon asked. "I'm very happy because I'm doing the things in my life that make *me* happy. Life is too short to be so miserable. I think you should find a man, Ada, and get your groove on and then some. Why not taste the forbidden fruit, just once?"

"I'd never cheat on my man because I believe in God, and I have morals. If I find out he's cheating on me, then it's time to move on. I don't want a cheating husband."

Fallon shook her head. "You're going to cause yourself a lot of unwanted pain and suffering taking that attitude. Just ignore his screwing around and find someone to take care of your needs or hire an investigator and get the goods on him. Then you can get a nice chunk of change from him in the divorce settlement."

"It's after five," I pointed out. "Don't you need to get home and fix that supper Donald won't be home to eat?" I asked Ada. I could have kicked myself for saying such a thing. What was wrong with me?

"You're so right about that," Ada said angrily. "My husband is probably screwing his whore."

"I think we need to break out the Jack Daniels and make a toast to ourselves," Fallon said. "The three most beautiful desperate housewives in Marynook," she declared.

"Here, here," I cried.

"Let me have a quick one before I leave to help me handle my lying husband tonight," Ada said. "Or maybe I shouldn't drink anything. I might find it too hard to keep myself from cutting off his balls or slapping the shit out of him. Or maybe both, preferably while his little whore is there so I can give her some of the same treatment. I want to make them suffer to the ends of the earth."

I stared down at the floor.

Five minutes later the three of us were getting drunk, all thought of fixing anyone's dinner flown out of our heads. I welcomed the numbing feeling creeping over my body.

The orgasms kept coming, my body shaking uncontrollably as the pleasure rolled through me. I was screaming out Donald's name while his tongue, buried deep inside me, made lewd slurping noises as my vagina contracted spasmodically around it. I had tried getting my husband to give me some oral pleasure, but he was just not interested. If he loved me, which he claimed he did most of the time, then he'd be trying to please me in bed. This man was pleasing me and he was not my husband. "Don't stop," I ordered. "Harder, use your teeth too. Bite that little bud."

It was ten minutes before he entered me, and started pumping, long slow strokes at first and then deeper and harder as his own orgasm approached. I closed my eyes and inhaled the intoxicating scent of aroused male, which pushed me ever closer to my next orgasm. I couldn't even remember how many I'd had.

He continued to pump, faster and faster, until he reached the brink and then tumbled over, screaming my name while I felt the rhythmic pulsing of his manhood as he spurted his seed into the condom buried in me. Breathless, he collapsed across my body, completely spent, our bodies still intimately connected as we tried to catch our breath. Finally he rolled to his side, pulling me into his arms to hold me tightly against him. Sex with him was so good. Why couldn't my husband please me like this?

Fifteen minutes later, I forced myself to meet his eyes as I told him, "We have to end our affair, baby. I'm so sorry but your wife suspects something is going on, and she's going to follow you. I don't want her to catch us."

"Baby, I love you, and I need you. Your hijinks in bed boggle my mind."

"What about your skinny little wife? Why would you want to screw my overweight ass when you can screw her?"

"My wife and you are two completely different people baby so let's not discuss her. When we're together, I feel so good. No one else has ever made me feel like you do. I can't let you end our relationship. I'll love you forever."

"Are you going to leave your wife for me?"

"Are you going to leave your husband for me?"

I stared at him thoughtfully. Would I leave Mark and our marriage just because I found someone who was better in bed than he was? Could I bear to see the hurt in Mark's eyes if I did it? Mark was always teasing me about sleeping around but he didn't really believe it. He had enough male ego to believe that he was the best stud ever. Did our years together count for anything? These were questions I knew had to be answered, and soon.

"Let's just continue our relationship the way it is," he said. "I'm hard for you again, baby. No one has ever affected me this way. Turn over on your stomach so I can massage your back. I know that will get you going again. I'm sure there's something you can do for me too."

He wanted me to perform oral sex. I'm a pro at that because it's the only thing Mark really enjoyed, although he was very reluctant to reciprocate. It took him forever to reach his orgasm, but from the moans that filled the room, I suspected that he considered it time well spent. I closed my eyes as Donald began massaging my back, feeling myself begin to heat up as he dug his hands deep into my back, soothing the tenseness from my muscles. His mouth and tongue soon replaced his hands as he slowly moved down my back, not neglecting any part of me as he slowly made his way down to my ankles, where he stopped and then began the slow ascent back up my legs, pausing at my knees to press my legs apart as he licked the inside of my thighs, working his way to my innermost being. He was a master at making love, and liked nothing better than oral sex, although Ada refused him that pleasure. She didn't know what she was missing. I felt another climax approaching as Donald's skilled tongue continued to work its magic and then I went over the edge, screaming as the pleasure sensations rippling through me shook my body. I had barely come down from my high when I felt an intense pain stab through me as Donald entered me from behind, pausing to let my body adjust to the feeling of him in my hitherto unexplored cavity.

"Just relax, baby," he said. "I'm not going to move until you feel comfortable." While he spoke, he reached under me, slipping his fingers between my legs, massaging my bud until I felt myself relaxing and letting Donald slip all of his manhood inside. The feeling of fullness was unbelievable but as Donald continued rubbing, I felt the first stirrings of desire and soon I was slamming back against him as he pistoned into me like a jackhammer. We reached our climax together, both of us crying out, and Donald slipped out of me, his mouth covering mine as his tongue probed, setting up a wild dance. I could never leave this man. Never in my life had I felt as much pleasure as he brought to me. I felt his manhood hardening and he entered me again, and we rode a cloud of heated bliss together. My body was so hot; I thought the sheets would catch fire as we continued our wild ride. It was another hour before we finally got dressed and climbed into our separate cars to go home to our spouses. I was so disappointed.

"You're looking like a glowing queen," a voice said in my ear. "Have you been sleeping around on your hubby?"

I opened my eyes to see Mark standing next to the bed carrying a tray of delectable smelling food. I was practically drooling. When I got in last night, I was too exhausted to eat and not looking forward to dealing with Mark before I went to bed, although my sister Shirley had agreed to cover for me if necessary. Luckily he was snoring like an elephant and never even heard me come in. Now here he was, serving me breakfast in bed. Mark knew how to cook and food was my weakness. I sometimes wondered if he fed me so much food in an effort to make me so fat that no man would ever look at me.

I stared at the platter of scrambled eggs and cheese surrounded by crispy, thick-sliced bacon and sausages. A separate plate held a pile of lavishly buttered toast, a small bowl of strawberry jam on the side. I smiled as I took a deep breath, inhaling the heavenly aromas. "It smells wonderful honey. How did you know I'd be so hungry?"

I sat up in bed as he handed me the tray, noticing that he had made me coffee instead of the diet soda I preferred. However, I wasn't going to say something that could spoil this wonderful meal. "What's on your agenda today? I thought since it was Saturday we could go to the beach."

"I'm going to hang out with my boys today, baby. Remember I told you Mark Jr. was moving, and we're going to help him. I'll be over there all day, and then I'll be too tired to do anything but take a shower and go to bed. We can go to the beach tomorrow, I promise."

I frowned as I bit into a piece of bacon, savoring the salty, smoky taste. This always happened. I wanted to do something with Mark and he always had other plans. I knew that on Sunday he would find another excuse for us not going out. I had seen it happen over and over. Maybe I just should just tell Mark the truth so we could each move on.

"Are you okay staying by yourself today honey? We'd love to have you come along if you'd like."

I laughed. "I'm sure I'd just be in the way."

"I promise tomorrow is just for us babe. I love you. Enjoy your breakfast. I want to finish moving as early as I can and get back home. There's a good movie on cable I'd like to watch tonight."

I smiled up at him. He really did try to be a good husband and father. Sometimes it was really tough. "Have a nice day, and give my love to the boys."

"I will." He kissed my cheek, and left me sitting in the middle of the bed, my enormous breakfast spread before me. I can't remember the last time Mark kissed me on the lips. I removed the tray, setting it on the bed as I hurried to the window to watch Mark get into his car and drive off. I caught a movement from the corner of my eye and looked over at Fallon's house to see her and James standing on the porch kissing like two teen-agers in the throes of first love. For some reason I wished it were Mark and me kissing. I loved him so much, and sometimes I wondered why. If he ever found out about my affair, our marriage would be over. I felt torn in two. On one hand, I wanted to tell Mark and get it all out in the open, even though it would destroy our marriage. The other side of me wanted things to go on as they were. I had a nice, considerate husband that I truly did love who cooked me wonderful meals and I had a dynamite lover who fulfilled all my other needs.

We were all at Ada's house this time, and for some reason I was feeling very uncomfortable. Perhaps it was because Ada had been staring at me for the longest time, this weird look on her face. It suddenly dawned on me that the cat was out of the bag and that perhaps I should get the hell out of Dodge, I stood up abruptly, saying to my friends, "I'm going to go home. I'm not feeling well. I'll talk to you all tomorrow."

"What's wrong Maude?" Fallon asked, peering at me a little drunkenly over her third drink. "You don't look too good. Sit back down and have a drink. That will perk you right up."

Ada, who had drunk as much as Fallon, said to me in a cold voice, "Sit down, Maude. You're not going anywhere until we have a little talk."

I stared at her, and slowly resumed my seat.

"What's going on?" Fallon asked. "I'm not too drunk to miss the tension in this room."

Ada stood up, walked over to the door and made sure that it was locked. When she turned back to face me her right hand was clutching a gun. What in the hell was she doing with a gun?

"Holy shit! Is that a gun?" Fallon screamed. "What are you doing?"

"I'm going to shoot my husband's bimbo and then I'm going to shoot him. I want him to see her fat body laying dead on the floor," Ada snapped. "What did you think I was going to do?"

"Well she's not here," Fallon said. "Put that gun away. You're making me nervous. Did you follow your husband like I said?"

"I hired a private investigator, and he caught everything on tape. Let's all watch it together," she said, a nasty smile aimed my way.

I panicked, knowing that my settled, easy life was over.

The tape came on and I stared at Donald and me, lost in the throes of passion. I couldn't believe she had it on tape.

Fallon was shocked, gasping as she recognized me and turned, hatred glaring in her eyes. "How could you do something like that to Ada?" she cried.

I was watching Ada, who stared in rapt fascination as Donald buried his face in me.

"Please turn it off," I cried. The tears were falling swiftly now. "I'm so sorry. We didn't mean for it to happen."

"How did it happen?" Ada asked as she pointed the gun straight at me.

"I don't know," I said miserably.

"You better start talking, and soon, because this gun is starting to hurt my hand."

"She's not worth this, girl," Fallon pleaded. "Don't go to jail for her."

"I'm waiting," Ada snapped, totally ignoring Fallon's pleas.

"I came out of my house a few months ago wearing shorts and your husband was all over me about my big legs. The first time we both laughed it off, but after the second or third time, I decided to call his bluff. So I asked him where he wanted to meet and he suggested the Hilton. No one was more surprised than I was when I got there and Donald was waiting for me. And then there's the fact that Mark hasn't been the most attentive husband the past year and..." I trailed off, letting the silence speak the words I couldn't bring myself to say.

"How long?" Ada said, her soft voice scaring me a lot more than if she had been screaming.

"Three months."

"Damn," Fallon said. "How could you do this to your best friend? You have no scruples at all, Maude. I thought you were such a sweet housewife. Looks can certainly be deceiving."

"Why would my husband want your fat ass?" Ada snapped. When I didn't answer, she went on, "Don't worry if you don't have an answer for me. We'll just ask Donald when he gets here. He's on his way home now and he's stopping to pick up Mark on the way. We're going to have ourselves a little party here."

"Mark doesn't deserve to hear about Donald and me like this," I cried. "Let me tell him in my own way, when we're alone. There's no need for you to humiliate him."

Ada walked up and before I knew what was happening, slapped me open-handed across my face. The force of the blow knocked me off the sofa and onto the floor.

Ada was livid and I thought the gun was going to go off in my face as she towered over me, shaking from the force of her anger. "No Maude, you have no right to ask for anything from me. Mark's going to learn about you just like I did."

"Ada, put the gun down before it goes off," Fallon begged. "No one is worth dying for."

"And how would you feel if you found out this fat slut was screwing your husband, Fallon? Don't you dare sit there and pretend you wouldn't want to kill the fat bitch."

"I'd beat her ass, but I wouldn't shoot her," Fallon snapped. "She's not worth spending the rest of my life in prison."

"You can't possibly understand the rage I'm feeling. When I think about how this bitch has been in my face, all sweet sympathy as she listened to me fuss about my husband cheating on me. They probably had themselves a good laugh about me too. Of course, that's always assuming they were able to talk. It looked like they spent most of their time eating. I almost died when I saw that she was the other woman. It would have been a thousand times easier to bear if I hadn't been betrayed by my friend."

"I tried to break it off," I cried. "Really, I did. But my libido got in the way. I just couldn't make that final break." Then, unable to stop myself, I added, "You know Ada, if you had even made an attempt to satisfy your husband's needs, he wouldn't have gone looking elsewhere."

"Because I wouldn't go down on him, or let him go down on me?" Ada said incredulously. "You knew how I felt. Why didn't you encourage me to do the things that I needed to do to keep my husband, you stank whore?"

"I'm sorry," I said softly. "I know there's no excuse and there's no way that I'll ever be able to explain it to you, but I was so depressed over my marriage. I didn't really mean to try and take Donald away from you. I was overjoyed that someone wanted me and thought that if Donald could fill my sexual needs, Mark and I would be able to continue our marriage."

"You should have been talking to your husband, not mine. Why couldn't you bang another man? Why did it have to be my husband?"

I shook my head but said nothing. I had no explanation.

"Are you banging my husband too, Fallon?" Ada asked, turning to face Fallon, while the gun remained pointing squarely at me.

"No, Ada. Your husband doesn't turn me on. I'm banging a twenty-five and twenty-seven year old. Why would I want Donald? I'm as appalled at Maude as you are. I had no idea she was the one getting her groove on with your husband."

Just then, the doorknob twisted and when the person on the other side realized the door was locked, he knocked. I jumped up when I heard Donald say, "Ada, are you in there? The door is locked."

"Open the damn door," Ada told me. "If you make one wrong move, I'm going to shoot."

I looked at her, blinded by tears of self-pity as I hurried to the door. I knew Ada wasn't playing around. I unlocked it, and stood quietly as Mark and Donald walked into the room.

"Lock the door," Ada snapped.

"What's going on here?" Donald asked. "Why do you have a gun?"

"I'm going to kill you for cheating on me and I'm killing Maude for helping you. I'm sorry to be the one to break the news to you Mark, but your wife has been a naughty girl. She told me that you suspected her of cheating and you were right. Let me show you both something."

Ada ran the tape again and I watched, totally numb, as Mark and Donald stared at the screen. Ada let it play out, using the remote to shut it down before she turned to Mark. "Your wife wasn't satisfied at home, so she went after my man," she snapped at him, spittle spraying from her mouth. "Why couldn't you bang your wife Mark? Why did you marry the bitch whore if you couldn't perform your husbandly duties? I blame you for not keeping your wife satisfied at home."

Mark ignored Ada and stared at me in horror. "You bitch!" he cried.

"Honey, let's send everyone home while we talk about this," Donald said. "I wanted Maude because she's a sexy woman and was willing to try anything in bed. You only know one way to have sex and you don't even enjoy that too much. This is as much the fault of you and Mark as it is Maude's and mine. A woman has to do everything in her power to keep her man in his bed at home. And," he adding, turning to Mark," a man has the same obligation to his woman." Turning back to Ada, he continued, "You knew making me happy in bed was the key to our happiness. How dare you get angry at us, you frigid bitch?"

I was stunned by Donald's words, but before I could react I saw Ada aim the gun at Donald and squeeze the trigger. My scream blended in with the others from around the room.

After what seemed like hours, but was actually only a second or so, I opened my eyes to see Donald lying on the floor, holding his leg as blood oozed between his fingers. Fallon was crouched behind the sofa, Mark beside her while I was frozen directly in front of Ada. After watching Donald bleed all over her beige rug, she pointed the gun at me, and I watched in horror as her finger slowly pulled the trigger. I didn't feel anything at first, but then I felt a piercing pain in my head, knocking me to the floor. I heard myself screaming as my world went dark.

I opened my eyes to total darkness. I couldn't see anything. Why did they have the room so dark? I was starting to panic when I heard Mark's voice. It took a moment for his words to sink in.

"Maude, you're in the hospital. The doctors have your eyes bandaged because of your injuries. I'm going to call someone now," he said. I felt him reaching over my body; I suppose to ring the call button, because a moment later I heard him say, "My wife is awake now if you can find the doctor for us."

Mark and I talked awkwardly, neither one of us wanting to discuss the topic uppermost in both our minds, until the doctor arrived.

"So, how are you feeling today Maude? Any headaches or pain anywhere?" the doctor asked as she walked into my room.

"Well, by head is awfully sore in the back," I replied.

"It should be. You fell flat on your back when you were shot and you're a mighty big woman," the doctor said. She continued, "I'm going to take the bandages from your eyes now. I need you to keep your eyes closed until I tell you to open them. Do you understand me?" she asked.

"Yes, I do," I replied.

"Okay, let's get started. Mark, would you please turn off the overhead lights? Maude's eyes will be very sensitive at first."

I heard the sound of the scissors cutting through the tape and then the agonizing wait as the bandage was removed. "All right Maude, keep your eyes closed. I'm going to lift off the eye pads," the doctor warned.

I obediently closed my eyes and suddenly felt a whisper of air on my eyelids as the pads were lifted.

"Now, count to ten and very slowly, keeping your head down, open your eyes," the doctor ordered.

I counted to ten and slowly opened my eyes. At first everything was black and I waited a moment for my eyes to adjust and focus. Another moment went by and I heard the doctor say, "What do you see Maude?"

"Nothing," I cried, panicking. "I can't see anything. It's all black."

"I can't see," I moaned. "I'm blind. What am I going to do?" It was later that day and Mark and I were alone in my hospital room, trying to accept the doctor's prognosis.

"I'm so sorry for you Maude," Mark said.

"Are you going to gloat about this from now on?"

"No Maude, I'm here to take care of you. I blame myself for what happened. I took you for granted, never giving a thought to your needs."

"Was Fallon hurt?" I asked.

"No, she and I were out of range. After Ada shot you, she dropped the gun to the floor and went to the desk to call 911.

"She's out of jail already. Donald refused to press charges, and I was sure you wouldn't either, so the police had no choice but to drop the case, although they wanted to get her for attempted murder. I contacted a buddy of mine who's a criminal attorney, and he got her off. She's going to divorce Donald. Right now she and the kids have moved in with her parents while she decides what to do. Donald is living in the house until it sells. Then he's moving to California to join a law firm there. He came to visit you a few times, but I told him that your relationship was over and he needed to move on. He actually took it pretty well."

I wept because I was never going to see Mark's face again. I also wept because Donald was out of my life. I was going to miss his lovemaking, but I resigned myself to the tedium of a life with Mark. I didn't know how I would be able to go on.

"Donald really did love you, and I can't blame him," I heard Mark say softly, cradling me to his chest as I sobbed my heart out. "The fact that you're blind tears me apart. Even if I wanted revenge, it wouldn't be this. When I saw that bullet hit your head, I thought you were dead."

"I want you to leave," I cried. "I don't want you here and I especially don't want your pity or your gloating."

"I'm here because I love you. I wanted to kill you when I saw that tape, but that's all behind me. The blame is as much on me as it is on you. I kept unfairly accusing you of having an affair and that's what put the idea in your head. I gave the desperate housewife a loaded gun and it went off."

"I can take care of myself," I cried. "Just let me die."

"Maude, you won't die from your injuries. I know it's hard right now, but you can put this behind you. I'll be here for you from now on and will give you the loving you so desperately need from a man. I love you, baby, and I'm sorry for taking you for granted. Ada was right about me. I put you into the arms of another man."

"I'm so sorry for everything, Mark. I promise that from now on, you're the only man for me."

It was a month later and I was slowly adjusting to life as a blind person. Mark was at my side every step of the way and I felt truly blessed as I slowly learned how to live again. As soon as the headaches cleared completely, I was going to a school for the blind where they would teach me the rudiments of daily life. In time, I might even get me a guide dog. If I had one, there would be no limit on where I could go.

The telephone rang and I reached out and put my hand on it immediately, thanking Mark yet again for the care he took in making sure everything was always returned to its place so I would not have to grope awkwardly looking for something. I felt for the button and pushed it. "Hello."

"How does it feel to be blind, you bitch?" I heard Ada say.

"I'm sorry for the pain I caused you Ada. I know you can never forgive me, but I wanted you to know that I forgive you for shooting me."

"Payback is a bitch isn't it girlfriend? I heard you and Mark were still together. I think he's stupid as hell. I'd have left your trifling ass wallowing around in the dark. I'm just calling to remind you to watch your back." In an abrupt change of subject she asked, "Are you still seeing Donald?"

"Ada, why would you be interested in anything about my life? And even though it's none of your business, no, I'm not seeing anyone. I'm completely devoted to my loving husband."

"Watch your back, bitch!"

I sat holding the receiver until I heard the operator's voice telling me to hang up before they unleashed that god-awful screech on me. As soon as I hung up, the phone rang again. Cautiously, thinking it was Ada again, I answered.

"Hi," said a familiar male voice. "How are you doing? I couldn't stand it any more. I just had to hear your voice."

"I'm doing fine Donald. Thank you for calling, but please, don't call me again. Mark and I have worked things out between us now."

"I had to call you, baby. I miss you so much I can hardly stand it. We need to meet again soon. I need you and your body."

"I can't see you," I said softly. "Not just because of the blindness. I can't see you because I've made a promise to Mark and I'm not going back on it."

"All right baby, but I want you to remember that I'm here. Any time you need me, you call. It doesn't matter when it is. Do you hear what I'm saying?"

"Yes Donald and I appreciate it. But you need to realize that I won't be calling you. I've made a solid commitment to Mark and I'm not going to break it."

"Even if he's not honoring his commitment to you?" Donald asked. "You do realize that he's started seeing Janey, don't you?"

I was stunned. Mark and I had known Janey for several years. I remembered Fallon saying Janey was seeing an older man. Had that man been Mark? I had never seen any indication that there was anything between the two of them when we were together. Maybe Donald was just saying that to try and make me leave Mark. Mark spent all of his non-working hours at my side. The only exception was a few hours he set aside for his kids, like he had this past Saturday. Although he had invited me along, I declined, as I always did. I never felt completely comfortable around Mark's children, feeling that they were always comparing me unfavorably with their mother. I thanked Donald and hung up the phone. For a few minutes I sat there, considering my options. Then I picked up the phone again and slowly punched in a number.

"Hello," said the voice on the other end.

"Hi Mark," I said, trying to keep my voice light and airy. "This is Maude. Your dad asked me to call and see if he left his sunglasses at your house. He's torn our place apart looking for them and he seems to think the last time he wore them was last weekend when you guys went out."

"Last weekend…Dad must be starting down the slippery slope to senility. I haven't seen him in at least three weeks," Mark replied, laughter evident in his voice.

Forcing myself to laugh too, I made some small talk for a few minutes before hanging up. My hands were ice-cold and shaking so badly I could hardly lay the phone down on the table. Mark was having the last laugh on me after all. What was I going to do? The tears fell uncontrollably as I contemplated my future. One thing I could see right now. I'd always be a desperate housewife.

On a cool April evening, I sat waiting for my friends Rashawn and Maureen at Bennigan's Restaurant in downtown Chicago. It was past our scheduled meeting time, but I wasn't upset. I could spend the time daydreaming about my wonderful husband Rick. I was a little surprised at Maureen being late. She was usually the first to arrive for our regular monthly meeting. It had been a month since I'd last seen Maureen and even longer for Rashawn. She'd missed the last three meetings, although we still talked on the telephone.

I cherished these times with my best friends. Our get-togethers were usually limited to this one day a month, since we were all holding down exacting jobs as well as needing time with our husbands.

I took a small sip of my MaiTai, knowing I had to make it last, smiling as I spotted Maureen coming through the door. I stood up so she could see me back in the corner and she hurried over, throwing her arms around me for a big hug and then pulling back, holding my hands as we looked each other over.

"You look so pretty," I said, taking in her jeans and matching windbreaker with a pretty blue shirt underneath.

"Thanks Jasmine. I feel pretty and sexy too," Maureen said happily. "I'm so glad to see you. That black dress is wearing you down girl. It makes you look good in all the right places and then some. I think we both have it going on, thank you very much."

I smiled. "I love it. Thanks for the nice compliment. I feel so good when I wear this dress. I'm even happier that we're all content with our bodies, even though they may not please everyone." As I saw the waiter approach, I told Maureen, "The drinks are on me."

"A white wine is fine," Maureen said to the waiter before turning back to me. "Where is Rashawn? I suppose I shouldn't be surprised that she's not here, but I thought she might be able to make it this time," she laughed. "I'm not going to worry about her. I'm just going to drink my wine and have a good time."

I shrugged my shoulders. "Maybe she's just running late as usual. Have you seen her lately? I haven't heard from her in days. She usually calls at least once a week to see what's going on, but she's pulled a disappearing act on me."

Maureen shook her head. "No, not a word. But I hadn't really noticed because I've been pretty upset the last few weeks. I think Marcus might be cheating on me. I just have this feeling girl, and it makes me angry as hell. I do everything I can to make him happy, and it's never enough. I want to scream I'm so angry."

I stared at her. "Do you have any proof that Marcus is cheating on you, Maureen? Don't go crazy unless you know for sure. It's so easy for us to suspect our husbands of cheating, but it would be terrible to accuse him and be wrong."

"No, but a woman knows these things. I understand what you mean, and Lord knows I don't want to believe it of Marcus, but he's not a saint by any means. I just have this feeling. Sometimes I wonder why he ever married me in the first place.

"I'm so sorry honey," I said. "I know this can't be easy for you, and I truly hope you're wrong. You need to ask him straight out if he's cheating. That's what I'd do if I were in your shoes. It can't be easy for anyone to find out their partners don't love them."

The waiter delivered the wine, and Maureen took a big sip. I knew how she felt because I was starting to wonder if Rick were cheating on me. He was spending a lot more time at his office than usual. "I think there's a possibility that Rick may be having an affair too." I said, feeling that I needed to be honest with her.

"Are you kidding me?" Maureen exclaimed. "I see the way he looks at you, and he's a man in love. Rick worships the ground you walk on Jasmine. When you come into a room, his whole face lights up. That is not the action of a man cheating on his wife. You are totally wrong about Rick, but I've got a feeling I'm right about mine."

"I don't have any evidence, but I hardly see him anymore. I know he has to work, but not all the time, Maureen. I just don't know if he's really working, or sleeping with another woman. My worst fear is that the woman he might be sleeping with is skinny. Isn't that dumb? I'm more worried about her size than the fact that he may be unfaithful."

"Do you think we're fooling ourselves, girl? I know we three are lucky to be married to handsome and powerful men, but I keep thinking perhaps we're living in a dream world. Why would our successful men want us? We're not Tyra Banks or Vanessa Williams."

She had a point there. "I keep asking myself the same question. Rick had his choice of women, all sizes. I didn't put a gun to his head to make him propose to me. He has to love me," I said, trying desperately to convince myself.

"But I'm never going to down myself, girl. If Marcus is cheating on me, then he's out of my life. It's been two years, and I'm not a fool. I'm a very pretty woman and if he's not my soul mate, then I'm going to keep looking and stepping. I'm going to find out the truth because what is done in the dark will come out in the light for sure."

"I keep telling myself that too. If Rick doesn't want to be with me, I'll bow out graciously. It would be horrible, but its better that we find out now and deal with the problem."

Maureen laughed, her big infectious laugh that had the people at nearby tables looking our way and smiling. "You probably did ask Rick to let you know if he was interested in another woman so you could divorce him and give him the happiness you feel he deserves. I'd give my man a kick in his balls if he left me for another woman," she said, still smiling, but underneath I saw the cold light of determination in her eyes.

"Without a doubt," I laughed. "I wouldn't force someone to stay with me out of fear or pity. What good would making both of us miserable do? I'd always love Rick, and I wouldn't do anything to cause him unhappiness. My life would be a vast void, but eventually I'd learn to cope and get on with it."

"That's for sure. I can't imagine life without Marcus in it, but if necessary, I can move on. It would be the hardest thing I ever had to do in my life, but I could work through it. It could even be that Marcus isn't the man for me, and my soul mate is just around the corner waiting for me."

I looked up inquiringly as a skinny woman approached our table. She looked very familiar to me, but I couldn't quite place her face. Then it hit me! She looked just like a skinny Rashawn. I must be losing my mind worrying about Rick and Marcus. Or maybe I needed new glasses.

"I don't believe it," Maureen cried. "That can't be Rashawn. She's skin and bones. No wonder we haven't seen her lately. She's been busy getting her skinny groove on and then some. I can't believe she'd do this to us. The girl has lost her mind."

"Surprise!" Rashawn cried. "Don't I look delicious as a size 9? I need a rum and coke to get my groove on. I'm so tired of exercising but my hard work has really paid off. Just look at me," she said, spreading her arms out to her sides and twirling around, giving us a good look at her thin body encased in a short red dress. It looked good on her, but...

Maureen and I exchanged glances. She didn't have any breast or booty to enhance the dress. "How did you lose the weight so quickly and, more importantly, why?" I asked. I was very interested in her reasons.

Rashawn waited for her drink before answering. After taking a long sip, she set her glass on the table and stared defiantly at us. "I went on diet pills and lived at the gym. All the sweating ruined my weave and my perm, but look at the results. Those diet pills really stop the hunger. You two should try them."

"You're kidding me, right?" Maureen said. "I've tried diet pills twice, and each time they made me sick. I fainted twice, and my stomach was hurting so badly I ended up in the emergency room. I remember having diarrhea for days on end."

"They work differently on different people," Rashawn said. "I'm never going to be fat again. The pills kept me from being hungry all the time. I was able to totally forget about food. I feel like a new woman and I love it. It's so hard to describe, but for the first time in my life, I honestly feel good about myself."

"What does Brian say?" I asked. "I'm sure your husband is pleased with the new you. Brian always told you to go on a diet. What man doesn't want his wife to lose weight? Has it helped straighten out some of the problems you've been having with Brian?"

"We're not getting along at all. Divorce seems to be looming on the horizon for us," Rashawn said. "I'm a new woman now and he doesn't understand me hanging out at night, and having the time of my life. I think I deserve a little freedom for all the hard work I put into changing myself. I'd also wanted to share my diet success with the two of you."

"No thanks," Maureen said and went on, with a trace of anger in her voice. "You do realize that you're no longer in the living large club, don't you? You just forfeited your club membership with the weight loss, Rashawn. I hope losing the weight was worth it."

"She's right," I said, feeling my own anger start to mount. "This club is about women who are happy with their big bodies, and would never do anything to compromise that position. I guess you were just lying all the time you were with us, Rashawn and your body is proof of your defection."

"This isn't a competition," Rashawn cried. "I just got exhausted with being fat, people talking about me; eating all the time. I was determined to make changes in my life, and I have. Look at the new Rashawn," she said, sweeping her hands over her body before sitting back in her chair and announcing, "I need another drink."

"Now we have to find someone else to join our club," I pointed out. "This isn't a weight loss club. It's a club for fat women, and you don't qualify any longer, Rashawn. Remember you made the rules, so you've got to stick by them."

"She's right," Maureen agreed. "The club is for large women. You're not welcome here anymore. I suggest you move your petite self into another club with women who are so stuck on themselves, they don't care about the rest of the world."

Rashawn was stunned. "What? I can't believe you two are so jealous of me that you're going to try and kick me out of my own club. I'm the one who started this club and made the rules. And I say the rules don't apply to the President, thank you very much. I should kick you bitches out and find two other women who might possibly have a brain between them."

"Don't you remember that we promised ourselves and each other that we would not lose weight after I almost died after taking those diet pills?" I asked. "How could you betray us like this? I'm not a bitch, either, you slut. I see that the only person you care about is yourself. I hope being skinny is the making of your dreams."

"I did this for me," Rashawn cried. "I want to feel good about what I see when I look in the mirror. I'm having the time of my life. Do you see those men over there in the corner? They haven't taken their eyes off me since I came in. I just need to give them a signal and they'll be all over me. I'm going to go shake my thing on the dance floor and get my groove on."

"And what about your husband?" I asked. "You should be at home shaking your groove thing with him, not trying to make out with strangers you pick up in a bar. Don't you think you owe Brian some loyalty for sticking with your fat ass?" In my heart I knew she owed Brian nothing. He had made her life miserable, but I was angry and wanted to lash out at her.

Rashawn shrugged, "I guess he's at home, but I really don't give a damn. I don't owe him a damn thing for marrying me. He made my life miserable. Every time I ate a meal with him, he'd ridicule me for packing on more fat. It didn't matter what I was eating, even if it was just a salad. What kind of husband is that?" she appealed to us.

But we weren't ready to forgive or make allowances. It was a deep betrayal of us on Rashawn's part. "So you wanted to be free," Maureen said. "Well, you are now. Free of Brian and of the Living Large Club. He shouldn't have married you if he wasn't happy with your weight. But we were. We loved you just like you were and never asked you to change."

"Well, now I can date all the men that rejected me when I was fat," Rashawn cried. "I'm going to lead them on and then dump them like a bad hair day. Payback is a bitch! The same men who rejected me when I was fat are ringing my phone off the hook. I'll get even with all of them!" she vowed.

"You have a new attitude to go with that new body of yours," I commented. "I hope you don't regret it. Payback seldom gives you any satisfaction, Rashawn. It usually backfires on you. I think you should work on your marriage now that you're thin. You just made Brian's dreams come true, and then some."

"Are you two jealous of me?" Rashawn snapped. "I look good and you both can't stand me. The thing is, Brian isn't in my league any more, and so it's time to move on. I don't want a man who couldn't appreciate me when I was large. It's too late for us."

"We're happy for you," I said. "I don't need to be jealous of anyone. You're going to have a rough time with men using you for a booty call Rashawn, because that is all they're going to want from you. Be very sure that's what you want."

"I'm sure Rick and his brother would love getting a taste of me," Rashawn snapped. "Why don't you invite me over to your house and let me rock your worlds? I hear its fun when the husband is watching. The three of us can have a good time."

"You're a slut," Maureen said. "Get out of my sight, and don't let me catch you near Marcus. He's my husband and he's off limits to the likes of you. I'm glad you got your groove on, but find your groove with another man."

Rashawn laughed. "You bitches are fat slobs. You don't know what you're missing. I'll see you both never, and good luck with your husbands because they might find themselves in my bed. If Marcus wants me, I'm not turning him down. I'm sure he needs a real woman, not a fatty, to wet his appetite."

I watched her walk off to the corner where she sat down with the men who were staring at her earlier. They were all over her and I shook my head in disgust. "Who are we going to find to take her place? I can't believe our best friend has turned on us. She's changed and her new attitude stinks."

"I don't know," Maureen said. "Rashawn was our best friend. I can't believe she has been a hypocrite all this time. I never thought she'd diet and lose the weight. I don't even recognize her. She doesn't care who she hurts, and I know Marcus trifling ass wouldn't turn her down."

"I know. She's too skinny for my taste. Are we jealous Maureen? I dream of being skinny, but I know it's never going to happen to me. I thought I accepted my weight, but looking at Rashawn, I'm beginning to lose all faith in myself. She looks real good, and the men love her."

"I'm really not," Maureen cried. "I'm never going to be skinny. My weight doesn't interfere with my work. I'm a damn good attorney, and my clients keep coming back to me, and they recommend other clients. I could retire right now and never have to work again."

"What about Marcus?" I asked. "I know you think he's not in love with you, but I think he is. Maybe he's going through a few failures in his life, and you need to get him to communicate with you. Marriages fail from lack of communication."

"Let's order and forget about Rashawn and men for the moment. I don't think I have any more words for Marcus right now. I'm so angry at his behavior. I just don't know what I'm going to do, so for now I'm just going to have a drink and forget the pain."

"We can forget men, but Rashawn is on the dance floor shaking her groove thing like it's never been shaken before. If she keeps that up, she's going to shake right out of that dress. I wonder if she's wearing underwear."

"She doesn't have that much to shake now," Maureen laughed. She stared at Rashawn. "I don't think she's wearing any underwear," she exclaimed. "The woman has lost her ever-loving mind. She's going to end up with AIDS if she doesn't slow down her ride."

"She's flat as a pancake," I pointed out. "I hope that she has plenty of condoms if she's going to get her groove on in the bedroom. She's playing a dangerous game if she really is going to seduce them and then kick them out. I hope she know what she's doing."

We both laughed and then ordered our food. Rashawn continued to entice the men with her skinny body. I hoped she was having the time of her life, and being skinny was the answer to all her prayers. The men were all over her, and Rashawn had the most beautiful smile on her face. She was truly having the time of her life.

It was three o'clock in the morning when I got home. I turned on the light and jumped at the sight of Rick sitting in a living room chair. "You scared the life out of me," I cried. "What are you doing sitting in the dark?"

"I was waiting for my wife," he said. "I can't believe you'd come home so late. I don't remember getting a call from my wife, letting me know that she was okay. I know when you get with your girls you forget that you have a husband at home."

"I'm sorry, but Maureen and I got to talking and we lost track of time, Rick. She's worried about her husband, and then we had to deal with Rashawn. You know how it is when you're out with the girls. We had so many issues to deal with, time flew right by us."

"What about Rashawn? That girl is just too wild sometimes. I'm sure she's making waves about me, telling you to get a divorce. She never liked me, and that's not going to change. I don't like you hanging around her."

"Usually, we can handle Rashawn with no problem. Tonight we were trying to keep an eye on her because she was making a complete ass of herself on the dance floor. She lost a lot of weight and the men were breaking their necks to dance with her." I sat down next to Rick. "You don't need to worry about me. If something was wrong, you would have gotten a phone call."

"I don't care if you're out with your friends. I'd just like you to call me if you're going to be out this late. I'm sure there are men who are spellbound by your beauty, and I don't want them making passes at my wife."

I frowned. "I'm surprised at you Rick. You're the one that's never home, always claiming that you're working late. I can't believe you have the nerve to give me the third degree when you're out doing who knows what."

Rick laughed. "Your insecurities are showing. I love every inch of you and don't want you to change a thing on yourself. I thought you said you were all right with all the extra work I would need to take on when I took the promotion at the firm. They gave me extra paralegals to supervise as well as that one high-profile case. I was just disappointed when you weren't home when I got here this evening. I won that big case today as well as an enormous bonus and I wanted to celebrate with you."

"I'm sorry I wasn't here Rick, but you know we three meet every month. You also can't blame me for thinking that you're with other women. I think about the women you work with every day. They see a handsome man and they don't give a damn about you being married."

"Why would you think I'm cheating on you? I never gave you any reason to doubt my love for you. I know it's difficult to believe that there are men who like women who have meat on their bones, but you're just going to have to work that out for yourself. I just don't know any other way to prove myself to you."

"There are so many skinny women out there, Rick. Rashawn is so gorgeous now. I bet if you take one look at her, you'll be all over her. I can't blame you for wanting a woman who looks good naked."

"Rashawn was gorgeous when she was dating my brother. She was comfortable with her body. That's what made her so attractive to him. I think she's trying to prove something to herself, and I hope it doesn't backfire on her. As for me, I'm in love with you, so Rashawn, or any woman, can't entice me."

"She surprised the life out of Maureen and me. We got so angry that she betrayed us; we kicked her out of the club. The rule was if someone went below size 14, they were automatically disqualified. So now we're searching for another woman to take her place. We joined this support group for help dealing with the problems of being fat, not to listen to Rashawn crow about being skinny."

Rick shook his head. "I thought you three were best friends as well as fellow club members. She shouldn't be kicked out of the club just because she lost weight."

"She has a new attitude with her new body and she thinks she's the queen or something. She thinks she's all that and then some, and we can't even talk to her. I'm not going to compete with Rashawn."

"Why don't you get undressed and give me that sexy body of yours. I don't give a damn about Rashawn as long as she doesn't try to ruin our marriage. I wish her the best. Right now I just want to make love to the most gorgeous woman in the world."

"I have something I need to tell you first, Rick. Do you remember a few weeks ago when I ran out of my birth control pills but thought it was the right time of the month to safely make love?"

Rick smiled at me as he nodded. I had a feeling he knew where I was heading.

"I'm pregnant," I said bluntly.

"This is wonderful news, baby. I wanted a child by the most beautiful woman in the world so much. I dreamed of your belly swollen with our child. I hope we have a little girl and that she has your exotic beauty. I'm the happiest man in the world"

"You aren't upset? We never talked about having children, and I didn't want you to think that I was trying to trap you. We've only been married two years and I really didn't plan on having a baby yet. There are still things I don't know about you."

"Why would I be upset? Some things are just out of our control. I'm thrilled about the baby our love made."

I flew into his arms. I love him so much I couldn't believe how much more love I felt for him at this precise moment. Maureen and Rashawn were having problems with their husbands, but mine was okay. "I'm the luckiest woman in the world."

"So am I." He kissed my lips and I closed my eyes as the sensations entered my body. My heart was aching with happiness as our tongues joined together as a tingling feeling paraded between my legs. I was on fire and Rick was the only one who could hose me down.

"I love you so much," I whispered against his lips. I never thought I'd utter those words to a man. I had dreamed of it happening sometimes as I was reading one of my romance novels. I had prayed that someone would love me unconditionally. Dreams do come true."

"Not as much as I love you," Rick said. "I'm going to treasure you for the rest of my life and our child will be blessed. We need to lay down a firm foundation of love for our child to fall back on when the interracial slurs start."

The whole time he was talking, Rick had been systematically removing my clothing and now I was naked. Rick tore off his clothes and we jumped into bed where he devoured me with his hot and ready lips. I could feel the heat rising everywhere Rick touched with his lips, causing me to moan in passion. My body was consumed with orgasm after orgasm, crying out with sheer pleasure as my body reacted to the satisfaction it was receiving.

Rick wanted me and he had barely entered me before his body shook with a powerful orgasm. He screamed out as his passion erupted his entire body and mine. We drifted on the magical sensations flooding our bodies. I thought I'd go on forever, and that was okay by me. My body shook one last time as Rick yelled out his final pleasure and then we lay spent.

I kept my eyes closed because I wanted to treasure this moment for the rest of my life. I thought my husband was having an affair, and let my imagination run a monk with me. I hoped Maureen was having a grand time. Marcus was hurting the only woman that would truly love him.

"Do you think the baby's okay?" he asked. "We made some explosive love, honey, but right now we need to be very careful because we don't want to hurt the baby. I'm going to treat you like a delicate flower. Do you need anything? What about a glass of cold milk?"

I smiled at my husband. "The baby's fine. A glass of orange juice would be perfect for me, but I'll get it in a few minutes."

"A son would be nice to play basketball with, but women are so independent I might be able to play basketball with my little girl," he laughed. "What did Maureen and Rashawn say about our news? he asked as he started to the kitchen to get my juice.

I covered my mouth with my hand. "I forgot to tell them after Rashawn took over the show. I'll tell Maureen the next time I see her. She's going to be thrilled for us. I don't know how Rashawn's going to feel about me being pregnant. Well, I do know she'd probably be a lot happier if the father was anyone but you," I said honestly.

"Are you jealous of Rashawn, honey? Please be honest with me. I'm sure she's jealous of you and Maureen. It's a normal human emotion."

I sat up, staring at him in all my naked glory. "How could you ask such a silly question? I'm never going to be jealous of anyone because it's a wasted emotion. I love me just as I am, and I'm going to love our baby too, no matter what."

"I think you are deep down inside, but she has nothing on you; her confidence in herself, and not caring what other people said. I admire that about her."

I shook my head. "We all dream of being skinny like Rashawn because we think it's going to make our life a little easier. Maybe keep people from gawking and making rude comments. But you finally have to live with your decision, whatever it is."

"You still think you're not worthy of me. You and I were destined for each other. I look at you, I see the most beautiful woman in the world. When you truly love someone, baby, you see the love that shines within you. It's really love."

I shook my head. "It's hard being confident when you're not petite. I know I love you with my entire soul, Rick. At times I know you love me too. The way you look at me, I see the soul of your love bursting forth to cover me in madness of our love. I'm so blessed."

"But you're a supermodel, girl, and you're in the spotlight all the time. You have to develop confidence in yourself, or you wouldn't be able to compete with the skinny models out there. I see you on a runway with the petite models, and you have it going on, and then some."

I smiled at his words. "And I have a large bank account to show for it. Modeling does wonders for my soul," I said. "When I'm wearing that outfit, I feel special because I'm a role model for other large women. You don't have to be petite to survive, and make all your dreams come true."

"So anyone would be glad to be in your shoes. There are some people in my office who are asking me how it feels to be married to a gorgeous supermodel. I tell them I'm the luckiest man in the world. I really mean that."

"I might be jealous of Rashawn when she was fat because she had it going on. She didn't give a damn what anyone thought of her, and she carried her weight well. Maybe she was just putting on a façade."

"She had the confidence, but you're getting there. If I want to sleep with another woman, you'll be the first to know and vice versa, but that's not happening. I have a good personal life, and a great job. In nine months we'll be complete with a baby. Who could want for anything else?"

"I'll kill you dead," I laughed. "I'll shoot your body so many times you won't know what hit you. If you ever think about hurting me, you're going to wish that you had never been born. I love you more than my own life, and there isn't another woman out there who will ever love you the way I do."

He laughed. "I'm never going to make you angry. Give me another kiss. I have the only woman who is going to love me the way a man should be loved. Never let anyone come between our love, baby. If so, then they're jealous and we can't let them win."

I stared into his black eyes. "Our baby is going to be very lucky. Black women have asked me why I fell in love with a white man. I told them that when I look at you, I see a very handsome man. I don't see his color. They'll never understand unless it happens to them."

"You're going to make the perfect mother. I hope our baby looks just like you, an exotic beauty. As for outsiders, we can't please everyone. They ask questions because they're nosy as hell and don't have a life."

The tears blinded me as I stared at him. "How did I ever get so lucky?" I didn't mean to be a crybaby, but these tears were tears of joy. I was sure the baby would make me shed a lot of tears. I was going to be a basket case in the next few months.

"Don't you weep on me now," he said. "I'm a mess when my wife is crying. I just hope those are tears of joy. God just gave us a baby, and our future has never looked as bright as it is right now, baby."

I hugged him. "I love you." I could say those three words to Rick for the rest of my life, and never get tired of saying them. I remember when I dated other men and the words came to mind, but I'd never utter them. It just never felt right. With Rick it was different and it felt so right this time."

"And I love you." Our lips met again and then our bodies shook as lovemaking became our only concern at the moment, and the thunder and lightening of our bodies took center stage. We had this chemistry that manifested when our bodies came together. No one could ever take that magic away from us. Never!

Maureen and I sat and waited for our new member to join us at Bennigan's. "How is everything going with Marcus?" I hoped she had some good news for me. I really and truly wanted her marriage to work out. What was going on with Marcus? I thought he loved Maureen.

"We're still distant," Maureen said. "I'm taking a few weeks off and we'll see if he goes out of town with me. If he refuses, then I know my marriage is over, and this time I mean it, Jasmine. Marcus has made a fool out of me for the final time. I have to move on."

"I'm so sorry," I cried. "You and Marcus seemed to be the idea couple. Why don't you get some counseling to work on your marriage? I think you have to try everything to make it work. If it's meant to be, then wild fire couldn't burn your marriage down."

Maureen laughed. "Give me a break, Marriage stinks half of the time. I give Marcus kinky sex to keep him from cheating on me, but I'm wasting my time. One time I almost got sick to my stomach when it went down my throat. I hate Marcus and at times I want to kill him."

"You do that stuff," I said. Women were doing it all the time to keep their men. I heard rumors that white men liked to go down on a woman, and they liked a lot of oral sex in return. Rick did go down on me, but he never asked me to satisfy him. What was wrong with that picture?

"You do whatever it takes to keep your man. My goal was to make Marcus happy. I knew the things he liked when we made love, and I was determined to grant his wishes. I was going to keep my man at home with me, and keep him so satisfied that he wouldn't need a mistress."

"But in reality you don't keep them at all. Most don't appreciate what you do for them. You can't compromise your ethics for a man."

"You're so right about that," Maureen cried. "I never told you about this but Marcus wanted two women to make love to him. I thought he was disgusting for thinking such a thing, but he told me that he wanted to spice up our marriage, so I let another woman make love to my husband."

"Hi you two," said a woman's voice. "I'm Linda." I was so stunned by Maureen's confession I just glared at the woman who had the nerve to interrupt our conversation. I couldn't believe Maureen's words. If Rick asked that of me, then our marriage would be over.

I focused on this Linda person. She was gorgeous and I recognized her from somewhere. "Hi. I'm Jasmine and this is Maureen." I really wanted to get more details about Maureen's confession, but this wasn't the right time and Maureen was now focused on Linda.

"It's nice meeting you both," Linda said. "I'm so glad to be here. I'm a large woman and proud of it. I've been trying to interact with a group of women who love their big bodies, so I was glad when I read your ad searching for another member. I do hope this works out."

"You look familiar," I said. Linda had it going on, but why did she look so familiar to me? I was still pondering the fact that Maureen watched another woman make love to her husband. Was Marcus having an affair with this woman? I had so many questions for Maureen, but she was drinking her third glass of wine while she stared at Linda.

"You might recognize me from television. I do the five and ten o'clock news on Channel 4. I don't like to be recognized so I don't make a big deal about it. Sometimes I can leave the house without being discovered, but most of the time I have to disguise myself or I'd never be able to go out."

"That's right," Maureen said. "You're a celebrity and your fans are watching. I can't believe you answered our ad, but Jasmine and I are glad to have you aboard. I watch you all the time because I admire you for still having a job. We big woman are alive and well."

Linda blushed. "I'm just a normal person with a good job that I love. There are petite women coming into the newsroom all the time who want my job with a passion, but I have a five-year contract and if they want to buy it out, it would cost them millions."

"You do a good job and you have that sense of humor. I'm laughing all the time. I look forward to turning on the news and watching your segments," I told her.

"Thanks. I have the highest ratings of all the reporters. We have fun on Channel 4. I'm so confident in myself I feel myself bursting with my high self-esteem. Basically I'm a happy person inside and out. I love myself because I'm a child of God. I know he loves me too."

"I like your attitude," Maureen said. "What would you do if you thought your husband was cheating on you? I'm just curious to know what a stranger would say and how would she react if this was happening to her? I'm sorry for being so forward, but we don't hold anything back in our club."

"The first job would be to make sure my hunches were right," Linda said. "We can assume anything, but we need hard evidence to prove those assumptions. Once you have the proof then the choice is up to you. I know women who have stayed with their cheating husbands and some who ran."

"That's not an answer," Maureen snapped. "I can't be with someone who doesn't want to be with me. If I let Marcus cheat on me, and forgive him, then he's going to do it again. I love him so much, but if he doesn't love me, then I'm wasting my time with him."

"Then there's your answer. You don't need an answer from me," Linda said. "I'm going to order a beer. The drinks are on me since this is my first time here. I'm looking forward to our meetings."

"A Mai Tai," I cried. Then I thought about being pregnant. "I'll have an orange juice, instead." I was going to miss my Mai Tai's, but the baby was more important right now. The minute I have my baby, I was going to celebrate with a string of Mai Tai's, I thought to myself. After giving birth, I was probably going to need it.

"Long Island Tea," Maureen said. "I need something different this time. I can't believe you're not having a Mai Tai, Jasmine. Is something wrong?"

I laughed. "My stomach hasn't been feeling good, so I'm going to take a break from the Mai Tais for today," I smiled. "I think I'm coming down with something." I don't know why I just didn't level with them. I was pregnant. Why was I playing games?

"I'm sorry for you pain," Linda said. "I'm fifty years old now and my first three husbands cheated on me. So far my fourth hasn't done the nasty. I'm still waiting for him to join the fun, but he might just be the one. I just kept trying until I got it right. I think Bill might be my mate. He's as fat as I am and we get along just fine. He loves me, and he shows me all the time."

"Wow," Maureen said. "You don't look fifty. I never would have guessed your age. You look like you're in your thirties, girl, and you do look good. You give us hope for when we get to your age."

Linda laughed. "I work out to keep my muscle tone, but I'm never going to be skinny. Remember skinny women are evil. I make sure I keep my weight stable. Yoyo dieting is the worse thing you can do to your body."

"I like Monique," I confessed. "She's a woman who loves herself. I read that she's toning down, but she's never going to be a petite woman. She's also coming up with a reality show for big women. Now I'm going to watch that because we big girls need the chance."

"We all do," Linda said. "She's a big woman and she loves herself. I admire her all over the place. When she comes back to Chicago she's going to do an exclusive interview with me. My producers are surprised that I landed the interview with her. They weren't so lucky."

"She has more confidence than any woman I've ever seen," I put in. "I look at Monique all the time because I want to have that confidence. She's in the public eye, so she's my role model for all time."

"Me too," Linda said. "I just love her. I can't wait for our interview. We do more than just deliver the bad news. We have segments on ordinary people, celebrities, and reality issues. I've been doing it for ten years now and I still love my job."

"Me too," I replied. "I dreamed of modeling when I was a teenager. After high school I did some local modeling, but I never went to New York to make all my dreams come true because reality was front and center. Now I'm modeling full time, and the money is out of this world."

"I've seen your picture in a few fashion magazines," Linda said. "You're a success story. I want to interview the sisters who have it going on and then some. I keep telling my producers that people are turning off the news because it's so damn depressing."

"I am," I smiled. "I have a nice life. I have to admit I don't watch the other news shows because it's very depressing. I turn you on because you interview ordinary people and I'd like to know what local people are doing around Chicago. It's good news."

"And you have a gorgeous husband," Linda pointed out. "You and Maureen would be a nice interview for the successful black woman. I'm working on successful couples, and successful career women. I don't want women with just jobs."

"I need another drink," Maureen cried. "My marriage is over, and the two of you are going on about jobs. Who gives a damn when your husband is out there sleeping with every woman that smiles at him? I love my man, but he doesn't give a damn about his wife."

I knew Maureen was hurting, and I wished there was something I could do for her. She was my very best friend. Maybe I could talk to Marcus and see what was going on with him? If he dared to cheat on my friend, then I will kick his balls. He'd deserve it and more.

"So do I pass?" Linda asked. "I was a little nervous joining a group because I don't want people to think of me as a celebrity. I met a few people who thought by associating with me that I could open doors for them. They had no idea that I wasn't about to be used."

"With flying colors," I said. "Everyone is always using someone, but Maureen and I are glad to have you on board with us. If you lose weight, then you're out of the club. I'll send you over a welcome package, and the rules and regulations."

"Welcome to the group," Maureen said. "If you'll excuse me, I'm going to the bathroom. I'm not feeling well. Maybe I shouldn't have had that mixed drink on top of all the wine. I think I'm going to throw up."

I watched as Maureen stood up and almost fell. "Do you need some help?" My friend was in bad shape, and had Marcus to thank for her pain. Why did he marry Maureen when he could have continued his playboy ways? I'd love to know what makes a man tick.

"No," Maureen cried. "I'll be right back." I hoped she made it in time. Maureen was doing too much drinking so I ordered her a cup of coffee to try and sober her up. Drinking wasn't the answer to her pain.

I stared after her. "She's hurting," I said. "Maureen would die for Marcus, and I thought he'd do the same thing for her. I'm sorry you have to see her in this state on your first day with us. She's usually this happy-go-lucky woman with plenty of dreams. She's just sad right now."

"I do understand," Linda said. "I hurt with all three of my husbands. When Maureen comes back I'll tell you about it. I did marry Bill for the right reason. He has been in love with me for ages but I always thought of him as a friend. I never once thought he'd be interested in me as a lover. I was so wrong. He loves me and I love him."

"It's a romantic fairy tale," I cried. "I can't believe Rick is in my life. He loves me, and I love him. Just thinking about him brings an ache between my legs. I'm sorry, but no man has ever melted my heart the way Rick does. I prayed for someone like him my entire life."

"You're such a gorgeous woman, and men should fall down at your feet. We do a segment every Monday on the large size woman, and most of the stories are success stories. We had a few who wanted to lose weight, but the majority was proud to wear a size 20. Society is a bitch where weight is concerned. God didn't make everyone petite, and as long as we like ourselves who are you or anyone to judge us?"

I smiled. "Nicely put. It hasn't been easy coming to those terms about my weight. You can't imagine the lonely times in my life. I thought I was going to die from being so bored, and lonely without a man. If I didn't have Rashawn, and Maureen, I'd be in a mental institute. I also had my books, and they kept me sane."

Maureen hurried back to the table and I was relieved she was in one piece. "What did I miss? I didn't vomit, but just used the bathroom. I think I'm going to be okay. Marcus isn't falling on his face because of me, so I'm not going to give him the satisfaction."

"I wanted to share some news before I forget this time," I cried. "Rick and I are going to have a baby." It was time to bring some happiness to this table, and get Maureen's mind on being a Godmother. I just hope she was happy about my news. I didn't want to hurt her feelings.

"I knew you were pregnant," Maureen said. "Congratulations! It's made my day that you and Rick are working out. I can't wait to be a Godmother. Your child is going to be blessed with everything and more. I'm going to baby sit to give you both some down time. It's going to be fun."

"Congratulations," Linda said. "A child is wonderful for a couple who is so much in love. I have five children with different fathers. I'm wishing the best for you and Rick. Maybe I can meet him sometime and see if he's as good looking in person as he is in his pictures. It's good to know that marriage is still working for some people."

"I can arrange it," I said. "I'm so happy about the news. I think I'm still in shock. Rick and I are still in the getting to know stage, and I never thought about having a baby. I just wanted to spend more time getting to know my handsome husband, but God has other plans for us."

"I'm going to be a Godmother," Maureen cried. "This is the best news ever. I have to go to the baby store and stock up on diapers, and the works. Then I have to plan a baby shower for my best friend. I know the perfect place for the shower. I just need to know if it's going to be a girl or a boy."

"So let's drink to a new life," Linda said. "Should you be drinking, Jasmine? You don't look pregnant, but we're not getting any younger, so we have to be very careful. I think you ordered orange juice."

"I did," I smiled. "The bartender is a good friend of mine and she's going to take good care of me. Besides, Rick will kill me if I don't take good care of myself. He's already pampering me by insisting that I have a tall glass of milk."

"Not to mention we practically live here at Bennigan's," Maureen laughed. "Why did you marry so many times, Linda? I don't mean to change the subject, Jasmine, but I was just curious about other people's marriage. Maybe it's something I'm doing wrong in my own."

Linda took a long sip of her beer. "I was insecure when I married my first husband, Tyler; I wanted to prove to myself that a fat woman can get married, but he cheated on me. I looked the other way for a while, and then I moved onto husband number two; he was a white man, but cheated on me with white women; husband number three, James, knew I had money and he wanted some of it. When I found him in bed with another man, I almost lost my head, but was relieved for some reason. John, the white man didn't care about hurting me because he really wanted a white woman."

"Where did you meet Bill?" I asked. Linda had a colorful life. I couldn't imagine being married four times, but never-say-never. I'm sure Linda didn't plan on marrying more than once, but it never works out the way you plan it.

"At a Channel 4 meeting," Linda said. "He's a general manager there. I saw him a few times, and he smiled at me, but I didn't give him the time of day. I had been married three times, and I told myself that three strikes and you're out. I really wasn't searching for a fourth husband."

"So you two work at the same station," I said. "This is just like a romance novel. You see your mate across the room at work. The sparks fly and the two of you ride off into the sunset, living happily ever after with your soul mate.

"I don't see that much of him, but we do go home together," she laughed. "Thanks for the fairy tale, Jasmine, but it didn't happen like that. I ignored Bill so much that he finally cornered me in the staff lounge and asked me out one day. I was so stunned I agreed to go out with him and the rest is history as they say. I need something to eat. I'm famished. "

"The fish is very good here," Maureen said. "I think I'll order some catfish. I don't believe in fairy tales," she went on. "I thought Marcus was my Prince Charming when I saw him across the room, but he was only interested in my big booty. Marcus is a booty man."

"I'm craving pizza for some reason," I pointed out. I laughed at myself. "I'll just blame it on the pregnancy. It's going to take some time to get used to this. Anyway let's order because I'm eating for two."

"I'll have the rib tips," Linda said. "I just love them. I can't eat them all the time, but if I could eat them everyday, I would. I might just do that and then some, thank you very much."

Silence took over our table as we concentrated on our food. Linda was going to be a great replacement to our group, but she'd never be Rashawn. I wanted to share my happy news with her. Rashawn was probably still too busy getting her groove on.

Rick and I had just finished making love. I relaxed in his arms. "How was your day baby? Did you win any more cases?"

"Very busy because I'm interviewing for an assistant. I can't do everything myself, and the paralegals are swamped too. I just can't find someone I really like to work with me. Paul is working out so far, so I might just make him my assistant."

"Is that good or bad? You should probably use a temp agency. I remember working for them a long time ago, and I liked it. I went to different jobs, and got to visit the other side of Chicago. I eventually got hired at one of those jobs."

"It is. Marcus and I had lunch today. I know you don't want to hear this, but he needed to talk and I was there for him. He's not looking good, and he needed someone to listen to him and I'm going to be down with my boy. Please stop looking at me with those cat eyes of yours."

I was stunned. "What? Why? Do you know he's ruining my friend's life? Maureen is drinking too much because she's so upset with Marcus having an affair. I love Maureen and I don't want to see her going through this stress with him."

"We're friends, honey, and he needs a man's point of view. I can't judge him, but I will be there for him. If he's making the wrong choices, then he still needs support. I can't stop talking to him because I'm married to his wife's best friend. That wouldn't be fair."

"Is he going to divorce her? Maureen is losing her mind over it." I know Rick is a good man who wouldn't leave Marcus alone. "I know you can't desert your friend. I'm just so mad at him for hurting my best friend. Why didn't he just leave Maureen alone if he didn't love her? I'll never understand men as long as I live."

"I don't know. He loves his wife, but he loves the skinny woman too. Marcus truly believes that men should have more than one woman to love. I just listen to him."

I frowned. "What kind of logic is that? Your friend is insane as hell. He can't expect Maureen to share him with another woman. I think Marcus should be slapped around until he comes to his senses, baby."

"Its insanity to us, but not to Marcus," Rick said. "He justifies his actions because Maureen is letting herself go. She's not trying to maintain her weight and she's eating like tomorrow is her last day on earth. He tried getting her to go to the gym with him, but she doesn't want to work out in front of a lot of people. He's trying, honey."

"The snake," I snapped. "Do you know the kinky things Maureen does for him? He should be shot. Why did he marry her if he's so obsessed with her weight? No one put a gun to his head. I thought he cared about her, but obviously he doesn't."

"I don't want to judge their situation, honey. I do know he loves, Maureen. He's not going to leave his wife for another woman. He just needs a petite woman in his life. The petite woman gives him something that Maureen can't, and the other way around with Maureen."

I shook my head. "I hope you don't get any ideas, Rick. I'm not sharing you with a petite woman. Marcus is sick for doing this to Maureen, and he needs to divorce her and move on with his life. I'm sure there's someone out there for her who doesn't need other women."

"I'm not Marcus," he snapped. "Don't you dare compare me to him? I told him that he was in some deep shit, but he thinks he's doing the right thing. He's in love with both women. I'm sorry about his problems, but I'm not Marcus, baby."

"Maureen is going to divorce him when she finds out. She's already suspecting that he's fooling around. There's no way she's going to condone this kind of unhealthy behavior in a marriage. Marcus knows she's going to divorce his ass when she learns the truth that he's in love with another woman."

"Only with one woman, and don't ask more of me. I can't betray his confidence. He's not going to divorce Maureen so she has nothing to worry about. I think the two of them need counseling, and I suggested this. He wasn't thrilled with the idea but he's thinking about it."

"So you expect me to keep quiet about Marcus when she throws it up in my face that he's sneaking around on her? I can't lie to my friend. He needs to be slapped, and kicked in the balls for his infidelity. I'm never going to look at him the same way again."

"Just listen to me, baby. Marcus doesn't want a divorce. I told you too much. He's going to talk to Maureen and explain everything to her. She's going to accept his conditions, or she will run to divorce court. It's up to us to be there for both of them."

"Then he's living in a dream world," I snapped. "I know my friend and she's not about to share her man with anyone. I can't believe this is happening to her. Maureen is a loving woman, and she's destroying her life with booze. Why did he get involved with a fat woman?"

"We just need to be there for them. For the record I told Marcus that he was wrong, but he told me not to judge him, and I can't do that, either. I know you're angry with him, and I am too, but we need to focus on our baby. There's nothing we can do for those two except be there for them, whatever happens."

"With bells on," I said. "I miss Rashawn and I'm going to be supportive. The baby is fine, but I'm always hungry and the doctor told me not to gain too much weight. I bought a lot of fresh vegetables and fruit so when I get hungry, I can at least eat healthy."

"Rashawn is making up for lost time. She's a party girl. I think more vegetables and fruit are fine ideas, baby, but you don't need to live off of them. I'm going to make you a healthy sandwich that tastes good and you can drink a glass of milk with it. There are exercises you can do to keep your weight the same, and nurture the baby, also. I've been reading this pregnancy book so I can understand your moods."

"How do you know?" I hoped Rashawn hadn't shown her face at my house trying to seduce my husband. If she had the nerve, the skinny bitch was going to pay in spades. After I got through with her she was no longer going to be my friend. The bitch was mud.

"A few co-workers at work were discussing her in the lounge. She has a reputation and it's not a good one. The woman is banging every man she can get her hands on as if she's making up for lost time."

"I'm sorry to hear that. I don't know what's going on with Rashawn? What about her husband? I'm sure Brian can't be happy about his wife sleeping around. I just don't know what is on her mind. She's not talking to Maureen or me. I hope she's okay."

"They're separated for the time being. Brian came to me requesting a legal separation. Black people are snobs when they get money, and the same thing happens to a woman who loses the weight. You have to make up for all the men that rejected you, and start living. I think this is happening to Rashawn. I can't believe she's really out of the group."

"She's the one that made up that rule," I snapped. "I didn't have confidence in myself when I joined the group, so she made sure that if I lost too much weight, I'd be out of the group. She has to live by her own rules. She knew what she was doing when she was taking all those diet pills."

"I know, but she's a friend. Of course she's in need of someone to talk too. I'm sure she's going through this attitude change, and she will need some adjusting. When she comes back to her senses and Rashawn will, of course, she's going to need you. It just takes some time, but friendship should be important."

"Not a skinny friend, Rick. She looks down her nose at everyone. I love Rashawn and that will never change. I know she's going through a nightmare of her own, and that's fine with me. When she's ready to talk Maureen and I will be there for her, and Linda."

"So true, but she went to see my brother to prove something to him. She tied him up to the bed, and then tortured him for rejecting her when she was in love with him. I think Rashawn has lost her demented mind. The man actually thought she was going to kill him."

"Is your brother okay?" He probably deserved the torture and then some. "Men are hurting women all the time, Rick and we're not going to sit around and take the pain any longer. I think your brother got what was coming to him, and maybe next time he'll learn from his mistakes."

"His ego is bruised, but he's okay. I don't think he's going to date another sister for a while. I don't know what he's doing now, but he was screaming that he's done with sisters because they're too violent for him. I laughed at him because he was so funny."

"I'm sorry. Maybe I will call her. Rashawn told me she was going to make all the men pay for rejecting her. I didn't think she was playing, and your brother was part of her revenge. I'm glad he's okay. I think once she gets this out of her system, she'll be able to move on with her life."

"Can I nibble on your neck? You have the most beautiful neck in the world, Jasmine. I just can't get over the fact that I'm married to the most gorgeous woman in the world, and then some. You take my breath away every time I'm in the same room with you."

I laughed. "You do the same thing for me, Rick with those black eyes of yours. I thought we were going to watch a movie to-gether."

"We can watch the movie but I'm going to nibble on that lovely neck of yours. You have the most beautiful neck baby. This is our time to spend together and I'm going to make love to my wife both mentally and physically."

"And flattery will let you nibble." I loved my man, and I wished Maureen and Rashawn could be as happy with their husbands. I wanted to share my bliss with my two best friends, and Linda. I couldn't forget about our new club member. I just wanted to share the contentment.

He laughed. "Then get over here because I'm hungry." I was hungry too, but I knew Rick wasn't starving for food. I was hot for him as much as he was heated for me. I don't think I'd ever stop wanting my husband. He turned me on sexually by his touch or his look.

I laughed. "Okay!" I inhaled the smell of Rick as I moved near him. I knew I smelled good, too. We mingled together as I went into his arms, and his scent energized my fat body into overdrive. I was on fire, and only Rick could light my passion in more ways than one.

Twenty minutes later I was deep into the movie INTOLERABLE CRUELTY. I adored George Clooney. Rick was having his fun nibbling on my neck, and the other part of my body. Soon we were making love in all the right places, and the television was a distant memory. Rick was the only man in the world who could make me forget George Clooney.

"My marriage is officially over," Maureen announced. "My husband told me that he was in love with another woman. Of course she was petite, and he wanted the both of us, but he wasn't divorcing me. She was aware of this and was quite content to be the mistress in the relationship."

"I'm so sorry" I cried. I thought Marcus would come to his senses, but that was wishing upon a star, and Marcus wasn't the one, thank you very much. Who did he think he was? My friend was in pain and he was the cause of all her pain. I was never going to speak to him again.

"Just give me three rum and cokes," Maureen cried. "The man expected me to go along with the program. He was having his cake and eating it too. He thought I should be grateful that he still wanted me."

"Men are a cake," Linda said. "I'm so sorry, Maureen. It's good that you know what's going on, but I feel for you. I know you can't win in this situation. I have to give Marcus credit for being honest with you. My first husband denied it so many times I lost count."

"It's okay," Maureen said. "I knew it was happening so I shouldn't be surprised. I'm not dense enough not to know that my husband is cheating on me. I give him credit for being honest, but it doesn't change the fact that Marcus isn't that into me. I heard that statement once. My husband just doesn't love me enough."

"It's been three months," I said. "I thought you two were working out your marriage. I can't believe he'd do this to you for a piece of ass. I'm so sorry this is happening to you. Maybe Marcus isn't into you. I heard the phrase on Sex and the City. It's the truth."

"So did I, but not with another woman." Maureen cried. "Her name is Michelle. He wasn't going to give me more information because he didn't want me to go over there and kick the woman's ass. I think if I had a gun in the house at that moment, I'd have used it on Marcus."

"I'm so sorry," I cried. "This can't be easy for you. Linda and I are here for you. If you need to get away for a while, we'd understand and give you some time for yourself. Maybe you could get some vacation time and take a trip. It might do the trick for you."

"Let's just change the subject," Maureen said. "I'm going to make partnership in a few months, so a trip is out of the question for now. When I do make a change in my life, then I'm going to New York for a while. I have some friends who are dying for me to come out there for a visit."

"You're kidding me," I cried. "This is a dream come true for you. I think a trip is exactly what you need. Of course you're not going to forgive your husband or forget him, but meeting with old friends and getting involved in their lives is therapy."

Maureen smiled. "It's the icing on the cake for now. I'm going to work my butt off to make my firm proud of me so I won't have time to worry about my marriage crumbling. Work is the key when your personal life crumbles right before your eyes. Marcus wants me to shut up and go along with the program. He better be glad I didn't have a gun, or his ass would be three feet under."

"Sounds like a plan to me," Linda said. "You have our support, Maureen. I met a woman once whose husband wanted the same thing in their relationship because he wanted to keep the sparks alive. She decided to turn the tables on him and found her another man. Let's say he wasn't happy, and now the two of them are happily married."

"She's right," I said. I took a sip of my orange juice staring around Bennigan's. It was crowded this Friday night. I looked at the dance floor staring at the many people that were shaking their bodies all over the place, and then I froze. Rashawn was on the floor dancing like a maniac and she was fat. I couldn't believe it, looking again to make sure it was her. I turned toward Linda and Maureen who were still discussing Maureen's promotion. "Look who's on the dance floor," I cried. I forgot about Linda's story for the moment.

Maureen followed my hand motion, staring at Rashawn. "I can't believe it. She's fat. The woman has gained all her weight back. She's almost as big as me, thank you very much. I can't believe this. One minute she's up and now she's down. This can't be healthy for her."

"Who is she?" Linda asked. "The woman has it going on and then some. Not only is she shaking her groove thing, but she also has a lot of men staring at her. I think she has all the attention she needs. I like her because she does have it going on."

"She's our former member," I said. "You took her place when she lost too much weight to be a member any more. I don't know what's going on in Rashawn's life, but something tells me it's not anything healthy because she's been eating. The last time we saw her she was pencil thin."

"Well, she's not skinny any more," Linda pointed out. "She's one of us again, so maybe she can get back into the group. I love being here, but if she's a friend, then I don't want to step on anyone's toes. I do hope you two keep me around because I look forward to our meetings."

"We can see that she has gained most of her weight back," Maureen said. "She must be a size sixteen now. She hasn't come over to our table, and I know she's seen us by now. I think she's avoiding us and I can't blame her. She has more problems than I do."

"It's hard to keep the weight off," Linda pointed out. "I went up and down so long; I finally just left it on and learned to live with it. You can really damage your health by dieting so much and losing the weight, and then gaining it back. It's not healthy and Rashawn needs to get a physical."

"We've all been there," I said. "I hope Rashawn does take care of her weight because she's going to need her health if she continues to dance the way she's dancing. The girl is the only one on the dance floor with all her moves. I thought she should always go into dancing."

"Why don't we call her over here?" Linda said. "I'd love to meet her and maybe she could rejoin the group. I have no intention of leaving but don't you think there can be four of us in the living large club. I think the more of us the better, and six members would be an even better idea."

"She might not be speaking to us," Maureen said. "And you have a good idea about expanding our club membership. I have a couple of friends that are eager to join us, and I'm going to give them a call. We big women have to stand together."

"I think she misses you both," Linda said. "I'm going to give you both a minute and take a break outside. Besides, I'm in need of a cigarette. I know smoking isn't healthy for me, and I'm going to stop in a few days, but it's going to take some time. I just need the cigarette."

"Thanks," I said. I stared at Maureen. "Should we talk to her? You know how stubborn Rashawn is and she's not going to make the first move. We have to go over there and give her a break. She's dancing too much and I know she's exhausted as hell. I would be."

"It's okay with me. I have nothing against her," Maureen said. "I just miss her. She can come back to the club without any problems since she has the weight back on. I'm going to recruit two more people, and then we'll have a six-member club with the same rules. I think six is enough for now."

"I agree. I'm going to do it." I walked over to Rashawn when the song ended. "Hi Rashawn! Why haven't you returned any of my calls?" She was surprised to see me, and I was glad to see her. "I've been eager to know how everything is going with you. Just because we're not club mates doesn't mean we don't care about you."

"What do you want, Jasmine? I'm busy, or are you here to gloat because I didn't manage to keep the weight off. Okay, I'm fat again, and that's fine with me. It was no fun being skinny, thank you very much. But I got my revenge in the process."

"I thought you could join our table. What happened to you? We were thinking about having six members with the same rules, of course. Why don't you just come back to us Rashawn? There are no hard feelings. You were skinny for a while, so it's time to move on."

"I see you have a new member so I wouldn't want to rain on her parade," Rashawn said. "I'm fine alone, and fat and the men are still eating me up alive. I don't know if my marriage is going to be saved, but I'm glad I got revenge on your husband's brother. You should have seen the look on his face. He was stunned as hell."

"But why are you fat now? I'm sure Rick's brother needed the pain," I said, trying to smother my laughter. "I don't blame you for giving him a taste of his own medicine. Men like that deserve what they get, but it's time to move on and get on with your life. There are other men."

"I started eating again. It's difficult keeping it off. I got so hungry at times; I just ate whatever the hell I wanted too. I'm fat for good and its okay by me. Being skinny wasn't so much fun after all. Men treated you like dirt, and they only wanted a booty call. I had a lot of men bothering me too. I couldn't get rid of them."

"Why don't you just join us Rashawn? The club hasn't been the same without you, but there's no President in this club. We're all equal members with the same rules and guidelines. Maureen is about to make partner and take a trip to New York City for a break. We miss you."

"For a minute," Rashawn said. "I do need a break. "I've been dancing all day so I need a cold glass of beer, and then some relaxation time. I'm moving on with my life. My marriage is probably over, but I'm not upset about Brian. He's not the man for me."

I smiled at her as we walked over to the table and sat down. I was so glad to have my old friend back looking the way she was supposed to look. If we stuck together there was nothing that could tear us apart, and that included men. They could never break us.

"Hi Rashawn," Maureen said. "You look great. I'm so glad to see you again. Sit down and take a load off. I want us to get back our club relationship because it's the only thing I can count on. I treasure our friendship and we need to stick together as women."

"I feel okay," Rashawn said. "How are you two doing? I see this other person is working out. I do miss the club, and its good seeing the two of you. I picked up the phone so many times to call you both but I'm stubborn as five mules and just couldn't do it."

"Linda is very nice too," I said. "Why don't you come back? We miss you. We used to have so much fun before men came into our program. We focused on our careers and made them work for us. Of course men had to come into our lives, but we're sisters first."

"So you're pregnant," Rashawn said. "Congratulations! You can't expect to keep the news from me. Rick's brother didn't think the marriage was going to last, and he was surprised when he got the news that he was going to be an uncle. I think Richard is jealous of his own brother."

"My baby is going to be very blessed with two Godmothers," I cried. "We miss you. I wanted to share the news with you, but you were on your own kick. I thought you needed to see how the skinny women lived would make you happy. I hoped you'd come back to the real world."

"I know, but I needed to live my life. Brian has moved out. He's divorcing me and it's my own fault. I had so much sex my body still hurts. I had to make up for lost time. Men still treat you like a tramp, and it doesn't matter what size you are. I met someone I thought I'd be falling in love with. He told me that he didn't date whores, and I was the biggest one in this city. I went home and bought everything fattening I could find and the rest is history."

"So you don't want to be skinny again?" Maureen said. "I always wanted to be skinny because I wanted the men staring at me with lust, and them whistling all over the place. I wanted so many telephone numbers; I'd be booked for the rest of my life."

"I'm a size 16 now, and I'm going to stay that way," Rashawn said. "It's great being a large woman and I'm proud of it. I had all the things you wanted and it was good for a while, Maureen, but you get sick of the men and the games. Some of them would do or say anything to get into your panties."

"And joining us again," Maureen said. "We're a pact and we have to remember that. If we lose weight, then we're out, but that doesn't mean we don't love each other. We can still stay together and communicate even though we're not in the group. I think we should change the contract."

"I was very hurt when you two kicked me out," Rashawn said. "I don't know if forgiveness is on the horizon. I know I made the rules, and I have to live with them, but I thought we were friends first. Friendship should be the most important issue in this group."

"It's your own fault," I snapped. "You made the rules so you have to stick by them. I think the three of us will be the best of friends because we've been together so long. Linda is a part of the group and when we find two more people they will be a part of the group also."

"She's right," Maureen said. "My marriage is over. And the three of us will remain best friends. We'll welcome the three new members, but this is a group and nothing more or less. We've been there for each other, and will support the decisions that we make, bad or good."

"I'm sorry," Rashawn said. "I resented you both for turning the tables on me. I want us to be able to get along. I love the two of you, and I don't want this happening again. I missed you both."

"Can I sit down?" Linda said. "I think I gave you three enough time to get reacquainted. I'm glad we're going to extend to six people. I think ten people in the group should be a good idea in the future. I just love people and I get a kick out of spending time with a bunch of women, and getting into their business."

"It's nice to finally meet you" Rashawn said. "I know the feeling about the group, and we're going to expand to six for the moment. If the six works out, then we can expand to eight and then ten. Right now we need to focus on the four of us and have a good time."

"The pleasure is all mine," Linda said, sitting next to Rashawn. "Are you going to join us? I know you seemed angry, but you needed to do your own thing. I understand how that feels to erase everyone from your life because there's something you need to do to survive."

"I think I'll come back, but let's keep the same rules," Rashawn said. "We can't be a fat club if someone loses the weight. Our clothing size is fourteen and if anyone drops below that, then it's time to leave. We're going to replace that person, and continue on with our plans."

"Can you live with that?" I asked. "We all should make the rules and stick by them. I'm never going to be skinny, so I'm going to be around for a long time. I think we should have a President in the group to keep everything organized and on a business level. We need someone experienced."

"With bells on," Rashawn said. "Now I'm going to pig out, get my groove on, and then dance the night away. I'm so glad to be back with my friends. I missed you all so much. As for being President, I think Maureen should do it because she's a legal mind with skills."

"How does it feel to be skinny?" Linda said. "Is it everything and more? I was almost skinny when I was in my thirties, and it was okay. I didn't have to worry about wearing anything and when it was hot, I was able to go to the beach and swim. I didn't have to hide myself."

"At first, but when you face reality, you realize it's not about the weight," Rashawn said. "It is how you feel about yourself. Three men called me a slut, and it woke me up. I'm nobody's slut. I was shaking my groove thing, and sleeping with a few men, but that was just a score I had to prove to myself. I'm not a whore by any means."

"Right on," I said, hitting her hand. "We're the ladies of Living Large, and we're proud of it. If you sleep around with a lot of men, Rashawn, it's the title that you put on yourself. You can't blame men for branding you in that category because you do it to yourself."

"I'm in," Maureen said. "With the three of you in my corner, I'm going to get through my marriage breaking up. I think I'll take the challenge of being the President. I'm going to go to my office and design new guidelines for us. This is going to be fun for me, and the group."

"And being back in the group will keep me in line," Rashawn said. "I have lives to go and save. I'm a doctor for heaven sakes, and as a sister, I should be proud of myself. So many black people dropped out the first year of medical school, but I'm a doctor."

"And I have news to report," Linda cried. "It's great knowing you all. I'm proud of the goals I've accomplished in my life, and wouldn't change that part of my life for all the tea in China. I'm a journalist, and I want to do more on the news to enhance it, instead of reporting the bad."

"It's fun to be fat," Rashawn said. "I don't have to worry about men all the time. Most of the time they don't give me the time of day, but at times, they do. I miss them hanging on my every word, but I don't miss them trying to get into my panties. I just want one man."

"I'll drink to that," I said, "but it will have to be with orange juice. I'm with you, Rashawn. I don't need the men buttering me up and staring at me with passion in their eyes. I just want someone who loves me, and thinks about me all the time."

"Let's make a toast," Maureen said. "I think we should make a pact, instead. If one member is excused from the club, we will still support the member forever, and move on. We love each other, and our friendship is binding. I think six members will suffice for now. Along the way we'll see how the group develops with the six."

"What's that?" I asked. "Friendship is the only pact we need, and rules to follow because we need them. Right now I'm going to be a mother and I'm frightened as sin so I'm going to need my support group. I think this club should be for a lot of things like books, support, and just having a good time. We should go to different places and do different things."

"We're the four of the Living Large club, and no one will ever break us apart," Maureen said. "In the next few months I'm going to need support because of my divorce. I never thought it'd happen, I knew Marcus wasn't the man for me, but I wanted him. Just please be patient with me."

"Exceptions to the rule of becoming skinny," Rashawn laughed. "Remember skinny women are evil as sin. We don't want to be skinny, and we're going to love ourselves being fat. We don't give a damn about men who don't like us. We're going to be proud for us."

"I agree," Linda said. "I'm blessed to have a good man in my life, but if he once mentions anything about my weight, then I'm going to kick him to the curb. If you want to be with a skinny woman, then you need to move on. I'm fat and proud of it, and I love me forever."

We embraced and then ordered our food because the ladies' of Living Large club were hungry as sin. I was going to have a baby;

Maureen had to deal with a man who was in love with two women; Rashawn had to get back to the real world; Linda was only just beginning. The Living Large club was definitely experiencing a new beginning.

Horrific Moments

I stared miserably at Banks as I struggled to find words to tell him that once again I did not want to make love to him. He looked so strong, lying there next to me, his impressive manhood once again deflated by me. How could I possibly make him understand? I loved him so much, but the thought of sex turned my stomach, raising the bile to the back of my throat so quickly that I had to fight to keep the nausea down. How much longer was he going to continue being the understanding husband? After all, it had been three months since we shared our bed for anything besides sleeping.

I turned to face him as he started talking, loving him more as I saw his struggle to keep from shouting at me.

"Penny, won't you please tell me what's wrong? What has you so afraid?" he asked.

I just stared at him, momentarily lost for words. If I told him the real reason, he'd never want me again. And ironically, if I didn't tell him, I was going to lose him anyway.

"All right Penny," Banks said, "You need to talk to me. It's been three months since we had sex. I'm trying my damnedest to be patient, but I need some answers…now."

There was no mistaking the undertones to his words. I needed to talk now or risk losing Banks forever. What could I do? There seemed to be only one answer. I steeled myself and turned to face him, feeling the trembling shake my body so badly, I could barely stand.

"I can't talk about it Banks. If you can't accept that and be patient for a little longer, we'll just have to agree to move on."

"Move on!" he shouted. "Are you out of your mind? You want to just give up two years of our lives and not even try to work this out? I was going to suggest we might get some therapy. I know you love me and, God knows I love you more than words can say. Why else have I been taking cold showers for the last three months?" he said, trying to inject a note of humor into our angry conversation.

I was in no mood to be humored and I turned on him in a fury. "Do you think I really believe that you've been faithful to me all this time?" I screamed at him as all my fears of the past months poured from my mouth. "I know you've been screwing around with all those bitches that throw themselves at you. No man can keep his pecker in his pants for this long, especially if his woman doesn't satisfy all his nasty little urges at home."

I jumped out of bed and grabbed my favorite yellow robe, pulling it on as I walked to the window to stare out at the gorgeous October day. Even though I knew it would be chilly, I longed to go down to the beach and just walk, trying to put this whole incident out of my mind, but I knew that was impossible. It was time for us to have this out, no matter what the outcome might be. I was truly afraid that this might be the end of my life with Banks. And even though I thought it might kill me to lose him, it would be easier to bear than the look on his face if he ever found out my secret.

I felt rather than heard him come up behind me and a second later his hands settled on my shoulders as he turned toward me and started talking.

"Penny, for the last time, will you please talk to me? Why won't you trust me enough to help you? What could possibly be so bad that we can't talk about it? Babe, we've been together for two years. I thought we had a great relationship. I understood that you wanted to wait for marriage before we had sex, but we've been married for a year now and I can count the number of times we've had sex on one hand. And it's not like we're making love…it's more like you're just waiting for me to get finished and leave you alone. I don't want a robot in my bed, I want a woman, a flesh and blood woman who enjoys sex as much as I would like to. What I don't want is a woman who just spreads her legs, waiting for me to come so that she can run and hide in the bathroom for hours. I hear the shower running and I know you're scrubbing the smell and feel of me from your body. Do you have any idea of how that makes me feel?"

I stared at him, speechless. What could I say? He was absolutely correct. I focused my attention back on him as he continued to talk.

"I've been running your behavior over and over in my mind and I keep coming back to one thing, Penny. It's the only answer I can think of for your behavior. I just want you to tell me the truth. Once we get your fears out in the open, we can try and overcome them. So, flat out Penny, were you raped at some time?

"Please trust me on this Banks. I love you and when I'm ready I'll talk to you. Right now, I'm not ready and you can't force me to talk. If you can't accept that, then maybe we really do need to separate for a while." I was quaking inside, but I forced myself to meet his gaze and I saw the anger spread over his face. I braced myself for what was coming. I knew it wasn't going to be good.

"I'm tired of waiting on you Penny. I've been waiting for two years now and you still won't talk. You need to get some help from a professional. When you get that help, you can find me at Rochelle's."

"So now I'm a sick bitch, right Banks?" I shouted. You don't love me at all. I thought I had finally found an understanding man, but I see I was really, really wrong. I guess the bitches out there are starting to look pretty good to you, aren't they Banks? I can't stop you from cheating. If you want to whore around and pick up some god-awful disease, go ahead but don't think I'm going to get AIDS just because my husband can't keep his pecker in his pants."

"Okay, that's it. I'm out of here. I just have one more thing to say to you Penny. I have never been unfaithful to you. I've never even thought of doing so although God knows I've had plenty of opportunities. You can reach me at Rochelle's for the next couple of weeks. She told me she was going to be taking a couple of weeks off and maybe she'll enjoy having her baby brother as a guest."

In spite of myself, I almost smiled. Banks' sister Rochelle was forty-five, four years older than Banks. She was a beautiful, plus-size woman and the star of her own weekly television drama called Fighting Bullets. I had great admiration for Rochelle. In spite of the obstacles in her path, she had persevered in her quest to become a television star and then, in spite of her popularity and wealth, she did not let it go to her head, remaining a wonderfully open and down-to-earth woman, as warm and loving now as when she was a struggling bit player.

My heart was breaking at the thought of losing Banks for as little as a day, much less two weeks. I had to try once more to reach him. "Please, Banks don't leave me," I begged. "If you can just give me a little more time to try and get my problems resolved, I promise you won't be sorry."

"I'm already sorry, Penny. If you can't talk to me, your husband who loves you more than anyone in the world, who can you talk to?"

"I thought maybe you could go to a hotel for a couple of weeks and let me talk to Rochelle. I really feel that she might be able to help me. She's so understanding and comforting. If Rochelle isn't able to help me, I promise you that I'll find professional help."

I wasn't prepared for Banks' response. "So I'm going to be the last man standing?" he shouted. "My wife can't talk to me, but she can open up to my sister? How do you think that makes me feel? I'm saying this for the last time...you need to talk to me. What kind of marriage do we have? I love my sister, but this is about the two of us and our life together."

I felt my own anger mounting. I thought Banks and I were soul mates. I was finding out that the only One you can trust totally is God. He's gotten me through the worst possible times in my life. I turned away as the tears started falling. "Just do what you have to do Banks. I'm going for a walk."

"No, don't go. I'll leave as soon as I get my suitcases packed." And Banks walked over to the closet and pulled out his suitcase.

I don't know what time it was when I heard the telephone ringing. It seemed like days since Banks had finished packing and walked out on me. What was I going to do without him? He was my husband and I loved him more than life itself. I hate you! I hate you! What did I do to deserve such pain?

The telephone stopped ringing, only to start up again almost immediately. I had no intention of answering it because I didn't want to talk to anyone, especially if by some chance it was Banks calling me. He had the audacity to leave me because I chose to keep part of my past from him. Who in the hell did he think he was? I'm sure he has some skeletons in his closet that he doesn't want to share. I wasn't getting all bent out of shape about it.

I stretched back out on the green shag rug, too worn out to even drag myself to bed. My mind went back through the years; finally focusing on the year I was five, which was the worst year of my life. I could lay all my problems at my parents' feet. I hated them then and to this day I still can't stand the sight of them. How could they let something like this happen to their baby? Parents are supposed to protect their children. How could they bring me into this world and then subject me to so much pain? It wasn't fair that I had to endure it. The tears fell unchecked as I gave in to my grief.

I woke again, but this time it was because someone was ringing the doorbell. I ignored it and a moment later whoever was there started beating on the door. After five minutes it became apparent that they were not leaving and I raced down the stairs and yanked the door open, ready to give someone a piece of my mind. I stood there speechless as Rochelle pushed past me, Banks right behind her carrying his suitcases.

"Banks, you take those suitcases back to your bedroom and un-pack them. I'll call you when we're ready for you to come back down," Rochelle ordered as she enveloped me in a rib-crushing hug.

Banks tried to say something, but Rochelle put up her hand, ef-fectively stopping him. "Banks, will you just listen to your older sister for once. Let me talk to Penny for a while and then I'll be ready to talk to you."

Banks looked at her, opened his mouth, and must have thought better of it because he closed it, not saying another word as he trudged up the stairs, lugging his heavy suitcases. We listened until we heard the door shut and then Rochelle took my hand, pulling me into the living room. While she made herself comfortable on the couch she ordered me, "Penny, make us a drink and then come and sit down. We've got a lot of talking to do." I felt a smile tug my lips as I hurried to the kitchen to get our drinks. I grabbed a couple of cans of diet cola as well as a paper towel to use as a coaster and went back to join Rochelle. As I handed her the drink, she pointed to the love seat and said, "Sit, girl. It's time to talk."

Before Rochelle got started I had a question of my own. "What's Banks doing back here? I thought he was going to visit you for a couple of weeks."

"Banks is here because I kicked his ass out of my house and brought him back home to his wife, where he belongs," she said, staring me in the eye and daring me to deny Banks his rightful place in our home. "He's a grown man now and it's time he stopped running from his problems. He needs to stand and face them. I brought him home myself to make sure he did come back and also because I thought this might be the time when he really does need a big sister's help."

"He doesn't want to be here," I shouted. "He's got another woman and doesn't want me any more. I'm not good enough to satisfy my husband in bed. The thought of sex makes me ill. This marriage is never going to work." I stopped in shock because Rochelle was laughing so hard tears were streaming down her face. She was a large woman whose big, hearty laugh filled the room. "I'm glad my pain makes you so happy," I snapped.

At my words, Rochelle started laughing even harder, bending over and clutching her sides, unable to stop the tears. Finally she seemed to be able to get a grip, using the paper towel to wipe her face and blow her nose before speaking.

"That big SOB upstairs loves you so much, he's never looked at another woman since he met you. He worships the ground you walk on and he'd do anything in the world for you."

I wanted to be angry at her, but Rochelle was so sweet and loving. I knew she was only trying to help and as I looked at her pretty face, still wet from her tears, I had to smile back at her.

That's better," Rochelle said as she took another big sip of her soda. "Now let's see if we can figure out what's bothering you and then we'll try to fix it. How does that sound to you?" she asked me, smiling again. As I stared at her, speechless, she went on, "Penny, I know Banks has not been unfaithful to you. But how long do you think he can go on like this? Do you expect any man to resist the charms of all the loose women out in our world forever?"

I began talking, but she interrupted me, holding up her hand. For some reason, I wanted to just slap that hand back. What right did she have to poke into my most private business?

I spoke anyway. "Rochelle, I love you and appreciate that you want to help, but this is not your business. I'm not going to explain anything to you."

Then you're going to lose your husband and your friend," Rochelle snapped. "We love you and only want to help. Now I think I know what your problem might be and you're going to sit there and let me have my say. If I'm wrong, just tell me," she went on more gently.

"A long time ago, we were talking about pedophiles and you got awfully quiet. I remember you left the room and didn't come back for ages. When Banks told me what was happening between you two in bed, it suddenly clicked." She leaned forward, grabbing my hands and holding them tightly. "Is that what happened Penny? Is that the big dark secret in your life? Oh baby, you need to realize that you're not a bad person. You were just a child, completely powerless against an adult." Unshed tears gleamed in her beautiful eyes as they held mine. "We need to let that snake out of the bag before he strangles you."

"Rochelle, I love you and really appreciate what you're trying to do. But you've got the wrong end of the snake, if you'll pardon the analogy. I don't have anything to tell you."

"All right, then let me tell you a little story, one I've never told anyone before. Ten years ago, I was grocery shopping and met a man named Raymond. He came on really strongly and even though my antenna was telling me to avoid him, I was so desperate to have someone in my life, I ignored my feelings and we moved in together. For two years I was in heaven. He showered compliments on me, telling me how much he loved my breasts and my big booty. Then our relationship soured. To this day I don't know what happened, but all of a sudden he started making fun of me, at first at home and then in front of our friends, calling me a fat cow and raping me when I refused to have sex."

Rochelle paused to take a deep breath and I winced when I saw the pain in her face. I saw what an effort it was for her to tell me this painful story.

"At first I blamed it on the fact that he had started drinking heavily. Every time he hurt me, I filed a police report but they couldn't do anything other than place a restraining order on him. In other words, if I were killed, he'd be their first suspect. One day he broke into my house and attacked me with a knife. For once, I was glad of my size because I was able to wrestle him to the floor and get the knife away from him. When he came at me again, I slashed him across the face, making a nice big cut that left an enormous scar."

I drew in my breath in horror as she continued. "Everything was quiet for a few months. I figured I had scared him enough that he'd never come around me again, but I did take a self-defense class and got a gun for protection. When Raymond got drunk and broke into my house again, I shot his ass dead. I was really frightened as I watched him dying on my floor, but not so frightened that I didn't make sure the son of a bitch was dead before I called 911. Then I called Bags Grin, the detective that had taken all of my calls about Raymond. He was also the one who advised me to take the self-defense classes and apply for a gun permit and taught me to shoot."

A secretive smile appeared on Rochelle's face when she said the detective's name and I wondered if Bags Grin might be the mysterious man in her life. We knew she had someone, but she never talked about him.

Rochelle saw my smile and wagged her finger at me. "Don't go seeing a big romance here Penny. The detective is just a friend. I'm not ready for another relationship right now. Truthfully, I just don't have time for one,"

Then why was she smiling at just the mention of the detective's name, I wondered?

"Anyway, back to my story," Rochelle continued. "I let the abuse continue because I thought I deserved it. I thought someone as big and fat as me wasn't worthy of a good man. That's why I now refuse to go on a diet. I'm me, and I'm not changing. I will not allow anyone to dictate how I will look, act or dress. I also know that what happened to me was not my fault. No one will ever be allowed to abuse me again, either physically or mentally."

"Whatever happened to you as a child was out of your control. You weren't the first, and God help us, you won't be the last. I'm so sorry that you had such pain, but it was in the past. You need to focus your attention on the here and now. You have a man who loves you with all his heart and soul and you have us, my parents and me, who love you like you were our own. In fact, you *are* our own," she finished softly, her love for me shining in her eyes.

I felt the tears well in my eyes as I looked at Rochelle. All of a sudden, I knew it was time to let my burden go. I looked around to make sure Banks wasn't in the room and Rochelle, knowing what I was doing, hastened to assure me that Banks was in the game room, well out of earshot.

I sat for a few minutes more, my eyes closed as I tried to decide where to start. Finally, taking a deep breath, I plunged in.

"When I was five years old, I thought I was the happiest, luckiest little girl in the world. My mother and father adored me although my father was my chief caregiver, while my mother, a legal secretary, worked fifty or more hours a week. When he would give me a bath, he loved to let me run around the house naked before he would pull me into his lap for story time. He would read story after story to me, all the while rubbing my legs, his hands rising higher and higher until he would be touching me in my special place. This was our little secret, he told me. Don't tell Mommy. I loved that Daddy and I shared a special secret.

Then one day it went dreadfully wrong. I had gotten out of the tub and went to climb into Daddy's lap for my story when he stopped me. "Baby, do you want to do something really special for Daddy? Something that he'll really like and will make him feel good?" he asked.

"Yes Daddy, I do," I laughed happily. "I want to make my Daddy feel good." I loved him more than anything in the world and I knew he loved me too. I would do anything for him because he was my Daddy and I was his Baby.

"He laid me down on the bed and pulled my legs apart and began shoving his fingers into my special place. It hurt very badly and I asked Daddy to stop hurting me. He told me to be quiet or he would really hurt me, but by then I was so scared I was crying. When he pushed his fingers far into me, I felt such an intense pain that I screamed. He found some tape and taped my mouth closed as his fingers continued to probe me. All of a sudden he started shaking and making these strange sounds before he fell on top of me. He pulled the tape off of my mouth and kissed me, his breath so nasty I almost puked from the stench.

"He smiled at me and said, 'you were a good little girl today and I'm really proud of you, but tomorrow you'll be even better. Don't forget that this is our little secret. Don't tell Mommy now.' After he left my room, I got up to go to the bathroom and found blood all over my sheet.

"This went on until I was ten years old. For my tenth birthday, my father raped me. His penis was so big it tore up my insides. I could barely walk at times. Looking back now, I can't believe that my mother didn't know what was going on. But he always told me that if I told my mother, he'd kill both of us. I couldn't take a chance on anything happening to my mother, so I just endured it as best I could." I stopped to draw a deep breath. This next part would be the hardest to confess.

"When I was fifteen, I finally had enough and I managed to stop my father dead in his tracks. I had recently watched a movie about a young girl who was being molested by her father. She hid a knife in her bed and stabbed him to death when he came into her room. I was determined that I was going to stop my father in the same way.

"I looked through all the knives in the kitchen to choose the best one. The blade needed to be sharp and long enough that it would reach his heart. When I found the one I wanted, I hid it under my pillow and waited. I knew he'd be coming to see me that night because that morning at breakfast, my mother had said she'd be working late. There was no mistaking the look he gave me as he told Mama that he'd take good care of me. I almost puked as he turned that look on me, but I held it in. I knew I'd be getting my revenge that night."

I stopped to sneak a glance at Rochelle, but I saw no condemnation in her face as she reached over and took my hands, holding them in her warm grasp as I struggled to continue.

"It's okay baby," she said. "Do you want another drink before you go on?"

The love and acceptance I saw in her face made it easy to answer, "No, thanks Rochelle, I'd rather get it all out now that I've come this far." And I found to my surprise that I really did want to tell my story to Rochelle.

"I was waiting, my hand wrapped around the handle of the knife, when my father walked into my room that night, his nasty little thang pointing at me from his naked body.

'Hey baby,' he cried, 'Daddy has a special treat for you tonight. I've been selfish and not giving my baby girl any pleasure, just taking it all for myself. Now you turn on over and let me get you screaming out in passion.'

"I stared at his ugly body, hating it and him. As he came closer to the bed and lifted his foot to climb in, I pulled out my knife and pointed it straight at his balls, pressing in hard enough for him to feel the sharp point of the knife. He stopped in his tracks, his erect penis shriveled up, and the fear in his eyes a wonder to behold. I pressed a little harder and a drop of blood appeared. He screamed, the terror making him piss, the yellow stream running down his leg.

'Now that I have your attention, you bastard, you need to listen to what I have to say to you. If you ever, ever, so much as even look at me, I'll cut off your tiny little dick and make you eat it before I call the police. Do you understand what I'm saying,' I said as I pressed the knife in a little more, causing him to scream."

'Yes, I understand. Please don't cut me. Come on baby doll, give Daddy the knife,' he said, holding out his hand like he really thought I'd give it to him. I laughed as I slashed his hand, watching the blood drip on my bed. He screamed and jumped back and I followed him, slashing my knife again and cutting his leg open. He ran running from my bedroom, crying like a baby himself as he tried to stop the blood streaming from his body."

Rochelle had a big smile on her face. "Wow girl that was brave. I'm so proud of you," she said as she leaned over to engulf me in a giant hug, which I returned, holding onto her as if I'd never let go. I felt wonderful, as if a giant weight had lifted from my heart. I've finally gotten up enough courage to tell someone what happened and she still loved me. Not only did she still love me, she actually approved of what I'd done.

"So what happened to you father?" she asked. "Did you call the police?"

"No, he grabbed some clothes and took off. We never heard from him again after the divorce. I always felt that my mother blamed me for him leaving although she never actually came right out and said anything. I guess she knew she was as culpable as he. A few years later he was dating another woman who had a young daughter and we heard that the father of that little girl killed him for molesting her. That little girl told her Daddy and he defended her, just like a Daddy should do," I said, trying to keep the resentment from coming through. Why couldn't my Daddy defend his little girl? "Justice was a long time coming, but my father finally got what was coming to him. I couldn't even cry for him when I heard the news. All I felt was a deep feeling of happiness that he'd never be able to hurt another child."

As I finished speaking, the tears fell. I cried for myself, for my ruined childhood, my barren adult life. I cried because I missed my husband. I wanted nothing more than to feel his strong arms wrapped around me, holding me as I wept for all the abused children of the world. I thought I'd never stop as Rochelle held me tight, murmuring soothing words as she led me up the stairs, helped me into a clean nightgown and tucked me into bed. The last thing I remember before falling into a deep, cleansing sleep was Rochelle bending over me, using a warm washcloth to wipe my tear stained face and kissing my eyelids as I fell into the first restful sleep I'd had since I was five years old.

Hours later I slowly surfaced from sleep, feeling a deep peace unlike anything I'd ever felt engulfing me. Even the sight of Banks, dozing in a chair by the bed, his laptop sitting on the floor next to him, didn't disturb my serenity. I lay there watching him sleep for a few minutes until he slowly awoke, his eyes darting quickly over to the bed as soon as he was conscious, a sweet smile forming for me as he leaned over to kiss my forehead.

"Morning Penny," he said. "Ready for some breakfast before we talk? Rochelle ran out and picked up some things for us and she told me to be sure and tell you that she bought you some bacon, sliced extra thick."

I smiled at him. Rochelle was a dear and she knew how I loved bacon, especially the thick slices fried nice and crispy. One day I had bacon as all three meals: bacon and eggs for breakfast, a BLT for lunch and a bacon and mushroom pizza for dinner. If I could have thought of a dessert made from bacon, I'd have eaten that too. Of course, I paid the price for all that bacon as I trudged miles on my treadmill, but it was worth it.

"No, I'm not hungry right now. How about you? Did you have anything to eat?"

"Let's not worry about me Penny. How about we just concentrate on you for now?" he said, a compassionate smile on his face, and I knew immediately that Rochelle had told him about my father. I waited for the anger at having my trust betrayed to rise, but as I looked at Banks, I knew Rochelle was right. It was time I faced my demons. If Banks couldn't handle it, I needed to put him behind me and continue my life. Somehow, though, seeing my husband sitting there, pure love for me shining in his face, I had a sudden feeling that everything might be all right.

"Rochelle told you, didn't she?"

"Well, not exactly. She knew you were going to make her promise not to tell me, so we stopped by the house of one of the soundmen from her show and got her wired. I could hear everything from our bedroom." He smiled at me, quite pleased at their cleverness and I found myself smiling back before we both burst in laughter. It felt so good to laugh with Banks again, but when he moved to sit on the side of the bed, the laughter stopped. We stared at each other for a few seconds and then Banks opened his arms wide, leaving the decision to me. Dare I take the chance? Hell, yes I would. There wasn't a second of hesitation before I threw myself into my husband's arms, feeling them wrap around me as he lifted me up and held me in his lap. I felt a moment of fear, remembering all the times my father had put me in his lap, but this was different. This was Banks, the only man I've ever loved and I knew I was safe.

I sat there, wrapped in a cocoon of love, inhaling his scent and suddenly I realized what I had almost lost. The tears started again and as they wet Banks' shirt, he pulled me even tighter, murmuring soft words that had no meaning as he too wept for innocence lost. My beautiful strong husband was weeping for me. It was too much to bear. I was so ashamed of myself for not seeking help long ago.

"Banks, can we lie down and get some sleep?" I asked, hoping he would realize that all I wanted to do was sleep.

"Sure, Baby. Let me go change into a dry shirt. Somehow, this one got all wet," he said grinning. I watched as he went to his dresser and pulled out a dry tee shirt, pulling his wet one over his head as he walked into the bathroom. I heard the water running and when he came out, he had a warm washcloth in his hand that he brought over to me. I realized that Rochelle had done the same thing for me earlier and I fought to keep the tears at bay. What a wonderful family I had found for myself!

I felt the bed move as Banks climbed in the other side and it took all of my courage to turn and face him. He didn't say a word, just gathered me close and said, "Go to sleep Penny. We'll talk in the morning." He closed his eyes and promptly went to sleep. I lay there in the warm circle of his arms, thinking I would just watch my beloved man sleep for a while, but before the thought was even finished, I too was asleep, a deep healing sleep.

Hours later I woke up. Banks and I had moved as we slept and I now had my back pressed into him spoon fashion. I felt something else too, that caused me a moment of panic. Something hard was thrusting against my backside and as I heard my husband wake, I dreaded the scene to come.

He pulled away from me and I heard him say, "Hey Woody, you need to go away for a while. I'll call you back when I need you."

I couldn't help it…His words made me giggle. Once I started, I couldn't stop and Banks said in an aggrieved tone, "Hey lady, don't laugh at poor Woody. Who knows what damage you'll do to his little psyche?"

I jumped out of bed and ran for the bathroom where I took a long hot shower. I was getting out of the shower when I realized I had forgotten to bring in my robe. I stood there indecisively for a moment, knowing I wasn't comfortable retuning to the bedroom in just my sheer nightgown, when I saw my thick, fleecy robe thrown across the stool. Once again, I was horrorstruck at the thought that I had almost lost this man. Belting on my robe, I returned to the bedroom but Banks was gone. I knew where he was though, as the aromas of freshly brewed coffee and bacon frying teased my nose and I realized I was starving. I was dressed in record time and raced down the stairs to the kitchen to help Banks finish up our breakfast, even though it was late afternoon.

We were both so hungry we barely said a word as we ate, but afterwards, the kitchen cleaned up; I knew the time had come for Banks and me to talk.

Carrying fresh cups of coffee, we went into the living room, sitting together on the couch. I opened my mouth to talk, but Banks forestalled me.

"Penny, you don't need to go over all the details again. I heard it all last night. What I want you to know is that I love you. I hate what happened to you, but that doesn't change my love for you. Now that I know what's wrong, I think, if you agree, we can work through this. This morning while you were sleeping, I went online and found thousands of websites devoted to abused children. There are four or five support groups right near us, as well as listings for doctors who specialize in adults who were abused children. Would you like to get online and see if we can find a compatible group for you?"

I smiled at him, my dearly beloved husband, my soul mate and knew in my heart that everything would be all right. How could they be anything else when I had Banks at my side? I grabbed his hand and we headed for the computer to begin our life over.

One year later

I was a little nervous as I waited for Banks to come to bed. Although we had indulged in some heavy petting, we had not made love since I began therapy. Tonight was the night and I hoped everything would go all right.

Banks walked in, a peculiar look on his face, and I realized he was as nervous as me, maybe even more so. For some reason, seeing Banks, my big strong protector, so scared made my own nerves vanish and I determined that, even if I couldn't find fulfillment tonight, Banks would have his.

"Don't say a word," I warned him as I took his hand and led him to the bed, where I fastened my mouth on his, my tongue delving deep into his mouth as I slowly unbuttoned his shirt. As I eased it off his shoulders and down his arms, my lips trailed over his chest, stopping to nip at his nipples, my teeth tugging the hair on his chest. I let my mouth continue to slide down his body as I threw his shirt aside and unfastened his pants. I could see that he was ready for me, his manhood straining against his tight briefs as I slid his pants down his legs, my mouth following, my tongue leaving a wet trail as I deliberately avoided the part that most wanted attention. I realized that I was no longer nervous. I was actually excited and could feel the wetness forming between my legs as I continued to make my way around his body.

I was back at his waist and I took the elastic of his briefs in my teeth, pulling back and letting it snap a little. His breathing was erratic, but so far he hadn't said a word. I pulled out the waistband of his briefs and peeked inside. I saw a turgid sword straining to be released. I reached inside and gently ran my finger around the helmet shaped head, feeling the moisture seeping out. "Hey Woody, you want to come out and play?" I said, finally pulling off his pants, allowing him to surge into my hand.

Above me, Banks made a strangled sound, half laugh and half groan of ecstasy, as I closed my lips around Woody, drawing him in as far as I could. Banks lasted about five seconds, attempting to pull out of my mouth but I wouldn't let go. I wanted to do this, for him and for me. I had never felt such passion in my life and I wanted it to go on forever.

Then it was my turn as Banks pulled my nightgown off me and let it drop to the floor before sweeping me into his arms and dropping me in the center of our big bed where he immediately joined me, pasting his mouth to mine, our tongues dueling as they chased each other back and forth. Then he left my mouth and started his own expedition down my body. As his mouth closed over a turgid nipple I tensed and he waited patiently until I relaxed before beginning a gentle suction that shot sensations into my innermost being. My insides were quivering and shaking when all of a sudden I was screaming as I felt my first-ever orgasm rip through my body. I lay there, unable to move, my insides in turmoil. I had never felt anything like this in my life. I felt Banks' hands running down my sides as he tried to help me calm myself.

"Wow! Could someone please explain just why I waited so long for this?" I said to Banks.

"Some people just like to postpone their pleasures longer than others," he said smiling.

"Well, I know one pleasure I don't want to postpone any longer," I said as I reached down and grabbed his rigid manhood, rubbing the tip around my most intimate parts as I felt the excitement begin to mount again.

"Are you sure, Penny? We can still have a lot of fun without…"

His words were cut off as I raised my hips and impaled myself on him, straining to take every inch inside my outrageously stretched flesh. And then there was nothing in my world except for Banks and what he was doing to me. I felt my pleasure mount and as I climaxed, he screamed and I felt the pulsations of his penis as he released jet after jet of his vital essence deep inside me.

Afterward, we lay entwined in each other's arms in our big bed, closing out the whole world as we talked in the universal language of love. I looked over at Banks, so worn out from our lovemaking that he barely had the energy to pull the covers over our naked bodies. I raised the blanket and contemplated once more my new favorite toy, reaching out to hold it in my hand, automatically rubbing up and down as it grew in my hand.

"Oh Baby, I can't. There's nothing left," he said.

I kept up my gentle stroking, not saying a word, letting my hands do the talking.

"All right, Penny, but I'm too tired to hold myself up," Banks said as he rolled over on his back, inviting me to climb the maypole. He held himself steady as I guided him in and I sank down, taking his full length, realizing that I was home, all horrific memories gone, erased by the love of this man. Finally after all these years, I was home.

Survival

I stood at the corner watching the men hunt down the prostitutes. I used to hate that word, preferring to call myself a whore or slut, because prostitute was too high-class for me. But then I thought, why not? I had a great size six body with large shapely breasts that were all mine, and the perfect ass. I made plenty of money and answered to no one but myself. I was a prostitute and proud of it. I had been conning the streets for eleven years. I had my own condo and plenty of money in my bank account.

It wasn't my fault that some women didn't know how to treat their men. I was here to entice a man into spending his money. Sometimes I made five hundred dollars for an hour's work. No wonder I loved some aspects of my job. Who wouldn't?

I was five years old the first time my mother's man Big came into my bedroom and molested me. He made me do things I hated and it made me grow up fast. When I was fourteen I ran away from home. I had tried to talk to my mother many times, but usually she was so drunk that I couldn't make her understand what Big was doing to me. Now that I'm older, with more experience of the world, I think she probably understood only too well what was happening. Hiding in the bottle meant she didn't need to take responsibility for me.

I blame my father as much as my mother for the way my life turned out. He was a weak son-of-a-bitch and couldn't handle my mother's drinking, so he took the easy way out and left when I was two. I never saw him again. I think if there had been other children in our family, someone for me to talk with and maybe help me fight off Big, my life would have turned out very different.

My mother sent me to school, but didn't involve herself in my school life. By the time I was nine, I was signing my report cards myself. I found out that I could give the boys in my class blowjobs at recess and I could earn lunch money. I was ready to enter high school when I ran away from home and I made the difficult decision to try and finish high school. I didn't have much money, but I found a cheap hotel and the manager offered me a proposition. In return for regular sex, he would let me use a storage room in the basement, where he set up a cot and a small dresser for me. In order to earn money for food and other necessities, I had to walk the streets, following the older prostitutes I saw to find the best pick-up spots.

I soon came to the conclusion that all any man needed was a body with a vagina hooked up to it. Soon, I had mastered the art of lovemaking and I was making enough money to afford a nicer hotel. The new hotel manager was also willing to look the other way when I brought my *friends* to my room, so long as I took care of him on a regular basis, and I had more clients than I could count. I was living my life my way, and I didn't give a damn about anyone's opinion of me. I paid my bills with money I earned and did anything I damn well pleased. Soon I had enough to put a down payment on my own condo. I still used the hotel for my work, not wanting my johns to know where I lived. I contacted most of my clients by phone, but sometimes I liked to go back to my roots and visit the street corners I worked as a teenager. That's what I was doing today, just checking out the competition and catching up with some old friends.

The rich men wearing their thousand dollars suits, most of them sporting wedding rings, still cruised the streets, searching for something their wealthy wives and girlfriends were unable to provide. I shook my head as a car stopped in front of me. I wasn't working today, but the driver of the green car caught my attention when he lowered his window. He was the most handsome man I had ever seen. Even as I shook my head and turned to walk on, I wondered what a man with his looks was doing here. He could probably have just about any woman he wanted. He cruised along beside me and I finally faced him and said, "Sorry, I'm not working today. Maybe another time."

"What's your name, Beautiful?" he asked me, still keeping pace as I walked down Fifth Street.

"My name doesn't matter to you, mister. I told you I'm not working today."

"So what would it cost me to get you to come into the office today," he asked with a smile.

I had to return his smile; he was so outrageous…and gorgeous. But I still wasn't going anywhere with him. I needed these days to rest and spend some time on me.

I had to give him credit for persistence. He still kept pace with me as he threw out his next come-on.

"Okay beautiful, how about $1000.00 for the night? I'll even take you someplace real nice for dinner. You can choose where you want to go."

"Listen mister..." I began, only to be interrupted by the handsome stranger.

"Latino, Latino Banks is my name. Real estate is my game and Beautiful; you've got some prime real estate on you. How about $2000.00 for the night and I'll throw in breakfast in the morning?"

I took a closer look at his face. He *was* Latino Banks, a multimillionaire real estate tycoon. But what was he doing trolling the street? Maybe he was a look-a-like, capitalizing on the uncanny resemblance. But why mess with hookers? He could go pick up some prime meat at any of the high-end bars in the city.

"Okay, Beautiful, you've looked me over long enough," he said, pulling his wallet from his pocket and opening it to show me his driver's license. "See, I really am Latino Banks, in person. Now here's my last offer. I'll give you $3000.00 for the night including dinner, a show and breakfast. That's it...take it or leave it."

"Lace is my name." I said, putting my hand out to open the door. The chance to make $3000.00 for one night's work was too good to pass up. I settled in the front seat, fastening my seat belt as I looked through the windshield at the cloudy September sky. It looked like it might rain later, but I wasn't worried. I didn't have to deal with anything but Latino Banks tonight.

"Lace...that's an unusual name. Is it your working name or your real name?"

"It's both. My mother loved fancy lace. She always had a piece of lace sewn somewhere on her clothing. She made a fancy lace layette for me and persuaded my father to let her name me Lacey. The hospital made a mistake and entered my name as Lace. Of course my mother loved it and never had it changed," I explained. I was surprised at myself. This was the first time I could ever recall explaining my unusual name to a john. But I didn't think Latino was going to be my usual sort of customer. Something about him drew me. It wasn't his looks; I'd had plenty of good-looking, even handsome men before. It wasn't even his wealth, although I don't think too many of my customers could match him in the money department. I did know I was attracted by his sense of humor. A man with a sense of humor could be butt-ugly and still attract me.

I was snapped out of my reverie by Latino's voice saying, "Hey Lace, I'm trying to get my Mack on here, and you're off day-dreaming about someone else. You need to concentrate on me for the next few hours, okay?"

I smiled at him. "I'm sorry. What did you say?" I didn't know what was wrong with me. I've met many men, but no one had ever captivated my senses like Latino.

"Now you've offended me," he said. "I'm your client and your only job tonight is to look beautiful and please me. Now you've got the first part down pat. You just need to work on the second part. And you should know that a big part of pleasing me is for you to listen to what I say."

I laughed. "I'm sorry. I was just wondering why you're down here picking up whores, especially black whores. It seems to me you could pretty well pick and choose any woman you wanted."

"I know that, baby," Latino agreed. "I have plenty of girl-friends. But I don't have to pretend with you girls. We both know our part and there's not a big song and dance beforehand. And I happen to be partial to black women. I've always dated them in preference to white women. Black women seem so much more alive and in tune with their bodies."

We drove past Roxie, a regular on this street who thought she was the bomb and then some. She had it going on with her tall, healthy body, without so much as an ounce of fat on it. All the men wanted her until I came along. She stared at the car, her face a mixture of aston-ishment and anger. Latino barely glanced at her as we passed her, but I knew they were acquainted.

"Is Roxie your usual?" I asked curiously. I wasn't angry with him. Hooking was a dog-eat-dog profession and you can never tell what a john would want on a particular day. We hookers tried to stay friends and look out for each other, but Roxie might be seriously pissed with me if I walked off with a regular, especially a free-spending regular.

"I've been with her a few times, but she's starting to take me for granted. I'm not getting tied down to any woman, much less a whore," he stated flatly.

For some reason that hurt me and being hurt scared me. I never allowed myself to be upset over what someone said about me or how I chose to live my life.

"Right! Whatever the reason you pick up prostitutes is your own business, Latino. I'm sure you have some kinky, sexy women in your bed that would probably die for you."

He mingled into traffic as I stared out the window. Latino smelled too good for my peace of mind. I didn't know what in the hell was happening to me? I was cold when I slept with men, but Latino was making me hot as hell.

"Are you close to your mother?" Latino asked. "Most women are, but I can't imagine your mother approving of what you do for a living. Or did your mother disown you when you became prettier than her? A lot of women actually get jealous of their own daughters instead of being proud of them."

"I'm sure you have plenty of glamorous type women in your life to talk to, Latino Banks. Why are you trying to make conversation with me? I don't usually chat with my customers. They prefer me to do things other than talking with my mouth." I don't know why I said that unless it was to unsettle Latino. I should have known it wouldn't work.

"I'm not the johns you usually sleep with," he snapped. "Don't ever put me in the same category. I do have other women in my life, but I'm with you now, and my focus is on you. Do you expect me to be alone without the touch and feel of a woman? It's not going to happen."

At least he didn't lie about his women, and I had to give him credit for that. I was curious to know what kind of woman made Latino Banks tick. For some reason I knew I couldn't be the one because we lived in two different worlds. "Why don't you tell me about your real girlfriends?"

"Why would you want to know about other women in my life? I'm not asking you about the men in yours and I'll bet you have a lot more men in your life than I have women."

Of course I wanted to know what kind of women made him tick. Who wouldn't be curious? "I really want to know," I replied, not sure if the statement was true or not.

"Racine is very special to me," Latino said. "She's a super-model so you would probably recognize her from fashion magazine covers. Bonnie is another model, not as famous as Racine and very ambitious. I don't see a lot of her because she does a lot of work in

Europe. She gives me a holler when she's stateside. Francine is an attorney and I date her more than the others. The other women in my life are transients."

I laughed, shaking my head at him. "At least you're an honest man," I said. "I think I like a man who doesn't play games with women. Why can't men just be honest with a woman? Just tell us, 'I want to sleep with you because you've got a great body, but I don't want to marry you.'"

"I'm not planning on getting married for a long time. I make sure the women I date understand that going in. I don't mind spending money or giving them a good time and most of them are happy with that. If they aren't, I break it off. But I've got to tell you Lace, none of them have ever captivated me the way you do. I never thought a prostitute would do this to me. Mimi warned me that someday I was going to pass a woman who would rock my world and I'd be so busy playing my little games with other women that I wouldn't even slow down enough to notice her. I can't believe the old girl got something right. I've been down this street hundreds of times and never noticed you before today."

The undisguised affection in his voice when he spoke about Mimi raised an unexpected feeling of jealousy in me. I couldn't stop myself from asking, "Who's Mimi?" fighting hard to keep the tartness out of my voice.

"Why Lace, are you jealous," Latino asked with a grin, turning to look at me as the car pulled up to a red light.

I shook my head. "No Latino, I'm not jealous. I don't believe in love, romance or relationships, thank you very much. I just want to have sex, get some pleasure out of it, and then move on. I'm not into a long-term commitment. Your voice just sounded so different when you said her name, I thought she might be someone very special to you."

"She is special…the most wonderful woman I've ever met. Without her, I'd be nothing. I owe my very existence to her." After pausing for a few seconds, he continued, "She's my mom."

I stared at this drop-dead gorgeous man. How could one man be so hot and exciting and yet infuriating, all at the same time? I wanted to slap him upside his head. I decided to change the subject. "Do you only date black women? I know Racine is black and if Francine's last name is Washington, I know she's black too."

"I just think black women are the most gorgeous woman in the world. I like a woman with a good booty, and black women seem to be better equipped in that department than white women, thank you very much. Plus the women I date are intelligent, and that really turns me on."

I was stunned by his words. "Are you color blind? There are just as many gorgeous white women out there, and they're kinky as hell. You should just watch them on cable," I laughed. "If you give yourself a chance, you might find a good white woman to live with for the rest of your life."

"I've dated white women, Lace, but I always go back to a black woman. They just turn me on. It's not that I'm color-blind. I see a gorgeous woman that appeals to me and she just happens to be black. Why does society always have to make color an issue?"

I shook my head. "You're weird, Latino Banks. I'm sure your mother isn't thrilled about you bringing black women home. Everyone isn't as okay about the other races as you. This may be the 21st century, but racists are still everywhere."

"So true, Lace, but if I worried about people thoughts about me, then I wouldn't be where I am today," he pointed out. "I take care of me, and what makes me happy is a black woman. My parents had plenty of black friends, and they encourage me to love everyone. And since they offer me unconditional love, they would love anyone I loved. Skin color would never be an issue. Besides, sisters have it going on."

"We do have it going on, and the black brothers don't give a damn about us. They don't appreciate what we can become. But if you don't get to know a white woman, you're never going to see if she's the one for you. I think you're wasting your time."

"Lace, I'm 45 years old. I've been having sex on a regular basis since I was 13 years old and one of Mimi's friends seduced me. I've dated women of every nationality and color you can name. I like them all, but I'm always drawn back to black women. I don't know exactly why, but I do know what I like. Now let's change the subject and you tell me a little about yourself. How old are you? How long have you been hooking? Why are you hooking rather than sitting behind a desk somewhere?"

I was very reluctant to talk about myself, but since he was paying I decided I could tell him a little bit. "I'm 24 years old and I've been a working girl since I was 13. I'm hooking because the pay is good, I set my own hours and everything I earn, I keep. I don't have to answer to anyone."

Deliberately changing the subject, I asked, "Where are you taking me for dinner. I'm really getting hungry."

"Let's go to the Rental Restaurant. I think it's the perfect place for the both of us. The food is out of this world plus it's so romantic, you could move in and never leave. I know you're a romantic, just like me."

Latino was surprising me all over the place. He had exquisite taste in restaurants. The Rental Restaurant was the most expensive restaurant in Chicago. You had to make reservations weeks in advance to get in. I didn't know that there were so many people who could afford to eat there, but the place was always booked up. I remember a john wanted to take me there after we had some good sex, but we couldn't get in. "Do you have reservations?"

"I don't need one," he laughed. "I own the place. The first time I ate there, I knew it was going to be my favorite restaurant and when I find something I like, I invest my money in it. Right now it's closed for remodeling, so you and I will have it all to ourselves."

"Get out of here," I cried. "Are you jiving me? That restaurant has the most mouth-watering food in the world. I went there once with a john who had reservations he didn't want to waste when his date cancelled on him at the last minute. He said if you don't use your reservations, you go on the Black List and you'll pay hell trying to get another reservation."

"Let me give you a little secret about me. Believe it or not, I'm a chef at heart. I love the kitchen and I'm going to take you to my restaurant and cook for you. I can take an egg and do wonders with it. You won't be disappointed."

I was speechless. I never expected Latino to be a chef. He could have said that he was a police officer and I'd have believed him. I stared at his hands. They looked soft, and I wanted to touch them for some reason. My body was so hot I thought I was going to suffocate if we didn't get out of this car. The window was down, but it wasn't doing anything for me.

"Cat got your tongue Lace?" Latino laughed. "That happens a lot when I mention that I'm a chef. Mimi's one of the best cooks in this city and she made sure I could cook."

Why was this happening to me? I had to get rid of Latino before I fell in love with him. My heart was beating so fast, I thought I would have a stroke. "Why don't you just take me home? I don't think dinner is such a good idea after all."

"I want to absorb your drugging nectar and you're ready to leave me. Let's just go have dinner and then go to my place. I won't pry into your private life any more. I promise. If you want to pretend that I'm just another john then do it. Whatever floats your boat is fine with me."

I smiled at his words. "You also have a way with words, Latino Banks. I've never met anyone like you before. I just don't think this is going to work so I want to go home. If you don't want to drive me, I'll call a taxi. You could go and see if Roxie is still available. I'm just not the one for you today."

"Lace, when did you become afraid of a man? You look the type to cut off a man's balls if he looks at you the wrong way. I just don't get what makes you tick. I thought I wasn't the only one who felt the erotic, intoxicating, engulfing heat. I'm usually a good judge of people."

I wanted to kiss him, but my lingering doubts were surfacing again. I wasn't stupid. Latino could become a major complication in my life and I needed to break off any association with the man. I couldn't let him wreck my perfect life.

"I want to dance and curl with your tongue; I want to take your swollen plums into my mouth, and feel the throbbing heat of your passion," Latino said softly. "I really don't know what's happening to me," he laughed. "I'm not usually like this. You bring out my wild side."

I never wasted time playing with words as I prepared for sex. I didn't kiss anyone on the lips unless they paid me extra. A few only wanted to kiss and for five hundred dollars, I gave them all the pleasure they wanted. I had men who uttered sweet nothings in my ears, but I quickly nipped that in the bud. What was happening to me?

"Are you going to let me invade your sweetness?" Latino begged. "I so want to be inside of you. I'm going to rock your spirit. Are you going to give this man what he wants?"

I laughed at him. "You need to quit, Latino? You picked me up for some wild sex and I admit that I'm hot for your body. I want to get to taste you, Latino and see what makes you tick."

Latino shook his head as we pulled up to the restaurant and he pulled into a reserved spot. "Let's hurry up and eat. Then I have a lot of plans for you, pretty lady. We're going to have a great time."

I smiled back, knowing we were going to have a great time too. I just had this feeling about this very seductive man. He wanted to rock my world, and I was going to give him the chance to do so while I shook up his world in more ways than one.

Renters' is the most elaborate restaurant in this city. It had two public floors but the third floor was for private parties only. It featured a lovely, romantic balcony with a spectacular view of the city. I sat down at a table for two as Latino poured me a glass of red wine. I took a long sip, trying to calm myself as he slipped into the seat opposite me. I couldn't believe this was happening to me. I felt like a queen instead of a prostitute. He took a swallow of his wine, and stood up, removing his suit jacket and rolling up his sleeves. "It's time to cook, Lace."

My eyes gleamed with excitement. It was going to be a fun night. Tomorrow I'd be back to my regular life and Latino would just be a perfect dream. He was making me so hot I was frightened. I'd never felt like this before.

"Your silence is rather unnerving, Lace. Why don't you tell me what's on your mind? I'm a good listener."

"You just look so ordinary when you take off your suit," I said. "I don't mean any disrespect, Latino. You look good either way, thank you very much." Why was I prattling away like this? I sounded like a star-struck high school freshman. I could kick myself.

"I can get into a pair of jeans with the best of them," he laughed. "You should see me on weekends. Every Saturday I play ball with a bunch of kids at the recreational center on the south side. Not only is it fun for me, it's also therapy. Some people read, but I like to bounce a ball back and forth. It gives me some free time of therapy. I love it and wouldn't stop for the world. On Sunday, I wear my sweats all day while I relax and maybe catch a game on television. I do have some fun, Lace. I'm not a businessman all the time."

Latino was surprising the hell out of me. I knew he could get down and dirty and that made me respect him more but I never would have guessed that he was a ball player. I thought he was a stuffy old shirt who worked 24/7. I was burning up, the heat of my body melted into his. What was going on? I didn't want to like this man, and I couldn't possibly fall in love with him. Or could I? Latino could really complicate my life, but I didn't really need to worry because he'd never marry a prostitute. What was I thinking?

Suddenly, I just wanted to get this over with. "Latino," I asked, "Do you mind if we eat later? I'm hungry for something besides food," I continued as I stood up and ran my hand down the front of his body, pausing to appreciate the large bulge behind his zipper.

Latino didn't say a word, just held out his hand to me. I too stayed quiet as I took his hand and followed him down the stairs. He made a left and we entered a spectacular apartment. Latino closed the door and stood there holding onto my hand for a minute before pulling me close to his body. I could smell his scent, a warm musky male scent of arousal. "I wanted to cook for you first, but I need to make love to that sweet body of yours so bad it hurts. I'm so glad you feel the same way about me."

"I don't want you to put me on a pedestal or think that you're the only man for me. Prostitution is the only way of life I've known for the last eleven years, Latino. You're not going to be able to just step in and change everything."

"I've been with plenty of women myself," he replied. "I'm not trying to change anything about you. I just think that you and I are going to make the world rock when we come together. If you need it, you can use the bathroom off the bedroom. I'll just make a quick trip down the hall and meet you back in the bedroom shortly."

"Did you have this same kind of plan with Roxie?" I shouldn't have uttered those words because I didn't want him to think that I was jealous of the time he spent with Roxie or any other woman for that matter. I just wanted to jump into bed with this intoxicating man.

"I was going home to do some work until I spotted you. I've seen you before, but I was never able to make the connection. I've always told myself that you're going to be my special whore one of these days."

I frowned at his words. "Are you trying to buy exclusive rights to me? Roxie understands that you might not sleep just with her, but she will fight for what she sees as her rights. She had you first. I'm not about to play games with her fighting over a man."

"Roxie sleeps with a hundred different men a month," he snapped. "She's hardly in a position to try and claim anyone for her own. My concern is with you." He started to walk away but turned back to say, "If you want to take a bath, I think you'll find everything you need in there. There's a green robe hanging on the back of the door. You can borrow that if you wish."

I stared after him, shaking my head. I thought I had seen it all, but I was deluding myself. I hurried into the bathroom, and after seeing the array of feminine bath products in there, decided to take a bubble bath. I could hardly decide what wonderful fragrance to try, but finally decided on a warm vanilla flavor. I luxuriated in the warm bubbles and as the bathwater cooled off, reluctantly opened the drain. I dried off, wrapping myself in the beautiful green robe before entering the bedroom. I couldn't believe the man had an apartment in a restaurant. I wondered how many women got to see this treat.

"Believe it or not, you're the first woman I ever brought here. This is a very special place to me. I don't bring anyone that's not special, and you fill that category very nicely. Don't ask me why because I can't answer that question for you," Latino said as he appeared in the doorway.

I was surprised at how he seemed able to read my mind. I decided to watch my thoughts a little closer from now on. For the moment, my thoughts were only on the man standing in front of me, wearing nothing but a white terry-cloth robe that did amazing things for his tanned body.

"Do I meet your exact standards?" he asked as he untied the belt and let the robe fall open. He was smiling all over himself, and I smiled back, unable to help myself. He had a body that could grace a swimsuit calendar, not an ounce of fat to be seen and all long, hard muscles…especially one particular muscle that I couldn't take my eyes from. Why did this man engender such feelings in me? It was getting harder and harder for me to remember that he was nothing more than a john, a man paying me for sex. Why did he affect me so?

"Please take off the robe. I want to see you naked," he begged. "I want to see every inch of you so bad, I'm about to burst. Hurry up!"

I smiled as I removed my robe, allowing it to fall down to the floor. I could feel the moist heat building between my legs, threatening to burn me alive if he didn't make love to me soon.

"Your body is so beautiful," Latino said. "I need to taste you," he said, pushing me gently backwards until I was lying on the green satin comforter, where he joined me after he dropped his own robe to the floor. His body, stretched across me, pressing me into the bed, felt so good. I wanted to treasure this moment for a long time.

"I just don't want to have sex with you, but to make love to you, Lace. I want to treasure this special moment. I'm not just one of your johns. There's something deep and magical happening to us," he said, once again reading my mind.

He was the most romantic man I ever met. I had really never been in love or met anyone so romantic before. Was I putting too much into Latino? He was just a man with a healthy appetite that I could satisfy. I felt an electric jolt as his intoxicating hands reached out to touch me. He circled my right breast with his expert and magical hands. I continued to keep my eyes closed because an orgasm was forthcoming. I was on the edge of exploding, and he was just playing with my breast. He then began fondling my left breast, and the thrills were running all over me. I wanted so much to rub between my legs because I was so hot. It was costing me a fortune not to scream out. I was ready.

As Latino kneaded my left breast with his talented hands, he lowered his mouth to my right breast, drawing the nipple deep into his mouth and gently nibbling on it. I moaned out with pleasure, unable to stop the orgasm that was building inside. "I need you now," I cried. "I want you now."

"Patience," Latino said softly, removing his mouth from my breast to move up to my mouth. He covered my lips with his, his tongue darting between my teeth, dueling with my tongue. I was aching inside, impatient to have him fill me. I had sex with my clients but I was making love with Latino. This time I was burning with need for him, sensational spasms of heat coursing through my body. I wanted him so much.

As Latino positioned himself between my legs, I suddenly remembered, "Do you have a condom?" Just the fact that I had almost forgotten made me realize how different it was being with Latino. I never had sex without protection.

He reached into the bedside table and pulled out a box of condoms, easing one over his erect manhood before sliding between my legs again. I was open and ready for him and he reclaimed my mouth as he filled me up, burying himself deep within me. I was hungry for this man, unwilling to end our deep, drugging kiss for even a moment. He felt so good.

At work a penis inside of me was just a job, but right at this moment I felt like Cinderella. I was going to keep my glass slipper on forever. I continued my moans as Latino pummeled me with his shaft. The heat was just too suffocating to last and I screamed as I rocked with the most powerful orgasm I had ever experienced. Seconds later, Latino tensed before his orgasm shot through him. I thought the walls were going to explode. Our bodies rocked like a bomb had exploded, multiple orgasms coursing through me, something that didn't often happen to me. I usually faked most of the time because the men wanted to make sure they did something to make you come. My clients didn't have a clue about a woman most private and secret spot. Her g-spot was the evolution of passion for a woman. Latino was able to manipulate me into multiple orgasms. I owed him dearly for my pleasure.

"Get on top of me," Latino cried. "I want to see that gorgeous body very close. I want to feel you."

I moved on top and began riding Latino like he was my bull. I shook the entire bed as I worked to experience more multiple orgasms. I was so hot as Latino plunged deeply into my wetness starting yet another orgasm, I thought I might faint. Latino too was on the brink of another orgasm and I was glad I was giving him such pleasure. Our pace increased as our bodies shook with one last orgasm before we collapsed on the bed, breathless, unable to move. What a man! No wonder he had all those women. If he made love to them the way he was making love to me, then I'd never let him out of my sight. I smiled bitterly. I really had no choice in the matter. I was a prostitute after all, and that was my only means of survival in this tarnished world.

It took a few minutes for our breathing to return to normal. I closed my eyes to relive the lighting bolts of pleasure. This had never happened to me before. I had climaxed so many times I lost count, and I was still hot for Latino. I felt like I could never get enough of him.

He reached for me again, and our wild ride began again. When we were finally too tired for any more lovemaking, we took a shower together and, wearing just our robes, headed back to the restaurant. I was so happy to be in his company, I couldn't believe it. Usually, once the sex was over with one of my johns, all I wanted to do was to get them out of the room while I shower and get ready for the next client. Latino Banks had it going on and then some. I could fall for him.

"I don't know about you, but I'm famished. What would you like to eat?" Latino asked.

"Pizza is fine with me," I said. "I'm so hungry I could eat a horse."

"How about if I make us some BLTs instead? I've got some hickory cured bacon and fresh tomatoes right from the farm."

Once again I was blown away. How could he possibly know my weakness for bacon? I could eat it every day of the week if it wasn't so fattening. I watched him rummaging through the fridge, setting the sandwich makings on the counter before turning back, his head and shoulders disappearing as he searched for something.

"Aha, found it." he said, backing out and setting a plate on the counter. "I knew it was in there somewhere. I don't know why they tried to hide it from me. I can always find it." He shot me a triumphant grin as he pulled the cover off a decadent chocolate cheesecake, covered with dark chocolate glaze.

"I need something to replace all that energy you drained out of me," he laughed. "And if you're worried about calories, don't. I plan on making sure you expend enough energy to use up every one of them."

A half-hour later, I was contemplating which half of an enormous BLT to tackle first. Latino had made it with thick sliced toast and tons of mayonnaise. I didn't even know if I could open my mouth wide enough to take a bite. "Tell me about your family. I'm really interested in knowing what makes you tick."

He smiled. "I have two brothers and a sister. They, and my parents, are scattered between Los Angeles and New York City. I do most of my business here in Chicago, but I have an apartment in LA and one in the Big Apple. I just love the Windy City for some reason. It's been very good to me."

"I see. I think it's time for me to be going," I said, completely forgetting that Latino was paying me for the entire night. I wanted to spend the rest of my life with him, but at the mention of his family, reality hit front and center for me. I could never meet his family or participate in that side of his life. I'd always be hiding in the background and I couldn't live like that."

"Not tonight, Lace. You and I have some more business to transact just as soon as we finish eating." He was smiling again as he reached in a drawer and pulled out a long thin knife and then searched in a cabinet for plates for our cheesecake.

"Listen Latino, let's just forget about it. We both had a good time so I'm not going to charge you. It was my night off and I can spend it anyway I want to."

"Lace, I want you to work exclusively for me," he said. "I'll give you the $3000.00 we agreed on for tonight plus a credit card for your day-to-day expenses. Do you need a place to live? I don't want you whoring around any longer. When was the last time you had an HIV test?"

"I'm a prostitute," I shouted. "I'm not going to let myself be dependant on any man. I have my own condo that I paid for with money that I earned myself. I don't need you to keep me. You and I can't be together openly, and I'm not sitting around waiting for you to grace me with a visit whenever you have the time. Besides, I have a good client base. If I'm off work for a few weeks, I'll lose them."

"There are enough women out there to satisfy your johns. You work for me now. I have some family business to attend to which should take about two weeks. When I get back, you need to be ready to come to me."

For some reason I resented the fact that he couldn't take me to meet his family. I know it was too early in the relationship. I was just a whore he hired for three thousand dollars. Why would he introduce me to his parents? I was truly losing it. I was a woman a man wouldn't take home to mother.

"Are you okay?" Latino asked. "Why are you always thinking about things? If you'd take the time to communicate with me, you wouldn't have to think all the time. I'm sure it's something negative, and it's not going to help our situation. Please try and stop the thinking because it's going to be the ruination of your life and relationships."

I frowned at his words. "This cheesecake is delicious. Did you make it yourself?" I knew I was changing the subject and so did he, although he ignored my question, instead asking me one of his own.

"Are you going to miss me while I'm gone Lace? I know I'm going to be thinking about you, fantasizing about what we're going to do when I get back. I hope that you'll be fantasizing about me too. There's not a minute of my day I won't be thinking about you. I'm ashamed of letting a woman get to me like this, but it appears that you have."

I ignored his words again. "I'll be too busy whoring around to think about you Latino," I replied sarcastically. Who did Latino think he was to make me fall in love with him? He was just a man. I wasn't going to miss him while he was gone and I didn't want to go away with him either. That was the bottom line.

"I don't think so," he snapped. "I won't have my woman whoring around on me."

"Then you can just call me a cab, Latino," I snapped. "I have a life, and you're not about to come in and destroy it. Who do you think you are?"

"You can either move in with me, or let me pay your bills, Lace. Don't you understand that I'm offering you a way out of a life of prostitution? We can even go to my attorney and I'll set up a trust for you. If anything happens to me, you'll be taken care of for the rest of your life. You can even have your own attorney go over the papers to see that it's all open and aboveboard."

"No one owns me," I snapped. "I can survive on my own. I've been doing it alone for a long time. Find Roxie to handle your manly needs because I'm done with you, Latino Banks. Who in the hell do you think you're talking to?"

"You and I are special, Lace," he pleaded. "What's the matter with you? Why are you spoiling such a splendid evening? We had a good time, an unforgettable evening. I'm not about to forget the way we made love, and neither will you. Don't even try to convince me that you didn't feel anything special between us."

"Reality is front and center," I snapped. "It's time to get with the real world. Prostitutes come and go, especially in the lives of men like you. I'm sure someone else will come along that will do anything you want, especially if you offer her $3000.00. My body might be for sale, but not my life."

"I'm going to give you two weeks Lace. I'll give you a call when I get back home. You want me, and I know I want you, and I'm willing to admit it. You seem to be the one with the problem."

I blocked out his words as I continued eating. I hated all men. They think because you make love to them they own you or something. They want you to be faithful to them, but in the meantime, they're out there sleeping around with every bitch in heat. The double standards bastards!

A week passed slowly and I missed Latino more than I thought possible. I didn't want to miss him. I resented him for not inviting me to meet his family. They didn't have to know that I was his prostitute. Was he really ashamed of me? Probably! Sometimes I was ashamed of myself.

By Friday night, I was jumping out of my skin. I reached for my cell phone when it rang. It was probably just another customer eager for my attention. "Hello."

"Hi," he said. "I just wanted to call so I could hear the sound of that gorgeous voice of yours. Are you missing me as much as I'm missing you? What are you doing with yourself while I'm gone? I hope you're keeping that sexy body warm for me."

"I'm trying to find something to do with myself," I snapped. "I'm usually busy at six o'clock in the evening. I'm bored out of my mind, Latino. What do you expect me to do with no work to occupy my time? I'm going out of my mind just sitting around."

"Go shopping, rent some movies, take a nap, watch television," he laughed. "I'm sure you can find something to take your mind off missing me, Lace. Why don't you go shopping and buy some new clothes? I would prefer something black and lacy and easy to remove. Don't get something with a lot of straps and buckles." I could hear the laughter in his voice as he gave me his outrageous suggestions.

I listened to all the noise in the background. "It sounds like you're having fun at a party, Latino. I'm bored out of my mind, and you're over there getting your groove on. I hope you're having a wonderful time," I snarled. I hated men!

"I'm at my sister's college graduation party. I met up with some old friends and we're having a wonderful time reminiscing about the old days. Are you jealous, Lace? It sounds good to me."

"I'm sorry I couldn't be there, Latino. Imagine me having the time of my life meeting your family and friends. I'm bored out of my skull, but you're having a grand time," I snapped. "I think this conversation is about to end. Thanks for calling, Latino, but I have to finish being bored."

He laughed. "I don't think so, and you do have a sense of humor. I like you, Lace, but introducing you to the most important people in my life is like giving you a loaded gun and telling you to shoot me with it."

"I'm good enough to sleep with, but not to meet that precious family of yours. Skip you Latino Banks and your precious family too. I wish I never met you. You and your family aren't good enough for the likes of me."

"I haven't known you long enough for you to meet my mother. She's the most precious person in the world to me. I tell my mother most things, but there's no sense telling her about you because I don't know what our future relationship will be. There's no use letting her meet you and really get to like you and then she never gets to see you again because you and I couldn't make a go of it. So there's no reason for you to get that attitude with me."

"I'll be your mistress when you find your snobbish wife?" I asked. "I don't think so, Latino. I'll be available when your boring wife can't do anything for you, but you'll buy my time just like any other john. I'm not tying myself down to any one man."

"We just met Lace and we should find out where this relationship is heading, or if it's even going anywhere before we bring in our families. I want you for more than sex. I want to spend time with you, explore your likes and dislikes, listen to you laugh. I don't know what kind of music you like, if you ever want to have kids and so much more."

"I never want to see you again, Latino. Leave me alone, and lose my telephone number. I don't want anything to do with you. No one messes with me, and lives to tell about it. I'm my own woman, and I'll be that way until this world ends for good. I just can't wait."

"I gave you $3000.00. You still owe me."

"No Latino, you gave me $3000.00 for one night. You got that one night and I hope you enjoyed it because it's the last one you get with me. No man owns me." I hurriedly clicked off the button of my cell phone before I started crying. There was no way I'd ever let him know how much I loved him.

I waited patiently for Bob to get his pleasure as I gave his penis my expert tongue. Finally, after thirty minutes he managed a small orgasm. I watched his few drops of semen fall to the floor while he screamed and moaned. Bob was sixty years old and I was always afraid he was going to drop dead on me.

"Let me do you baby," he panted, trying to get his breath back. "I do want you to get pleasure. You're so gorgeous and I want to eat you. I bet you smell so good. I'm hungry for that sweet smell of yours."

"I'm sorry Bob. I have another appointment," I said. "Besides, it's my job to give you pleasure. Watching you pump it out is all the thanks I need." He actually believed that watching his old tired penis squeeze out a few drops turned me on. Man, I was too good!

"I'll see you next week, and I'll take my Viagra. Have you thought any more about letting me set you up in your own house so you don't have to live in this seedy hotel? You don't deserve to live like this."

I smiled at him even though he reminded me of Latino. He *was* a sweet gentleman, always giving me a big tip and offering to bring me pleasure with his mouth since his penis wasn't up to the job since he had been sick. He genuinely worried about me living in this fleabag hotel but I wasn't going to let him know I had a nice condo of my own. I'm sure part of the enormous tip he gave me each week was so I'd have some extra spending money. "Thank you Bob. I really appreciate your offer but I'm very happy as I am." I waited patiently for him to leave, and then counted the money he had given me. Once again there was a large tip. I was rolling in the money.

Four hours later I was wrapping myself in my soft plushy robe after a long, hot shower. I was exhausted and longing to just fall into bed and sleep for days but I couldn't stop thinking about Latino. I thought he'd call me, and apologize for hurting my feelings, but the man didn't have a clue. I reached for the newspaper I'd thrown on the bed when I came in, and began reading the entertainment section. I was stunned when I saw Latino's face smiling up at me while his arm encircled the shoulders of a beautiful young black woman wearing a gorgeous evening gown. The caption below the picture read: *"Latino Banks, the 45 year old Chicago real estate tycoon, parties with his fiancée, Margaret Thomas. The 30 year-old self-employed court reporter tells us they are planning a Halloween wedding."*

I read the announcement again and then I threw the paper across the room. How dare he do this to me? I hated the bastard. I hoped he dropped dead before he got married. I had never before cried over a man, but this was the exception. I was crying like a baby because the man I loved was marrying someone else. I fell asleep still crying.

The pain didn't get any better as Saturday and Sunday slowly dragged by. I worked as usual but my heart wasn't in it. All I wanted to do was brood about how much I hated men in general and one man in particular. Monday I was off. I couldn't stop thinking about the way

Latino and I had made love. That memory was embedded deep inside my soul, and it was never going away. I had to find something to do instead of sitting at home thinking about a man who was out partying with Margaret Thomas. I finally decided to go shopping. That always cheered me up, no matter how far in the dumps I was.

Except for today, when the first person I met as I stopped in the store restaurant for a cup of coffee was Roxie, all ready to gloat about Latino's engagement.

"I see your man has moved on, girl," she said. "I told you not to go and get all serious on Latino because he likes sex, but won't take you home to meet the family if you know what I mean. I thought he was so in love with me that I was going to be the next Mrs. Banks. I was a stupid, naïve fool just like you."

I looked at Roxie and then rolled my eyes. "For your information, Latino Banks is good in bed, and nothing more. I'm a prostitute and I don't have dreams of finding my Prince Charming and living happily ever after. I can take care of myself very nicely."

"I think you need to go home," Roxie snapped. "You look like shit. What's going on with you, Lace?" She stared at me, and then she covered her mouth and laughed. "My God, Lace, you did fall in love with him. Are you crazy? Men like him don't marry women like us. We're whores and no matter what we say or do, we'll always be a whore to men."

"Are you available?" I stared at the man standing next to my table. He was black and looked like a dumpy boo. I didn't say anything, just got up, left money for my untouched coffee and left the restaurant. The guy followed me as I walked out the door mumbling under his breath about whores who thought they were too good for a man and finally I turned around and said, "Listen mister, I don't know who you think you're talking to, but if you don't walk away from me right now, I'll fix you so you won't ever bother another woman again." Then I opened my purse and gave him a glimpse of my gun.

He finally got the message and hurried away. Even when I wasn't working, men still recognized me as a whore. No wonder Latino didn't want anything to do with me. A blue car pulled up next to me and the window rolled down. I ignored it and kept on walking. It was so depressing that anyone could tell I was a hooker just by looking at me.

"I thought dinner would be nice," a familiar voice said. "You know how damn hungry you make me. Actually, you make me hungry in more ways than one, but right now I'm talking about food for the stomach."

Where in the hell was his green car? I stared at him, unable to speak, trying frantically to think of some way to get out of this situation without making a fool of myself. Once again, Latino read my mind.

"I thought you might recognize the green car and manage to avoid me. How are you doing? Did you miss me while I was gone?" He acted as if nothing had changed in the time he was gone and maybe it hadn't for him. Maybe all men considered marriage a duty forced on them by society in order to carry on the family lines and women on the side were their reward for a job well done. Or else the whole bunch of them was incapable of being monogamous.

"Where is Margaret?" I snapped. "I saw your announcement in the paper. It was a good picture of you."

Latino laughed, and I wanted to kick his ass for it. "Don't believe everything you read. The name of the game is selling papers. A waiter almost bumped Margaret with his tray and I put my arm around her to get her out of the way. The photographer happened to catch the shot and Margaret gave them the caption. She's been trying to tie me down for a long time and thought if it was in the papers and our parents saw it, I wouldn't back out. Her mother and mine have been friends since high school and they always hoped that Margaret and I would marry." He paused to take a breath before continuing, "Now Lace, I have to warn you that I'm fair game for the paparazzi. Your picture will be in the paper as soon as word gets out about our engagement. I'm sure some enterprising reporter is going to ferret out your background too. Can you handle it?"

"What the hell do I care it you're followed around by every daaaaaaaaaa.....WHAT DID YOU SAY? WHAT ENGAGEMENT?" I screamed at him.

"Well, I think I'm talking about our engagement, yours and mine. Do you think you can handle the press? I know your background is going to come out and I want you to be prepared to handle it."

"I don't believe you," I cried. I could kick Latino's ass for doing this to me. I was all ready to hate the man, and now he had to go and knock my socks off. What in the hell did this mean? "What about your family? What's your mom going to say when you tell her you want to marry a whore? I asked bitterly.

"I think Mimi will say how happy she is that I've finally found someone to love. I think she will say that our past is our past. We can't undo it, but we can let it remain in the past. I think she will say she already loves you because I do. I know she'll say all of that because she already has. She's coming to Chicago tomorrow to meet you. She's very anxious to meet the woman who has finally tamed me down," he laughed.

"So now I'm good enough for you," I snapped. "I'm confused Latino Banks. One moment you're not going to introduce me to your precious family, but the next minute you're singing my phrases to your mother. I think you're the one with the double standards."

"Your way of life was never much of an obstacle to me Lace. What was an obstacle is giving up my freedom. I wanted to be very sure that you were the one for me, the one for whom I would give up all other women. Anyway, I went away to see my family. I mainly wanted to see if I was going to get over you. I thought about you every minute; the way you smell, and taste. I need you, Lace. For some reason I want you in my life."

"I don't want to be your whore," I snapped.

"I didn't ask you to be my whore," he snapped back. "I asked you to marry me. I want to court you, take you out for dinner and dancing and the theater. I want you to meet all my friends and I want to meet your friends. I want to get to know everything about the woman I want at my side the rest of my life, the mother of my children."

I couldn't believe what I was hearing. Latino wanted to marry me and have kids with me. He must be crazy. I'd never in my life thought about a having child. I wouldn't know what to do with one.

"If you don't want kids in your life, I can understand that Lace. What I meant was that maybe we could adopt a couple of kids. There are so many black children with no family and no one willing to adopt them, I thought we could open our home to some. Maybe take in a family and let the children be raised together by a mother and father who love each other and them. We could give them a home where they'll want for nothing, but won't be spoiled. Where they'll be sheltered and safe. We don't have to decide now. Just keep it in the back of your mind and we'll talk about it in a year or so. For now, if you want to train for a new career, that's fine. If you like, you can work in my office and I can help you get your realtor's license," he offered.

I was lost in a daydream, a dream like nothing I had ever had before. I had always thought that if I had continued to college I would have liked to be a nurse or maybe a teacher. Now I saw myself walking around my dining room table, with five or six children seated there, heads bent over their homework as they waited for Mom to get to them. In the kitchen, Dad was keeping an eye on dinner as it cooked. There were pictures hanging on the refrigerator with funny magnets and a big calendar was marked up with kid's activities. But the best thing about the dream was the love, pure simple unadulterated love. Love for your child, for your spouse, for the little dog sleeping in the basket in the corner.

"What are you thinking about Lace? You have the funniest expression on your face. There has to be a dream you had when you were growing up. I think now is the time that you exorcise the career demon because I need my wife to be fulfilled. You don't need any time on your hands because I don't want my wife bored out of her skull."

I laughed at his words. I thought a house full of children would keep me pretty busy. But I decided to keep that thought to myself for a few days and make sure it was what I really wanted.I didn't make any attempt to wipe away the tears. I wasn't ashamed of them.

."Latino, first of all I want you to know I love you too and even though you didn't really ask me to marry you, I will. But right now, I need some time by myself to think. Will you give me that time? I need you to trust me that I really have to have this space right now." I waited quietly for his answer and wasn't disappointed.

"Of course you can Lace. When will you call me?" he asked quietly.

"How about if you come to my place tomorrow at 11:00 am? We can talk things out and get ready to meet your mom."

"Lace, why don't you let me get you a suite in one of the hotels downtown? I hate the idea of you staying in that squalid little hotel," Latino said.

"That's something else we need to talk about, Latino. Right now, I want to do a little more shopping before I go home. I'll call you tomorrow," I said as I climbed out of the car, stopping to give him a soft loving kiss before I left him.

As soon as he pulled away, I headed to my condo, barely closing the door before I powered up the computer. I pulled up Google and started searching, taking pages of notes as I made several phone calls and took in copious amounts of information. Then I sat reading them over and over before finally going to bed, where I lay and dreamed about Latino for the rest of the night.

At 7 a.m. I called Latino and he answered on the first ring. I was laughing as I said; "I guess it's not too early to call you then."

"Lord no, I've been up since 5 a.m. waiting for you to call. I'm sitting right outside your place now. I'll be up in a minute."

"Wait a minute Latino. I don't live at that crummy hotel. I just use it for work," I explained as I gave him the address of my condo before jumping out of bed to get ready for him. I figured I had about twenty minutes before he could get here. I was wrong. Fifteen minutes later, he was ringing my doorbell. I opened the door and pulled him inside, throwing myself into his arms. He swept me up and whispered urgently, "Where's the bedroom?"

Without a word, I pointed to the bedroom door and he practically ran in, tossing me on the bed and, undressing faster than I would have thought possible, falling down next to me, covering me with kisses as he untied the bow on my robe. Luckily for him, I had anticipated this scenario and the robe was all I was wearing.

Later, both of us sated and pleasantly drowsy, Latino thought to ask me about my condo.

"I would never let a john into my home, Latino. That's why I always used the hotel. I used to live there but as soon as I had enough money for a down payment, I moved. You're the only guest I've ever had here," I confessed, suddenly aching as I thought of all the lonely years I had spent.

"You mean I'm the only man that's ever been in this bed?" he asked, sounding suspiciously happy.

"Yes Latino and don't sound so happy. It's very unbecoming," I said, punching him in the arm. "I need to talk to you. I've decided on a career. Are you ready to talk about it?" I asked as I got out of bed and donned my robe.

"Yes I am," he said, pulling on his trousers and trailing after me to the kitchen, where he started the coffee while I got out the bacon and eggs for breakfast.

"Let's talk after we eat, okay?" I asked him, running my eyes over his muscular chest with the light dusting of hair, feeling the longing starting up again.

Later, dishes done and the kitchen restored to order, I took Latino's hand and led him into my spare bedroom where I had my computer. I sat him down in one of the chairs and turned the computer so he could see the screen too. I powered it up and then I started talking.

"I always thought that I would like to be a teacher or a nurse if I had continued on in school. You reminded me of that yesterday when we were talking and I realized that I really did want to be a teacher." I watched his face carefully for signs of anger...maybe he really didn't want me going back to school. Maybe he wanted me sitting around the house waiting for him to come home, the master, the breadwinner. But there was only alert intelligence in his face as he waited for me to go on.

"So I found this school, here in Chicago. If I double my course load, I'd have a teacher's degree in three years. I've got enough money to keep myself until then. The question is, would you be willing to wait for me that long?" I held my breath as I waited for his answer. What he said next would determine the course of our lives. I had to know that he trusted me to take care of myself and that he would let me do so. He had to love me enough to let me go.

"My darling, if I have to let you go to prove I love you, then go with my blessing," he said. "Will I still be able to see you? I don't think I could bear to be away from you so long."

I smiled to myself as I opened up a web site and found the picture I wanted to show Latino. "I thought this could be my first class," I told him, watching closely to see if he understood. "Of course, the agency will only adopt them out to a stable family, with a mother and father both, preferably with more grownups for backup. How do you think your mom and dad would feel about living part time in Chicago to help take care of the grandkids?"

I had spent the previous evening searching for adoption agencies that specialized in placing black children. We had an excellent agency right here in Chicago and the lady I spoke to was very encouraging. I told her everything about me, holding nothing back. On my own, they would probably never consider me, but when I threw in Latino's name, that changed everything. When I told her we wanted a family of kids, at least three, but more were fine, she was ecstatic.

"You realize that it's going to take a long time to be approved Latino, but if we got married right away, we could get the approval process started. And I'm sure you know people in high places who could help speed it along, don't you?" I asked.

Suddenly, I was yanked off my feet and into Latino's arms, causing the chair to squeak alarmingly. There were tears streaming down his face as he smothered my face with kisses, murmuring soft words I couldn't understand. When I felt something wet on my face, I opened my eyes to see tears streaming down Latino's face as he stared at the computer screen, watching our children, memorizing their faces.

A year later, Latino and I celebrated our first wedding anniversary. Joining in the celebration were his mother and father, who had moved back to Chicago permanently, his brother and sisters and their families and our own five children. Right now we were still their foster parents, but Latino and his parents were pushing the paperwork through the system. By our next anniversary, they would be all ours.

I looked up and met Latino's eyes. The past year had been difficult; getting approval for fostering was harder than we had thought it would be, thanks to me. But we persevered and now we had our family. I had another present for Latino, one I would give him later, when everyone had gone home and the children were in bed. I hoped he liked it because there was no returning this one. I was three weeks pregnant.

As I looked around the table at my beloved family, I realized that I was a survivor. And because of that love, six more precious souls were going to be survivors too. I was planning on dedicating the rest of my life to that goal. It was the greatest career I could ever have.

Sins of the Preacher

I shook my head as my husband stood in front of a congregation of over five thousand members preaching about the sins of the humans. He had some nerve. I wanted to march up there and confront the snake. Who in the world did he think he was? He was a hypocrite of the worse kind. How could he preach about the righteous when he was committing the biggest sin of the history of mankind, and in the eyes of God? He was committing adultery.

How did I know this? I had my husband followed. I was a preacher's wife, and hired a private investigator, who just happened to be my friend, Confess Moore. He gave me the scoop on my husband infidelity and pictures to prove it. I couldn't believe that my husband was eating a black bimbo when he wouldn't give me any oral sex. "I don't believe in such crass," he replied. He should be shot dead for his sins. I continued to listen to the snake.

"Now I love my wife, Penny, and she's the only woman I think about," the preacher replied. "I may look at other woman, but I don't touch them. I'm married, but I'm not dead."

"Amen," a few men chorused.

I shook my head again. I wished I could let the entire congregation know what my husband was doing. Of course it might ruin the healthy lifestyle I had been living for fifteen years. I didn't have to work, my children, Daisy and James were attending private school; I shopped all day, and did whatever the heck I wanted to do. I really had to think about my actions. If I exposed Land for the cheating bastard he was, then his rein as the preacher would be over. Our marriage would come to an end, and then I'd have to find a job. Did I want too?

I had my teaching degree and license because Confess was insistent that I have some kind of skills if my marriage didn't work out. There was always a need for a teacher. I could work, but I didn't want to work. It had been my dream to find a man and marry him enabling me to stay at home and be a housewife. Land presented me with my dreams, but overlooking his cheating ways was getting on my last nerves. He had the nerve to want to make love to me, after he had been with fifty other women. I lost count. Can I just turn my head and let Land continue to embarrass the heck out of me? I bet the entire congregation knew the man was cheating on me.

As I stared around the Church, I noticed how most of the women were hanging onto Land's every word. Three of them were sleeping with my husband, and I wanted to kick their buts. In time, I was going to devise a master plan, and Land was going to pay. I had to find a way to make sure that I got something out of the deal because I had no intention of being homeless. I had to talk to Confess. He'd have the answers for me.

In the meantime, I focused back on my husband.

"If you continue to sin, you're going to hell," Land replied. "I don't care how many times you come to this Church; it won't wash away your sins, unless you repent. If you continue to sleep with married women or men then your life is a waste because you don't care. When your flesh is falling off from the pain of burning, then you'd wish you had ceased your sins. It's just not worth it."

"Amen, preacher," a woman said.

I turned toward the voice, staring at Mamie Franks. She was in the pictures with my husband, and he was eating the life out of her. She was sitting there with the Holy Ghost, next to her old husband, Jimmy, who was seventy-five years old. Mamie was twenty-nine so what was wrong with that picture? Jimmy had more money than the banks of Chicago, which is why she married him.

Mamie was tall, petite, and gorgeous. All the single and married men wanted her, and my husband had her. The way she was staring at him, I knew she wanted him to please her here and now. I wished I could kick the bitches' ass. I shook my head because I was in the house of the Lord. I had to stop thinking like the devil because he wasn't going to ruin my life.

I was relieved when Janice Greene, one of the choir members stood up to sing. I focused on the song because my devil thoughts were just too much for Church. I wasn't going to let Land send me to hell with him.

After smiling my fake smile, and shaking everyone's hands, I was relieved when I walked to my car. I waited for Land to join me, but he was too busy entertaining the women. He just didn't have a clue. He thought God didn't know what he was doing or me for that matter. I was glad the children were visiting my parents in Florida for the summer because I was going to make sure that Land never cheated on me again. I just had to think of something.

After fifteen more minutes Land joined me at my car since I was doing the driving today. "How about going to out to dinner?" Land replied. "I think it's time I give my wife some tender loving care. You're the most beautiful woman in the world."

I rolled my eyes at him, wanting to give him a piece of my mind. Who did he think he was lying too? The man had just gone to Church. I didn't want to go anywhere with the snake from Satan. "I have plans with Confess," I happily stated. "Maybe you can find one of your harems of women to take out to dinner. I'm not available."

He frowned. "Confess needs to get a life," he snapped. "How do you think it looks for a preacher's wife to be having dinner with another man? He's handsome for a man, and you're not ugly. I forbid it."

I laughed. "Are you going to give up your women? Mamie is practically lusting for you."

He laughed. "You're the only woman for me. I have a tall and petite wife who looks like Robin Givens. I think I'm the luckiest man in the world." He admired me from head to toe. "Every man at this Church is jealous of me because I got Penny May. Why would I have to cheat on you?"

"I'll see you at home, Land, but don't wait up."

"Do you want me to cut off your allowance, Penny? Don't play with me."

I had money saved, and almost five thousand dollars too. Did the snake think I was stupid? "I'm going out with Confess, and then I'm coming home. I don't care what you do." I opened my car door; glad I had my keys in my hands. After five minutes I mingled into traffic, staring at Land still glaring at me. He had some nerve. Mamie would satisfy his every urge without a doubt.

Land couldn't stand Confess because he thought he was interested in me. I laughed because Confess and I had been friends since forever. I met him about ten years ago at a book convention. He was promoting his nonfiction book, WHY DO MEN CHEAT? Of course it was still on the New York Times bestselling list for fifteen weeks straight. I was so proud of my best friend. He had been writing for most of his life, and now he had three more books coming out this year. Confess was the most talented man in the world. Chicago was lucky to have him. Of course I had no plans with Confess, but I was going to visit him. He was probably glued to his computer.

Confess lived in a beautiful house in South Holland, Illinois, not to far from Chicago. He also had a condo on Lake Shore Drive, but when he needed some privacy from his adoring fans, he hid out at South Holland. No one knew about his place away from home, but me, and maybe his publisher, agent, and a few family and friends. This was a good day to visit my friend. I smiled because I looked forward to seeing Confess. He made me feel so special and appreciated me. I was sure my husband was too busy eating Mamie's private parts to give a heck about me. One day Land was going to burn in hell for his sins.

It was fifty minutes later when I stared at Confess' house. I had a key, but I'd never use it. Confess dated lots of women and had no itching to settle down with just one of them. He was waiting for his mate, but so far he wasn't finding her. Everyone I knew wanted to bed Confess, and probably got their wish. I rang the doorbell praying that he was home. I rang the bell more than once because Confess had an office in the back of his house and sometimes he didn't hear the doorbell. I waited, tapping my foot on the ground.

Finally the door opened and I smiled at the most gorgeous man. "Hi. I'm glad you're home."

"What a pleasure," he exclaimed. "Why didn't you call?"

I frowned. "Do you have company?"

"No. I was just making myself something to eat. Let's go into the kitchen. You look great as usual, but you're just to skinny."

I frowned as I followed him into his immaculate kitchen. Confess' house was gorgeous... I loved his green cabinets, which wasn't seen in most houses. Confess had his entire house built to his specifications, and it was fabulous. "What are you cooking?"

"My famous spaghetti with garlic bread," he exclaimed.

I smiled. "I'm glad I did come over. You know I love your spaghetti and garlic bread."

"Then you're right on time. Why don't you kick off your high heels, and come relax with me. You should have changed into jeans or something. I have a shirt you can wear."

"Then give it to me," I cried. "I do need to relax."

"You know where the bedroom is, and find something to your liking."

I smiled, and hurried up the expensive spiral stairs. The woman who married Confess was going to love this house.

In this immaculate bedroom, I removed my dress and everything and kept on my panties and bra. I found my favorite blue shirt and smelled the bounty smell. I smiled as I got into it. My feet were bare but I was comfortable because Confess' house wasn't too cold or too warm, but just right. I stared at myself in the mirror. I looked sexy as heck with my long legs showing, and my flat butt. I wished I had more of one, but I still loved my body. I hung up my clothes, and then hurried back downstairs to the kitchen because the smell of food was intoxicating.

"We can eat in the dining room," Confess said. "I was going to call you over for dinner."

"Land wasn't happy about me coming over here."

"Don't get me involved in your domestic disputes," he cautioned. "I'm not the one."

"I'm sorry, but he wanted to take me out to dinner because he had been neglecting his wife. The man is clueless."

"Sit down and take a load off. Baby, your husband is stupid as they come. The way you look in my shirt makes me want to take it off and have my way with you."

I laughed. "Don't play with me. Can I help?"

"You can go down to the basement and find a wine for us."

"Is this a special occasion?"

"I have my best friend with me."

I smiled at him. "I love you."

"And I love you."

I hurried to the basement.

Ten minutes later Confess and I were eating and laughing. I had so much fun with him, and the wine was loosening me up. "So what's going on with your love life, Confess? Who is the current woman in your life?"

"I was dating Natalie, but she had a problem with you. She told me that the reason why I couldn't commit to anyone was because I was in love with my best friend. I laughed in her face."

I stopped eating staring at him. "She's wrong, Confess. We're only friends."

"Natalie didn't hear me, Penny because she had her mind made up."

"Then you should go after her. I think she's very special to you."

"I did want to see her again. I usually don't date the same woman more than a week."

I shook my head as I devoured my wine. "This wine is delicious, and you're a playa."

"I'm waiting for the right woman to channel all my buttons. I don't think Natalie is the one."

"She's the only woman you discussed with me more than once, Confess. What are you waiting for? Natalie is gorgeous, and she's rich. She has her own money, and the two of you wouldn't have to fight about the finances. She's also petite, and gorgeous, and she has a brain."

"And she's white."

I waved my hand at him. "That's just a minor obstacle. Color doesn't make the world stop. I think she's really into you, and the two of you could make it work."

"Why are you so gone on Natalie?"

"I like her, and I explained to her that if she hurts you, I was going to beat her ass."

"Today is Sunday," he exclaimed. "Didn't you just come back from Church?"

"When are you going with me, by the way?"

"Let's not change the subject, girl. I'll be there real soon, and God knows my heart."

"He also wants you to worship him from time to time. What are you thinking?"

"I will go, okay. Natalie preached the same thing to me the other day."

"I really like Natalie. Do you want me to talk to her?"

"Just leave it alone because she's never going to listen. I do miss her."

I smiled because I was going to talk to the woman. Was she insane? I drained my wine and reached for the bottle. "This is really good."

"Why don't you pour me some before you drink the entire bottle?"

I pouted. "I did not drink all of this."

"Who are you fooling now?"

I reached for his glass, and poured him a portion, and then added the rest to my glass. I took another long sip, savoring the taste. I then put down my glass and focused on my best friend. "Did you find out any new information on my husband?"

"He's sleeping with Mamie, Janet, Judy, and Lillie."

I rolled my eyes. "The bastard!"

"I'm sorry, baby. Your husband can't keep his thang in his pants."

"I should divorce him and get everything he's got, and then some."

"My friend can get you a fair settlement, and you still won't have to work, but I believe a woman should either have a career or hobby. Sitting at home all the time is boring as sin. I also have a friend who is searching for a qualified teacher on a part-time basis. It's a college right here in South Holland, and you can teach English."

I was getting excited, and I knew it had nothing to do with the wine. "I like it."

"Remind me to give you her card."

"Thanks, Confess for looking out for me. I have to end this nightmare with Land, but I want to find a way of making him pay. I can never forgive him for eating Mamie like she was a hot pork chop. When I asked him to go down on me, he had excuses like I had the plague or something."

"That's because you are a preacher's wife, Penny, and it's nasty to go down on his wife. I think in this case, Land was protecting and respecting you all at the same time. This is probably why he sleeps around with other women. They're probably whores who give him what he wants."

"Are you justifying his actions, Confess? You can't be serious," I shouted.

"He's a hypocrite, true and far, but he does have some legit reasons."

"Can you get a tape of him cheating on me?"

"I can, but what are you going to do with it?"

I smiled. "That's for me to know, and for you to find out. You'll have to come to Church to see the episode I'm going to film."

He shook his head. "Church isn't the way."

"I think it is," I shouted. "The snake is always preaching about adultery, and he's sleeping around. I can't stand him preaching to me or anyone when he's sleeping with every woman at the Church. I can't let him continue to make a fool out of me, Confess. I do have my pride."

"Honey, pride doesn't work in Church."

"And when was the last time you were there?" I shouted.

"Ouch!" Confess said.

I stared at my best friend. "I'm so sorry, Confess. I love you and I never want to hurt you."

"I have to finish my three chapters for my new book. I can get the tape in a few days. I want to know what you're going to do so I can try to salvage your reputation in the process."

"It's too late for that," I stated. "Land has ruined my life and my reputation along with it. Is Natalie in town?"

"I think she is for the rest of the week," he stated. "She's show-casing her fashions in New York next week. I had made some plans to join her there, but I guess that's over with."

"You have to let your pride go and talk to her. Pride isn't going to win."

"She's the one that stormed out on me," he shouted. "Why do I have to run after her? She should be knocking down my door with plenty of apologizes, but it's not happening. I haven't talked to her in five days."

"Are you keeping score?" I laughed.

Confess rolled his eyes. "I do miss her, okay."

I got serious and touched his arm. "I know, baby. Natalie isn't stupid and she will come to her senses. I read that she was having a fashion show for Rat Fashions on Friday."

"She is, but I won't be there."

But I will, I said to myself, taking a bite of garlic bread. "You sure can cook, Confess."

He smiled. "I'm glad to be appreciated."

"I love you, Confess, and you will always be appreciated by me. You're a talented writer, and a professional investigator. What woman wouldn't want to spend the duration of their life with you?"

He took a long sip of his wine. I felt for my friend because Confess was truly falling in love. I never thought I'd see the day. Natalie and I were going to have an interesting chat on Friday. I couldn't wait.

"Do you want some dessert?" Confess asked. "I made it from scratch."

I stared at him. "Are you talking about banana pudding?"

He smiled. "I made it just for you."

I got up from the table and hugged my friend. "I love you even more."

It was four hours later when I walked into my house. I turned on the light and jumped at the sight of Land. I couldn't believe he'd be home. I stared at him. "What are you doing here?"

"Waiting for my tramp of a wife," he snapped.

I stared at him. I was tipsy from the wine, and in no mood. "You're the whore, Land."

"I should slap you for dishonoring me," he snapped. "What were you and Confess doing?"

"Having dinner, and enjoying each other's company. Confess likes spending time with me."

"I offered to take you to dinner," he snapped again. "What more do you want?"

"I want nothing from you, Land. I'm going to bed."

"Let me make love to you. I want to eat my wife."

I always had the fantasy of someone going down on me. I'd have liked it to be my husband. "What?"

"Take a shower, and then let me eat you."

"Why?"

"You're my wife, and if this makes you happy, then I'm going to make all your dreams come true."

"What is the catch?"

"Do you want me too or not?" he snapped.

"Don't do me any favors."

"I love you, Penny. Let me show you how."

I couldn't believe his words, but I wanted him. I hurried into the shower, and then minutes later I met Land in our bedroom. He was already naked. I stared at his 45 year old body. Land still had it going on and then some. I was 45, and so did I.

"You look good baby. Come over here to me."

I complied as I laid on the bed.

"Spread those legs, baby," Land said.

I did, closing my eyes. I couldn't believe this was happening to me.

Land didn't waste any time, and the minute his tongue located my pleasure zone, I screamed out because his tongue tickled for a minute, and then the pleasure of sensations evaporated my entire body. I rocked from the thrills of pleasure as his tongue continued to give me pleasure. I knew it'd be like this as I let the feelings of the most wonderful specks of pleasure electrified my entire zone of passion. I had to hold onto the bedpost because Land was giving me all the pleasure I needed and deserved. My body felt so good, and I loved having his tongue eat me. It felt so good just like a dick but the tongue was a dangerous weapon all by itself.

I continued to multiply with orgasms, and I thought my body would never stop the shaking of thrills. I thought about him doing this same thing to Mamie, but I didn't give a damn. I shouted out for the last time, and waited seven minutes before my body came down to earth. I was burning from the coals of my being as my body continued to shake.

After twenty minutes I began breathing normally as I stared lovingly at my husband. "Thank you," I cried. "I loved it."

"I could tell," he laughed. "I'm going to do this more often."

"Why are you changing your methods? What are you trying to prove?"

"That I love my wife, and I might do other things because I also respect her. I thought doing this to you would be dirty, but if you like it, then who am I to stop you from enjoying your pleasure with your husband? And besides, I don't want Confess doing this to you."

I frowned sitting up in bed. "Is this the only reason?"

"Of course not," he shouted. "I'll be in the office getting some work done."

I stared after the snake and then hurried into the bathroom to take a shower. A man like Land would never change and his sins were going to wash down on him. As I washed between my legs, I still felt some thrills still lingering and I closed my eyes to let the orgasms take over. I moaned to myself because I was still lingering with my passion. It took another fifteen minutes before I could finish my shower. I just loved oral sex.

The fashion show was a huge success I thought as I waited for Natalie to finish greeting her guests. She was definitely a striking woman, and very successful as a fashion designer. She was up there with the other famous fashion designers, establishing her own following. I was truly proud of my white sister. Natalie noticed me a few times because she kept stealing glances at me. I smiled at her, and then waited until she was alone. When I finally found the opportunity, I hurried over to her. "Hi Natalie," I said. "Are you going to avoid me forever? I saw a dress I'd just love to have."

"What do you want?" Natalie said.

"I need to have a private word with you."

"Can't you see I'm busy?"

"This won't take but a minute," I sarcastically replied. "I'm sure you won't lose any money."

"You're a bitch," she said.

"It takes one to know one. Do you want to air our business right here in front of everyone?"

"We can go into my office?" Natalie snapped.

"I followed the size ten women with the right curves, and everything to match. Confess always liked women with meat on their bones. Natalie was still a skinny woman, but she was built in most of the right areas.

Natalie closed the door. "You have five minutes."

I found a seat at the desk and stared at her. "I'm here to do you a favor so get over the attitude."

"I thought you were here to tell me to leave Confess alone," she shouted. "I dumped him so he's all yours."

"Did you forget that I have a husband?" I snapped. "I don't want Confess. He's my best friend, and he will continue to be my best friend regardless of you being in the picture or not. He told you this fact, and I'm telling you. My friend is unhappy and when that happens, then I'm not a happy person. You don't have to waste this precious time being jealous of me. I have my own demons to deal with, but they have nothing to do with Confess."

"Males and females can't be friends," she said.

"Then you need to read his latest book," I snapped. "Yes they can."

"I miss him so much," she cried. "I thought he'd call me back."

"He's angry at the moment, and he's waiting for you to call because you're the one that dumped him. Why don't you give him a call? This is the first time my best friend has fallen in love, and I like you for some reason. I don't want my friend hurt."

"You really do love him as a friend."

"With all my being," I snapped. "I might not be married long, but Confess will always be there for me. If you can't understand our relationship Natalie, then you don't need to be with Confess. I don't want you getting all jealous on him every time he spends time with me, and calls me. I expect you to understand that I will never go beyond friendship with Confess. We tried it once, and it almost ruined our relationship as friends. I can't trust women, so I have Confess to take their place. We're better off being just friends."

"I'm sorry," she cried.

I stood up and embraced the woman. "I'm just glad I was able to talk to you. Confess is a good man. He's handsome, and very sensitive. You better nurture him because I'll be on your ass like a bat out of water. He'd die for me, and I'd die for him; Confess will die for you too. What are you waiting on, Natalie? The show is over and it's time for you to go and get your man. Give Confess my love when you see him. My job is done here."

Our embrace ended. "How can I ever thank you?" Natalie said.

"By loving Confess and never cheating on him," I said. "He needs honesty in his life, and a woman who only wants him. I promise that if you treat him right, you'd never regret the day you ever got involved with him. Now go on!"

Natalie hugged me again, and then she grabbed her purse and car keys, not to mention her coat. It was a beautiful Friday evening, but it was November, so winter was trying to stalk us. I stared after her, and then I smiled. Five minutes later I frowned because it was time to take care of my own business.

"My subject is once again on sinning," the preacher said. "I keep coming back to this because it's very important to me. I know half of the men and women here today are cheating, but you're singing and getting the Holy Ghost. How can you look at yourself in the mirror?"

I shook my head as I stared at Confess and Natalie. The two of them were back together, and I was glad to have them at Church. Confess was so grateful to me for bringing Natalie back into his life, so he owed me a favor. Of course coming to Church was my favor. I smiled, and then I focused on my lying husband. He was about to go down.

"Are you sure about this?" Confess said. "I have the VCR ready."

I shook my head. "I've never been sure about anything in my entire life. It's time for the sins of the preacher to come to life. You can go in the back and I'll let you know when to play the tape."

"Okay."

"Are you okay?" Natalie asked.

I smiled for the first time in a long time. "I'm just fine."

"Is the woman or man worth your life?" the preacher said. "I love my wife. I wouldn't think about cheating on her? She means everything to me and then some."

I knew that was my cue as I stood up, walking to the podium. "Honey, let me speak for a minute." I stared at the shock on his face. "I'd like to share something with the congregation since you're still preaching about adultery and infidelity," I smiled.

"Honey, what are you doing?" Land asked. "Have you lost your mind? We didn't discuss any changes in the sermon."

"I wanted to surprise you honey," I smiled again. "Why don't you sit down?"

He reluctantly sat down. "Hello everyone, I'm Land's wife, but most of you know this. I'm stating my name for the visitors. I'm sorry you have to be witness to the sins of the preacher."

The congregation made some noise.

"My husband preaches every Sunday about cheating, but he's the main one doing it with Mamie. How many times has he gone down on her?"

Mamie covered her mouth in shock, and Land was speechless.

"Don't just take my word for it," I shouted. "Let me show you."

Confess heard his cue as the lights went down, and the slide show began. The entire congregation was stunned as they watched their preacher eat Mamie, and about ten other women; the compromising positions he found himself in. He was naked in every picture, and everyone got a load of that big cock of his. I smiled at the shock on Land's face.

"That's my wife," a man shouted.

"And that's mine too," another man shouted.

"You slut," another man said.

"I want a divorce, another man repeated.

"How could you Janice?" her husband shouted. "I trusted you."

"How could you do this?" Land shouted, after finding his voice. "I'm going to be expelled from the Church. Where will you be without me and my money? You don't work?" he whispered.

"When I finished with you in court, I'll be rich," I shouted. "Did I dare to mention that I have a part-time job teaching English at a prestigious college? I also found me a nice little apartment with the children, of course. You're going to continue to pay child support for your two children and alimony to me. My lawyer will be calling yours."

"You bitch!" he cried. "How could you do this to us? You have ruined my reputation."

I slapped his face as the Church went silent. "You did that all by yourself when you continue to preach every Sunday about sinning, and you're doing all the sinning. You have no right to stand up here and tell anyone how to live because you're a hypocrite. How dare you!"

"You will suffer for this," he cried.

"I don't think so, Land. You do weep what you sow, and your time is up."

"I guess you'll be living with Confess," he shouted.

"I'll be living in my apartment with my two children. I'm taking care of me, myself, and I, thank you very much. Get away from me, and if you come near me, I'd have you thrown in jail."

"I have children," Land shouted.

"The courts will decide about them," I shouted.

Natalie joined me staring at Land. "I didn't know this was your husband," she said. "He tried hitting on me more than once, and I turned him down. I didn't even know that he was a preacher."

I shook my head at Land. "Whatever!"

"Let's go," Natalie said.

I stared at Land, feeling sorry for him. I then watched as Mamie ran over to him. "I'll be by your side forever," she cried. "I love you, Land, and I'm the only woman for you."

Land brushed her off as he hurried toward the exit. "Get away from me whore."

Mamie stared at him in shock, and then her tears blinded her. I smiled at Mamie. "It takes one to know one. Let's go Natalie."

An hour later Natalie, Confess, and I were having lunch at popular restaurant in South Holland. "You really busted your husband," Confess said. "Are you okay?"

"I explained to the children what was going on, and they weren't happy, but they knew their father was sleeping around. My oldest, Tammy is really hurt, but she'd get over it. Of course they still love their father, and I'd never take that away from them. I just don't want the lying snake in my life."

"I admire you so much," Natalie said. "It took a lot of guts for you to air your dirty laundry in front of the members of the Church. Did the board of trustees fire Land?"

"The same day," I said. "I was glad to do it because they deserved to know. Land will never change. I'm just glad he's out of my life." I lift my wine glass. "Let's toast to new beginnings. I start a new teaching job next week, and I just love my condo."

"I'm glad I could assist," Natalie said. "I really didn't use the condo."

"Thanks for letting me buy it from you. I just love it."

"Please change the decorations because it's yours."

"I will."

"Natalie and I are engaged," Confess said.

I stared at Natalie's ring. "How did you ever keep this from me?" I embraced Natalie and then I embraced Confess. "I'm so thrilled for the two of you, and happiness all over the place."

"I know you're going to be my maid of honor."

I was touched. "Are you sure?"

"Of course she's sure," Confess said. "You brought us back to each other and we'll always be grateful to you."

"Land is living with his father for the time being," I laughed. "The man is certifiable."

"Do you still love him?"

"I did, but the love was soiled. Anyway, let's move on because there are bigger and better things for me in the future. I'm only just beginning."

"I love you," Confess said.

"I love you too," Natalie said.

"And I love the both of you."

Six months later my life was progressing nicely. Land was still living with his father, and unemployed. The church gave him a year's severance pay in lieu of notice, but he squandered it all and was now penniless, depending on his father for everything. He kept ringing my cell phone, but I ignored him. There was nothing Land could say to me. Our life together was over because once a cheater, always a cheater.

June 5, 2004 – Saturday

I sat at the table, contemplating the boring day ahead of me. What a way to spend a day off, doing laundry, grocery shopping and vegging out in front of the television. I might even squeeze out some time from my busy schedule to read one or two of the fifteen or so books sitting in my 'To Be Read' pile.

I was forty-two, and while fairly content with my life, I felt like I was missing something. And I knew just what was missing. I was at heart a romantic and I wanted love and romance in my life. I've been divorced for fourteen years now, and although I was proud of my ability to take care of myself, deep down inside I was still hoping for my knight in shining amour to come along. I wanted someone to snuggle up to at night, someone to talk to. I didn't need a man to keep me; I could do that on my own. I just needed someone to love and to love me. I wasn't about to give up on romance. I don't think you can ever be too old for love.

I grabbed my laundry basket and headed to the basement, glad that I had my own house complete with washer and dryer. I shuddered at the thought of going to the Laundromat on a Saturday morning with everyone in the nearby apartments vying for a chance at the machines.

Five minutes later the washer was running and I was back in my pink bedroom, wondering what to do first. I decided to rush through the house cleaning while the laundry was going and then I'd be free for the rest of the day. I tried to keep my weekends as free as possible. Although I loved my job as a litigation paralegal, it kept me busy. I had to spend a lot of time in court with Knight Mann, the attorney for whom I worked, and still make time to get the office work finished. He expected a lot from me, but he worked just as hard himself, making his job his number one priority. Five years ago, he had hired me the day I graduated with my associate degree and trained me to do the work his way. He worked me hard, but he paid me very well for it so I had no complaints. We seldom had any personal talk in the office, but once in a while he would mention something about one of his many personal relationships. Right now he was dating a woman named Darla, who expected him to give her a lot more of his time than he was willing to.

I opened my closet door with a frustrated sigh as I stared at the chaos around me. There was no time like the present. I worked quickly, determined to have the rest of the day for myself.

Five hours later, my house was clean and neat, the laundry finished and put away neatly. I decided to watch the tube for a while so I went to make some popcorn, feeling the irritation with myself rising when I realized I was out of microwave popcorn. Deciding that I couldn't watch TV without my popcorn, I grabbed up my keys and was heading out the door when Knight called. Damn, I was angry. Knight had a bad habit of calling me any time he thought of something about one of our cases, but he promised me he wouldn't bother me this whole weekend.

"Hello!" I barked into the phone.

"I'm so glad I reached you, Kendra. I have a really important statement that needs to be done right away and I'm too busy. Can you do it for me?"

I frowned. "You promised not to bother me this weekend Knight."

"And I wouldn't if this case wasn't important. It's vitally important that you get this statement for me."

I began playing with a long strand of hair, something I did when I was angry. I thought I would explode as I stood there, indecisive.

"This is really important," Knight said. "I'd love you forever."

I frowned again. "Can't it wait until Monday?"

"No, it really can't Kendra," he said. "The man's name is Malcolm Saint. He's accused of murdering his girlfriend. I need you to take his statement and listen to him. He and I were friends a long time ago and I want to represent him, but I need to know if he's lying or not. I trust your judgment, and I need you to do this favor for me. If you do, you can have Monday off. I don't know how I'll survive without you, but I'm willing to make the sacrifice."

I thought about having Monday off. "Do I have to go into the office?"

"He can come to your place, or you can meet somewhere public. If you go to a restaurant, get a receipt and I'll reimburse you."

The restaurant idea sounded good. If I had to give up some of my precious free time, I might as well get a free meal out of it. Besides, I didn't want a stranger, especially someone who could be a murderer, coming to my house. "Give me an hour and I'll meet him at McDonalds."

Knight laughed at my choice of restaurant. "I knew I'd love you forever."

I smiled. "I don't want you to love me, I want Monday off."

"You've got it. Thanks so much, Kendra. I love you."

"Whatever!"

I hurried upstairs to change my clothes, pulling out my favorite yellow top to pair with my jeans. It took me a few minutes, but I finally found my yellow sandals and I was ready to go meet Mr. Saint.

I was the first to arrive at McDonalds and then realized that I had no idea what Malcolm Saint looked like so I had to call Knight. He was a big help...look for someone wearing red. I told him what I was wearing, just in case Mr. Saint called him and went to get my lunch.

Five minutes later I was dipping piping hot French fries into ketchup, closing my eyes as I savored the delicious flavor. I don't think anybody makes better fries than McDonalds.

I was snapped out of my potato and grease orgy by a voice saying, "I guess you know that you're just eating a box of grease, don't you?"

I was angry at the idea of a stranger presuming to judge me. I was an adult and could decide for myself what I put into my body and I turned to tell this presumptuous man that, but found myself meeting the amused eyes of one of the most handsome men I had ever seen. "Are you Malcolm?" I had to find out instead of gawking at him.

"Yes I am, Kendra. Knight told me to look for a beautiful yellow canary. He was certainly right," he said, smiling at me, revealing the whitest teeth I had ever seen.

I was surprised to feel myself blushing and it irritated me. I wasn't the type of woman to be bowled over by a pretty face. "Why don't you sit down Malcolm? I don't want to be as rude as you, but I think I'm old enough to choose my own food. I don't eat them all the time, but when I do, I enjoy them."

"I can see the passion on that pretty face of yours. I'm sure your husband appreciates that."

I frowned. "Would you like something to eat?" I wasn't about to discuss my personal life with a perfect stranger. If he wanted to believe that I was married, then it was fine with me.

"The frown doesn't do you justice."

I blushed again and then remembered why we were here. I ate the last of my fries before wiping my hands on a napkin and pulling a yellow pad and marker from my briefcase. "We should get down to business. I need the details of your relationship with the victim."

"I thought I could order something to eat first."

"By all means," I smiled. "The number 3 is good."

"I prefer the fish fillet," he said, heading to the counter.

He turned back as I muttered under my breath, "Oh yeah, you won't get much grease in that," smiling widely at me before continuing to the counter.

I stared after him. Malcolm Saint was tall, dark and handsome. He almost looked white, but his hair was definitely black. I wondered if he had a white parent. He was medium sized, mostly muscled, and he was fine. He couldn't have killed his girlfriend, or could he? I just met the man, but the inside of my body was going crazy. It had been two years since I had sex, and Malcolm was bringing out some familiar longings.

I studied my pink fingernails as I tried to get hold of myself. What was wrong with me?"

A few minutes later Malcolm joined me at the table with a tray loaded with a fish fillet, fries, a soda and two apple pies. I looked at the tray, mentally calculating the grease factor, but nobly kept my mouth shut and got down to business.

"Are you ready to start?"

"Knight is very lucky to have such an efficient paralegal."

"How did you meet the victim?" I wasn't about to listen to his line. The man could be a murderer.

He smiled. "We can get down to business first, of course."

That was all we'd get down too. I poised my pen over my tablet, waiting for him to answer.

He began eating. I liked the way he chewed. I shook my head, sure that I was losing my mind. How could eating a fish sandwich be so sexy?

"Are you okay?" he asked, chewing seductively.

"I'm fine. Let's begin."

"Are you taping me?"

"No, I'm taking it down in shorthand."

He smiled. "She's brilliant too."

I smiled back at him. Okay, he won that one.

He chewed for another minute before he focused on me. I didn't like him staring at me, but had no choice in the matter. I couldn't possibly object to him looking at me while we talked.

"I met Rita five years ago," Malcolm began. "She was modeling and I was the photographer. She made it pretty clear that she wanted me, and me being a man, I went for it. We started a relationship and it went okay for a while. Rita spent most of her time traveling, so we didn't see that much of each other. Then I fell in love with her and I thought she felt the same way about me. Then I learned that she had men in almost every city where she did regular work. She told me once that one man couldn't satisfy her every need, and she needed more but I didn't really believe her. I found out the hard way when I decided to surprise her in Los Angeles and found her in bed with a man and another woman."

I was stunned.

"The two women were having sex," he continued, "and the man was getting off watching the two of them. I had never seen two women together and I have to admit it was hot. I even got off myself. After that, I came to my senses and ended my relationship with Rita."

I was diligently writing despite the unsettling heat spreading through my body.

"I was very upset," Malcolm continued, "because I loved her and planned to propose to her. I'm just glad I found out what she was really like before we became engaged."

"Did you see her on the night she was killed?"

"She was stalking me but I ignored her calls, even changed my number. A few days before she died, she accosted me at work and I threatened to get a restraining order if she did it again. I spoke to Knight about it, but I never followed up on it because she stopped pestering me. I just assumed she found another man and had gotten on with her life."

"You dated Rita for five years, correct?"

"Yes, but we were separated most of that time. We both traveled a lot so when we managed to be in the same city we tried to spend a lot of time together. The longest continuous time we ever had together in that five years was one three-month stretch in Los Angeles. Even then, we were both working and didn't spend that much time with each other. Rita was wild, and she never stayed in one place long. Looking back now, I wonder how many other men she had while we were there."

"Why did you hook up with her?"

"She turned me on in more than one way. To really understand, you have to be a man."

"But she was turned on to women and men."

"She fucked them both," he snapped. "I wasn't thrilled when she wanted two women to make love to me so she could watch. I thought the woman was crazy where sex was concerned. I didn't like her views."

I laughed. "Most men would love to be in your shoes."

"Most men, but I'm not one of them."

"Whatever!"

"Did your husband hurt you?"

"We're not here to discuss my personal life. Anyway, where were you on the night that Rita was murdered?"

"I was here in Chicago."

"So was Rita."

"We were both here for a fashion show. She managed to get herself assigned to the one that I was working and made it a point to parade her men in my face. She enjoyed showing me that she didn't need me."

"Did she get you back?"

"No, but I promised to talk to her. We had arranged to meet at Red Lobster, but she never showed up. I sat there for an hour or so waiting on her before I went home. The next morning I found out that she was dead, shot in the head at point blank range. It wasn't me. I didn't love Rita anymore and revenging myself wasn't worth spending the rest of my life in prison."

"Do you suspect anyone?"

"I would say any of the dozen or so men she flaunted in front of me, or one of her boyfriends from around the world. Someone really wanted to destroy her beautiful face. Hell, it could even have been a woman. "

"Did you notice anyone hanging around her?"

"That's a good question. Rita had men following her every move. I can't remember a time when I didn't see her with a man in tow, but I don't remember any one particular man. She really enjoyed the attention."

"Did you kill her?" I asked abruptly.

He stared me right in the eyes. "No!"

I looked into his eyes and for a minute I believed him. I couldn't let my hormones dictate right from wrong. "I'll type up my notes and send them to Knight. I'm sure he'll be in touch," I said, putting away my notebook and rising from the table. "It was nice to meet you."

"Thank you for meeting me on your day off. I really appreciate it."

I smiled and left, refusing his offer to walk me to my car.

June 6, 2004 – Sunday

I sat in the pew at church and I listened to Minister Jacob Jones preach about finding the right soul mate and not giving in to temptation too early in the relationship. Sometimes I thought that Minister Jones lived in the stone-age because women and men were sleeping together on the first date. I wouldn't do it, but... I had been aching since I met Malcolm and that was crazy.

"You want to go out to dinner with us?" a female voice asked.

I smiled at Janet, a fellow church member. "I'm sorry, I can't, but thanks for the invitation. I already have plans."

"Then I'll see you next Sunday. I hope you have a great week," Janet said.

"You do the same," I smiled. Janet and her husband left and I watched them walk to their car. When was I going to find a husband? I walked to my car and smiled when I saw Knight leaning on it. "What are you doing here?"

"Waiting for you, of course," he smiled. "How was church? Hey, I didn't know you had legs," he said. "I thought you had some grotesque hairy sticks that you needed to keep hidden in long pants all the time."

I hit him on the arm. "What's going on?"

"I was just anxious to talk to you about Malcolm. Can we go somewhere?"

"What did you have in mind?"

"Are you hungry?"

I was.

"Then let's go to Bennigan's."

"My favorite place," I cried.

At Bennigan's, I took a sip of my Mai Tai as I said to Knight, "I just love this place.'

"Me too," he said. "You look great."

"So do you Knight. I never thought I'd see the day when you'd be wearing jeans."

"I know, but I do get to take a day off once in a blue moon, thank you very much."

"What's on your mind, Knight?"

"What did you think of Malcolm? I have to file an Answer to the allegations from the D.A.'s office, and I'm not sure what to do. I might be too close to Malcolm to see things clearly. Did you know my parents were his foster parents most of his life? His own parents deserted him and after bouncing around the welfare system for a while, he wound up with us. Something clicked and he wound up staying with us permanently. I look on him as my brother. "

I stared at him. "I don't really know. Malcolm is very charming. I need more time with him to know if he's lying. He says that he's a one woman man."

"That's for sure. He spent five years of his life with Rita. The woman was a whore."

"You speak from experience."

"I do. When I was in Los Angeles a few years ago, I spent time with Malcolm. One day Malcolm was working and Rita entertained me. She flirted with me so seductively we ended up sleeping together. Malcolm never found out, but I wonder if I should tell him the truth."

I was flabbergasted at Knight's confession.

"Rita was the kind of woman that you couldn't turn down. She had the body and the looks and she was the bomb. The woman was a whore, but she was only thirty-three, way too young to die. She wanted me to go along with the program but I couldn't do it to Malcolm. At least she was honest enough to admit her faults, although Malcolm refused to believe her."

I shook my head. Who was this Rita person? "Did you love her?"

He shook his head. "She was only sex for me and she knew how to play the game."

"I don't think you should say anything to Malcolm. It's over with now. Why hurt him any more?"

"I'll think about it some more before I do anything. For now, what do you think about this case? Should I take it?"

"Since he's your friend, I think you owe it to him. He might be guilty or innocent, but he does have a right to a fair trial with good representation. There are a lot of guilty people walking the streets and innocent people rotting in jail. The justice system doesn't work all the time."

He smiled. "Why don't you go to law school?"

I took a bite of my lasagna. "I'll just leave that to you."

"I'll get the papers ready for you to type on Tuesday. I'd appreciate it if you would spend more time with Malcolm and get to know him. He's a very charming man and he can manipulate the best of us, but he's very sincere with his relationship. He only dates one woman at a time."

"Do you want me to seduce him, Knight? That isn't in my job description."

"Of course not, Kendra, but when was the last time I saw you with a man? You're the most gorgeous woman in the world, and you should be in love."

"Are you in love?"

"No, but that doesn't mean I don't want the best for you. Just have some fun with Malcolm. I pray that he's innocent, and my gut instinct tells me he is, but I've been wrong before. Besides, I'm biased because he's my best friend. I need your input."

"Who is filing this suit?"

"The D.A., Lucy Mayes. She is bent on winning this one."

"Find a sucker and prosecute him to the fullest extinct of the law."

"Of course, but I'm not going to let her make the sacrifice. Rita's Sister, Glenda is overweight, but she loved her sister, and tried getting her to settle down. Rita loved Glenda, and did everything for her. Glenda never has to work again, and she lives in a mansion, and her two children are in private school; they have trust funds, and could go to any college they want. Rita provided for her only sister."

"Do you think Glenda had something to do with her death?"

"It did cross my mind, but Glenda had made some good investments, and she's about to open up a boutique of crocheted items. She's very good, and has a good business head on her shoulders. She went to college on Rita's money and majored in business management. Rita was going to invest in the shop, but she was murdered before she did."

"So Glenda wouldn't gain anything from her sister's death."

"We're on the same page," Knight said. "You're the best paralegal in the world."

"And I took an online course at that."

"But you surprised the hell out of me."

"I surprised the hell out of myself," I smiled. I'll entertain Malcolm for you."

"It's not a death sentence," he laughed. "I'm sure Malcolm was flirting all over the place with you."

"He was, but all men flirt."

"Not Malcolm, baby. When he sees someone he wants he goes after them."

"I'm not for sale Knight."

"He's a good man who will only get better when he gets this cloud from around him."

"Time will tell. Did Glenda like Malcolm?"

"She thought he was the perfect man for Rita."

"Oh!"

"Enjoy your day off and I'll see you on Tuesday."

"Where is Malcolm staying?"

"With me. You have the number."

I laughed. "I've never chased after a man before."

"If I know Malcolm he'll be calling you so jump to the bait."

"I want a raise," I laughed.

"And you have it," Knight said. "I love you." We embraced and then we got into our separate cars and drove off. I was wondering as I focused on my driving if Knight was putting me in the middle of the nightmare from hell.

June 7, 2004 – Monday

I decided to make the most of my day off and slept until noon. I took a shower, ate a bowl of cereal and watched my favorite soap opera before booting up my computer to search for information on Rita Taye.

She was the top fashion model worth millions. Her only sibling, Glenda, was the benefactor of her estate. I'd need to talk to Glenda about her sister. I put her name in the search box. She was a volunteer at several Chicago hospitals and seemed to be well-known. I emailed her, hoping she'd agree to talk to me. I had to find out what kind of woman Rita was and her sister would know more than anyone.

I continued my search while I waited for Glenda to respond.

Ten minutes later the ringing of the telephone disturbed my search. "Hello," I shouted.

"Are we PMS'ing today?"

I felt my heart began beating too fast. "No."

"Then I caught you at a bad time. Knight told me that you were off today. I thought we could visit Jerry's Photos. I'm debuting my photos there, and it'd be a pleasure to share them with you."

Jerry's Photos was a very prestigious gallery on Lake Shore Drive. "I'm impressed."

"So you'll go with me."

"Do I need to dress up?"

"No, but Knight says that your legs are to die for so I want to see them."

"Are you flirting with me?"

"I am, baby. Is that okay?"

"I don't know. You might be a murderer."

"I need for my legal team to believe in me."

"I'll be ready, Mr. Saint. What time?"

"I'll pick you up at six this evening, so you have plenty of time to enjoy your day off."

"I'm enjoying it, but I like to ask you a quick question."

"Okay," he said.

"What do you think about Rita's sister, Glenda?"

"She's a gorgeous human being, and I love her. She's the only woman who understood me and believed in my gift. She told me that if I married Rita, she might just settle down. She also kept warning me that Rita wasn't all there in a nutshell, but she was worth it. Glenda tried helping her, but she just wouldn't listen to anyone, but herself. She was the only person who knew what was best for her."

"What about her parents?"

"They tried with Rita, but they couldn't do anything with her. She was having sex when she was only eleven. Her mother put her in a group home when she was ten, but she ran away so many times, they gave up; she stayed with an aunt for six months, and then the aunt kicked her out when she fucked her husband. I'm sorry for the language."

"Do you think her father molested Rita?"

"I do believe it, but Rita denied it to me and her sister. We could never prove it, either."

"How did Rita act around her father?"

"She doted on him."

"Are her parents still alive?"

"They live in Florida. Glenda keeps in touch with them, and they visit their two grandchildren, but Rita didn't communicate with them after a time. She was never that close to her mother. Glenda was the only person she would listen too, and she loved her. She did what she wanted to do, but she gave Glenda the time of day. It's such a waste because Rita had so much life to live. Glenda always believed that Rita was going to settle down. I'm very sorry she's dead."

"So you do have remorse."

"Of course I do," he snapped. "I never wanted her dead. Rita didn't believe in rejection."

"Thanks for the information. I emailed Glenda. Do you think she'll talk to me about her sister?"

"I'll give her a call and have her call you."

"Okay, that will be a big help. Thanks a lot."

I smiled. "I'll see you tonight then."

"And I can't wait."

The gallery was crowded for the invitation only showing and I was thrilled to be here. The photos were out of this world, and Malcolm's display took the front wall. "I love it," I cried. "Where did you find the gorgeous children, and the beautiful flowers? You're romantic after all."

"I don't think so."

"But I do," I cried. "How can I purchase this?"

"You don't have too," he said.

"I know that, Malcolm, but I love it. Flowers are my passion."

"It's going to be released in a book of photography this September. I'm really excited about it. Morgan Publishers saw the potential in my work, and they have given me a five-book contract. I'm in the money. I love displaying my work and the money doesn't mean a damn thing."

"I am duly impressed," I cried. "You have green and the pink. Pink is my favorite color. Thank you so much."

"Thank you. I'd be glad to give you an advance copy."

"I want to pay for mine," I declared. "I'm not a charity case, thank you very much."

"By all means," he smiled. "Let's see the rest of the photos."

"Okay."

June 8, 2004 – Tuesday

Back at work I couldn't concentrate because I was too busy thinking about the wonderful time I had with Malcolm at the gallery. We enjoyed the rest of the show and then went to a nearby restaurant for dinner. It was so romantic, and I had a great time. Okay, I was falling for Malcolm, but I didn't know how he felt about me. Was he just playing with me so he could get me into bed? I wasn't a booty call by a long shot.

"Are we dreaming about Malcolm?"

I stared at Knight. "I was dreaming about my work."

"Right." He sat down next to me. "How is the investigation going?"

"I'm writing a brief of my findings so far, and I'm going to meet with Glenda at noon."

"Now that's a good idea. I never thought about that."

"I know. I told Malcolm about it, and he arranged it. I was on the Internet and found out some good things about Glenda and I emailed her. She's very popular in the community of Chicago."

"She warned me once not to fall in love with Rita because she could never be faithful to just one man. She saved me from falling under her web of deception."

I frowned at him. "You three act like Rita was on the throne or something."

"She had this way about her and she knew how to use it. Even women wanted her."

"I'll be taking to Glenda and then my brief will be ready before the end of the day. You should take the case because Malcolm is your best friend, and we should die for them."

"Do you have one?"

"I did, but she stabbed me in the back," I cried.

"What did she do?"

"She was jealous of me and for some reason I didn't know it. She did everything she could to ruin my life, and she almost did. I conquered the demon web of deceit she was trying to weave. She slept with my boyfriend and that was the last straw for me. I wanted to forgive her, and I did, but I'll never forget. I'm never getting that close to another woman again."

"Malcolm has never stabbed me in the back, and I love him."

"Then he's going to need your help."

"I love you, Kendra."

"Will you stop saying that, Knight? I had a huge crush on you once upon a time."

"I know that Kendra. I do love you, but as a friend only. I'd die for you."

I felt the tears forming. "Thank you." I knew Knight could never be more than a friend, of course. Who was I fooling?

"Malcolm is the perfect mate for you. I trust him with you, which is a good thing."

I peered at him. "I don't think so, but thanks for the thought." I was attracted to Malcolm but he had a lot of issues I just didn't want to deal with."

"Don't erase him because you'll be an old maid before you know it. Love doesn't happen often so give it a try. I wouldn't put a burden on you. Malcolm has some very good traits. He just hooked up with the wrong woman?"

"We all hook up with the wrong man or woman."

"You two had a great time at the gallery."

I smiled. "Malcolm is very talented."

"He's very talented, and his book will be on the New York Times best seller lists for weeks."

"I agree," I said.

"Now get back to work. I'll be in court for the rest of the day. Call my cell phone if you need me."

"I will, and break a leg."

"I always do," he laughed.

I stared out the window. So Malcolm enjoyed himself very much, and so did I. I smiled.

Glenda suggested we meet at Water Tower Place on Michigan Avenue. As I stepped into the glamorous building, I was reminded why this was the place to visit in Chicago. It was very prestigious. I browsed through the stores, window-shopping as I killed twenty minutes before I met with Glenda.

At noon on the dot, I felt a tap on my shoulder. I turned around to greet Glenda Hayes, a tall, strikingly beautiful woman. She was pleasantly plump, but she wore her size well. Her hair was in curls pinned up in a catchy style to enhance her beauty. "Hello," I said.

"Hi. So you're the woman who has finally captured the heart and soul of Malcolm. It's been a long time coming, but I love it. Let's go into Cat's Restaurant. It's my treat."

I wasn't about to argue with her because the restaurant was extremely expensive. I followed the stunning woman, noting the interested looks thrown our way.

Ten minutes later we were inspecting each other over sodas at a quiet table where we could see everything going on around us.

"Are you hungry?" Glenda asked.

"Maybe a little later," I said.

"Me too," Glenda replied. "Malcolm is a very special man. I love him."

I was touched by Glenda's words.

"I know he didn't kill my sister."

"Can I take notes, Glenda?"

"Of course," she cried.

"Why did you insist on prosecuting him?"

"The D.A. is the one doing the prosecuting and not me."

"The D.A. has a vendetta," I pointed out.

"I know," Glenda said. "But the truth has to work for Malcolm."

"Who do you think could have killed her?"

"A man took her life, and it could be one of hundreds that she dated. Rita kept a record of all the men in her life and the D.A. is investigating them, which is why Malcolm was, and still is, a suspect. The list is endless and I'm sure the D.A. will find the suspect before Malcolm goes to trial."

"Who is the D.A. on this case?"

"Lucy Mayes and I informed her that Malcolm is not a suspect."

"Knight is just filing his Motions."

"The D.A. is ready; she has solid evidence to convict. Rita had about three hundred people and more at her funeral and most of them were men. I was sure that I was staring at the murderer right in the face. The bastard will pay for killing my sister," Glenda snapped. "They will pay. I miss her so much, and I think about her all the time. She had so much potential in her life, and she wasted most of it with men."

I stared at her because I felt her pain. "Do you think a woman could have killed her?"

"What do you mean?"

"Malcolm said that Rita was sleeping with men and women."

"Rita was a sick person."

"But she was bi-sexual?"

"Yes she was. You know, your theory could be right. I believe you could be onto something because Yvette was a stalker in a crazy way. She harassed Rita on many occasions and showed up at a few of her fashion shows demanding to see Rita. She should definitely be investigated."

I wrote diligently on my yellow legal pad. If my theory was right, Malcolm could be free and clear. "What can you tell me about Yvette?"

"Her name is Yvette Coats. She's in her late 30's, beautiful and she loves women and men. She's bi-sexual, and she was obsessed with Rita. I remember mentioning it to Rita, but she laughed it off. Yvette was just a cutey pie and Rita adored her. She was nothing to worry about. My God she could have killed my sister."

I shook my head because it could be true. Who'd think a woman killed Rita. I couldn't wait to give the news to Malcolm. Was I very eager to see him again? I smiled to myself because I couldn't wait.

"Malcolm does make you smile," Glenda said. "I'm glad he's interested in someone who is worthy of his praise. Most of the women he meets are whores in every sense of the word. Thank God he has met you. I hope the two of you make it work."

I smiled. "I just don't know."

"Let's order something to eat and talk about Malcolm. I'm going to school you on the most wonderful man in the world.

I smiled again.

June 9, 2004 – Wednesday

It was noon before I looked up from my computer. I had been typing briefs for three cases since I started this morning and I was on a roll. If I didn't take lunch I wouldn't have to work late this evening.

I kept staring at the telephone for some reason. Okay, it was noon and I hadn't heard anything from Malcolm. Maybe I should just go into Knight's office. He was bound to mention the man.

"Hi."

I smiled at the sound of Malcolm's voice. "Hi."

"Were you just thinking about me?"

"Of course not," I lied. "What are you doing here?"

"I came to invite you to lunch."

"I'm really busy. I was going to eat a sandwich at my desk."

"How about me joining you at your desk?" he asked.

"Are you serious?"

"As a stroke," he laughed.

"I usually order something from Macy's."

"Then give me the menu and let's order from Macy's."

I smiled at him as I handed him the menu. As our hands touched, the electricity jolted through my system. I hurriedly pulled back my hand, and stared down at my shoes. I didn't want him to see my reaction because I was hot as hell. It was time to admit my feelings and stop playing these childish games. I wanted Malcolm, and those were the facts. I didn't know how he felt about me, but I wasn't just a booty call.

As we were munching on corned beef sandwiches and sodas, I told Malcolm about my luncheon with Glenda. "I think Rita might have been murdered by a woman. Do you know a friend of Rita's name Yvette?"

"I do. She tried seducing me once or twice, but I wouldn't give her the time of day."

"What is your opinion of her?"

"I told Rita that she was obsessed with her, but Rita always laughed it off. A couple of times she showed up on the job making a scene, and trying to stake her claim on Rita. The woman was something else."

"I'm going to look into this Yvette person. Do you think she could have killed Rita?"

"Yvette told Rita that if she couldn't have her, then no one would. She found Rita in bed with another woman, and I thought Yvette was going to kill her. It was a very ugly scene, Rita explained to me."

I registered his comments in my head. "Where was Yvette on the night Rita was killed?"

"I have no idea," Malcolm said. "I stayed away from the woman because there was just something about her that irked me. I have a feeling that she wasn't far behind. Rita told me once when we were making love that she felt like someone was always watching her, even then, when it was just the two of us. She couldn't erase this feeling."

"Did you feel anything when you were with her?"

"No. I thought she was taking drugs or something."

"We have to find Yvette."

"If anyone can find her, Knight is the one."

I want us to exclusively date," he replied, changing the subject. I think we have something special happening, and we should see where it's going."

I stared at him. "Are you asking me to be your girlfriend?"

"I am," Malcolm said. "We're attracted to each other, and the electricity is apparent. Let's just date for a month or two and see where it's going from there. I'm positive that I have met my perfect match."

I smiled to myself. "Maybe your plan can work."

"Good," he laughed.

I laughed with him.

September 5, 2004 – Sunday

I smiled at Malcolm as we walked outside after church. The weather in Chicago was getting cool and I closed up the flaps on my coat. "What would you like to do?"

"I have some business to take care of," Malcolm said. "Why don't I join you later at your house?"

"Are you okay?" I asked.

"Why do you ask?"

"You haven't been yourself lately. It's as if you've been in dreamland or something."

"We've only been dating three months and you're acting like a wife."

I was stunned by his words. "What?"

"You go home and I'll talk to you later," he insisted.

"How are you going to get there, Malcolm," I snapped. "We came in my car."

"I can take a cab."

"Then don't bother coming over until you get your attitude in check."

"Maybe I won't," he snapped back. He stormed off. I felt the tears forming but refused to let them fall as I got into my car, slamming it. I was so in love with Malcolm, but it seemed like he was about to move on. Why did he do this to me? I thought our relationship would be much longer, but I guess I was living in a dream world.

Yvette was in prison for five years for murdering her lover, Rita. The private investigator nailed Yvette for the crime, and then she admitted it to her mother who called the police. How could she kill someone she loved? The D.A. was livid because she couldn't put another win on her belt of success stories. I shook my head as I reached for my cell phone and dialed Knight's number. I knew it was Sunday, but knowing Knight he was probably working on another case.

"Hello," Knight said.

"Hi."

"Hey baby. Is everything okay?"

"I don't know. Malcolm has been acting very strange lately. Do you have any idea what's going on with him? He's shutting me out. I thought our relationship was working out nicely. Does he want to break up with me?"

"Probably falling in love scares him," Knight said. "I'd just give him some space and when he's ready he'll come to you with opened arms. Malcolm loves you and that's the truth. He's not going to dump you, so you have nothing to worry about."

I wasn't convinced. "I don't know."

"Don't dwell on the negative. I'll talk to Malcolm."

"Thanks Knight. Who are you dating?"

"I've been talking to Yvette in prison."

"What?"

"She just needs someone to talk too."

"Yvette likes women."

"And she likes men too."

I shook my head. "It's your business, Knight, but you could do a whole lot better."

"I'll see you on Monday."

"Okay." I disconnected, staring outside my car window. There was nothing else to do but go home although I'd be spending it alone, of course. I kept the tears at bay because a man just wasn't worth it.

September 12, 2004 – Sunday

It didn't take a genius to figure out that Malcolm was a dog and then some.

How dare he treat me in this fashion? I was leaving church and he was leaning on my car. I was stunned to see him, and I was also angry. It had been a week of hell for me. I had been staring out the window, waiting for his call, for hours. I thought I was going to lose my mind when the telephone didn't ring. I reached my car. "What do you want, Malcolm?"

"We need to talk. I'm sorry for hurting you."

"What's going on?"

"I can't be in a relationship right now. I'm having a baby by another woman and I need to be with her. I told myself that I'd never give up on my child the way my parents gave up on me. I love you, Kendra, but my baby needs a mother and a father. I have to marry Jada in a few days. I'm so sorry."

I couldn't believe this was happening to me. "I love you, Malcolm. When did you sleep with this woman?"

"Before I met you," he said. "She's almost nine months."

"Get out of my life, Malcolm and don't come back," I cried. "Just leave."

He stared at me for a long while before he walked off.

I waited for him to get out of my sight, and I cried hysterically. I was in love with Malcolm. Why did this have to happen to me?

October 12, 2004 – Tuesday

I looked at Knight but I couldn't concentrate on the case he was working on. My heart was still broken because of Malcolm. I couldn't stop thinking about the man I loved.

"Honey, Malcolm is a good man."

"He's a very married man," I cried. "I can't believe he's going to be a father."

"I was stunned when he told me after he talked with you. He's in love with you, but he's marrying the mother of his baby because of the way he was treated by his parents. I do admire him for it."

"So I have to make the sacrifice."

"I was at his wedding, Kendra. I'm so sorry for you. I thought Malcolm was the one."

"The woman is Hispanic for heaven sakes. Malcolm does get around."

"I'm sorry for your pain."

"But you're sticking by your friend."

"That's what friends are for, Kendra. I don't agree with his actions, but he made his bed and now he has to lie in it. They aren't in love with each other. Malcolm wants you to be his mistress. What do you think of the idea?"

I laughed at Knight. "You two are certifiable."

"I told him that he was sinful for thinking of such an action, but he wants you in his life."

"Let's get back to work," I shouted. "Men are dogs!"

"I'm sorry honey. You haven't gotten over Malcolm and he hasn't gotten over you either. Jada does her own thing with her man on the side. The two of them don't sleep together because she has her own man."

I shook my head. "What kind of marriage is that?"

"A marriage of convenience," Knight said. "When he first told me about his marriage I thought he was sick, but this is the extent of their marital relationship. He wants to be a father to his son, and nothing is going to stop him from being there, but he also wants the love of his life too. Why don't you just talk to Malcolm? He's coming by the house."

"I don't think so," I snapped. "I'm not so desperate that I'll settle for a married man. I go to church on Sunday, and you expect me to commit adultery. Malcolm isn't all that, believe me."

"I'm sorry," Knight said.

I shook my head again. "Men will never change. Let's finish this."

"Please don't be angry with me."

"Why should I blame you? This is what I expect of all men."

Back at home I stared at myself in the mirror. I was a fine woman and one day I was going to find the man of my dreams. Malcolm had lost his mind. He expected me to be his mistress. I was still so in love with Malcolm and what was I going to do about it?

November 1, 2004 – Monday

My breast was ripe from his expert hands as I fought the feelings of passion. He was enticing my plums and apples in sexual fashion and I was grooving to the beat of the drum. He sucked the nipples and I cried out his name. I was too hot and my breast loved every minute of it. I wanted him inside of me. I wanted to feel that hard dick rotating into my cove of pleasure.

"Take me," I cried.

He didn't hesitate as he added a condom and then moved onto me. I felt his penis inside of me, and began rocking to the heat of my sexual pleasure. I was high as a kite on my loving, and he was giving it to me. We rotated together as our bodies heated up to the pitch of ecstasy. I closed my eyes because we were both coming, and I wanted to feel every minute of my sensations. They came, and I screamed out, letting my body shake to the groove of the orgasms turning my body into a pleasure zone of thrills. It took me about fifteen minutes before my body stopped bouncing from the pleasure. I opened my eyes staring into his eyes. The pleasure I had just received was still centering my being. I made sure the orgasms were spent before I lay spent.

It took another five minutes, and then my body ceased.

I wasn't finished with the thrills when he entered me again, and we both rocked to, 'IT'S GETTING HOT IN HERRE' BY NELLY.

That was my favorite song, and my booty was floating on cloud nine as the sensations lit up my world. I was hot as a bomb, and the pops were circling my love zone.

He began screaming out and I felt his juices enter the condom more than once. Finally our pleasure of ecstasy was spent, and our lips met in the most unbelievable kiss. I loved his lips on mine, and he didn't disappoint. He bit my tongue a few times, and I screamed out my love of pain. I bit his and we continued the process until our tongues were spent, and then we again, rotated the process until our lips were raw from all the kissing. I could make love for the rest of my life with this man because I knew he was my world, and I was his in a nutshell.

"I love you," he cried.

I smiled as I bit his lip. "I love you too, Malcolm."

So far so good, I said to myself. I've been married for three years to the man of my dreams. It wasn't an easy task to get here, believe me. Lucas had been married to Jody for eight years. I was so jealous of her because she had Lucas, the man I had been in love with for a long time.

Lucas was forty-six, a handsome man. I called him my black beauty. We had been together for years when he caught me in bed with another man. It was all Lucas' fault, but he wouldn't accept my reasons. He spent all of his time in his studio trying to design new and innovative clothes and he neglected his woman in the process.

Lucas is a very passionate man and when we made love the world ended. He was the only man who could entice my body into an overdrive of sexual madness. Lucas was truly the only man for me. There wasn't another male in sixty miles who could turn me on the way Lucas does.

Enter Jody, a tall, gorgeous, black beauty. Lucas fell in love with her the minute they met. She was a supermodel and turned plenty of heads. I knew our relationship was over the minute he met her. Why did she have to fall into Lucas' lap? Why?

I did everything I could to break them up, but they managed to find each other again. I slept with all the men who wanted me because I was so angry that Lucas couldn't fall in love with me. I was the only woman he needed and should love in his life.

Jody and Lucas ran off to Las Vegas and got married. I was the first person they told when they got back to Chicago. Jody showed me her ring, loving the hurt and tears on my face. I wanted to beat her ass for stealing my man, but it was too late. Lucas was a married man now.

When Lucas went to the store for wine to celebrate, Jody showed her true colors. The minute he closed the door, Jody lit into me.

I wasn't surprised by her actions because she was a bitch in heat. Lucas was so blinded by her beauty he didn't see the inner demon.

"You bitch," she said. "Lucas is my husband now, and if you come anywhere near him, you'll die. I'll kill you with my bare hands. Do I make myself perfectly clear? You had your chance with Lucas, but you lost. Move on! You're a pretty woman. I'm sure you'll be able to find another man."

"Lucas is the only man for me," I shouted. "He may be blinded by your beauty, but when it wears off, reality will set in. Enjoy Lucas for a while because he'll be coming back to me. He's my man, and I'll wait for him. Have all the babies you want because I'll be raising your children one day."

"Dream on," Jody snapped. "Why did you cheat on Lucas if you're so in love with him? He was devastated when you betrayed him. The difference between you and me is that I really love Lucas and I'd never cheat on someone I love. What is your excuse?"

It was a mistake," I yelled. I couldn't believe that Lucas would discuss our personal business with Jody. "Lucas was working all the time and he forgot about me. I was lonely because of his job, and I'm only human. I'm sure you have plenty of skeletons in your closet. Who are you to judge me?"

"Move on Reese. Lucas is happy with me, and if you care anything about him, then you'll leave him alone and let us be happy. Love is the most powerful emotion in the world and sometimes we don't have to be together to love someone. Lucas is my soul mate. I'm sure yours is right around the corner. I know that Robert is in love with you. What's wrong with him? He's handsome."

I was shocked for a minute. Robert was a good friend of mine but I never knew he loved me like a man loves a woman. I loved Robert as a friend. I never thought of him as anything more or less. Jody was just a confused bitch. She didn't know anything. "Robert is my friend so mind your own damn business."

"Open your eyes, bitch, and focus on Robert. He loves you and he's wasting his time because you're so blinded by the light. Robert is an attorney, and he's handsome. What more could you want? Lucas is off limits so leave him alone, and play your games with someone else. Do I make myself clear?"

Back in the present I knew Jody could be a very dangerous opponent. I did a lot of online research on her. She was in the public eye, so there were plenty of articles written on her. I needed to find the skeleton in her closet because something told me that Lucas could be in danger if he ever crossed her. Why did I believe that Lucas was in danger by being in contact with Jody?

I searched for years before I found what I needed. His name was Anthony Paci, and he was the most dangerous man in the universe. Why would Jody get involved with a mob boss? I searched for information for Anthony Paci, and found way more than I needed.

The article was about Jody. I couldn't believe it, but he was searching for her. Her real name was Linda Blair. I printed out the article. I knew Jody was full of surprises. Why would she get involved in dangerous territory? Why would she talk to a mob figure? Was she stupid or something? The man would kill you as soon as look at you. He was searching for Linda aka Jody who disappeared off the face of the earth. Well he had finally found her. I just had to devise a way of making it happen without him knowing my name.

I wasn't about to be killed after he got the information he needed. I saw the Godfather movies more than once. The mob didn't care about killing someone when they were done with them. Maybe I could talk to Robert. He was smart, but I couldn't risk him getting involved.

I read the article again, searching for contact information. There had to be a way I could pull this off. I couldn't go to Lucas because he was so blinded by Jody, I mean Linda. I was determined to get Jody/Linda out of Lucas' life, and this is the way to do it. I just had to think.

Six months later Lucas and Jody were still going strong in their marriage. Jody was now pregnant so I couldn't go along with my plan, and it was killing me. She waited eight years before finally getting pregnant. Of course she had plenty of miscarriages in the process, but she might just have this baby.

I was thrilled for Lucas because he always wanted a child. I couldn't give him one because of the two abortions I had. I never told Lucas the truth. I just couldn't, but Robert knew everything about me. He was my best friend. I had to contact him because he'd never betray me. Jody/Linda was due to give birth any minute, and once the baby was born then my plan would be put into action. I smiled because Robert would know what to do.

It was a beautiful evening in May. Robert and I were sitting on the balcony of his condo in Palos Heights eating take-out fried chicken. I enjoyed hanging with Robert. He was a good friend and I'd always love him.

Robert was 42, a nice ordinary guy, working hard at his law office all week and spending his off time cooking gourmet meals for his friends. Robert loved eating and it showed in his big belly. I loved his cooking, and always had to fast the next day because I ate too much. I was a size six, and planning on staying this size forever. "What's going on with you, Robert? Are you dating anyone?"

Robert smiled at me. "I believe I might have found someone who captures my attention. Her name is Carolyn More. I met her at the bookstore, and something clicked between us. I hope she's the one because it has been a long time for me. I really like her, Reese. I called her right away and we talked and laughed for hours."

I was frowning for some reason. What was wrong with me? I should be happy for Robert. He had been alone for a long time, and it was time for him to meet the woman of his dreams. I smiled. "I'm so thrilled for you, but you know I have to check her out. I'm your best friend, and I have to make sure she's not going to hurt you."

Robert smiled. "I'm going to introduce her to you when I know she's the one. Let's not jinx it right now. I'm taking her to the movies tomorrow. I'm very excited about this. I've been alone too long."

"I do want the best for you, Robert. I hope she's the one, but go slow with her. Make sure this Carolyn person isn't looking for you to pay her bills. You know how we women can be? I don't want a broke man in my life. Lucas had money for me."

"I thought you were moving on about Lucas?" Robert frowned. "He's married and he's moved on with his life. I don't want to see you hurt, girl. There are a lot of men waiting to go out with you, Reese. I know a few who want to meet you."

I shook my head, sipping my lemonade. "I don't want to meet any men right now," I snapped. "I need to get Lucas back and make him my husband. I need you to do something for me. I don't know how to do it without getting caught. I trust you with my life."

Robert shook his head at me. He didn't want to get into any trouble because of me. I didn't want to get him into any trouble, either. "If this has anything to do with Lucas or his wife, you can count me out. I love you, Reese, but I'm not about to go to prison because of you."

I laughed, trying to break the ice. "This isn't going to get you into trouble, Robert. I need to do something and I don't know how to do it without being held responsible. Let me explain before you chew me out. I found out something about Jody. Her real name is Linda Blair."

Robert stared at me. "Are you serious? Anthony Paci, the mobster, is searching for a woman by that name. I wonder if it's our Jody. Do you know if he finds her he's going to kill her for running away with fifty thousand dollars?"

I was stunned. "How do you know, Robert? This kind of information is private. I hope you're not into mob work because you're going to die for sure, and then I'd have to get involved. I was thinking about telling this Anthony person Jody's whereabouts."

"If so, then you're killing her, and your conscience will haunt you for the rest of your life. It's not that easy to hurt someone so you can have the prize. Lucas is a good person, but he's happy with Jody. Why would you ruin his happiness because you think you want him?"

I was angry now. "Do you think I care about Jody? She made her bed and now she has to lie in it. I want Lucas to find out about his wife. He needs to know so when Anthony finds her, he won't hurt Lucas. The man has a right to know about his wife. It's my duty to tell him."

"It's your duty to mind your own damn business," Robert snapped. "I wish you would find someone to rock your world so you can get over this obsession with Lucas. You cheated on him and he's never going to forgive you."

"I'm sure he cheated on me too," I snapped. "Don't you dare go righteous on me? Men are cheating all the damn time, but when a woman does it, they can't forgive. How many damn times did I forgive all the men in my life? I was lonely and I told Lucas how I was feeling, but he didn't give a damn. How can I give Anthony Paci the information without him finding out who I am? Can I do it with a fake email or something? I don't want him finding out that I'm the one and then come after me. He's not going to be grateful to me."

"A man like that won't be, but there's a way," Robert stated. "I could do it for you, but I won't. I like Jody and I'm not about to get her killed because you want her husband. Let me set you up on a blind date, and then the two of us can move on. Peter is dying to date you."

"I can't be with another man," I snapped. "Are you even listening to me? I'm your best friend, and right now I need your help. I'm sure Anthony will be so thrilled to find Jody he wouldn't do anything to hurt her. He just wants his money back, and maybe her."

"We can't think for Anthony Paci. He's a mob king, and he's dangerous, you fool! He's going to shoot and not bother asking questions. A man with his resources and connections should have been able to find Jody a long time ago, but she was able to outsmart him. I'm not going to have her death on my hands. I suggest you go out with Peter and have some fun."

"Okay, set me up with him for tomorrow night." I was going to find a way of doing this myself and to hell with Robert. I couldn't blame him because he was trying to save me from myself, but this was something I had to do. Jody was living a lie, and she wasn't about to take Lucas down with her.

"You're going to have a good time with Peter, girl. He's handsome, rich, and gorgeous. I think the two of you will hit it off perfectly. He's an attorney in my firm, and he's searching for the right woman. He saw you once, and he's interested.

I needed sex, so this Peter person was as good as the next person. I'd have a conversation with him, and then move on to the bedroom and make love. I guess it'd be all about sex. I'd have an orgasm, he'd get his, and then I'll move on. Those are the simple facts.

"What's going on in that head of yours?" Robert asked. "I told you to forget about ruining Lucas' life. He's about to have a baby. You've ruined your chances with him, so it's time to move on. How many times do I need to tell you?"

"I heard you loud and clear, Robert, and thanks for doing the right thing by me. I do need to forget about Lucas. He's the only man I'll ever love, but loving someone means letting them go. I'm going to have some fun with Peter. Why don't you and Carolyn join us?"

"Because Carolyn and I have other plans, but when the time is right you'll meet her. I want you to be nice to her and not make her feel bad. I know how sarcastic your mouth can be at times."

"I wish you the best, Robert. So you're not going to do the email for me?" I was trying to get some information. "My boss was thinking about me adding another email to my account. I told her that it'd cost some money, and she's as cheap as they come so I can't do it."

"Tell your boss to go to yahoo. They have free emails accounts. I'm going to go into the house and call Carolyn because I told her that I would. I don't want her to think I don't keep my word, of course. It's time to move on because there are other fish in the sea."

There was no other fish for me, but the emailing was going to happen. I was sure that Jody/Linda or whatever her name is will not die. I believed that I was doing her a favor. When Anthony found her, then I was going to be there to help Lucas to pick up the pieces. I couldn't wait to be his wife."

I watched Robert as he walked into his house. He was finally falling in love, and if he could find a woman, then Lucas will come to his senses sooner than later. I couldn't wait to meet this woman and I prayed she really liked Robert. He wasn't Shemar Moore, but he was very nice. Robert was going to find his happiness and so was I.

The next day I met Peter, and Robert was correct. He was tall and gorgeous, and white. I dated a few white men before and they were all the same. Men had the same thing between their legs, so I didn't give a hoot about their color. We were going to have sex because I was itching for some sexual contact.

Peter took me to a nice, expensive restaurant on Michigan Avenue. It was my favorite place in Chicago. The restaurant was booming as I stared at my menu. I was going to have something fattening because I needed the energy to keep up with Peter. Robert didn't tell me that he was 32 years old. What was he thinking?

"Is everything to your liking?" Peter asked. "I couldn't believe it when Robert gave me your telephone number and told me to call you. I thought I had died and gone to heaven. I saw you a few times when you came to visit Robert, and I thought the two of you were dating. I was relieved when Robert informed me that you two were best friends."

"Robert is full of surprises. He's been trying to get me married off for the longest. He also didn't mention the fact that you're a young man. I'm not into age or color, thank you very much. I just like to know the facts when I'm with someone. I don't like surprises."

"Some women are age conscious and some don't give a damn. I met a few who did, so I told him to keep my age out of the picture. I'm mature for my age and you look to be in your early thirties, so why worry about such a petty thing."

I smiled because I didn't look my age, so I know Peter wasn't trying to flatter me. "Thanks for the compliment and we're going to have sex because I'm horny as hell, Peter, so you don't have to keep the compliments coming. I know you're going to rock my world."

He laughed, and I laughed with him. Peter and I were going to get along just fine. He wasn't about to play games with me. "Have you been with a black woman before, Peter? If not, you're in for a rude awakening of passion."

"I haven't, but I heard that black women had it going on in the bedroom. I work with a lot of brothers, and in the staff lounge, they're talking about the good times they had the other night, and so forth. I'm not going to dare talk about us. I think you and I will have a lasting relationship."

I shook my head. "I'm going to have a cheeseburger and fries and a milk shake. I'm in need of something fattening. I get sick of eating food that won't make me fat. I want to pig out, and not give a damn about my weight. It's time to move on to some loving."

Peter laughed. "We're definitely going to have a good time. I've never met anyone like you before. Robert told me you had it going on and he was right Have the two of you ever gotten together before? I know it might be personal, but I was just wondering."

I took a sip of my white wine. "Robert and I fucked a few times one night when we got so drunk we didn't know what we were doing. The next morning we were angry with ourselves because our friendship was almost lost. Robert and I didn't talk for weeks. We're never going to let that happen again."

"I did that once with a good friend of mine. Her name was Lacy and we were both ending relationships. We got drunk and found ourselves in bed the next morning. It was great sex, but for some reason we began acting differently with each other. Sex ruins a friendship."

"I agree with you," I said. "Robert and I will only be friends. He's finally met someone and I hope she's the right woman for him because Robert is a good man and he needs the loving of a good woman. I do want the best for him, and maybe this Carolyn person is the one."

"What do you want for yourself, Reese?" Peter asked. "I have a feeling that you're very sad. I know you're pining over someone. He has to be the most foolish man in the universe. If you were in love with me, I wouldn't let you go, you'd be my wife."

I smiled. "Thanks, and I think you mean it too. I'm in love with someone, but he got married, so I have to move on. I made a mistake and I apologized, but he's not willing to forgive and forget, so I know he's not the right man for me," I lied. If I kept telling myself this maybe I could find happiness with Peter. "Why don't you talk about you?"

Peter smiled. "I'm going to have what you're having. Anyway, you know my age, and I'm an attorney. I'm hoping to be a partner within the next five years. I was a paralegal when I was nineteen. I loved the paperwork but then one day I went to a courtroom with my boss, I knew there was nothing else I wanted to do. I had to be in the courtroom. I applied to law school and, as they say, the rest is history."

"I wish you luck with all of your dreams. I'm a court reporter and I only work three days a week. I work extremely hard on those three days, but I love having all that free time and it works for me. I don't regard it as a career though; it's just a job that pays enough to let me live the kind of life I want to live."

"All people have dreams," Peter said. "Working three days a week is a blessing for working women. There's a lady paralegal at my office that works the same schedule as you. She refuses to spend her life working and missing out on so much. I agree."

"Its interesting work," Peter said. "I do admire court reporters. I think you're going to make it in this world. Why don't you concentrate more on a hobby? What do you like to do when you're not working? I like painting. Maybe I can show you my studio some time."

I was surprised. "I think painting is wonderful. I used to want to design baby clothes." I laughed before Peter could, but he wasn't laughing at all. He had a nice smile. "I was invited to a couple of baby showers and I couldn't find anything I liked. I thought about making something myself, but I never followed up on it."

"Then it's time that you make that happen," he said. "Painting is very therapeutic for me. An attorney's job is hard, so the painting clears my mind, and gives me strength, faith in God, and the ability to perform. Why don't you research it on the internet?"

He was serious about this. "I can do that," I said. "I just thought it was so funny. I haven't even told Robert my dream because I was afraid someone would laugh at me. I used to make clothes for my dolls. I still have them somewhere in the back of my closet. I think I did a good job."

"The next time we get together, I want you to make all your dreams come true. Life is so short, and you don't want to regret the things you could have done when you were here. I planned on getting married and having two children. It's the next goal in my life."

"I'm sure you're going to find your soul mate. What do you do when you believe and know in your heart that someone or something is right for you? I know I can be a good wife to Lucas, but he doesn't want to forgive me. I'd never cheat on him again. I love him so much." I couldn't believe I lost control in front of Peter. He could be the man I wanted to date. I couldn't even get the sex out of the way.

"I understand your honesty," Peter said. "I believe that if you're meant to be with someone, then you're going to be with them when the time is right. If you believe that, then move on with your life now. When the time is right then you and this Lucas person will find each other. I think if you love someone enough, and you can't be together, then your love will let him go. Please don't stalk the person because it's not healthy."

I laughed. "I'm not a stalker, and you're right about moving on. It's difficult for me because I love him so much. I'm going to carry on. Let's eat, and then we can go to your place and have a good time. I'm going to live for the moment, and maybe you'll be the one to get my mind off of Lucas. I want ketchup and plenty of salt on my fries." I laughed, and Peter laughed too. He might just be the one to keep me happy, but Lucas was the only man for my happiness.

Peter was in his early thirties and he owned a nice house that he decorated in shades of orange, which actually turned out to look very nice when I had a look around his three-bedroom, two baths home. I loved it. The man had it going on. "Your place is gorgeous."

"So are you," Peter cried. Our eyes met, and then I walked over to him. I knew I was going to have sex with this man, and I was looking forward to it. I had a feeling that Peter was going to do things for me that I couldn't get Lucas to do. Maybe I needed another man in my life.

I removed my clothes and stood naked in front of Peter. I was proud of my body, and the way Peter was staring at my firm ass and breasts, I thought he was going to come in his pants. "Why don't you

stop staring, Peter and come over here and give this body some pleasure."

I didn't have to say another word. Peter hurriedly removed his
clothes. I stared at his naked body. He was built in a healthy way. What
I noticed about Peter was that his manhood was standing at attention. It
looked like it needed my loving touch and I was ready to give it to him.

I stood in front of him, bent down to his manhood and went to
work on pleasing my man of the moment. I saw the shock on Peter's
face, but when my mouth began working his manhood, he began
moaning and screaming out his passion. I smiled and continued my
ministrations until Peter was bursting with his pride and joy.

When he came back down to earth, he eagerly grabbed me and
began kissing me all over. I began moaning because it had been a while
for me, and his mouth was giving me pleasure. I closed my eyes and
dreamed of Lucas as Peter continued his ministrations on my love nest.

He excited my breasts until they were exhausted from his lips,
and then he went down to my pleasure zone of passion and his tongue
went to work. I screamed out because my body was rotating with
pleasure. I was coming, and I couldn't believe I was coming so soon. I
wanted to prolong my orgasm, but it wasn't happening as my body
ripped with shocks of sensations. I exploded inside and out, thinking I
was going to faint from the orgasms. They kept coming, and my body
kept shaking. I cried so loud you'd think I hadn't had sex in years.

When my body finally stopped shaking, Peter asked for a condom. I supplied him with two, and he entered me. I didn't feel any pain
because I was so moist with pleasure. He pumped me and I pumped
him, and the two of us rode a ride of sexual gratification. Peter had my
body rotating with pleasure, and when he screamed out my name, I
knew he was getting his pleasure.

Our bodies continued to rotate with love again as Peter turned
me over and we continued to ride with the punches. He entered me
from behind and I screamed out from the pain, but it didn't last long as
he rode me, and I rode him. Our tongues met because Peter was a
tongue man. I didn't like it at first, but Peter was an expert as he mated
with my tongue.

His hands were between my legs, and I exploded inside again,
shouting out my passion this time. I couldn't believe how sexually
satisfied I had been. Peter wasn't selfish in the lovemaking department,
and I was having the time of my life. My eyes were closed as my body

burst with pleasure. Peter was exciting every pore of my sexual appetites. We continued our maze of pleasure for another hour, and then we lay spent from exhaustion. I was so tired I couldn't get up to run into the bathroom. I needed to get into the shower. I didn't want to linger with sex on me especially from a man I didn't plan to love for the duration of my life.

"Are you okay?" Peter whispered. "I'm so tired I can't move. What they say about black women is true. You're the most passionate woman I've ever met, and you make a lot of noise so it makes me feel good because I know I'm satisfying you."

I laughed at him. "I guess you've been with women who don't utter a sound. How do you know if they're enjoying the sexual lesson you're giving them? I can't help my passionate nature. I scream my passion out because I'm so hot and you turned me on the minute your tongue went to work."

"I'm a pro in the lovemaking department, but I'm not going to toot my own horn," he laughed. "I'm going to take a shower as soon as I can get off of this bed. You can use the bathroom downstairs. You should find everything you need. I thought we could listen to some soft music, drink wine and talk."

"Sounds like a plan to me." I don't plan on leaving, but if I went home, I knew I was going to get straight on the computer, and email Anthony Paci. He left his email address for contact.

Peter smiled. "I'd love to have you spend the night with me. I'm just sorry I didn't think of it first. I didn't want you to think I was a cad or something. You can stay in the guest room, or sleep in bed with me. We're adults, and we can do what we want."

"I think I'll sleep with you Peter because I just don't want to be alone for some reason. If you want me to sleep in the guest room, that's fine with me too. I don't want to suffocate you but I'm just feeling lonely right now. It's weird to me."

"It's okay, Reese. I'd love to have you in bed with me and hold you close. It's fine with me. Let's get our showers and find something to eat. What about some strawberries, cheese and crackers with some white wine?"

I smiled. "That sounds perfect to me, Peter. Please don't make me fall in love with you. Lucas is the only man I want to be in love with, so slow down being so nice to me. I can't afford to find someone like you. For now, I want to just have sex with you again."

"Now that sounds like a plan to me," he laughed. "Let me show you to the bathroom. After that I'm going to ravish you with my body, and shake that groove thing of yours again."

I smiled at him. I was ready for him to ravish my body again. Peter was okay for a white man. He was good in bed, and I was having the time of my life forgetting about Lucas for the moment. Maybe he wasn't the right man for me, and there were other fish in the sea. Peter was very attracted to me, and we could be compatible. I was definitely going to find out.

I hurried into the shower and cleaned my body well. I was going to make love again and I wanted to smell good. Peter's bathroom was well stocked with everything I needed and more. I wondered how many women he brought home. I put it out of my mind because I was here and I was going to enjoy every minute of it.

It was the wee hours of morning and Peter and I were still talking. I wasn't sleepy, and believe it or not, I was having the time of my life. Peter was a very interesting man. He had a lot of stories to tell and I was a good listener. I didn't find myself bored at all. This was the therapy I needed to get my mind off of Lucas.

"I think we should try and get some sleep," Peter said. "I'm exhausted from our lovemaking for the second time. Girl you wiped me out with that great body of yours. I'm going into work late tomorrow, so I can fix you a good breakfast."

I thought the tears were going to overwhelm me, but I yawned instead. "I think you're right. I'll just lie on the sofa and close my eyes. I might sleep until noon. I'm off tomorrow I think. Dammit, I don't even know what day it is."

"Maybe you're finally realizing that there are other men out there who want to be with you. Lucas isn't the only man in this world. I'm going to take your mind off of him. I'd like you to sleep in bed with me. I have the perfect shirt for you to put on."

I was naked and loving every minute of it, but I didn't want Peter to get used to my body. I yawned again. "Why don't you get me the shirt because I'm getting sleepy this time? Thanks for a wonderful day, Peter. You made me feel good. I owe Robert, big time."

"I do too," he laughed. "Let me get you a shirt. I want you to sleep like a baby. It's three o'clock so I need to get some rest. Tomorrow is Saturday so we both can sleep in. I do have to go into the office for some paperwork, but it won't take long."

I yawned for the third time, covering my mouth. I was going to sleep good this morning because my sexual urges have finally been filled. I dreamed every night of Lucas making love to me. Even when Peter made love to me the first time, I only saw Lucas' face. The second time I saw Peter's face. Maybe I was moving on. I hoped so.

I spent a wonderful weekend with Peter, making love, eating, talking and going to a movie. It seemed like Peter was going to be a good lay for a long time. I had to keep him in my life. Now I was back at home and sitting in front of my computer. It was time to get to the business at hand. It only took five minutes for me to open a new email account with yahoo using a phony name,

I reread the article by Anthony Paci and typed a short message telling Anthony where he could find Linda. I hesitated for a moment and pushed send. There was no turning back now, the deed was done. I smiled, happy that I was going to be with Lucas after all. I'm sorry, Jody/Linda, but it's time for you to go back to Anthony because Lucas is all mine.

A month later, Peter and I were still a couple. Robert was thrilled about it. I had fun with Peter, but I was still waiting for Lucas to contact me. I had to find out if Anthony had contacted Jody/Linda, but I couldn't call him because I'd give myself away. I waited patiently by the telephone, but Lucas forgot that I even existed. Sometimes I hated the bastard for being so cold to me. What was he thinking?

One evening, Peter was dropping me off at my place when I noticed a figure sitting on the steps. It looked like Robert at first. I kissed Peter and waved goodbye, watching until his car was out of sight before hurrying to the stairs.

"Robert, what..." I was stunned beyond words as I stared at Lucas. He didn't look like himself at all. He smelled like he had been drinking, and his clothes were dirty and wrinkled. "Lucas, what's going on?"

"I need to talk to someone," he cried. "My life is over. I know I told myself that I'd never speak to you again but you're the only person I can talk too. Where have you been, Reese? I've been sitting here for hours. I couldn't remember your telephone numbers."

I reached for my keys. "Let's go into the house, Lucas and we can talk about it after you take a shower. You need a large cup of black coffee too. Where is your wife? I told you I wasn't going to pick up the pieces when she hurt you. It's time to move on, and I've done that and more."

"I saw you with your white man. I never thought you'd change to another race, Reese. You told me that you didn't date white men. I thought I'd be the only man in your life. I see you didn't wait for me very long."

I laughed as I pushed him into the living room. He fell to the floor and I shut the door with a bang. "I should throw your ass out of here. How dare you get angry with me because I'm kissing another man? I'm not married to you, and I do have a life, thank you very much."

"I'm sorry," he cried. "Jody is gone. Some man in a suit, surrounded by bodyguards, came to the house and pointed guns in our faces when we were asleep in bed. I thought I was going to die, but they took Jody. She begged him not to hurt me, and she'd go freely without any problems. The woman is about to have my baby. I think she went into labor, but I couldn't do a damn thing about it."

I smiled to myself but I quickly changed it to a frown as I looked at Lucas. "Who are these men? I don't understand someone coming into your house with guns and taking your wife. Did you call the police? There's something wrong with this picture. Did she act like she knew the men?" I sat down on the sofa trying to keep myself from laughing out loud.

"One of the men kept calling her Linda, and she called him Anthony. I remember her asking him how he found her."

"Lucas I'm so sorry for you and Jody. Did she contact you after this mess? What's going on with your child? Let's call the police and get her back. They'll know what to do, Lucas. You can't just let her go without a fight." I had to play the game, and I was a good actress.

"If I call the police, the men will find me and kill me. I can't risk it." He shook his head. "This Anthony person told me to forget about Jody and move on with my life. She was his and would always be his. Then he told me the baby would be safe with another family. Reese, I'm never going to see my wife or child again. I think he's going to kill her."

I felt guilty as sin. I didn't want the woman to die. What had I done? I just wanted her out of Lucas' life. "Lucas, we need to call the police. Maybe you'll be able to save her life by contacting them. This

Anthony person can't get away with barging into your home and kidnapping your wife."

"No," he shouted. "I was warned more than once. I shouldn't have told you anything because I'm risking your life too. I just didn't know where to turn. I have a feeling I'm never going to see my wife again. What in the hell am I going to do without Jody? She was my soul mate."

I frowned and shook my head. Lucas didn't have a clue. I was his soul mate. "Let's get you into the shower and some coffee inside of you and get you to bed. We can talk after you get some rest. You're exhausted, Lucas. In the morning we can find a solution to this problem."

"I knew it was right for me to come to you. Tomorrow we'll find my wife, and this nightmare will be over. I just need to get some sleep. My life flashed before my eyes when that gun was pointing at me. I thought I was going to see God real soon."

"I'm glad you're alive and well Lucas. Everything is going to work out. Jody was probably involved with this man and she got away. He's been searching for her. You said that the man kept calling her Linda. Who in the hell is Linda? Something isn't right."

"He said he had been looking for Linda, and she was very clever. She'd pay for abandoning him. No one ever ran from him and lived. This can't be happening to me. I need my wife." He wept like a baby.

I was surprised because Lucas had always been a proud man. He'd never shed a tear for anyone, and now he was on the floor weeping like his life was over. He was really in love with Jody and she was the only woman for him. I came to this conclusion, and realized I didn't care because I wanted Lucas.

On Saturday morning Lucas slept until 10:30, wandering into the kitchen, fresh from his shower, where I was cooking bacon and eggs with French toast. I prayed that Jody wasn't dead as I switched on the small television in the kitchen to check the news.

He sat down at the table. "How could you cook at a time like this? My life is over and you're cooking. You're a selfish bitch."

I put my hands on my hips. "This is the second time you've insulted me, Lucas, and I won't have it. Go home and take care of your business and leave me the hell alone. I have my own life and man to deal with. I'm trying to feed you so you can think on a full stomach."

"I'm sorry," he cried. "I never let myself get in this state before and I'm losing my mind. I need to hear something about my wife. What's going on with her? She has to come back to me, or I'll die. She's my life. There's no other woman out there for me."

I wanted to kick him in his balls, but I controlled the urge. Lucas was hurting, so I couldn't bring him down. I had to be supportive since I was the reason for this madness. I heard something on TV that caught my attention and I shushed Lucas, turning the sound up so I could hear. The reporter was talking. **"The body of a woman was found in the alley behind an abandoned building on the West side of Chicago. She was shot in the head and set on fire. An unnamed source tells me that police have identified her through her dental records, but refuse to release her name pending notification of her family."**

I covered my mouth in shock as Lucas crumbled to the floor and screamed. I can't believe Anthony would kill her and burn her body. Of course one of his henchmen did it because the bastard didn't have the guts. I killed Jody/Linda. My life was over. I took Lucas' into my arms, and wept with him. Why?

It was nine months later and Lucas and I were dating now. I told Peter he had to move on, and he wasn't thrilled about it. He was in love with me. I liked him too, but Lucas was the only love of my life. I knew he didn't love me, but since I had been there for him, making all the funeral arrangements and dealing with his and Jody's family, he trusted and respected me. One day we were so exhausted that we fell into bed and made love. I had my man, and I was the happiest woman in the world.

Lucas called me Jody many times in these bouts of passion, but I ignored it because he was never going to get over his wife being killed so horribly. He could never find out that I had something to do with her death because Lucas would kill me in cold blood and not bat an eye.

I was in the kitchen cooking Lucas' favorite dinner, fried chicken and rice, when the telephone rang. "Hello." I didn't have time to socialize with anyone because Lucas would be home soon.

"This is Peter, Reese. I just wanted to hear your voice. I know you told me not to call you, but its difficult being in love with someone and trying to forget about her. I know you're with Lucas. I'm not going to break that up or stalk you. I love you, and I know you have feelings for me. Think about the times we shared. I love you."

The telephone clicked and I stared at the dead phone. Okay, I missed Peter more than I thought possible, but he wasn't my soul mate. Lucas was the only man for me, and he was coming around. The news media reported that Jody was married to this mob figure and ran out on him. The woman told so many lies; I can't keep up with her.

The door burst opened and Lucas flew into the kitchen. He grabbed me and twirled me around a few times. "Lucas, what are you doing to me? I'm going to drop the frying pan. It's great seeing you in this mood, but what's gotten into you."

He put me down. "Let's get married, Reese. I want to spend the rest of my life with you. We can go to City Hall to get married and have a short honeymoon later. I'm in love with you, and you're the only woman I can trust. Jody lied to me so many times I lost count."

The tears enveloped me because dreams do come true. "Are you sure about this? Jody was divorced from Anthony so the two of you are still legally married. I know she's dead, and that makes you a widow, but you need to make sure. I won't have you use me."

He laughed. "I should have married you in the first place. Let's get married. I want to do it right now. You have been so supportive of me, and I wouldn't have survived the funeral with Jody's family. You can also give me a baby because I want children. Let's do it."

I frowned because I couldn't give any him any children. Should I tell him the truth or not? I thought about Peter for some reason. Why would Peter enter my brain right now? He was just someone I used at a time when I needed a man in my life. "Let's get this show on the road."

By the end of the day I was Mrs. Lucas Pope. I couldn't believe this was happening to me, but I was now married to the man I had been dreaming about since we met. I was his wife and I wanted to shout it to the world. I stared down at my ring. I was Lucas' wife.

After the ceremony we went to a restaurant on Michigan Avenue to celebrate. Carolyn and Robert were our witnesses. The two of them were in love with each other, and wedding bells would be ringing for them very soon. I watched Carolyn and Lucas dance.

"So you mastered this plan, and a woman had to die in the process, not to mention her unborn child," Robert whispered in my ear. "Do you have any guilt feelings that you're with a man who lost his wife because of your jealousy? I told you not to get involved."

I rolled my eyes at Robert. "I didn't send the email, thank you very much, so don't you dare blame this on me." I snapped. "I moved on with Peter, who I was falling in love with until Lucas showed up on my doorstep. The woman was going to be found because the mob is the mob. This isn't my fault, Robert. I thought you'd be happy for me. I love Carolyn. She's plump and the perfect woman for you, and she loves you. Why don't you focus on marrying her before she drops your ass? She's not going to wait for you forever. Did you see the way she lighted up when Lucas and I got married? The girl wants to get married."

"I'm going to propose to her soon, but I'm still angry with you," Robert shouted. "Look me dead in the eyes and tell me you had nothing to do with Jody's murder, and then I'll never bring up the subject again. I feel partly responsible for her death and it's eating me up alive."

I looked dead in Robert's black eyes. "I didn't have anything to do with Jody's death," I calmly lied. "I wasn't the one who lured Anthony Paci to her. I don't know how he found out, but it had nothing to do with me. I wish you'd go back to being my friend and loving me."

Robert smiled and took my hand. "I believe you, so let's move on. I'm glad for you and Lucas, and I'm thrilled about Carolyn. I'm going to propose to her on her birthday in May and we can get married at the end of the year."

I smiled at Robert. "I'm so thrilled for you, and wish you the best with Carolyn. I'm also glad that we both have finally found happiness in our lives. I'm with the man I love and you're with the woman you love. I don't think life can get any better than this. I'm so happy."

"Do you ever think about Peter, Reese? I can't believe he had to go and fall in love with you. Right now he's dating this bimbo, and believe me she's a bimbo. She's only twenty and she doesn't have a clue about anything on this earth."

"I was falling in love with Peter, Robert, but Lucas came back into my life, and he's the man I want with me for the rest of my life. I love him and I'm not the woman for Peter. I think about him from time to time and I wish him the best in finding his soul mate."

I was glad when Carolyn and Lucas came back to the table. Lucas was so handsome in his black suit, and he was healing from the pain Jody caused him. I mean he was moving on with his life because there wasn't anything else he could do. Jody wasn't coming back.

"Let's dance, Wifey," Lucas said. "And then we're going home and make love. I want you pregnant very soon because I need children in my life. If we get started right away, you'll get pregnant before the end of the year."

I frowned as I took my husband's hand and we walked to the crowded dance floor. It was so good being this close to Lucas. I closed my eyes to savor the moment, and then opened them, staring at my husband. "I love you so much," I cried. "I love you so much, Lucas."

"I'm falling back in love with you, Reese," he replied. "It's going to be a long time before I can get over Jody, but having you by my side, it's going to help me. I'm going to make you happy, and you're going to give me a child. I can't wait to see your belly growing."

"Lucas, I want to spend time with my husband," I said. "I want to know you before we bring children into the world. I need to be with you because when children come along, we won't have time to make love or do anything."

"It's okay. I'll be there for you and our child. He's going to think I'm the mother. I'm going to change his diapers, and give him his bottles when you stop breast feeding him. I'm not going to be one of those fathers who are never around until their child is sleeping."

I closed my eyes for a second, before opening them and staring around the room, avoiding Lucas' eyes. How was I going to tell him that I couldn't give him any children? My eyes swept across a table in the back of the room and then I looked back and focused on the woman, stunned. It couldn't be her. She was dead and burned.

The woman smiled at me and waved. I stopped dancing and said, "Honey, I need to go to the bathroom. I think I drank too much water."

I didn't wait for his consent as I ran to the bathroom. What was happening to me? Was the guilt eating me up alive? I sat down in a chair and stared at myself in the mirror. Jody was dead. There was no way she was smiling and waving at me.

The bathroom door opened and I jumped up, looking into Jody's eyes. She wasn't dead after all. I covered my mouth with shock. This couldn't be happening to me. "You're dead," I cried.

"I'm not dead, you bitch," Jody cried. "I staged my own death. Now I'm free because Anthony is dead, and I want my husband back.

You thought you could turn me in and then live to tell about it. I knew it was you. I can't prove it so I'm going to make a deal with you. Get out of Lucas' life, and never talk to him again. His wife is coming back, so you two aren't married after all. If you ever contact Lucas again, you're going to pay for turning me in."

"He's my husband, and I love him," I cried. "I can't desert him. He was devastated when you abandoned him. He needs me, and I love him. I need Lucas in my life. I'm sorry you got caught, but I had nothing to do with it. Please just disappear where you came from. Where is the baby?"

"The baby was stillborn, but I'll give Lucas another child. I'm going to tell him how you lied to him. How you can't possibly have any children because of the two abortions. Do you want me to rain on your parade? I'm going to be your worst nightmare, bitch!

"I love Lucas. What's wrong with you? I can't just leave him. What do you think it's going to do to him? I'm going to contact Lucas in a few days and let him know that I'm alive. He's going to be thrilled to hear from me, so I don't think he's going to spend any time mourning you. I think your Peter might be still waiting for you. The man is a sucker for a gorgeous black woman. You have one week to get out of Lucas' life. Remember I'll be watching your ass. Do not repeat this conversation to Robert, or he will die. I've been with the mob, so don't mess with me."

Jody quickly left the bathroom. I let the tears fall, and then wiped my eyes and hurried back to Lucas. This was my last day with him, so I had to make the most of it. I couldn't believe Jody wasn't dead. How did she manage to escape Anthony Paci? How could he be dead?

It was May and I was staring at Carolyn and Robert as they pledged their love for each other. Robert proposed when I came back to the table that fateful night, and Carolyn agreed. Now it was a year later and my best friend was tying the knot with his soul mate. Carolyn was gorgeous in a pretty green dress. They both looked so happy.

Lucas was back with his wife and he didn't once contact me. He just dropped out of my life and never again contacted me once Jody swooped back into his life. I still hated the bitch.

Carolyn and Robert were now man and wife. I watched as they kissed and then I hurried over to the bar. I needed something to drink. I grabbed two glasses, and drained both of them. I coughed, and reached for a third one. I was going to get drunk as a skunk.

"So I see you made it after all," the male voice said. "Robert told me what has been going on in your life. You should write a book, believe me. You were with a man, who thought his wife was dead, but found out that she's alive, and staged her own death to get away from the mob. The book will sell millions."

I stared at Peter, appalled at being trapped in a conversation with him. He had been standing next to Robert as his best man with his bimbo girlfriend smiling at him. She looked like she was fifteen. "Are you here to gloat? You'd better hurry because I think your girlfriend needs to get home before her curfew."

Peter laughed. "Jamie is my niece, thank you very much, and she's sixteen. I'm keeping her while her parents are on a second honeymoon cruise. I tried calling you when I found out the pain you were going through. Why didn't you call me back?"

I had been trying to keep the tears at bay since I got to this wedding, and now Peter had to interfere. I drained another glass of wine, and reached for my fourth one, but Peter grabbed that one right out of my hand as he escorted me outside the hotel. I didn't want to cause a scene, so I walked quietly by his side.

Outside I broke away from him. "How dare you touch me, you snake! Leave me alone, Peter. I'm sure you've moved on, so let me do the same. I made a lot of mistakes in my life, but those are the breaks when you're involved with people who you think love you."

"I'd say the same thing," Peter snapped. "I fell in love with you when I knew you were involved with another man. I guess we can't help who we fall in love with. I'm still in love with you, but that will change when someone else comes into my life. I wish you the best."

I was surprised that he was still in love with me because I didn't deserve it. The tears fell this time and I just let them. I missed Lucas, but I was quickly getting over him. I left him when he told me about Jody, and he didn't once ask me to stay. I thought for a minute that he'd choose me. The bitch managed to get pregnant again.

"Why don't we congratulate the bride and groom and then go back to my place and talk," Peter suggested. "I know you just need to weep for hours and then get it out of your system. I'm still in love with you, and I'm going to be there for you. I guess you'd kick me in the teeth again, but I'm dense as hell."

I went into his arms, and I wept like I had never wept before. Peter held me tight, touching my hair, and massaging my back. I felt the heat of temptation enter my soul, but right now I was just glad to see him and thrilled that he hadn't given up on me. "I'm so sorry for hurting you. I thought Lucas was the only man for me," I cried.

"Well as you can see he's not the man for you, so stalking him isn't the answer," he cried. "I want you to move onto someone that will treasure you for the rest of your life. I love you, girl, and I could kick myself for loving you at all. I do."

I stared into his eyes. "Will you marry me Peter Holmes? I want you to spend the rest of your life with me. I need someone who can handle me, and I think you're the perfect man for the job. I'm going to need a lot of patience."

Peter laughed. "I've never been proposed to before, but ask me again after a few months. We both need time to heal. I tried forgetting about you, and I told myself when I came to this wedding to stand by Robert, I was going to ignore you. I know that it's not all your fault because I let myself get involved with you. I love you."

I kissed him before we walked back into the Hilton. Robert and Carolyn accepted our congratulations, and then Robert whispered to me. "I knew you'd get it right. You should be glad that Peter is in love with your ass. I hope you don't do anything to ruin this relationship. I'll be on my honeymoon in New York City for a few weeks, but I'm going to check on you."

I embraced Robert. "I'm in good hands with Peter so don't you dare worry about me. I want you to treasure Carolyn and not do anything to hurt her. I've learned a lesson in all of this mess. I wished the two of you more happiness that I can imagine lasting a lifetime."

We all embraced and then Robert and Carolyn got into their limousine and drove off. I took Peter's hand and we walked to my car, with his niece Jamie tagging along. Maybe I was going to have happiness after all. We reached my car, and I froze. I couldn't believe it, but Lucas was leaning on my car. Why was he here? I stared at Peter and then Lucas. I couldn't move…

My name is Silk, and I'm the bomb. I'm thirty-one years old and my body is to die for and then some. Sisters would literally kill to have a body like mine. Of course my career is using my body.

I'm a stripper and I love taking off my clothes and giving men and women a look at the beautiful body I possess. My breasts were large and full and my ass is big and beautiful. When I introduce my body to men, they drool all over themselves.

I love my job. Most people can't say that. I make lots of money and I only work four, four-hour evening shifts a week. I'm working a job that allows me to give my son Jason everything he needs and wants. He's six and he's the apple of my eye. I'd do anything for my son.

The down side of my happiness is my boyfriend Ray. He loves me very much and I love him, but he can't handle the men staring at my body. He comes to most of my shows, but I can tell that he hates being there. Ray could take care of me with his accounting job, but I need my own independence and I don't want a man taking care of me. I'm I.N.D.E.P.E.D.E.N.T.!

I was sitting in my dressing room waiting for my show to begin. I've worked the 11 p.m. to 3 a.m. shift at Sammy's, a very reputable nightclub, for five years. The owner, Sammy, is sixty-five and she used to strip until she got too old. Now she runs the place. Sammy is like a mother to me. I love her.

"Hi."

I looked up at Rusty. "Hi. Are you almost done for the day?"

"I am, but I don't want my boyfriend, Al to find out what I'm doing. I love him, but I hate lying to him constantly. He thinks I'm a babysitter for this rich family."

"Are you buying him things and making more money that he is?"

Rusty laughed. "I am."

"Is he taking the gifts and money you shared?"

"He does with bells on."

I frowned. "Then Al needs to shut up."

"I know, but honesty is the best policy."

"Ray doesn't like my line of work, but he's dealing with it. I tried working nine to five and it doesn't work for me, Rusty. Jason is growing up so fast and he's in constant need of gym shoes, clothes, etc. I have to take care of my man."

"And I have three children."

"Then don't feel guilty about it. As long as we have the body, then flaunt it. There are a lot of sisters who would love to be in our shoes."

Rusty laughed. "Thanks for the pep talk, but I'm going to tell Al the truth. If he can't deal with my line of work, then I have to kick him to the curb. The lies are killing me."

"Do what you have to do, girl?"

"I'm going home. There's a big crowd tonight so have a good time."

"I always do."

I stared at Rusty. Most men couldn't handle strippers so Rusty might be alone for while, but it won't last long. She's a very beautiful woman, and there are men banging down the door to get to her. I hope Al is no fool.

I had five minutes before the show began.

On stage I stared at the many men and women. Most of the customers were men all ready with their money in their hands. This time I'd dance from "It's Hot In Here" by Nelly. I loved his songs, and worked with a former dancer who taught me the moves. I paid her handsomely, but Shirley was worth every penny. She was an attorney now, but she danced when she needed to pay off a student loan. Shirley was one of my best friends because we had a lot in common.

Nelly began singing and I began dancing. I had the biggest smile on my face because I loved this song, and the men were whistling and having the time of their lives. It made me feel good that I was giving them pleasure. I quickly removed my bra, showcasing my large breasts. I had no intention of wasting time giving the men what they came for. The minute my breasts were exposed, the room exploded as men ran up to the stage and threw me money."

I kept the games going as I danced around the pole a few times, and then quickly removed my black skirt. I was naked except for my black thong and dancing to the beat of the music. I always wanted to become a dancer, but Jason came along, and I had to give up my dreams for the moment.

Men begged to touch me. I sometimes let a few of them touch me when Ray wasn't around and this was one of those times. I frowned because he told me that he'd be there. I hadn't talked to him all day and I was a bit worried. What was going on with my man? Ray was always working late because he loved his CPA status, and definitely had to please his clients. I'd call him on his cell phone when I take a break.

Nelly was ending his song, and it was time for the climax. I slipped off my panties and stood straight, very proud of my size six body as the men yelled and screamed, and money flew at me like rain or snow. Five more songs came on. I continued my dance moves naked to the core, and loving every minute of it. I was a star, and I didn't have to say one line. This was my world.

At three o'clock in the morning Big Red, the bouncer of the club, walked me to my car. Some of the men stalked me and wanted to have sex with me. I used to give a few of them my body but when I met Ray five years ago, the sleeping around ceased. I loved Ray and he was the only one getting my body.

We reached my car and I smiled at Big Red. "Thanks for the walk. You're my teddy bear."

Big Red laughed. "You better not let my wife hear you."

I embraced him. "I know. Tell Patty I love her."

"I will. Do you need me to follow you home?"

"I'll be fine."

"Okay."

I got into my car, locked the doors, and reached for my cell phone. I dialed Ray's number and waited for him to pick up. When I got his voice mail, I frowned. "Where are you Ray and what are you doing?" We spoke to each other every day. It wasn't like Ray to ignore me the entire day. I made sure no one was stalking me as I pulled out of the parking lot and mingled into the slow traffic. There were a few cars along the road, but it should only take me about fifteen minutes to get home.

I hurried into the house and flew immediately to my telephone, checking the voice message light. I had two messages, and I quickly pushed the button as I turned on the light.

I was standing in my living room, of my condo on Lake Shore Drive. My mother and sister, Chelsea called. What was going on with Ray? I picked up the telephone and dialed his home number. I got another voice mail.

I sat down on the sofa, beginning to worry when the doorbell rang. I hurried to the door, opening it and staring at Ray. I breathed a sigh of relief when I saw him and threw myself into his arms. I was so happy to see my man. I knew he was my life. "Where have you been?"

"This is a very nice welcome. I'm sorry honey, I meant to get to the club, but I had a client, and he wanted to go out. I had to take him to another club."

I frowned. "Why?"

"I didn't want him staring at my woman."

"I see. Why didn't you answer your cell phone?"

"My client told me to turn it off when I was conducting business with him. I had to keep my cool, but I had no choice in the matter. How did it go today? I'm in fear of something happening to you."

I left his grasp and closed the door. "It was nice as usual, and I made tons of money."

"Whatever! I need a drink."

"I'll get you one, baby, and meet you in the bedroom. Jason is with mother for the night."

"I'm taking him to a basketball game tomorrow."

"I know, baby, and he's so excited about it."

"What about his father?"

"John is out of his life for the duration. Can we not talk about him?"

"I'd love to adopt him."

I stared at him. "Let's take one day at a time."

In the bedroom I hurriedly showered and got into bed naked, waiting for Ray. What was he doing? Five minutes later he walked his naked butt into the room and I stared at his hard on. He was ready for me. I wanted to taste my man, and I put out my arms, and Ray ran into them. He went to work on caressing my entire body. I moaned with loud bouts of satisfaction. This time I could scream because Jason wasn't home.

My pleasure zone was exploding with happiness as Ray used his tongue to excite every pore of my pleasure zone. I was screaming out this time because my body wouldn't stop shaking with pleasure. I was bouncing all over the place. Ray continued until I was exhausted from the sensations.

He immediately entered me because he was hot as fire, and just holding it in until I got my pleasure. Ray rocked in a matter of seconds as he screamed out my name. I felt his juices enter me, and we forgot the condom this time. I was safe from having any children. After Jason, I made sure my baby days were over.

We continued our lovemaking for another hour, and then we slept in each other arms. I was so lucky, and at times I thought the bomb would fall. I just kept having this feeling.

The next day, Jason was home from school at twelve-thirty because of a half-day. My mother had picked him up for me. Ray was long gone. "Hi baby. How is my handsome man?"

"Hi mommy! Can Grandma take me to McDonalds? I want a Happy Meal."

Jason knew he ate at McDonalds only on special occasions because I didn't like the greasy food. "Is there something that happened today?"

"I got an A on my spelling test."

I was so pleased. "Let me see it."

He proudly held up his spelling test, and I smiled at him. "Then McDonalds is fine. Go into your room and change your clothes."

"Okay," he exclaimed. I embraced my man, staring at my mother. She was silent for some reason. "Mother is there something wrong?" She was 59 and still beautiful. I was glad my parents were still together after thirty-five years.

"I'm just worried about you and your dangerous career. I keep having these nightmares about you."

I frowned at her. "Mother don't let the devil win. I'm fine at work."

"I wish you'd find something else to do. You have plenty of money. Why don't you go to law school?"

I laughed. "Just because Father is an attorney doesn't mean it's for me. I like dancing."

She shook her head at me. "Okay, but just be careful."

"I will. How is Chelsea doing?"

"She's ready to have her baby. I can't wait until next month."

"Me either. Don't forget we're going to New York to be there for her."

"I wouldn't miss it for the world. I love New York City."

"Then let's go to McDonalds."

"Okay."

"The Hustle" was on and I was dancing my ass off to the beat. I loved the song, one of my favorites. My naked booty was shaking all over the place; the men were screaming, and staring, and silence was golden as every eye was on me. I was about to rip my bra off when the lights went out and a bolt of electricity from the sound stage hit me. I screamed and passed out.

It was three days before I was able to open my eyes. It took me a while to focus on Ray and my mother. I could tell that they both had been crying. I reached out my hand and touched my face. I was bandaged up, and I felt the tears forming because I couldn't remember anything. "What happened to me?" I cried.

Ray and Mother rushed over to me. "I'm so glad you're alive," Mother cried. "It's been three days."

I stared at Ray. "What's going on?"

"Honey, you were in a terrible accident. The lights went off, and there was a bad connection, and you were literally electrocuted. I'm so sorry," he cried.

I was burned," I cried. "Where?"

"On your face and arms, honey," he cried. "The doctors did everything they could for your face, but you're going to have a scar on the left side. I'm so sorry."

I couldn't believe what Ray was telling me. "A scar!"

"Once you heal we can try to have a plastic surgeon look at you," Ray said.

"But it's hopeless," Mother said. "You could be dead, honey. I'm so happy."

"Where is father?"

"He was here for a short time, but had to leave because he's in court for two weeks. He sends his love."

"I need to see the scar," I cried.

"Not for a few more days," Ray cried. "I was there when it happened. I couldn't see anything. It went pure dark."

"I need to be alone," I cried. "Please just get out."

"You need us," Mother cried.

"Where is Jason?"

"He's with Aunt June. You need to call him when you can. He's been crying up a storm about his mother."

"Just leave me alone," I cried. "Please!"

"We'll give you a moment," Ray said, "but we'll be back. Don't try to get rid of us because it's not going to work."

I turned away from them and let the tears fall. How could this have happened to me? I can't dance with an ugly scar on my face. My face is my life. I'm the most beautiful woman in the world. I hysterically wept.

The bandages came off in two weeks, and my mother, father, son and Ray were all staring at me. I could tell it was bad. "Let me have the mirror," I cried.

Ray handed me the mirror and I stared at myself. The scar was horrible, and I looked like a monster. I screamed hysterically. Five minutes later a nurse and doctor ran into the room and gave me a shot to calm me down. I was never going to be the same again.

I stayed in my house for a week, not going anywhere because I didn't want anyone to see me. Jason cried when he saw me, so I let him stay with my mother who called and came to visit me every day with my father. I didn't want anyone to see me. I was staring out the window at the beautiful July summer day. I was in my room with a scarf wrapped around my face, and the tears running. I wept all the time because my dancing career was over. I could never be a stripper again.

My door opened and Ray walked in. "Hi honey, I bought you something to eat."

I stared out the window. "I'm not hungry."

"You're losing weight, baby, and it's not good. This is a Caesar salad and a diet coke. I'm not going to leave until you eat. I thought then we could take a walk on the beach. It's such a lovely day."

I laughed. "Are you kidding me? I'm not a circus act for everyone. I'm never leaving this house again."

"Honey, I love you. What do you think about suing the club? Your father thinks you have a case."

"It was a freak accident, and I'd never hurt Sammy. She has been good to me. No!"

"I'll let your father know. Please come and eat."

"Just leave it there, Ray. I thought I told you to find someone else. I'm not good enough for you. I had this feeling that something was going to happen to spoil my happiness. I was right."

"Silk, things happen for a reason. Maybe it was time you stopped stripping."

I stared at him as if he had lost his mind. "You're stupid, Ray. Stripping paid my bills; took care of my son, and me. I know nothing else."

"You have plenty of money, and don't belittle me because you're in pain. I love you."

I removed my scarf. "Look at me, Ray. I'm ugly as hell. Do you see this ugly red scar right in the middle of my face? It's hideous. I can't stand to look in the mirror."

"I see it, but so what? You're still the same person, Silk, and the woman I love and want to spend the rest of my life with. Jason says you're still his very beautiful mother."

"But he got into a fight the other day because someone saw me, and told him about it. They made fun of me, and Jason hit the boy in the mouth, and got suspended for two days. This is the real world, Ray, not some fantasy land."

"Eat, and I'll check on you later. I have to take Mr. Abby to another club. The man is horny as hell."

I frowned. "Have fun looking at the beautiful women."

"I will only be thinking of you."

"Whatever!"

He kissed me on the cheek and took off. I stared after him, shaking my head. Ray was so sweet, but he didn't need to stay with me because of pity. I loved him, which is why I wanted him to move on. I was just too ugly. I stared at the tray of food and moved over to it. I was hungry and began eating. I was never going to be the same again. Why did this happen to me? Was I just too vain?

Three weeks passed and I was still barricaded in the house. Mother and Ray did everything for me because I refused to go out. I was sitting in the living room when the doorbell rang. I ignored it because Ray was out with Jason at the park, and Mother went grocery shopping. I'd just let it ring.

Five minutes later, whoever was at the door was still ringing the bell. I walked over to it. "Who is it?"

"Sammy and Rusty. Open up the door because we're not leaving," Sammy said.

I frowned. I didn't want to see anyone. "This is not a good time."

"We're not leaving," Rusty said.

I had no choice so I walked to the door and opened it, making sure my scarf hid my scar. "What are you both doing here?"

"Just to see how you were doing," Rusty said. "Can we come in? I need a drink of water."

"You know where the kitchen is, and we can go into the living room."

Sammy followed me into the living room and Rusty hurried to the kitchen. "How are you doing?" Sammy asked.

I stared at her. "I'm miserable."

"We miss you at the club. It hasn't been the same. I'm losing money."

"Why don't you replace me, Sammy?" I asked. "I'm not the only gorgeous woman in the Windy City"

"I wanted to leave your spot open for you, Silk."

I shook my head. "I can never dance again. The men would boo me."

"I think you're wrong about that. They want to see that body of yours."

"And my face, Sammy," I cried. "Don't play with me."

"Your face is still gorgeous, but they come to see your breasts and booty, girl."

"I can't," I cried.

Rusty walked into the room drinking her bottle of water. She sat down next to Sammy. "I miss you, too. I'm not you, and the scar doesn't look that bad. I can get my sister to make up your face, and it won't be seen that much. She's the best make-up artist in this city, and then some."

"And there's a foundation you could use on your face to cover the scar," Sammy said. "I sell MK products, and I might have the perfect foundation for you. Let's try and make this work."

"The scar isn't going to disappear," I cried.

"It's probably with you for the rest of your life," Rusty said. "But you could be dead, and it can be hidden. My sister has done wonders for sisters with bad acne. Can I call her over?"

"No," I screamed. "I'm ruined for life."

"I don't think you are," Rusty said. "Make your body continue to work for you."

"I'd be a freak out there," I cried. "No!"

"What are you going to do when you run out of money?" Sammy asked. "Jason has to eat."

"I have plenty of money," I cried.

"Whenever you're ready to come back to work is fine with me," Sammy stated. "Take six months off because you deserve it. I think you should marry Ray and go on a honeymoon. He loves you."

"Just leave me alone," I cried.

"It's not going to happen," Rusty said. "I'm going into the kitchen and call my sister. She'll move mountains. My sister has won awards because of her make up expertise."

I closed my eyes because no one was listening to me. Rusty went into the kitchen to make her call, and Sammy continued to talk to me. I wasn't hearing any of it as the tears drowned my sorrows.

"I'm going to get my MK bag," Sammy stared.

An hour later I was staring in the mirror at myself. I was still beautiful and the scar was hardly noticeable at all. If I wore my hair long, it wouldn't be seen at all.

"What do you think?" Rusty cried. "I told you my sister was the best."

I stared at Rusty, and then her sister, Kate. "It's almost invisible."

"That's right," Kate said.

"And this is the best foundation for you?" Sammy said. "I'm going to stock you up on this foundation."

"How much do I owe you for the makeup?" I asked.

"I can get you five bottles for $150."

"Let me write you a cheek," I cried.

"Do you want to work tonight?" Sammy said. "Your spot is still open."

"I want to see Ray's reaction."

"That'd be a good test," Rusty said.

"Then we should be going," Sammy said. "I have business to contend with. I'll look for you, but if you're not coming, then ring my cell phone to let me know. Sherrie is on stand-by."

"She's very good," I cried.

"And she's working on being a plus-sized model," Sammy cried. "I have men who love larger women. I didn't think it'd work out, but she's happy and so are my customers."

"I'll let you know," I said. "Kate, how much do I owe you? Let me get my purse."

"It's on the house," Kate said.

I smiled. "Nothing is free, so please let me pay you."

"Seventy-five dollars," Kate said.

I reached for my checkbook and began writing. "How about the five bottles for $150.00?"

"Are you sure?" Kate said, smiling.

"With bells on! You've done wonders for me."

"Follow my instructions and you'll be good as new," Kate said. "Here's my business card in case you have any questions."

"I'll use it," I cried. I wrote out a check for Sammy and handed it to her. "Thanks for everything. I have friends after all."

"And don't you forget it," Rusty laughed.

I stared at her. "How is Al doing?"

"I told him the truth and he was angry for a while," Rusty cried. "I thought my relationship was over, but he came back and it's working out. Al loves me after all, and I'm so blessed. Once I save enough money I'm going to go back to school. I want to be a teacher."

"Really," I said, surprised. "I'd have never pictured you for a teacher."

"I know," Rusty laughed. "It's been a life long passion of mine, and Al convinced me to pursue it. And he's not changing careers for me. I'm going to be stripping on a part-time basis while I attend school full-time. I know where I come from, thank you very much."

"I like that independence in you?" I cried.

"We need it," Rusty said.

"Let's go," Kate said. "I have two other appointments."

"Do you make a lot of money, Kate?" I asked.

"I don't have to work a nine to five job any longer," Kate said. "I love my work because I can turn an ugly ducking into a swan."

"You certainly made a difference with me," I cried.

"I didn't have much to do," Kate laughed. "You're a very gorgeous woman, so most of the work is already done."

"Thanks for that," I cried. "I love you all."

"And we love you," Sammy said.

I embraced everyone, and then stared at myself in the mirror. The scar was still evident, especially up close, but from a distance you couldn't see it at all. I was still beautiful with my long pretty hair. Maybe I could pull this off.

I had just taken a shower and was walking into the living room when the door opened and Jason and Ray walked in. I sat down on the sofa in my green lounging gown. "Hi. Did you have some fun, Jason?"

He ran over to me, and then stopped, staring at me. "Hi. You look different, Mommy."

"How so, baby?"

"Did you do something to the scar?" Jason cried. "I don't see it."

I smiled all over myself.

"He's right," Ray said. He surveyed my face. "Where is it?"

"Just covered by foundation and makeup," I cried. "Are you both serious?"

"You look pretty, mommy," Jason cried.

"Will you marry me?" Ray cried. "I love you."

Jason started bouncing up and down. "I saw the ring, Mommy. We went to pick it out. Say yes! I love Ray."

The tears blinded me as I stared at the two loves of my life. "Ray, the scar is still apparent."

"Jason, can I talk to your mother?" Ray asked.

"I'll be in my room," he said. "Don't let her say no."

"I'll try my best," Ray laughed. "You know how stubborn your mother can be."

He nodded his head and then ran upstairs. I focused on Ray. "Why do you want to marry me now?"

"I love you, and I'm your biggest supporter. I love Jason."

"I love you, Ray more than anything. I don't want you regretting marrying me. I'm still ugly."

"Not in your wildest dreams," he cried. "Now I hate your job, but I'm with you all the way. Let's go to Las Vegas and get married. We can do it this weekend, and then you can go back to work. I know you love me, but you miss dancing so I want you to make your dreams come true. It's the only way for happiness, baby."

I ran into Ray's arms. "I love you, and let's get married."

"Thank you," he cried. Our lips met and then we made love on the floor after we checked on Jason, who was fast asleep. My world was still winning.

Michael Jackson's 'Smooth Criminal' hit the airwaves. I stared at the men and women screaming. There were so many people in the club there was standing room only and a line out front waiting to get in. Sammy said they were glad for me to be back. I was seeing the evidence. I began dancing and in five minutes the nervousness disappeared and I danced my ass off.

When I was naked the screams shouted out the room, and the tears blinded me as I continued dancing. I was back, and it was only in the eye of the beholder after all. I smiled at my husband as I continued to dance.

My Perfect Husband

John Barnes was tall and handsome with a milk-chocolate complexion. I wasn't bragging about my husband, I was telling the absolute truth. John and I shared a bond of love that would last through eternity. I knew I had found my Prince Charming and my soul mate. John is the perfect husband.

You might say that there is no perfect human being, especially a man. Men are so dense and evil and out to get any booty they can. You can never find a faithful man. Yes you can, and I'm a witness to it. There are some people that have everything in life they want and then some, whereas other people seem to have nothing but chaos and pain in their lives. I constantly asked myself how I managed to have such a wonderful man in my life. Why did John Barnes want me?

I'm an attractive woman of 42, but I'm not beautiful. I'm tall and carry my size 16 body well, although I dreamed of being a size 6. I gained weight easily and had to watch what I ate. My passion was the #3 meal at McDonalds. I loved their quarter-pounder with cheese, fries and a diet soda. I ate what I wanted to eat, and made exercise a part of my routine. I had no choice because I couldn't give up my McDonalds.

I remember my first date with John. We were sitting in his car one summer day and he asked me, "What would you like to eat?"

"#3 at McDonalds is fine with me."

"Are you kidding me?" John laughed.

"I don't think I am," I replied seriously. "It's my passion."

"Then we're going to McDonalds," he said, his beautiful laugh ringing out again. "Are you sure? I was thinking about a nice restaurant downtown or something. You don't have to humor me."

I laughed. "Maybe another time, but I have a taste for my favorite meal."

"Okay," he laughed for the third time. John was unlike anyone I had ever met. I had men in my life; I was even married for ten years, but no one ever haunted me the way John has, and in a good way. I know he's my soul mate.

I smiled at the thought. We went to McDonalds and ended up spending two hours there, just talking. John was a character with lots of stories to tell me from his younger days. He was ten years older than me but maybe that's what I need. I had been alone for a long time, and to have someone around me with more life experience was wonderful. I'd been living in a bubble for a long time and John opened up a new world for me. I've been to places I never thought would be possible and met a lot of people. It has been a joy for me to discover there's a wonderful human being inside of me, and it took John to bring this out.

I remember praying for the perfect man. I knew I was probably asking for too much. I wanted one so much and I believed you get what you pray for. However, it might not be what you wanted in the first place. It worked out for me. I just wanted to find someone who loved me the way I am. Why not? Is it possible? Nothing is impossible with the assistance of God. He answers all prayers in his own way and I felt blessed when he sent me John Barnes.

John and I met one warm, sunny Wednesday. I had the day off and instead of resting, I decided to hop on the bus and hit the big sale at the Target store on the south side of Chicago to hunt for some bargains to stretch my money. I strolled through the store, hunting for the things I needed, glad that it wasn't too crowded.

I was heading for the checkout when I noticed a man watching me. He was tall and heavy-set with a lovely smile. I looked away, pretending to be interested in some bathroom towels. When I looked up again he was walking over to me. "Hi."

I blushed for some reason. "Hi."

"Are you going to buy those towels?"

"I was thinking about it," I lied.

"I see your favorite color is green," he said. "I'm John."

I blushed again. "Yes it is. My name is Juicy."

He laughed. "Are you kidding me?"

"My mother wanted to name me something strange."

"I like it," he laughed again.

For some reason, his laughter didn't offend me. I was normally hot all the time, but I felt the heat intensify as I spoke with this perfect stranger.

"It's nice meeting you, Juicy. I've been watching you since you walked into the store. No woman has captured my attention the way you have."

I was wearing a long black skirt paired with a purple tunic top. I didn't feel attractive at all. Was he blind?

I couldn't respond.

"You don't believe me," he said. "I'm not just stringing you a line. I'm sure you meet so many men; I'm wasting my breath. But I had to give it a try. You're the most beautiful woman in the world."

I blushed again, and then smiled. "Thanks." I have long hair that curls nicely, and I have a pretty face. I just needed to work on my body.

"Can I get your number?"

I looked at him, carefully checking out his ring finger. There was no ring there, or any signs of one. What was I supposed to do in a situation like this? It had been a while since a man asked me for my telephone number.

"How about if I give you my number and then you give me yours?" John suggested.

I could deal with that plan. I reached into my purse and took out a pen and a small pad. I wrote down my cell phone number and handed him the slip of paper. The instant our eyes met, the music began playing in my head for some reason. Was I losing my mind? I felt the music and the electricity all at the same time. What was happening to me?

He took my number, handed me his, and the fireworks began. I eagerly put his card in my purse. "Thanks."

"Can I call you tonight?"

"Okay," I nodded.

"I'm on my way to an appointment. I'll talk to you later."

"Okay."

He smiled as he walked away. I watched him get into a white car hoping he really would call me. He probably wasn't going to call, but it'd be nice if he would. John was handsome and fat. That gave us something in common. He just had a big stomach, but he didn't shy away from his body. I could tell that John liked himself. I had to get more confidence in myself. I smiled as I finished the rest of my shopping. I couldn't help thinking about John. I patted my purse, and then opened it to make sure I didn't lose his card. This was real, and not one of my romantic dreams.

John called three times that night and I missed the first two because I was playing my music too loud to hear the phone the first time and then I went to check the mail and missed the second one. The third time I was right next to the phone when it rang. I held my breath as I punched the 'Talk' button. Getting to know someone was so difficult. I was afraid that he was going to be a waste of time. I didn't feel that at my age I had any time to waste. I'll never forget our first conversation.

"Hello," I said. I had never been so nervous in my life. There were other occasions, of course, but this one was the most nerve-wracking ever.

"Hi. I'm glad you didn't give me the wrong number."

"I don't play those games," I replied.

"I'm pleased about that because I'm too old to play the games."

I was relieved he said that. It was something we had in common.

"So tell me something about yourself, Juicy."

I smiled at the mention of my name. I used to hate it, but I'm used to it now. My late mother had her own reasons for my name. I still missed her like crazy. I'd pick up the telephone to call her, but she would never answer the telephone again.

"Is everything okay, Juicy? I assume that you're not married or seeing anyone or you wouldn't have given me your number. I don't want to trespass on another man's turf."

Was he for real?

"I'm not married or seeing anyone right now."

"That's hard to believe," he said. "Any special reason why?"

"I not sure," I replied. I wasn't about to tell him that I was fat and men didn't want a fat woman. I had to develop personal confidence so I didn't talk down about myself to people. I had some confidence about my hair and face. It didn't involve looks all the time. I wanted to go beyond looks.

"Are you going to tell me about yourself?"

I could kick myself for being so quiet. "I'm sorry. I'm 42 years old."

"Wow! You don't look it," he exclaimed. "Baby you look good for your age. I'm 52 years old."

I smiled at the compliment, but I heard that often. "Thanks."

"I drove a bus for CTA until I retired. I got bored with retirement and got a janitorial job at a factory. Now I'm learning to use computers. I never knew they were so much fun."

"I love my job. I'm a paralegal at a local law firm."

"How fascinating! When can we go out to dinner?"

"I don't know."

"Well then, when do you have some free time?"

"I'm off on Wednesdays and Sundays."

"How about I pick you up around seven o'clock on Wednesday and we'll go out for dinner?"

"Okay," I said. I wanted to scream, but I controlled the urge.

"Where should I pick you up?"

I gave him my address. "So you live in Pine Shores."

"I've been here for five years now. I love the area."

"It's a very nice area."

I laughed. I'm not rich by a long shot. I just spend my money wisely."

"Most people can't say that. I had fun on my job with the CTA. I have some stories to tell you."

I couldn't wait to hear them.

"Why did you want to be a paralegal?"

"I'm fascinated with law, but I prefer dealing with the paperwork you get as a paralegal over that of an attorney. I work on some interesting and challenging cases and especially like doing research. I got my associate degree online and I'm going back in the fall for my bachelor's in paralegal science. Online schools are much more convenient than traditional schools. I work a lot of overtime, mostly in the law library researching a precedent. I wouldn't be able to do so much if I had to stop and go to school."

"Your job sounds fascinating. I've never met a paralegal before."

"I've met a few bus drivers."

"You mean you dated a few."

"I did, but..." I didn't know what else to say. I had no intention of telling him that I hadn't dated in three years. I meet men all the time, but no one interested me.

"Are you always this quiet?" he laughed.

I laughed with him. "I daydream a lot. I'm sorry if it bothers you."

"It's okay. I like a smart woman who thinks a lot."

"Thanks."

"Do you have any children?"

"My daughter is 23 and Tiffany, my grandbaby, is 5."

"I have four grown sons."

"Wow," I said.

"I was a busy man. I've been married twice. I won't burden you with all the gory details of my failed marriages."

"Oh!"

"I just want to be honest with you."

"I appreciate that. Most men lie through their teeth."

"I'm not most men, but I've done my share of lying. When you get older you just don't have time to play the games."

"I agree," I said. "I'm not about to play any games with a man."

"I'm glad to hear that. I want us to be honest with each other. The truth will make a relationship last for a long time. I'm a difficult man to live with and then I married a younger woman who did nothing but play games."

"So now you want the older woman," I laughed. "Most men your age look for young trophy women."

He laughed. "A lot of men do, but I'm not most men. I'm attracted to you. I'm not a sex-hungry man. I can take it or leave it. I think we have that in common."

He was right up my alley. I wanted someone to love me, but sex wasn't that all-important ingredient in my marriage. I craved the emotional aspects of a relationship. I need the unconditional love.

"So I have some appointments, but I'll see you at seven on Wednesday. I can't wait."

"Neither can I," I said.

"I'll call you again before that. It's nice talking with you, Juicy?"

"The same, John," I said. I hung up the telephone and smiled all over myself. I couldn't wait until Wednesday. What was I going to wear? I had to talk to my best friend about John.

"She had a motive for killing her husband," I said. "She caught him having an affair four times. I'd say she was a much-scorned woman. When I interviewed her she was bitter about the affairs and glad her husband is dead. I don't see any remorse in her."

"But why would she kill her husband?" Sean asked.

I stared at Sean. "Are you for real? The man was cheating on her, and he got his third girlfriend pregnant? The girlfriend was going to keep the baby and herself on the child support she'd get from him. Mickey James was something else. I'm sure if I keep investigating, more women will emerge."

"So you don't like Mickey James?" he asked with a smile.

I was sitting in Sean's office, and we were going over a new case, trying to decide if Sean wanted to handle it. "I'm not here to judge anyone Sean. She had the motive. I'm not saying she pulled the trigger herself, but she could have hired someone. Mickey James was shot seven times. I think it's a crime of passion. Someone wanted him dead, and made sure of it."

"I need these comments in your brief."

"It's all there," I said.

"So you think I should refuse her case."

"When did you start to rely on my opinion?"

"Don't be silly. I'm always interested in your opinion."

I smiled at Sean, a tall, good-looking black man. He and his wife Betty had five children that they loved almost as much as they loved each other. I had never seen Sean so much as look at another woman. There were good men out there. I thought about John and smiled.

"Why are you smiling?" Sean replied.

"I'm always smiling."

"You are, but this is different. Who is he?"

"Just someone I met at Target, but I'm not going to say anything more."

"I'm glad he's brought that gorgeous smile out. You're so pretty."

Sean always had a nice word for me. "Thanks, but let's get back to business."

"My brother is still waiting for a date."

"I know, but Linc isn't my type. I'm not going to be another notch on his belt."

"He really likes you."

I laughed. "He likes women with curves and he likes them for one reason. He's not about to take me home to meet his mother."

Sean and I shared a laugh and got back to work.

I owed a lot to Sean. He hired me right out of school. I had no experience in a law firm, but I had good skills, a quick mind and a high GPA. Sean tested me and felt I could handle the work. That was six years ago and somewhere along the way we had passed from boss and employee to friends. "I'm going to interview a few of the defendant's friends. I think she might have been having an affair too. In her last testimony she said she was with her friend when she found her husband's body."

"Does she have an alibi?"

"It's not solid," I said. "I'm going back to the bookstore. Her latest novel has a wife murdered and the only suspect is the husband. It sounds a little too coincidental for me." Our client is a popular mystery writer.

"I thought about that, but I think she's too smart to do something like that."

"Okay," I said, writing on my legal pad. "Why did Mickey have to cheat on his wife? She's a beautiful woman and her body is to die for."

Sean shook his head. "There are so many rationalizations for cheating."

"Bypass the beauty and look at the real woman. She could be a devil."

"I'm looking into every angle, Juicy. A beautiful face doesn't blind me to the inner beast. But if she becomes our client, our job is to get her an acquittal."

"Hopefully the district attorney will ferret out the truth and the jury will see it."

"Ann is pretty damn good at her job."

"I'm banking on that. I think I'm going to accept this case."

"Are you sure?"

"Positive. I need you to get going on discovery and interviewing. I'd like to be in court by late June or early July. The media is going to have a field day. I want you in the courtroom with me."

I was proud of the trust Sean placed in me and determined that I would never let him down.

"Are you getting all teary-eyed on me?"

"I just love you so much. I wouldn't be doing the job I love if you hadn't taken a chance on me."

"You're the best Juicy. I knew that when I saw the results of your tests and you've never disappointed me. I'm blessed to have you as my right hand woman. I want to see you happy in a relationship. I hope this person turns out to be the one for you. I'd like to meet him sometime soon."

"Time will tell. I've got a million things to do in my office," I said as I gathered up my paperwork. "I'm going to interview the defendant one more time before I give you my findings. Then you can make the final decision about taking her case."

"That sounds fair. I'll see what you come up with."

John and I were sitting at a nice 24-hour restaurant at 31st & Archer that John had casually mentioned he owned. I was studying the menu while he studied me. I looked up and smiled at him. "What's wrong?"

"Nothing's wrong. In fact, everything is very right for me. Your hair looks great today."

I smiled. "Thanks. What's good to eat? I didn't eat any lunch today."

"I know for a fact that everything on the menu is good here. I'm having the greens dinner with potato salad and the works.

"A Caesar salad sounds good to me."

"Are you sure that's all you want? You must be hungry if you didn't eat any lunch," John said.

I blushed a little as I assured him the salad would be plenty, even though we both knew I could eat three of them.

Twenty minutes later I was munching on some delicious chicken bites from my salad while John spread butter on his cornbread. "So how was work?" he asked.

"Work is always fun. Right now, I'm interviewing a potential client to see if we're going to take her case."

"Anyone I know?" he asked.

"I can't discuss a pending client, but if you can recall a mystery book author that's been in the news lately, you should figure it out."

"Really? She's a friend of mine."

I stared at him.

"We dated a long time ago, before she got married. She was a wild woman and we had a good time."

I didn't know if I wanted to hear this. "How did it end?"

"She dumped me. I was devastated for a while, but since I had done the same thing to a few women during my playboy days, I figured I deserved it. It also taught me a valuable lesson about honor and responsibility. Now that I'm older, I just want to settle down with someone."

"Do you think your friend is capable of murder?"

"I don't think she cared enough about him to kill him. She's earned plenty of her own money, so even if they divorced and split everything down the middle, it would be equitable. But who knows what happens in the privacy of someone's home. She could be a completely different person. I'm a perfect example of changing. I used to date a different woman every week and if she didn't hop into bed with me on the first date, I dumped her. Now I haven't been to bed with a woman in almost ten years."

It was my turn to stare at him. "Really? That's hard to believe."

"I know a lot of people, from all walks of life, because I'm a hustler and have the gift of gab. I have more women friends than men, but it doesn't mean I sleep around. I'm older now, and I can't do everything I used to do. I think I wore myself out," he laughed.

I laughed with him as he revealed his most intimate secrets to me.

"Am I scaring you off?"

I shook my head. "I don't scare that easily."

"Good! I'll try to keep you happy."

"That's difficult, John. No one can be happy all the time."

"Life is what you make it."

"I can't argue with you there. I also believe in the power of prayer."

"Did you ask God for your soul mate?" he asked.

I laughed. "How did you know?"

"I asked God for the same thing. I think God is right here with us."

He was a man of God. That was a double dosage for me.

John kept me laughing all through dinner as he told me about his antics during his younger days. I had so much fun listening to him;

I almost forgot to eat. The man was certifiable. I had never been so happy in my life.

After that dinner, John and I became a couple. We did everything together and at the end of the year we married and I moved into his house. John's house was perfect in every way except it didn't feel like it belonged to me, and that was worrisome. We lived there for a year before buying our own house in the historic district of Longwood. Our house was a mini-mansion, with four bedrooms, two bathrooms and a large kitchen. I was having the time of my life and I owed it all to John. I was the happiest woman in the world. I had my perfect man who made it all possible. I was living the dream life. I had a good job and a good husband. What more could I want?

Of course, John was not without faults. He loved to cook, but when he finished, the kitchen looked like a hurricane had come through. He was not a neat person outside of the kitchen either, but I loved him. If I had to clean up after him, then so be it. I figured it was an even trade since I hate to cook. Then there was the matter of the television. John liked to fall asleep with the TV on. That was fine, but he also liked the sound turned up as high as it would go so he could hear it. For some reason, he was too vain to admit he needed a hearing aid. I had to wait until he fell asleep before I could turn it down. John was also a fusser. His Virgo personality often showed through and it took me some time not to take his words seriously. I did eventually learn to ignore him.

I know I had plenty of faults, and John mentioned them often. We'd stand there arguing our heads off and then all of a sudden one of us would start laughing and we ended up laughing at each other. That laughter was one of the best parts of being with him. I loved him so much and he returned that love, showing me every day, in a million ways, just how much. I wanted to grow old with John Barnes. I prayed every day that he would take care of his many health problems. This was the only area where we had major disagreements. John thought he could ignore little signs like the pain in his chest, the numb fingers, the breathlessness and it would just go away. I knew he was wrong...dead wrong.

* * * * *

I was on my way to the hospital to visit John, who was lying in a coma after his heart attack. Although I knew he was a prime candidate for one, I couldn't believe it had really happened. John and I were at home; he was watching football and I was catching up on some work. He got up to fix something to eat when he grabbed his chest and fell to the floor. I grabbed the telephone and called 911, trying hard to stay calm enough for the operator to understand me. I ran and unlocked the front door for the paramedics and then dropped down next to John, grabbing his hand and praying, "Please God don't take John away from me. I love him so much. You didn't let me meet this man just to take him away from me. I can't bear to be without him. It has taken me so long to find the man of my dreams. You can't do this to me. I love him." He was so cold, and I held his hands, blinded by tears, until the paramedics arrived and started working over him.

I sat in the quiet hospital room, the only sound the soft beep of the monitors, watching John lying there hooked up to the machines. He was so silent and pale. God was giving him the rest he needed, and when he had enough, he'd be joining his wife. Everything was going to be just fine. His sons, friends, and the rest of his family visited him at intervals. I stayed with him all day on Wednesdays and Sundays and came back to be with him after work. I went nowhere except the hospital and to work. I wasn't going to leave my husband. Wild horses wouldn't keep me away.

"Hi honey, it's Juicy. Remember how you laughed when I told you my name? I love you so much and I know it's not your time. Even though you said that you didn't have a long time, you were wrong, John. I love you, and you love me. We're going to grow old together. I'm glad you're getting the rest you need, but it's time to come back to me. I miss your cursing and fussing. The house is so clean I can't stand it. I need you to come and make a mess so I can yell at you. Can you believe it?" I laughed softly, fighting to keep the tears at bay as I look on his still pale face, memories engulfing me.

When we got married at City Hall followed by a five hour long reception at his cousin's church with family and friends, it was the one of the most memorable days in my life. We were both exhausted when we headed to our hotel in the Wisconsin Dells for our weeklong honeymoon. It was perfect. I closed my eyes, remembering the first time John made love to me. I was on fire when he kissed me, my body exploding with multiple orgasms as he caressed me.

When John touched me, my pussy was leaking my intoxicating juices of love. I screamed when he entered me, rotating my body to meet his. John would climax almost as soon as he entered me, and our bodies did the dance of love as we screamed out our mutual pleasure. We made love again and fell into each other arms. Our love knew no boundaries.

I wiped the tears as I remembered our lovemaking. John thought he was old, and lovemaking was a thing of the past. I brought sunshine back into his life. John loved my size sixteen body and would get an erection every time he saw it naked. I loved his big body too. We shared so much and I never wanted that to end.

Sometimes I wished life could be different and no one had to die. My mother would be living now, and see the happiness that John has brought into my life. She'd be so pleased for me. "Don't leave me, John. I know we all have to die, but it's not your time. Please come back to me. You're just tired, but please hurry and get well. Your family needs you. Please!" I got into bed with John and held him as I continued to weep.

"Juicy, it's me."

I opened my eyes, thinking it was John but it was my best friend, Roni. "Hi Roni. When did you get into town? I thought you'd be in New York for another month," I said as we hugged each other.

Roni was a plus-sized model, who had recently relocated to New York. Her husband Harry was a cardiologist still living in Chicago. He was also the doctor in charge of John. I knew there had been problems in their marriage due to the long separations, but neither of them wanted to sacrifice their careers. Finally Harry had been offered a comparable position to his present post at New York General Hospital and would be moving to New York in January.

"Let's go into the cafeteria and get something to eat. You've lost a lot of weight since John became ill. If you don't take care of yourself, you'll be the one in the hospital. The nurse said she'd call if anything happens."

I stared at John. "I don't want to leave him."

"He's asleep, so he won't even know you left him," she said softly.

I kissed John on the cheek. "Honey, Roni is here, but I'll be right back. I love you."

In the cafeteria, Roni went up to the food line and came back to the table with a tray of fries, cheeseburgers and shakes. The girl didn't have a clue. "I'm not hungry, Roni."

"You have to eat," she said.

I rolled my eyes at her and reached for a fry, eating it in two bites. "Are you happy now?"

"Not until you clean your plate."

Fifteen minutes later I looked at the empty plate. Roni had been right. I was hungry. I looked up as she spoke to me.

"You know, Juicy, Harry was telling me how bad John is doing. He's on total life support. He thinks you should consider letting him go. It's been a month and he's shown no signs of recovering. John's sons have asked him about pulling the plug, but he says it's entirely your decision.

"It's out of the question," I snapped. "My husband isn't dead and he'll be sitting up and talking before you know it."

"I know this is difficult," she replied.

"You don't have a clue," I shouted. "No one pulls the plug on my husband. His family might want to give up, but I'm never giving up. John loves me and he's coming back to me."

Roni shook her head. "Harry is a good doctor and he's convinced that he's gone, honey. I'm so sorry, but I had to tell you. I just thought you should know. His sons want him to rest in peace."

"I don't give a damn about them. John is my husband and I'll make the decisions for him," I screamed. A few people were staring at me, but I didn't give a damn. I was not giving up on John.

"His sons will be here tomorrow," Roni said

"And?" I snapped.

"They want to talk to you."

"They can talk all they want" I said. "This is my soul mate and he's not going anywhere as long as I can help it. Do you understand where I'm coming from, Roni? It took forever for me to find my soul mate, and no one is taking his life. How could his sons be so insensitive? How could you condone it?"

"They're honoring his wishes," she said

"I'll be in John's room." I stormed out of the cafeteria, almost hitting the wall as my tears blinded me.

Three months later I was beginning to give up hope, but I wouldn't let the negative thoughts get me down. I had gone to Church this Sunday morning to celebrate God and pray for John who was still sleeping. I knew God was going to hear my prayers. I just had to wait on the Lord, like Psalm 27 says. It was my favorite Psalm.

"Hi honey, it's Juicy. Church was wonderful this morning. I said a prayer for you, asking the Lord to open your eyes and beam your beautiful smile at me. I know he'll grant it, honey. I love you so much."

The door opened and John's four sons walked into the room. I glared at the handsome young men, looking so much like their father. "Hello."

They embraced me before turning to their father. "How is he doing?" Larry asked.

"He's the same," I replied.

"It's been three months," Hal said. "Christmas is almost here."

"I need to take a break," I said. "I'll be in the cafeteria if you need me."

"You don't have to leave," Jackson said.

"I was just giving you four some time with your father, alone," I said. "I'm not pulling any plugs, so don't talk to him about that. He's going to open his eyes and I'm going to be sitting right here when he does. Respect my wishes and talk to your father about life."

"He's gone," Phil cried. "I miss him so much."

"He's just getting the rest he needs," I said. "You know how hard your father has always worked. Don't argue with me, I'm not changing my mind so let's celebrate life." I stood up walking to the door. "I'll see you four later and remember...life."

I hurried to the cafeteria, returning greetings as I walked along. I had gotten to know a lot of the staff in the last three months and some of them seemed almost like family. I was so appreciative of the care they gave John. I was thrilled that he was so loved.

I sat in the cafeteria and took out my writing pad to make notes for an interview and deposition I had to conduct tomorrow. I had so much going on in my life, but I loved my life, and John. I felt very blessed.

When I returned to John's room, his sons stayed for another hour or so and then went home. I sat by his bed, holding his hand and reading to him. I glanced at him and was stunned to see his eyes were open and he was looking at me. "John, can you hear me?" He blinked at me, unable to answer with the breathing tube in his throat.

"My God," I cried, feverishly pushing the call button. "Are you coming back to me? Let me get your doctor."

I put my arms around him, holding him gently until the nurse hurried in. She took one look and grabbed me up, twirling me off my feet, both of us laughing like crazy before she left to summon a doctor. I think everyone I had met in the hospital the last three months managed to stop by some time during that endless day and congratulate us. John was weak as a kitten and he had a long way to go, but he was breathing on his own. He'd be back on his feet in no time. I smiled to myself, remembering the stunned look on his sons' faces when their father smiled at them. They couldn't believe he was alive and well, crying as they embraced me and thanked me for saving their father's life. I loved my perfect man, and I'd do anything for him. Soon we'd be back home together, ready to face the rest of our lives, no matter what happened.

I examined myself carefully in the mirror. I had to admit that, even at 42, I still had the figure to wear the gorgeous green mini-dress. The gold flecks embedded in the green satin caught the light as I moved, and I looked good. I checked the time again. I had plenty of time before I needed to meet my best friend Lynn. I was taking her out to our favorite club to celebrate her 42nd birthday. I was looking forward to spending some time away from my husband. Lately I had been asking myself why I put up with him. Surely I could find someone who appreciated me, as my husband Lloyd, never has. I don't know why he married me. I loved him, which was the only reason why I put up with his mess, and deep down inside I knew he loved me too.

"Where do you think you're going?"

I jumped at the sound of my husband's voice. I was hoping to leave before he got home. "I told you last week. Lynn and I are going out for her birthday."

"I can't stand that fat bitch. She's always trying to screw with your head and make you leave me. You're not going anywhere with her. You need to go fix my dinner and then we'll do something nice together."

I frowned at Lloyd. "Lynn's my best friend. I've always cele-brated her birthday with her. If I can't go out with her, then she's coming over for dinner. It's not like I'm your slave and you can dictate who I can and can't see. What's wrong with you?"

"If you keep on talking I'm going to fatten your lip," Lloyd snapped. "I make the rules, and you follow them. Lynn is a bad influence on you. She needs to spend her birthday at the gym losing some weight. The woman is fat as a cow and I don't want her fat ass hanging around you. Why don't you encourage her to lose some weight instead of spending her time getting up in your business? It's the reason why she can't get a man. When are you going to see the light?"

I couldn't believe he was talking to me like this. Part of the reason was because I let him, but he wasn't going to stop me from spending time with Lynn. She was all alone, and I wasn't going to let her down. I reached for my purse and wrap. "I'll be home late, Lloyd so don't wait up for me." I headed to the door and as I opened it, Lloyd slammed it so hard I thought it was going to fall from its hinges.

"I said you're not going out tonight. What part of that didn't you understand? We're spending some quality time together, and Lynn can go to hell where she belongs. Go and change your clothes and wash off that makeup. You look like a slut in heat."

I tried to get out of the door, but Lloyd was to strong for me. "Move out of my way, Lloyd. You're not going to bully me this time. I'm sick of you bullying me. I am a grown woman, and I can do what I want. I told you way in advance that I'd be spending tonight with Lynn. How dare you try and boss me around? Get away from the door!"

I thought Lloyd was going to move from the door, but instead he grabbed me and threw me down to the floor. I missed hitting the cocktail by an inch as my head hit the carpet instead.

"You're not going anywhere," he shouted. "You have five minutes to change and get some dinner on the table. I'm hungry and I want some respect in my house."

"I hate you, Lloyd. I hate you," I screamed.

"Shut up," he snapped, kicking me in the side. "I should mess up that pretty face of yours, and that will keep you in the house. You should be worshipping the ground I walk on. I'm the breadwinner in this family and it's your job to take care of me. Don't you ever forget it?"

"I'm not your slave," I cried.

"Yes you are bitch. Now quit whining and get up and do what I told you to do."

"You're just like your father. Big strong man beating up on a woman," I taunted. "I thought you were going to be different. You promised me that you were nothing like your father, and you hated the man for abusing your mother. Now here you are doing the same thing to me. How could you be so cruel?"

He put his hands around my neck, and I screamed. "I should choke the life out of you," he snapped. "Don't you ever again bring up my father to me? He's dead and buried. I love you Lonnie, but your mouth is going to make me do something you're going to regret.

Didn't that black eye tell you something? I'm not playing here. I'm going to take a shower, and then I want you ready for me. We're going to make love."

He stormed out of the living room, and I wept hysterically. What was I going to tell Lynn? She told me on many occasions to leave the bastard and never look back. I could move in with her. I made up my mind to do that tomorrow when he went to work. I was going to pack a few things, and go stay with Lynn. She'd protect me until I could get the police involved. I wasn't going to live my life being beaten by my husband. Eventually he would kill me. When Lloyd got home tomorrow, I'd be gone, and he'd never abuse me again.

I closed my eyes as Lloyd pumped into me screaming out his pleasure. I couldn't wait until he was finished. I used to love making love with Lloyd because he was the only man who could make me feel good. Now he was practically raping me. I didn't want him inside of me. I was going to shower for hours trying to get his stench out of me. I hated him, and I never hated anyone as I did Lloyd. He's the most cowardly human being I've ever met, and one day he was going to pay for his sins.

"Don't just lay there," Lloyd snapped. "Give your husband some pleasure."

I put my hands around his neck thinking about strangling him, but he'd kill me first. Why do men like Lloyd live? I've been married for six years, and the first two years were wonderful. After the third year Lloyd showed his true colors. I couldn't believe the first time he hit me. Lloyd is an attorney and we went to his company Christmas party. I was mingling with his friends because I had a gift for gab and I loved meeting new people. Lloyd's co-workers loved me and told him how gorgeous I was, which I thought was good. The minute we stepped into the door, he attacked me, slapping my face and throwing me to the floor. I had never been so stunned in my life. I'd never forget his abusive words.

"Don't you ever act like a slut with me at my party," Lloyd snapped. "All the men wanted to take you to bed and you gave them the opportunity the way you were flirting with everyone. You're my wife so act like it. I'm going out," he snapped a minute later as I still lay on the hall floor crying.

I was relieved when he slammed the door, and I waited a few minutes before I picked myself off the floor. I stared at the marks on my face, standing out against my light skin. I was glad I didn't have to work because I didn't want my co-workers staring at me with pity.

I came back to the present with a snap when someone knocked on the front door.   I knew it was Lynn and hurried to the door. I opened it a crack and peeked out at her as I said, "This isn't a good time, Lynn."

She pushed her robust self in. "Are you ready to party all night? You look good, baby, but remember I'm the birthday girl, and you can't get all the men. I'm trying to find my Prince Charming."

I started toward the bathroom. "Lynn, I can't go with you to-night. I'm so sorry."

She looked me up and down as if I had lost my mind. "What did you just say to me?"

"Lloyd wants me to spend some time with him, and he's right. He's been working a lot lately and misses me. I want to spend some quality time with him. Please understand this time. I'll make it up to you." Then, very quietly so that Lloyd couldn't hear me I said, "When he goes to work tomorrow, I'm moving out. Can I stay with you for a few days while I figure out what I'm going to do?"

Lynn embraced me. "Of course you can. I'll come over and help you."

I shook my head. "This is something I need to do on my own, but I'll be there."

"This is the right thing to do, sugar. I can see the marks he made on that gorgeous face of yours. Sugar, you don't need this abuse from that bastard husband of yours. There are so many good men out there, and one is just waiting for you."

I smiled at Lynn. We had been best friends since high school, and she was like a sister to me. What would I do without her in my life? "Lynn I don't have a job. How am I going to make it on my own?"

"Brush up your typing skills, girl. You're good on the computer too. I'll help you find a job. Lloyd didn't want you to work so you would be dependent on him. God will make a way for you to survive because he doesn't want to see you being beat up by your husband. He loves you, as I do."

I embraced my best friend. I truly loved her. I heard the shower turn off and said hurriedly, "I want you to leave now, Lynn. I'll call you tomorrow and we can get the show on the road."

"What show on the road?" Lloyd snapped, walking back into the room.

"Just girl talk, honey," I said. "Lynn was just leaving."

"She better hurry up and get her fat ass out of here," he snarled. "I don't want her in my house."

"I love my fat ass," Lynn snapped right back. "You bully! Do you get a thrill out of beating your wife? I dare you to hit me. I'll kick your butt, you mother! Put your hands on me and you'll regret it. Hit me big man!"

"Please just go, Lynn," I cried. "Just leave."

Lloyd walked over to Lynn and pulled his hand back. She immediately pulled out a gun and pointed it at him. I was stunned because I didn't know she carried a gun, but it sure had an effect on Lloyd.

I stared at the shock on Lloyd's face. The coward was afraid of a little gun. I wanted to laugh in his face.

"You're not so big now," Lynn said. "Give me a reason to blow your balls off, you coward! I'd love to see you screaming and begging for mercy for your damn balls, you snake in heat! I can't stand the sight of you, you animal! Hit on me, and you'll never hit anyone else again."

"I'm going to call the police," Lloyd finally said. "How dare you pull a gun on me?"

"Go right ahead," Lynn said calmly. "Then we can talk about how your wife got those marks all over her face.

"You better get her out of here," Lloyd said. "I want her gone."

I stared at Lynn. She was so angry I knew she could shoot him right between the eyes. "Lynn, I'll talk to you later."

"I want him to disappear because I'm not about to leave and then let him beat you again because of me. Why don't you find something to do? Or take a walk or something. My friend doesn't deserve the way you've been treating her. You need to seek some counseling or something. What's wrong with you?"

"I'll be back," Lloyd snapped. "I want her gone when I get back."

Five minutes later he was out of the house running for his life."

Lynn just laughed. "I think you should take this gun."

"He's going to hurt me because of your stunt," I cried. "Lynn, why did you have to pull a gun on him?"

"Are you serious?"

"He was just playing with you."

Lynn put her gun away in her purse. "I always take my gun with me and he was about to punch me. I'd never let a man hit me and get away with it, girl. What's wrong with you?"

"Lloyd loves me, Lynn. He just has to come to terms with his past."

Lynn laughed. "And you need counseling yourself. Someone is going to get killed and I don't want it to be you. Please, just pack up your stuff now and leave with me. We can go out and celebrate my birthday like we planned and you can just go home with me. But tomorrow night, you'll be on your own. I'm going out on a first date."

I stared at her. "What? Who?"

"His name is Manny and I met him at the supermarket. I'm not going to get my hopes up too high, but he's nice. We're going to the movies and then dinner. He's also big, so we have that in common. I've been seeing him around and he kept talking to me, but I ignored him, of course. He was insistent this time, so I gave him my number just for the hell of it. I didn't think he was going to call."

"I'm so thrilled for you and I can't wait to meet him."

"You will when I think the relationship is going somewhere."

"I'm so happy for you, Lynn. It's been a long time coming."

"God is good. I hope he's the one."

"Lynn, I think I'm going to stay here tonight. I have some things that I just can't leave and I'll never get them packed before Lloyd gets back. I don't think he'll try anything knowing you're so close and have a gun you're not afraid to use."

"Are you going to be okay?"

"I don't know," I cried. "But I just can't leave everything here. He'll destroy it."

"Then I'm going to stay here with you."

"No, you just go. I'll talk to you tomorrow."

"But we're going to make it his last time. Please take the gun."

I stared at the dangerous weapon. "I'll feel better knowing it's in the house."

"Then keep it for me, and I hope you never have to use it, or someone doesn't use it on you. Please put it in a safe place for keeps. I love you so much."

"I'm sorry I missed your birthday."

"Manny will take me out to celebrate. I'm going to be fine."

"I love you, Lynn. You're my only true friend." I embraced her as the tears blinded me. "Now go and have a great time. I want all the details when you get home."

"I love you, and please be careful. Just don't say anything to him."

"I'm going to try, thanks. I love you too." We embraced again and then Lynn left. I was so glad she had finally met someone, and I prayed Manny was her Prince Charming.

I was sleeping for the first time in a long time when I felt his presence. I opened my eyes. He was walking over to the bed. I could tell that he had been drinking. I closed my eyes and pretended I was sleeping and prayed he didn't bother me.

He walked into the bathroom and shut the door. A minute later I heard the water running. Sometimes I had a feeling that Lloyd was cheating on me. He'd stay out late, and then the minute he came home, he'd run to the bathroom and jump in the shower. I didn't even care if he was sleeping around. I just wanted him to divorce me so I could move on with my life. I was sure he wasn't abusing the women he was pumping. I held my breath as I waited for the first punch.

Fifteen minutes later, Lloyd turned off the water, walked into the room, and got into bed. He was naked, and I continued to hold my breath. Finally he turned over and five minutes later he was snoring. I stopped holding my breath as the tears fell. I prayed for a break today and fell asleep still crying. Maybe Lynn was right in showing the gun to Lloyd. He might have finally learned his lesson.

The next few days were wonderful. Lloyd was being very nice to me and he didn't once put his hands on me or abuse me verbally. I didn't see the need to pack and move in with Lynn. Of course she was livid with rage when she found out about my actions. I cut her off, and told her to mind her own business. I knew what I was doing. I hated to be angry with my friend, but right now Lloyd was acting like he was during our first two years of marriage. I was going to ride in the niceness.

I was cleaning the house from top to bottom, listening to my favorite radio station 106.3 a few days later and singing along with the music. I felt great. My husband was his old loving self. I smiled as I continued vacuuming the floor and dusting the furniture with the dust mop. When I was finished I was a sweaty mess and took a shower, donning my pretty green nightgown and robe set that Lloyd had bought for me.

The house was shining and dinner was in the oven when Lloyd walked in a few minutes after six. I had just woken from a nap, and looked up. "Hi honey. Are you ready to eat?"

"Why are you napping at this time of day?"

"It's the evening, honey, and I've been house cleaning all day. I'm just about to run the last load of laundry. Let me get you something to eat."

"I need to take a shower first."

Something inside of me snapped. "Honey, you just left work. Why do you need a shower?"

"I like to take two or three a day, Lonnie. What's wrong with you?"

"I'm sorry for questioning you."

"Why are you wearing that nightgown around the house? It's too sexy."

"I wanted to wear something sexy for my husband when he came home."

"Who's been in my house? Who are you banging?"

I was stunned by his words. "Honey, please don't do this. I love you and only you."

"Who is he?" he yelled.

"You, of course, Lloyd," I snapped. "Why do you have to spoil things?"

"You're the one whoring around, Lonnie. Who is he?"

"I'm going to finish the laundry, Lloyd. I'm not about to have this conversation with you."

I walked toward the door, but Lloyd grabbed me and threw me to the floor. "Don't you ever walk away from me when I'm talking," he snapped. "Who do you think you are?"

"I'm sorry," I cried. "I thought you were finished with abusing me."

"I was until you managed to make me angry. I'm not having a wife sleeping around."

"You're the one that's whoring around," I shouted. "Why do you need to take a shower?"

"I have more than one woman, but you're my wife. She's just a slut," he snapped. "A man needs more than one woman when his wife can't meet all his needs. Don't you ever question me! Francine knows how to treat her man."

I was stunned. "Francine is one of my friends."

"She was," he laughed. "The bitch talks about your naïve ass the entire time. She's so right."

"You bastard," I cried. "You and Francine can rot in hell."

He kicked me a few times and I hid my face so he wouldn't kick me there. "I hope this makes you happy," I cried. "Why don't you just kill me and get it over with? I'm sick of your abuse, Lloyd. Just do it so I can finally rest in peace away from your trifling demeanor. I hate you!"

He continued to kick me like the sun wasn't shining. I saw my blood pooling on the floor as I managed to get up and crawl over to the living room table. I reached for the gun and then I pointed it at him. I was in so much pain I couldn't even hold it steady. "I'm going to kill you," I cried. "You'll never hit me again, you poor excuse for a man. You son of a bitch! I hate you!"

He laughed. "You're not about to shoot me," he raged. "I'm going to beat your ass with it."

"Don't move," I shouted. "I'm not playing here."

"Give me the gun, Lonnie, and we can talk about this."

I shook my head, feeling the pain boiling through my body. "Move, bastard, and I'm going to shoot your balls off. Lynn should have killed you when she had the chance. You'll never hurt me again, you bastard from Hades. I'm hope that you burn in an eternal tornado of fire."

"I'm sorry," he cried.

"Is big bad Lloyd frightened of a little, bitty gun? Why are you almost pissing in your pants big man?"

"Give me the gun, you bitch! You don't have the guts."

He moved, and the gun went off. I stared at Lloyd as he fell to the floor, holding his chest while blood trickled through his fingers.

"You shot me, you bitch!" he cried. "Call an ambulance."

I stared at the snake making a mess on my clean floors. I knew once he got out of the hospital he was going to hunt me down and beat me for the rest of my life. I couldn't let that happen. I stared at the bastard.

"What are you waiting for woman? I am bleeding here."

"Rot in hell, bastard!" I fired five more shots and dropped the gun as I stared at Lloyd's bloody body. The snake was dead, and he would never hurt me, or any woman, again. I was finally at peace.

I continued to stare at his body for hours until the door opened and Lynn walked into the room. She stared at the bloody mess, and then she embraced me before going to call 911. I was going to spend the rest of my life in prison, but I didn't give a damn. Lloyd was just like his father. I was sure the both of them were baking in the fires or Hades.

"I do," Lynn said happily.

"I do," Manny said.

I smiled as the bride and groom kissed, and the minister pronounced them man and wife. It was a year later, and I wasn't in prison. Thanks to Lynn, who had hidden a video camera in my house, the prosecutors got to see the way Lloyd had repeatedly abused me. I got probation, and had to perform community service for five years at a recreational center on the west side of Chicago.

I also had all the money in the world because Lloyd never got around to changing his Will. I'll never have to work and I wanted to open up a center for abused women, and children. I thought it was a fitting use of Lloyd's money, something he would absolutely hate. As for dating, I couldn't subject myself to another man at the moment. I didn't trust them, and I needed time to heal. I was just glad for my best friend.

I embraced her at the reception. "I'm so happy for you, Lynn."

"So am I," Lynn cried. "Manny is my soul mate."

"I like him myself," I cried. "You look so gorgeous."

"I feel beautiful, and Manny loves me. If I lose any weight, Manny is going to divorce me."

I laughed. "Is he serious?"

"Like a heart attack. Are you going to be okay? I'll be on my honeymoon for three weeks. Why don't you come with us? It'll be good for you."

"I don't think so, but thanks Lynn. I owe you so much. If it wasn't for you I'd be in prison for a long time. I miss Lloyd so much. I'm sorry he wasn't the man for me. I still love him."

"Lloyd is burning in hell, and it's because of his father. He watched his father abuse his mother, and she ended up killing him. And now he has done the same thing with you. He should have sought counseling or something. It might have saved his life. I love you, girl."

"And I love you. Please go and have a good time."

"I'm going to call you when I get to Los Angeles."

"You do that, but enjoy being with your husband because he loves you so very much."

"I know." We embraced one last time, and then I embraced Manny, and watched as they got into the limousine and rode off. I let the tears fall as they blinded me from happiness. Lynn was happy and that was a good thing.

I picked up a glass of wine, and drained it before I walked out of the building. I was going to go home and think about my husband. Why did Lloyd have to be so bad? Why? He was truly the love of my life and we could have had a great life. I walked to my car and searched in my purse for my keys. Then I noticed the woman. "Who are you?"

"I'm the woman that Lloyd loved, but you took him away from me, and now you're walking the streets as free as a bird. He was going to divorce you and marry me."

I stared at the slim woman, long hair, and cute complexion. Lloyd did have good taste, of course. "I'm sure he didn't abuse you the way he abused me."

"Lloyd didn't have a mean bone in his body. How could you just shoot him in cold blood?"

"Why don't you review the police tapes, and look at the abuse he inflicted on me, and then we can have this conversation again. Lloyd lied to you about me, and those are the facts. Get the hell out of my face!" I pointed my gun at her. "Don't ever contact me again." She stared at the gun, and then she ran off.

I stared after her until she was out of sight. My gun was definitely my protection, and no one would mess with me again. I got into my car and drove to the nearest bar. I was going to have me a few drinks and then I was going to find a man to entertain me until the wee hours of the morning.

I was never going to fall in love again or be abused by any man. I'd do all the abusing this time. I smiled to myself. I was going to have a good time, and heaven help the poor sucker who messed with me. I continued to laugh hysterically as I drove. Lonnie was only just beginning!

I gloried in the pressing of his lips on mine. It was heaven as our lips blended together like bees to honey. The desire was racing through my body at the powerful kiss we shared. I couldn't wait until the more dramatic lovemaking took over. My lips parted, our tongues touched, as we tasted each other. I closed my eyes as the feelings overtook my body. Our kiss intensified as I again gloried in the wonderful feelings that were overtaking my hot and ready body. I wanted this man right now and I was going to let him know the error of my sexual ways.

He was on fire, his heart eagerly pumping. I heard the steady beats that would escalate as the emotions took over. I was a pro at making love. I abruptly ended the kiss, staring into his heated face. "Let the lovemaking begin." I removed my short negligee and let him get a glimpse of my perfect body with curves in all the right places. My breasts were the perfect size to please the tastes of any man, as was my booty.

He stared at me, unable to move. I knew he was sated; which was okay by me. At the sight of my precious body, all men were speechless for a moment. I had to do all the work. I smiled all over myself as I walked over to Lee and took his hand, leading him to the bed like a dog on a leash. He was so commanding I wished I had my black whip. I had a feeling I could do anything with Lee and he wouldn't scream or bat an eye, unless it was for passionate purposes, of course.

I liked it rough occasionally and I slammed Lee to the bed, stripping off his shorts and staring at his hard maleness. I knew he was ready for me. I was steaming for him, so I gently added the protection I had ready in my hand, and went to work on getting the pleasure I needed. I was a hot sex machine and men were my dogs. Lee was panting as I pumped, trembling on the verge of an explosion, the most powerful sexual gratification in the world.

A minute later I felt the pleasure release me at the same time Lee moaned out my name. I smiled at the sound of his voice. We both reached the ecstasy of forbidden fruit. The orange of sex was the phrase I thought in my head for the moment. I didn't know where it came from, but it was front and center for some reason.

When Lee lay spent, he put his hands on my breast and ignited more fire into me. He became the aggressor and threw me to the bed. He took my breast into his mouth, sucking and giving me the pleasure I craved. I was still hot and never wanted this session to end, but knowing I had another man coming by shortly. I just couldn't get enough of sex. I loved it. Sex was the only thing I knew how to do well. It was my job, and I excelled in it.

I closed my eyes as Lee's mouth suckled my breast. I began moaning, the fire again building between my legs, and I pushed Lee away and fell on top of him, adding more protection as I thrust like never before; screaming out my pleasure. Lee was panting and I was screaming. Within seconds we both exploded like thunder. I closed my eyes again as the pleasure literally took over. I was spent for the moment.

A few hours later, I stared at my shrink, Janet Greene.

"Why do you think you need sex?" she asked. "Is it because you're hot all the time? It's the only thing you want day and night."

"Twenty-four/seven," I replied. I didn't know why I needed to see her three times a week. I started it because I thought something was terribly wrong with me. Why did I need sex all the time? I had been seeing the doctor for a month now. I was still hot, but it felt good talking to someone. I was alone in the world and my shrink was like family to me.

"Tell me about your childhood," Dr. Greene said.

"There's nothing more to tell, doctor," I said. "I was raped by my father and two older cousins. My mother didn't believe me when I finally told her, so I left. I've been prostituting myself since I was fifteen. It's the only thing I know. I used to work in a high-class house, but the madam was taking all of my money and giving me a percentage, which amounted to pennies. I wasn't working my ass off for small change. I went out on my own and now I'm thirty and doing okay."

"It's a dangerous life, Satin. You have so much potential. You're beautiful and modeling comes to mind."

"I thought about it doctor, but black people don't make as much. I'm not about to compete with a bunch of white women. My body works for me. I keep it in good shape and eat the right foods. You don't see an ounce of fat on my body. I consider myself self-employed if you know what I mean. I majored in lovemaking and graduated with honors. I love my job. I get paid to live in a condo, and my bank account is larger than working on a nine-to-five-job. Modeling just isn't worth it."

"Have you tried it?" she asked.

"I did once after a john beat me up a few times and I was going to get out of the business. I worked at a restaurant, but my boss wanted me to work overtime. She wasn't paying the cash. I worked in plenty of stores as a cashier, but the money was short after taxes; I did McDonalds and Burger King for a year but I knew that there had to be something else for me."

"Did you think about going to college?"

"I finished high school and that was enough of a challenge, believe me. I never wanted to look back. I do have some sense, thank you very much. I like what I'm doing. There are men out there and some of them are so weak and stupid, I take advantage of them. One man was almost sixty years old, and all he wanted to do was touch me. He gave me five hundred dollars for services rendered. I live for those old goons."

"Do you ever fall in love? There has to be more in this life for you. What about children and having a family? Does marriage appeal to you?"

I laughed. "Doctor you've been working in a hospital too long. Read my lips. I sleep with them and they go home. I take care of myself and AIDS will never happen to me. I'm never without a condom, and plenty of medical assessments. I know how to take care of myself. There's no chance of me ever getting pregnant."

"What about your sisters?"

"I have two of them. Why?"

"No reason," she stated.

"Joann is thirty-five and we used to be very close. She had moved to New York City and we lost contact. She's a successful supermodel."

"Why don't you use a private investigator to find where your sisters are now? Family is very important in my eyes. I'm sure they are dying to hear from you, also."

"I think it's a good idea, but they have to know what I do for a living. I'm not ashamed or hiding anything from them. I don't want Joann or Ana judging me."

"I'm sure they won't judge you," the shrink frowned.

"Ana is living in Paris the last time I checked. She recently got married, and she's a very famous photographer. Her book will be out in June. I wonder what my mother is doing since you're on this kick about family history. I inquired about my mother and she was on drugs, living with some bad apple. I'm glad my sisters and I are doing well, and my mother didn't corrupt us, so to speak."

"So am I," the shrink replied.

"Who is the investigator, and I'll call him?" Satin promised. I stared at the doctor. She was forty and still a beautiful woman, married with four children. How did she stand the strain? "I don't know, Doc. If Joann thinks she's going to change my life and find something better for me to do, then she's wasting a lot of time. No one can understand but me, myself and I. My life is my own. I'm taking care of me."

"His name is Bobby Greene," the shrink insisted. She reached into her desk drawer and handed me the information.

"I'll call Joann when I find her, but I'm a prostitute, and there's nothing she can do about it. I mean it, doc. If she can't abide by my rules, then we shouldn't get together. I don't want to be judged, either."

"We have already covered this topic," the shrink pointed out.

"We can meet for lunch or something. I'm not ready to open up my world to her until she has accepted what I do for a living."

"I know the game. This will be good for you. It's imperative to have someone else in your life, Satin. You just can't depend on yourself. Joann is a very understanding person. I talked to her for two hours, and this is the impression that I got. She's also engaged to be married. Maybe there's hope for you yet."

"Whatever! Our time is up. I'll see you at our next session." I hurried out of the office and ran to the elevator. I had another John in less than fifteen minutes. I had to get all ready for him.

Duke sat on the bed in my apartment in Hyde Park. He gazed at the outline of my delicious body; barely visible through the long opaque negligee I was wearing. Soft sexy music was playing on the CD player. I had every intention of stripping for Duke who deserved it and more. I smiled as the gown slipped lower, revealing my breast. I began to dance to the music. At one point in my life I wanted to become a dancer. After one week of classes, I was exhausted and dropped out. I was now doing exactly what was meant for me.

The warmth lighting up Duke's face made me smile. I knew my seductive moves were working. When the music ended, I let the gown fall to the floor, seeing the shock on Duke's face. I was as ready for him as he was ready for me. This time I stood in the center of my bedroom and waited for Duke's actions. The plan was all up to him. I didn't have long to wait as Duke hurriedly removed his clothes and stood naked in front of me. By the size of his manhood, I knew he was over the limit in sexual heat. I smiled as he attacked me like a madman, and we fell to the floor. Duke didn't waste any time trying to enter me. I stopped him, making sure the condom was adjusted correctly before I let him enter me. I closed my eyes and let the familiar feelings take over. It was the most magical and intoxicating feeling in the world. Duke was like a man possessed as he yelled, screamed and thrust as though he had been in prison for five years and just gotten out. I thought he was going to knock me into the apartment downstairs as the room shook with his pumping.

Finally he exploded. I felt my body rock with pleasure as we exploded in unison, relieving the powerful forces of nature. After a moment, I guided Duke's hands on the button of my pleasure palace. He didn't disappoint as he went to work on keeping my groove going.

In less than ten minutes I was hot again. Duke knew where to highlight my button. I felt the erotic sensations overcome me, throwing my head back and closing my eyes as desire took over. I was about to blow like dynamite as I rocked back and forth in a bliss of heated fervor. I screamed as the orgasm lit up my insides, rocking me to the core. This was my forte I thought as I shook for the last time. I lay spent before I slowly opened my eyes to see the smile on Duke's face. The two of us were Adam and Eve. I liked Duke because he was almost the best in the lovemaking department. I took his lips as he responded, all ready for my tongue. We ate each other exploring the hardcore of each other mouths, and then lips.

I felt the feelings in Duke's groin lighting up his body. The kiss ended and we satisfied each other again, shouting and shrieking with unbelievable pleasure. This was the third time for us. Only Duke and I could make love so many times and not get tired of each other.

For the last time we rocked with passion then we snuggled up in each other arms as I inhaled his clean, musky male aroma. Duke was the only man I let hold me. I had limitations but I was only human. Duke was black, beautiful, and single for some stupid reason. He had a great body and made good money as a fitness trainer. He was working on his own training video; pursuing a lot of exciting goals in his career. I was so very proud of him.

"I want you to marry me, and stop this madness," Duke said.

I jumped off the floor with a frown. "Let's not go there, Duke. You're about to spoil a wonderful moment. We make good love, but I'm not about to be tied down to one man. I don't love you."

"I love you, and that's enough for the both of us. And I feel that you might be falling in love with me, Satin. You wouldn't know it or admit it because I'd ruin all your laid out plans. I'd destroy your securely nestled life. I make enough money for the both of us."

"I take care of myself, Duke. I think you should leave because you're making me very angry. If you can't abide by my wishes, I'm going to cancel you out. I'm not about to change the rules in my game. How in the hell would it look if I were married and sleeping around? I like variety in men, Duke. You're great, but I'd get tired of the same thing. You won't let me tie you to the bed and I can't whip you. There are men I can entice to my bidding."

"How gross, Satin," he snapped. "There's more to you than this."

"When did you have the chance to know me, Duke? We've been banging each other for months now. You're not a scholar on the attributes of Satin Jones."

"If you don't marry me I'm going to end our relationship. I love you, Satin, but the thought of you sleeping with another man boils me into a range of demons. I don't like it. I think about you when I'm not here, wondering what the men are doing to you, and it kills me. I don't want a man touching your body because that's my property."

I walked to the door and opened it. "It's time for you to leave. Duke, I'm not going to marry you, so save the proposal. Let's take some time away from each other."

"That's fine with me. I know you care deeply for me. When you come to your senses, give me a call. But don't wait too long. Women are proposing to me often. One day I'm going to take one of them up on their offer. I'm forty years old and I'm ready to settle down. I dream about you being pregnant and giving me a son. I like the picture."

"I'm going to take a shower. When I get out, I want you gone Duke."

In the shower, I let the water sluice my body. I leaned back on the wall to relax, closing my eyes. The door slammed so I knew Duke was gone. Why did he have to change the rules? I liked Duke, and that's saying a lot for me. I hated myself for it. Why did I have to like any of my johns? Duke was a john for heaven sakes. Nothing more or less, but he was different. Not sleeping with him again was going to kill me but I had to deal with it. Duke would miss me for a few days, then he'd be calling my private number, begging me to schedule some time with him. I knew how a man's mind worked. He was in love with me. How could he possibly stay away? Duke will be back very soon. I just had to keep cool and let the games follow the usual course. I've spent my entire life playing games. Will it ever end?

Two weeks later I found myself staring at the water, feeling the serenity; not as justified as I would normally be. For some reason the water wasn't working it's magic. It was so beautiful on this Sunday afternoon. I took off on Sundays, giving some peace and soul issues to my being.

But the truth was that I missed Duke, and that was the real deal. I missed him like I never thought possible. I wanted to kick myself or shoot myself in the head. Why did I have to fall in love with Duke? That was the only explanation for feeling this way. I thought he'd have come to his senses, but he didn't call. I tried calling him once, but he didn't pick up. Was he moving on with his life? The fact that he was banging another woman irked me. Damn! I couldn't wait to get back to work on Monday when I had four men lined up. I wasn't going to give Duke another minute of my time. My body will be performing acts that he'd never contemplate, so who needed Duke Maples? I didn't, not one damn bit. He was just a man, and there were plenty of them to go around. In addition to the four scheduled for Monday, I have seven lined up for Tuesday. I wouldn't think about Duke I promised myself. He didn't mean anything to me. Not a damn thing!

Ten minutes later I picked up my telephone to call him again, hating myself for my weakness. I waited through seven rings and was ready to hang up when he answered. "Are you going to marry me and change your life style?"

I was muted. "What?"

"I know it's you, Satin. You do have feelings after all. You're in love with me. I love you so let's make it official. I was thinking about going to Las Vegas and getting married; then showcasing you with the honeymoon of your life. What do you think? Then we can find a new career for you. I won't share my wife with another man."

I stared at my telephone. Was Duke living in a dream world? "I can never be faithful to one man. Listen to me, Duke. If I marry you, then I'll be cheating on you. I couldn't do that to you, Duke. I do have feelings for you."

"Marry me, and you won't need another man. Let me make all your dreams come true. You can go back to dancing or start up another business. There is something else out there for you. I trust you with my life, Satin. Or you can just be my wife and travel the world with me. I'm going to start my own business and hire other trainers. It'll be fun."

I liked his plans. The sane side of me wanted to fit in with them, but the insane side knew I couldn't hold up my end of the bargain. I'd get restless, and start sleeping around, going back into business for myself. I wouldn't hurt Duke for all the money in the world. "I can't."

"Then don't call me until you come to your senses. Don't wait too long either. I have a date so I've got to go."

I was jolted. "Who is she?" I cried.

"Her name is Tina if you must know. I'm not sitting around waiting for you to come to your senses. I'm going to have some fun in the process. Tina and I are just friends so don't get jealous on me. I'll talk to you later."

I heard the dial tone and couldn't breathe for some reason. Who was this Tina and why did I give a damn? Damn! I was glad I was meeting Joann at a restaurant at the Water Tower Place. I needed something to do. Damn Duke! Was he trying to make me jealous? If so, it was working. How did this Tina look? Was she black or white?

Where were they going? I should have asked him. Why was I falling apart? I didn't like me at all.

Joann was beautiful. I was about to give up on her, having waited for ten minutes when she walked up to my table. She was tall, and had a nice short haircut, highlighting her almost yellow face. She wore a pair of jeans and a blouse with high heel pumps as she sat down. "Hi. You're beautiful."

"I can say the same thing about you."

"So is Ana. Mother did something right."

"I guess so. Do you want a drink?"

"A rum and Coke is fine."

I motioned for the waitress... "So you're a fashion model."

"I am. I graduated from John Robert Powers and then headed for New York City. I love it out there because it makes my career but I love Chicago too, so visiting you will give me the chance to come back home."

I noticed her engagement ring. "Wow!"

"Thanks. Ruben is the man for me. We met at the park and I instantly knew he was the man I was going to marry."

The waitress dropped off the drinks and took our food orders, sauntering off to another table before going up to turn in the orders. I took a sip of my double scotch on the rocks. "What is his line of work?"

"He's a Senator."

"Oh," I exclaimed. "You move in high circles. Does he know that your sister is a prostitute?"

"I don't like hearing those words."

"I guess not. Imagine polluting the senator's world."

"It's not his business, Satin. He wouldn't understand. I told him you were in public relations. He wants to meet you and Ana, which I hope I can arrange. I also informed him that mother and father were dead so keep that lie going."

"It's not great starting off a marriage with secrets and lies."

"Whatever! The SOB doesn't want any scandals to ruin his career, so I have to be clean. I love him, Satin. When you fall in love, you'll move mountains for that person."

"How do you know you're in love?"

"The butterflies and the ringing in the ears for me; you think about that person all the time; you want to be with him, and you can't live without him in your life. It's love."

"I see," I said.

"I have a feeling we're not talking about Ruben and me."

"Of course we are," I asserted.

"I could always read you, Satin, so out with it. I've missed you so much. Remember how we used to talk for hours when our parents thought we were sleeping. I want to thank you for saving me when our father tried to rape me. I still feel guilty about that. I can understand why you're in this line of business."

"Believe it or not, it's water under the bridge. I handled father, but you and Ana couldn't. Hopefully he's rotting in hell now so let's not discuss him. I have no parents. They're dead. I was proposed to, Joann. I think I'm in love with him, but cheating on him will be the ruination of our lives together. I couldn't do it to him."

"You're in love because you're thinking about him. Wonders never cease."

"I'm going to lose him. The deadline will soon be up for me to accept his proposal. Duke is very handsome, and women are throwing themselves at him. He's out there with a date right now. Her name is Tina. If I knew where he was going, I'd be on his tail right now."

"You're in love," Joann laughed. "I'm glad for you. Maybe this Duke person can save your life. Why don't you give it a try? Are you still seeing the shrink?"

"That's my sanity, believe me."

"You know what I think? A double wedding would be great. I'd love it."

"Let's not get carried away," I said, but the idea did have possibilities.

"I need another drink."

Joann and I talked for five more hours and we embraced before getting into our cars. I was glad to finally know one of my sisters. Joann was very nice after all.

"What is wrong with you?"

I stared at James. "I don't really know. I'm usually hot for sex, so maybe I'm coming down with something."

"Or your monthly is about to flow. Let me have some fun and you just lay back and enjoy."

"What are you going to do?"

"Teach you a few new tricks I learned from the master, you, of course," he laughed.

I laid back on the bed feeling relieved. I waited for James to entice me with his lovemaking techniques. I closed my eyes. This had never happened to me before. Was I losing my touch? Lovemaking was my life, and now I was completely dead.

But my body lit up a little as James captivated me with his magical hands. He had definitely been listening when I was teaching. I was ready to explode off the bed. Maybe I wasn't losing my touch after all. In five minutes I collapsed with an orgasm, fighting the spasms of feelings. "Wow, Duke I loved that."

I covered my mouth in shock when I realized the name that came out of my mouth. James had a frown on his face. "I'm so sorry. I didn't mean it. Let's just continue where we left off. Get a condom. I'll give you the pleasure you deserve and more."

James agreed, but I could tell that he was just going through the motions. He donned the condom before he entered me. The fire was gone for both of us. We just rocked with the essence of the situation. I was more than angry with myself as James rocked with pleasure before jumping up, searching for his clothes. He was silent and I didn't like it. Duke was ruining my business. "James, let's reschedule. I want to make this up to you."

"I think not," he snapped. "Find this Duke person and make love to him. I won't be a stand-in."

"I'm a prostitute, so don't get holier-than-thou on me," I snapped. "Did you actually think that you were the only one? If so you're mad and stupid as hell."

"I know you're a hooker, but you used to be a high-class one," he snapped. "Calling me another man's name stinks to high heaven. I suggest you take a vacation. You're slipping and I don't like it. When you get your act together, give me a call. You need the rest."

I couldn't believe his words, watching as he hurriedly dressed and slammed the door. The nerve of him, getting angry with me because I made one ghastly mistake, the bastard! It's not the end of the world. Who in the hell did he think he was? I threw my pillows at the door, crying as I watched them fall to the floor. Why did my world have to change because of Duke? Why?

Another two weeks had passed and I hadn't heard anything from Duke. I didn't pick up the phone to call him either. I guess he was having a grand time with Tina and didn't once think about me. I didn't give a damn, I thought as I stared at my sister and her new husband dancing. They looked so happy and made the perfect couple. I was glad that Joann decided to have the wedding in Chicago. Even Ana was having a grand time, dancing with her husband. Two married sisters, and it was never going to happen to me. I stood by the door and watched people come in and out. I needed a drink so I grabbed a glass from a passing waiter and drained it, then waited for him to come back around. I wanted to go home, but home wasn't the place for me. I lost my thrill and zest for life because of Duke. Okay he had finally moved on with his life. He should have been man enough to let me know that. Who did he think he was? I wished him the best with Tina. I hoped the two of them floated in water. Damn!

"Are we pouting now?" asked Ana.

I stared at Ana. "I'm going home. I'll talk to you later."

"Who is that handsome man? He's late for the festivals."

I followed her gaze staring in shock at Duke. He looked fine as wine. I wanted him for breakfast, lunch, and dinner. "He's a friend of mine."

"That must be Duke. Joann had a difficult time talking him into coming to the wedding. He was so furious with you he wasn't about to show up. Joann had her mind made up. I'll talk to you later."

I stared after Ana, wondering what Joann was thinking for interfering in my life, but the sight of Duke brought tears to my eyes. I missed him so much. I knew he was the only man for me. I didn't need anyone else. Duke would be able to handle all my sexual desires. "Hi."

"I was out of town on business or I would have called you. You look great."

"Thanks. You don't look so bad yourself. What are you doing here?"

"Your sister is paying matchmaker of course. I told her I wouldn't attend, but the urge got the better of me. How are you doing?"

"I missed you, Duke. I'm not about to play any more games. I need you."

"Will you marry me?" he asked.

"Not here, Duke." I stared around the room noticing that the room became silent. Everyone was staring at us as if we were making a movie or something. "We're the center of attention."

"That's okay," Duke replied.

I watched in horror as he took out a small black box, and got down on his knees, heedless of his white suit. I wanted to run and hide as he took my hand and smiled. "I love you so please spend the rest of your life with me, and only me."

The tears fell as my sexual desires were parading in overdrive. "Yes I will."

He stood up, embraced me and then kissed my lips. After the kiss, he slipped the ring on my finger as the entire room applauded, with Ana and Joann running toward us to embrace me. I smiled because I was happy for the first time in my thirty years. All the pain and suffering was worth it.

Alone at last in my bedroom, Duke and I had made love for hours. I stared at his naked body as we lay in bed. "You're going to need patience with me."

"I know honey."

He was playing with my breasts. "But right now my patience has exploded over the limit. I want you."

"Do you sexually desire me again? Your appetite is getting much better. I love the food."

"Get on top of me and make me yours," he purred.

I gladly obeyed as he quickly entered me and we both fulfilled our sexual desires once again. I was completely satisfied as my desires were spent, satisfied, and then spent again. Duke was definitely the only man for me, and he'd always captivate my every sexual desire.

Day 1

I was getting married in ten days. I still pinched myself to make sure this is really happening to me. I am 42 years old and about to marry the man of my dreams, Hirsch Mays.

Thanks to my best friend in the whole world, singing sensation and superstar, Kimberla, I didn't have anything to do but show up. I was sitting in my condo on Lake Shore Drive, staring out the window on this beautiful November morning. It was cold in Chicago, but the sun was shining, and it was just great to be alive. I had a month off from work. I still couldn't believe this was happening to me.

I met Hirsch through Kimberla. He's a music agent, and when I went to hear Kimberla's concert in Los Angeles, Hirsch was there in the audience. He was tall and handsome. The minute our hands touched I was electrified.

After Walker left me, I thought I'd never find a man to share my life with. I was glad I didn't marry Walker because he was the most selfish man in the universe. He wanted to pursue his acting career and when he finally got the break to do a drama for television, he was packing his bags before the ink was dried on his three-year contract. I thought about moving to New York City with him, but he didn't even ask me. He had the nerve to tell me that he needed all his energy to make this drama work for him, and he didn't need any distractions. I had been with the man for three years, and he had the nerve to dump me.

His drama, THE CASINO, was making the ratings, and Walker had made all his dreams come true. He didn't even have the decency to call me. I had heard on television and read in the entertainment section of the paper that Walker was *the* bachelor now, and he had so many women, I lost count. I was glad he moved on with his life, but the pain was still there. I never got the closure from him.

When Hirsch continued to pursue me, I wouldn't give him the time of day at first, but he made me laugh, and that was the key ingredient for me. I had never laughed so much with Hirsch that I began to take interest in him. He was one of the most successful agents in the world. He was white, but I didn't give a damn about his color. I was in love with the most wonderful man in the world.

Hirsch ran his own law firm and he was an entertainment attorney for many celebrities too. I met a few when I went to different parties with him. I loved him and I knew he loved me. I shouldn't be thinking about Walker because he was just a distant memory.

I sighed as I thought about my wedding. I was getting married at my childhood Church on the south side of Chicago, and then having my wedding reception at Orchestra Hall on Michigan Avenue thanks to Kimberla. She was something else and I was thrilled to have her as my best friend.

She was a major singing superstar now, but she never dumped me and moved on with her life the way Walker did. Kimberla continued to be my best friend. I was there when her first single was played on the radio, and when she won two music awards, and five Grammies. I played her CD's all the time. I was so proud of and devoted to my best friend.

I was getting married, and the tears fell because I just couldn't believe it.

Day 2

Since I really had nothing to do I was kind of bored. Hirsch was in San Francisco on business, so I wouldn't see him until the wedding. I couldn't wait to become Mrs. Hirsch Mays.

His parents, Sarah and Raymond Mays adored me, and I adored them. My parents, Lisa and James Roberts weren't convinced that Hirsch was the ideal man for me. They wanted me to marry Walker because he was black and my children wouldn't have any problems by being mixed. I thought I'd spend the rest of my life with Walker, but that wasn't in the cards. I can't marry a man who doesn't think I'm important enough to be in his life.

I had no siblings, so Kimberla was the only person I could really talk too. She was there for me when Walker left me. I stayed home from work and wept for days because I just couldn't face the world. Walker had no idea the way he affected my life, but I was sure he moved on with his life. Men didn't suffer when they ended a relationship, but women had to bear the burden of heartbreak, and try to move on with their lives. I wanted a man to weep and cry for me. I think I've found that in Hirsch. He was my Prince Charming and knight all in one. How could I have been so lucky? Hirsch was only 43, and while most men his age wanted younger women, the sparks flew the minute Kimberla introduced us. We had so much in common.

I was sitting in my office staring at my designs. I was an architect and I loved my job and Hirsch supported me in my career goals. He had never met a woman architect before, and wasn't intimidated by my choice of a profession. I was in the process of building our dream house right on the Lake.

On the other hand, Walker didn't think my choice of careers would work for me and thought I was living in a dream world. I needed to find a more sensible career. I should have known at that point that he wasn't the man for me. What was I thinking? Walker was only 30 years old, so I was certifiable for getting involved with a younger man. He didn't know where he was going. I was on the right path and still educating myself. I loved my job and most people couldn't say that.

I focused on my sketch pad. Although I was off for a month, I didn't have much to do. I couldn't wait to have my Bachelorette party on Day 8. I was on pins and needles waiting for it to happen.

I concentrated on my sketching.

An hour later the ringing of my cell phone distracted me. "Hello."

"Hi baby. It's good hearing your voice."

I smiled at the sound of Hirsch's voice and gave him my full attention. "How are you?"

"I'm fine now hearing your voice. I couldn't go another minute without talking to the love of my life. In eight days you're going to be my wife. I can't wait."

I closed my eyes for a moment. "Me either. How is everything going out there? I miss you so much, baby."

"I'm busy as five bees, negotiating contracts all over the place. The work is endless for me. I love it though. I'm in the office with Cynthia James. She's trying to get more money on her contract with her sitcom."

"My God she's a huge star."

"She's that, but I hope she gets the money she wants. Everyone can be replaced, and she's so big she wants the money to go along with it. I hope she's not putting her foot in her mouth, but that's her business. It's my job as her attorney/agent to negotiate the best deals for her, and to follow my client's wishes. That's why I get the big bucks."

"And you're very good at your job."

"I do have some news for you."

"What's that?"

"Walker is back in Chicago."

I was speechless. He couldn't be.

"I thought that would surprise you. He's doing some publicity there for a movie he's in. Maybe the two of you need to talk so you can get that closure you've been searching for. I think it's a good idea so we can start off our marriage on the right foot. I know you love me, and no other man will take my place."

I couldn't believe him. "Baby, I don't need the closure from Walker. He's a part of my distant past. I was once in love with him, but now I'm in love with you, honey."

"I'll be marrying you in eight days, so the choice is yours. I have to run. I'm going to call your later, baby. I love you more than anything. I have your picture with me, and everyone is saying that I'm the luckiest man in the world. I can't wait to see you in your wedding gown."

I felt the tears forming. "I feel the same way, honey. I love you."

"And I love you." We made kissing noises before hanging up the phone. I couldn't believe that Walker was in Chicago. I didn't read anything about him being back in his home town. I hoped he had the good sense not to call me. I had nothing to say to him. Hirsh was so wrong. I had closure because I was marrying the most wonderful man in the world. I never had to lay eyes on Walker again.

I shook my head because the memories came crashing down on me. Why did Hirsch have to bring up Walker's name? Didn't he have a clue that I couldn't stand the man, and I wanted nothing to do with him? He didn't exist for me. I had moved on, and he has too.

I tried focusing on my sketches, but after five minutes, I put the marker down. It wasn't going to work because the seed had been planted. Did I want to see Walker again? It wouldn't hurt to give the bastard a piece of my mind, but he just wasn't worth me getting a headache over. If it wasn't for Kimberla, I'd have died because of that snake. I didn't want to live because I was so in love with Walker. What did that tell me? Was I really over him? I shook my head, confused as ever.

Day 3

I was meeting with Hirsch's parents at Water Tower Place. I arrived right on time and was showed to their table by a waiter all in black. This was the most expensive restaurant in the city. I smiled at them as we embraced and sat down. "Hello!"

"You look lovely, Sasha," Raymond said. "I keep telling my son that he's the luckiest man in the world."

I blushed. "You two are very handsome yourselves," I replied.

"What would you like to drink?" Raymond asked.

"A Mai Tai is fine," I replied as I looked around the restaurant. "This is very nice."

"How are you doing, dear?" Sarah asked. "I know you have to be very nervous."

"I am," I cried.

"And you miss my son," Raymond said.

I thanked the waitress for my drink, and took a sip. "I spoke to him just yesterday. I love him so much and I thank God I met him."

"Are you over this Walker person?' Sarah asked.

I was glad the drink was sitting on the table because I was shocked.

"I told you not to just blurt it out," Raymond scolded.

"I'm sorry," Sarah said. "I saw him on an interview once and he kept talking about you."

"What did he say?" I asked.

"That he regrets the way he ended the relationship and he'd give anything to take that day back," Sarah said. "He could never fall in love with anyone else because you'll be the apple of his life forever. He didn't use your name, but it was you, of course."

"Are you investigating me?" I snapped. "Are you here to stop this wedding?"

"Not on your life," Sarah cried. "We know you're the right woman for our son. He has told us that many times. I've never seen him so happy before."

"He knows all about Walker because I told him." I reached for my glass and took another long sip of my drink.

"We know, honey, but do you have closure with this Walker person?" Sarah asked.

"I don't mean any disrespect, but why are you two in our business," I snapped.

"Because Hirsch is our only son, and we want the best for him."

"I'm the best for you son," I stated. "We love each other and in seven days I'll be his wife, and no one will come between us."

"I'm sorry you're so defensive," Raymond said. "We love you, Sasha, but you need to understand our point of view. There have been so many women trying to win Hirsch's wallet instead of his love. He's a good man and he deserves a woman who loves him more than life itself. He needs someone who'd die for him."

"I will, without any hesitation," I cried. "I never thought I'd find the man of my dreams. I gave up when Walker and I broke up. I focused myself on my career and nothing else mattered. When I met Hirsch, the electricity was there, and I fell in love with him the first time I met him. You don't have to doubt my love for your son. I have my own money and my own independence."

"That building you designed on Michigan Avenue is gorgeous," Raymond said. "The Children's Library is going to be the best thing that ever happened to Michigan Avenue and Chicago will truly benefit from it. You're a very talented individual for a woman."

I chuckled at him because he was trying to be funny.

"Just understand where we're coming from," Sarah said. "We love you."

"And I love you both," I cried.

"Do we need to do anything," Sarah said. "Do you have something, blue, borrowed, old and new?"

I smiled at her because they weren't so bad after all. "My dress is new; I have an old watch from my mother; borrowed is Kimberla's very expensive earrings and I just need something blue. We both are working on that."

"I have the blue," Sarah said.

I stared at her as she reached into her purse and took out something wrapped in tissue paper. I stared at it. When she removed the tissue paper I gasped at the most beautiful bracelet I had ever seen, the glowing sapphires interspersed with twinkling diamonds. "It's gorgeous," I cried.

"I made it for you myself," Sarah said. "It's a hobby of mine. I want you to have this and treasure it for the rest of your life. I'm not giving this to just anyone. I'm giving it to my beloved daughter."

I looked at Sarah through my tears. "I don't know what to say," I declared.

"I told you she was going to weep," Raymond stated. "I can't stand a weeping woman."

Sarah frowned at her husband. "We know, Raymond."

"I didn't know you did such perfect work," I said.

"I make jewelry for my clients," Sarah said. "It keeps me from being bored."

"You truly have a gift," I cried.

"Wear it with pride," Sarah said. "It's going to look so pretty with your wedding gown. I can't wait until the day you become a part of our family. I can't wait either for the grandbabies. We never thought Hirsch would give us any children."

I smiled. "I can't wait to have Hirsch's baby."

"Stop the weeping," Raymond snapped. "Let's order."

"We're going to meet with your parents later on today," Sarah said.

"They're looking forward to it," I cried.

"Here is the box for the bracelet," Sarah said. "I can't wait to see it on you."

I reached for the box as the tears continued to fall. I'm sorry," I cried. "I'm acting like a little baby."

"You have feelings," Sarah said. "I like that in you."

"Can we order now?" Raymond said. "I can't stand this weeping."

"I don't know why I love him," Sarah said, "but I do."

"And I love you too," Raymond laughed.

I smiled at the two of them because they were so in love with each other. I wanted to share my life with Hirsch and have happiness the way they have.

We ordered and talked about everything under the sun during the meal. I was having the time of my life with my new mom and dad. It was great knowing the color of our skins would not interfere in our lives. Hirsch's parents were wonderful, and I was blessed to be in his family.

Day 4

I decided to sit on the beach and enjoy the 70-degree weather. The citizens of Chicago never knew what to expect weather wise.

There wasn't anyone else on the beach this Monday afternoon as I stared at the water, wanting to dive in, but knowing the water temperature was hovering around 40. There was also the matter of my hair. Kimberla was going to redo it for me, but I wasn't about to walk around like I had an afro or something.

I smiled out of pure happiness, wishing everyone could be as happy as me. It's the most wonderful feeling in the world, and then some. In six days my other dream will be coming true.

"I thought I'd find you here," Walker said. "You haven't changed about loving the beach."

I couldn't believe that Walker was standing in front of me. "What are you doing here?"

"Looking for you, Beautiful."

Walker was older, but he was still tall, dark, and handsome. "What do you want?"

"I just wanted to see you. I met your fiancé. I never thought you'd marry a white man. I hope I'm not the one who changed your mind about black men, Sasha. You belong with one, and I think you're making the biggest mistake of your life."

I didn't want to talk to him. My heart was beating fast and I was feeling faint. I had to hurt him so he could leave me the hell alone. "Get out of my face, Walker. I'm sure your bimbo women are waiting for you."

"I still love you," he confessed. "I know you're marrying this white man because you're vulnerable. You think you can't trust black men. I made the biggest mistake of my life by leaving you. I should have taken you with me, but I've made something of my life, and my career is booming. I need you to share the limelight with me."

"What did you say to Hirsch?"

"That I was still in love with you, and you felt the same way about me."

"You bastard!" I cried. "What gives you the right to interfere in my life? You chose your career over me and I've moved on. Did you expect me to just stand here until you got your acting career off the ground? I do thank you for leaving me," I went on. "It gave me the opportunity to evaluate my life, and realize that you aren't the man for me. I think you're the most selfish human being on this earth, and right now you're proving it. How could you wreck my happiness for your own gain?"

"I'm sorry, but I think I'm doing the right thing. No one can ever match the love we shared."

"Get out!" I cried.

"Let's get together one last time. I want to take you out to dinner. Your white boy is okay with this."

I shook my head. "His name is Hirsch."

"He's a great attorney for actors. I know his reputation. You did well, but he's the wrong color."

"Who are you to judge?"

"I'm the man that you'll always love."

I laughed. "Your ego is unbelievable. I don't want to have anything to do with you, so get that through that thick skull of yours. I'm sure there are plenty of women to take my place. Let me be happy, Walker, and move on with your life. If you ever loved me, then you'd leave me the hell alone. Hirsch is the love of my life and he's going to make me happy."

Before I could move, Walker grabbed me and pounced on me with his lips. I tried moving away from him, but he held me in a death grip, and I couldn't move if it wanted to. The kiss lasted forever it seemed, before Walker broke it, smiling all over himself. "I'll see you at Bennigan's tomorrow night. I suggest you be there because that kiss tells it all."

I stared after him as I wiped my mouth, darting glances around the beach. No one was present, so I let the tears fall. What was happening to me? I let Walker kiss me, and it was the ruination of my life.

Day 5

I was lying in bed when the doorbell rang. I opened my eyes and checked the bedside clock. It was one o'clock in the afternoon. I didn't want to get out of bed but whoever was at the door was persistent. The doorbell rang again, so I got out of bed and went to the door wearing only my oversized tee shirt as I opened the door to my mother. I smiled at her. "Hi. What are you doing here?"

"And what are you still doing in bed?" she asked. "It's the afternoon."

I closed the door and walked back into my bedroom. My mother followed as I got back into bed. "I'm just tired," I said. "I'm so exhausted Mother."

"Why do you have the attitude?" she asked.

"I'm sorry, Mother."

"Is something wrong?"

"I'm just nervous. In five days I'm going to be a married woman. I get more nervous as it gets closer. I can't wait for Kimberla to get back to Chicago. She knows how to have fun."

"Why don't you talk to me about it? Is it Walker?"

I stared at her. How did she know?

"What do you mean?"

"I know he's in town, honey. The media follows him like a robot on wheels."

I smiled because my mother could be funny at times. "Why don't you sit down?"

She sat down on the end of the bed. "I want you to get up and shower, and then we can talk."

"Mother, this is the first time I've had a moment just to lie in bed, and I want to do it. I don't want to take a shower. I want to enjoy my time off and have the time of my life doing it. I need the sleep."

"You can't hide in bed from Walker."

"I hate him, mother. Why did he have to come back?"

"He wants to see you."

"He's insistent that I meet him for dinner at Bennigan's tonight. I just can't do it."

"Is it because you still have feelings for Walker?"

"I think I do, Mother. When he came to the beach, I was humid as hell."

"Then you need to meet with him and get the closure you need. If you're still in love with him, Hirsch has a right to know because you don't want to hurt him. He's a good man."

"But you two didn't like his color."

"We were biased, honey, but after getting to know Hirsch and his parents, we realized they were no different than us. I had them laughing all over the place and we had a very nice time. Your father even enjoyed himself, and that's not a piece of cake with your father."

I smiled. "I'm glad Dad had a good time. I don't want to ruin lives."

"It's best to make sure before the wedding. You have five days left. Go and meet with Walker."

"He kissed me, mother, and I let him do it."

"He probably caught you off guard, Baby. Walker is a smooth criminal."

I laughed. "Mother, you're something else."

"I know, baby. Let me tell you a story."

"Okay." I sat up in bed, and leaned on my elbow.

"I love your father more than anything, but he wasn't the first love of my life. In high school I met Brian, and we dated for four years. I thought we were going to get married, but after high school he decided to enlist in the army. He signed the papers, but didn't let me know his plans. I'm thinking we'd set up house, and he had other plans. He wanted me to go with him, but I couldn't do it. I realized that Brian wasn't the man for me.

I was heartbroken, but shortly after I met your father, and he wined and dined me, I fell in love with him. Four years later Brian came back into my life, and he insisted on meeting me. I didn't lie to your father, and told him about Brian, and he told me to go and get him out of my system. If he didn't see me at our favorite beach in two hours, then he'd know that I chose Brian."

I was fascinated by her story. "You chose Dad."

"I did, and I never regretted it. I love your father more than life itself."

"So you met Dad at the beach."

"I ran to him, and the tears in his eyes told me that I had made the right choice."

"So I should just get Walker out of my system?"

"That was my life, honey; you have to make your own."

"I'm confused, Mother."

"It's natural because you're about to get married, and the devil is trying to ruin a relationship and marriage. Satan doesn't want to see you happy, so please don't let him win."

"I love Hirsch, Mother. I didn't go to him because I was vulnerable. I love him."

"And do you still love Walker?"

I stared at her, blinded by my own tears. "I don't know."

"Then meet with him, and end the relationship once and for all. If not, then be with Walker. Your father and I only want your happiness, and you have to make sure. Your father always kept a watchful eye on me because he thought I'd leave him for Brian. You have to make sure that Hirsch is your soul mate, or you're going to be sorry."

"I hate Walker for coming back into my life," I cried. "Why couldn't he just leave me the hell alone?"

"Hate is such a strong word honey," she cried. "It always happens when an old boyfriend finds out that you're getting married, and he's no longer in the picture. I know this is very difficult for you because I've been there, but you have to follow your heart."

"I love you so much, Mother."

"And I love you. I need you to pick out the china patterns, and then I'll be on my way. I've been working with Kimberla on this wedding, and we have everything in place. Your wedding is going to be the event of the season."

I shook my head. "Don't remind me, mother. I know Hirsch is somewhat of a celebrity."

"Good luck with Walker baby, and whatever decision you make, I'll be right here for you."

I got out of bed and embraced my mother. "You and Dad should have had more children. You two are the best parents in the world. There are so many men and women who don't deserve any children. I'll never understand that."

"I love you too, and thanks. I could only have one child. I'm grateful for having the smartest and most beautiful child in the world. I'm so proud of you, baby. When I tell people that my daughter is an architect, they're impressed. You make your parents so proud."

I held my mother tight. "You two raised me well. I just hope I make the right decision in my personal life."

"You will do the right thing for you because your happiness is the only thing that matters."

She was so right about that.

"I have to get going, Sasha. I still have lots of things to do before the wedding. I'm going to talk to the catering service and then call Kimberla. I'm having the time of my life and then some."

"I'm happy for you, Mother, and thanks for talking to me."

"You can always talk to me, baby. I told you this all your life, and I mean it."

"Thanks." I stared after her, and then frowned. What was I going to do about Walker and Hirsch?

Day 6

The restaurant was loaded with people, but I found Walker sitting in the back with his many fans. He was signing autographs and talking about his movies. I stared at the scene for a while. Walker always wanted to be an actor. I thought when he first told me about his career goals that he'd be wasting this time. It wasn't easy, but he was determined to make his dreams come true. He graduated from Columbia College with an associate degree in drama as well as receiving degrees from two performing arts schools.

Finally he had accomplished his dreams, and I was proud of him. I never thought he'd leave me behind, but most men did when they made it big, and Walker was no different. I frowned at him, remembering that he deserted me, and not the other way around.

"Sasha you can sit down," Walker said. "My fans are gone for the moment."

I just looked at him as I walked over to the table and sat down. I was wearing jeans, high heel black boots and a white turtle neck sweater with my leather jacket. I wasn't about to get dressed up because it wasn't a date. Walker was dressed in beige slacks and a shirt with the collar opened. He looked good, but he always knew how to dress.

"You look good enough to eat," Walker said. "I like."

"I need a drink," I cried.

"I ordered a Mai Tai for you. I know that's your favorite."

"Thanks."

"Will you stop being hostile to me. I love you, and we had some good times," Walker laughed. "I remember when I chased you all over Grant Park because you were so angry with me, and wouldn't come back to me. I had never seen you so angry before."

I remembered that time, and smiled. "I was in a rage because you were looking at other women right in front of me. I thought it was disrespectful," I snapped. "I bet you're still the same way."

"As long as I didn't do anything but look, what was the problem, Sasha? There were other women in the world, and I like women. I didn't take them all to bed with me. During our relationship, I was more faithful to you than ever. I loved you more than my own life."

"But you chose to leave town without me," I snapped. "It's too late for us, Walker. I'm in love with a good man, and I won't hurt him because of you."

"Let's get some food in our bodies. Are you still a size five?"

"My size is none of your business," I told him.

"You look fantastic, Sasha. I can't blame Hirsch for wanting you, but he's the wrong color. Black people need to stick with their own kind. I'm sorry you had to go out of your race for happiness. I came back here to take you with me. Let's get married and live in New York City. I need a wife, and you're the only one I can trust."

I drained my Mai Tai and then I laughed at him. "You've lost your mind."

"I know this is all of a sudden for you, so I'm going to give you some space. You have four days left before you're married. I want you to come to me on the 9th day, and we'll make love and live happily ever after. Break it off with Hirsch on the 8th day so he can find someone else. It won't be difficult for him because he's a very handsome man. I'll be going back to New York then. I have plane tickets for you. Our flight leaves at noon and I expect you to be there. I won't disappoint you this time. I love you."

I shook my head. I don't think so! Who did he think he was? I ordered fish and concentrated on my food. The man didn't have a clue.

Day 7

I still had last minute details to take care of for the wedding, but I couldn't concentrate on the list Kimberla had faxed to me. I was thinking about my dinner with Walker. We had a good time with Walker talking about the many memories we shared, making me laugh out loud. We used to bike ride all over Chicago, and swim naked in the water. The police almost arrested us, but Walker talked us out of going to jail. He had a knack for words which was why he was an actor. We jumped off a cliff together; we jumped out of an airplane, and climbed the top of a mountain. We went camping for two weeks, and slept outside in the summer months. I did have so much fun with Walker.

Hirsch and I didn't do much, but I loved him and he loved me. I was going to spend the rest of my life with him. Walker could go back to New York and find another woman to keep him warm in bed.

My cell phone rang and I picked it up to talk to Hirsch. "Hi. How is everything?"

I felt the tears forming as I listened to Hirsch's voice. "I'm just going over last minute details of our wedding. How are you doing?"

"Just missing my woman," he cried. "How are you and Walker doing?"

"He's about to go back to New York."

"Are you sure, Sasha? I don't want you marrying me because you want to teach Walker a lesson? This is the most important decision of your life, and you need to make the right one."

"Why are you being so kind to me, Hirsch? I thought you'd be ranting and raving like a maniac for the woman you loved. Instead, you're trying to give me away to Walker. What's your problem? Do you want me to call off this wedding because you don't know how to break it off? Talk to me Hirsch, because I'm getting mixed vibes here."

"You're not about to put the decision on me, Sasha. Let me know your decision."

"Do you love me, Hirsch?"

"I do with all my soul, but if you don't feel the same way, then there's nothing I can do to change your mind. The choice is yours. I'll talk to you soon."

I listened to the silence on the telephone. What in the hell was I going to do?

Day 8

I was at my Bachelorette party, but I was still so confused. One hundred of my best girlfriends, family and co-workers were giving me gifts for my honeymoon. I was trying to have the time of my life, but I was still so confused. I had two days before the wedding to decide if I wanted to spend the rest of my life with Walker or Hirsch. Walker was pressuring me with his constant telephone calls, and Hirsch was giving me the silent treatment. I just didn't know what to do.

"Let's talk about the party," Kimberla said. "I can't believe your mood at your own pre-wedding party. What's the matter with you?"

Kimberla was my best friend, but sometimes she just didn't understand my mind. I was thrilled for this very expensive party, but I was confused because I didn't know who I wanted to spend the duration of my life with. When was she really going to understand me?

The party continued for three more hours. Kimberla had hired a cleaning crew, so we were sitting on her bedroom at her condo on Michigan Avenue. I was staring out at the water, and Kimberla was pacing the floor.

"Will you sit down Kimberla?" I said. "You're getting on my nerves."

"Not until you level with me. What's going on?"

"I'm confused, and I don't know who I want to marry."

"Hirsch is the answer to your prayers," she shouted. "Why would you want to have anything to do with Walker? He's the most selfish human being in the world, and then some."

"He still loves me, and I still have feelings for him."

"You're confused, girl. Hirsch loves you like a man should love a woman. If Walker's career moves to another level, he's gone again. Are you willing to give up a winner for a loser?"

"Hirsch isn't even pressuring me, Kimberla. I don't think he gives a damn. Who should I choose?"

"Hirsch, but I can't make that decision for you. I thought you had your life in order."

"So did I until Walker came back into the picture," I cried. "I've been remembering some of our good times together, Kimberla. Walker and I had so much fun together. Hirsch and I are so boring together. I miss the adventure with Walker. I think I want that kind of suspense in my life."

Kimberla shook her head. "You're crazy. Life isn't about adventure."

"So I should vegetate in a serious relationship and forget about the fun."

"I will stand by you whatever choice you make, but you need to let Hirsch know if you're not going to marry him. You're about to ruin a family who accepted you with open arms as well as your family who handled having Hirsch in their lives. Now you're about to create a tornado from hell. I do want you to be with the man you love."

"I love Walker and Hirsch in two different and special ways."

"Who do you love the most, Sasha?"

I stared at her because I just didn't have an answer for her. Again, what was I going to do?

Day 9

I had to end this madness right here and now because tomorrow was my wedding day. I wanted to be with Walker, and I wanted to be with Hirsch. Why couldn't I marry both of them? I was losing my mind. I was lying in bed because I couldn't think of who I wanted to spend the duration of my life with. The telephone shrilled into the room and I reached for it. "Hello."

"Hi. This is Walker. What are you doing?"

"Lying in bed," I said. "Tomorrow is my wedding day."

"Don't I know it," he declared. "Can you be ready in ten minutes?"

"No, Walker. You can't keep pressuring me."

"I'm going to take you somewhere to help you think of the man you want to be with."

"You're pressuring me. I need to make the right decision."

"I'll be there in thirty minutes. Wear jeans."

"Walker don't..." he had the nerve to hang up. What was I going to do? Ten minutes later I smiled as I hurried into the bathroom to grab a shower. I knew it was going to be fun.

I was right. I stared at the miniature people on the ground. I was in an airplane and Walker was piloting an airplane. I was so impressed that he had his pilot license. "Where are we going?"

"Just to Wisconsin for a few hours," he laughed.

I shook my head at him. "Are you crazy? I have last minute preparations for my wedding tomorrow. I'm getting married at noon."

"You don't have to keep telling me that you're about to marry a dull man."

"Hirsch is a lot of fun, Walker."

"Then why are you up here with me?"

I stared out the window. "I don't know."

"I'm sorry I hurt you, Sasha, and I'd give anything to take it back. I have the fame and fortune, but I can't survive without having you to share it with me. I've dated women, but I keep coming back to you. I want you to become my wife, and be happy with me. You and I have so much fun and adventure and that's what a marriage needs. I don't want you becoming a bored housewife with three children. It's not for you."

"I do have a career," I snapped.

"When those children come along, you won't have the time to build buildings, baby."

He was so right about that. Hirsch wanted at least one child. We were both older and didn't have the energy for more than one. I smiled. "I'm going to marry Hirsch tomorrow, Walker. I just can't trust you. He's stable."

"You're making the biggest mistake of your life," he cried.

I stared out the window. "I don't think so."

I had a wonderful time in Wisconsin because Walker was crazy and he got my mind off my wedding. This would be the last time I spent with Walker, and then it was time to focus on Hirsch. I thought he'd call me today, but it was almost five o'clock and there were no calls from Hirsch. What kind of man didn't call his fiancé on the eve of their wedding? I was beginning to ask myself a lot of questions about Hirsch. Did he care about me at all?

I stared over at Walker. "It's time to go Walker. I'm sure my mother and Kimberla are having a heart attack searching for me. I have to get back to Chicago. Thanks for the trip."

He moved toward me and kissed me. I tried resisting, but the passion was just too much. Our kiss intensified as my body lit up with pleasure. I closed my eyes as our tongues bonded, and the passion grew even more inside of me. I was on fire.

When the kiss ended, our eyes met. I stared at Walker. "I think we should go now," I shouted.

"A bedroom is my guess," Walker said. "I want to make love to you."

I shook my head, and then wiped my mouth. "Take me home."

"Your wish is granted, Sasha, but I'm very disappointed. I'm going to love you for the rest of my life and that will never change. I'm also going to wait for you to come back to me. I'm a very patient man."

"I'll meet you at the plane."

Five hours later Kimberla and my mother were furiously shouting at me. I didn't care because I was as confused as ever. Hirsch is a person I can trust, so he was definitely the man I was going to marry. "I'm here now, so let's get ready for the wedding of the century. I am ready to spend my life with Hirsch Mays."

"I'm glad to hear that," Kimberla said.

"I'm going to check on the catering service," my mother replied.

I smiled because Hirsch was the only man for me after all.

Day 10

"You may kiss the bride," the minister said.

I smiled as my veil was lifted and my eyes locked with my husband's and our lips met. We kissed passionately for a few minutes and then our eyes met again in love.

"I love you so much," he cried.

"I love you too, Walker." We kissed again to celebrate being man and wife.

A Woman Scorned

It had been five years and I couldn't wait to see my boyfriend. I couldn't believe I let him go away to Paris to pursue his doctoring goals without me, but I did. We emailed each other everyday, talking when the rates were cheaper. Now he was coming home and I was on pins and needles.

A lot had changed over the five years. I didn't look the way I used to look. When Phil first left I was a size six, and he adored my body. Now the stress has taken its toll on me and I was a size sixteen.

I had to meet him at the airport, and I was nervous. Phil always told me that I was his woman and he'd love me through thick and thin. We were going to get married when he graduated from medical school. I found myself staring at my bridal magazines.

In three hours I'd see Phil, my tall, dark, and very handsome man. It wasn't easy letting him go to a foreign country, but I trusted him with my life. We kept in constant touch, thanks to the computer and modern technology.

I stared at myself in the mirror trying to find something slimming. I didn't want Phil to look at me with disgust. I tried losing the excess weight, but it was impossible. I'd lose five pounds, and then buy some ice cream and gain ten pounds. I was thirty-eight so the weight wasn't easy to take off and keep off. I even emailed Phil that I didn't look exactly the same, but he chalked it up to old age. Phil would still look good at 60. I had never missed anyone like I did Phil.

I was wearing a long summer dress. I heard that black was slimming and when I checked myself in the mirror, I looked good to eat. I liked myself now because my breasts and ass were bigger, so Phil had a lot to hold onto. I remember when he complained that my ass was too small and my breasts weren't large enough. Now he had a lot to hold so he should be pleased as a boy on Christmas Day. I'd wear high heel sandals to make me look taller and disguise the weight. I was five ten so maybe he wouldn't notice. Who was I fooling? Phil noticed everything. He was definitely going to notice I gained a lot of weight. Going from a size six to a size sixteen was a major feat. I couldn't believe it myself when I got on the scale. The weight just took it upon itself to devour my body.

But Phil wouldn't care because he loved me. He was going to prove himself when I meet him at the airport. I smiled. My man was coming home, and I just couldn't wait.

I was nervous as Phil's flight was called. In five minutes he'd be looking at me. I wore my hair long, hanging down my shoulders so he'd recognize me. I kind of wished that it was wintertime so I could hide myself in a coat, but it was eighty degrees this lovely day in May.

I closed my eyes and prayed Phil would appreciate the new me. I couldn't survive if he rejected me because I had gained a little weight. Okay, it was a lot of weight, but that was beside the point. I was still Leann Washington, and I'd always be her.

I opened my eyes and he was staring around O'Hara Airport. Okay, he didn't recognize me, and I didn't know if that was good or bad. I was still the same person. I waited for our eyes to meet, but when they did, Phil looked away. I felt like puking. He didn't even recognize me. I had to face the music. I took a deep breath and walked over to my man. "Hi Phil. It's me."

He turned toward me and the shock on his face was apparent. His mouth opened wide as if he was looking at a ghost. "Honey is something wrong?"

"Is that you Leann?" he finally replied. "You look so different, honey."

I smiled, trying to play it off, but I was hurting inside. "I'm the same, but it has been five years. What do you think?"

"You put on a lot of weight. What happened to that size six body of yours?"

I was livid with anger, but I wasn't about to let him see the effect his words were having on me. "The stress was just too much, baby. I missed you like crazy, and my body went into depression."

"You used to care about your weight."

The bastard! "Now I have more for you to hold. Let's go home so I can show you my new breasts and rounder ass. You're going to love the new me, Phil. I'm still the same woman inside. What's your problem?"

He didn't look a day older, and he looked all good with the same skinny body. Why did women get fatter and men didn't change at all? I was at least expecting Phil to have a gut. He was 40 years old and still very handsome. He made me sick. "Let's go and get your luggage."

"Okay," he said.

I could tell that Phil couldn't get over the sight of me, and I was angry as hell. Who did he think he was? Men could lose their hair, and get a gut, but when it happened to a woman, they didn't want to be bothered. I was going to show the snake that I still had it in me. When I finished making love to him, he'd never discuss my weight again.

In the car as Phil drove I stared at his profile. What was he thinking? Did he still love me? I was going to find out. "So did you meet any woman in Paris?"

"I met them, but they're my friends. I didn't have that much time to socialize, Leann. I had studying and making the first year of medical school. Now I'm a doctor."

"So you'll be interviewing for hospitals."

"I have about five interviews lined up staring on Monday. I should be working very soon. I'm going to get a job. How is your business going?"

I had my own word processing business. "It's very stressful, but I'm finally seeing a profit. I had to fire Shelly, so I've been doing a lot of the typing myself until I hire someone to take up the slack. I have five employees and I'm looking to expand. I'll be busy all next week" I touched his leg. "I want you right now, Phil."

"I can't concentrate on my driving when you're doing that. Just wait until we get to your place."

I frowned because Phil and I always made love in the car. The bastard! He was changing because my body wasn't a size six anymore. I was so angry with him I stared out the window and didn't say anything else to him. At least the apartment was the same. He wouldn't be able to fault me on it, the snake! Sometimes I hated men. I felt the tears forming but I wasn't going to weep in front of Phil. He just wasn't worth it.

"The apartment is still the same," Phil stated. "Nothing has changed, Leann, but I'm still shocked that you let yourself go like this.

The stress couldn't have been that bad. You didn't once tell me about your weight in your emails."

"And why should I?" I snapped. "Look at the way you're acting, Phil. You didn't even recognize me at the airport. How dare you treat me this way? I love you."

"And I love you, but I'm just surprised. You can't blame my actions."

"I thought we were together for better and for worse."

"Honey, I love you, but the weight has to go. I like my woman small and petite."

"But that's not going to happen. I'm a size 16 now, and I still look good. Believe it or not, the men are breaking their necks to get to me."

"I'm sure they are, but we're talking about me, Leann. I like small women."

"So what about loving me unconditionally?" I snapped. "Those were just words, and you didn't mean them?"

"I'm tired, Leann; it's been a long flight. I need to get some rest and then we can talk about it. I've been working hard and I need to rejuvenate myself. Is that okay with you?"

"I thought we'd make love. I miss your body."

"I'm just not in the mood. I'm sorry, but when I wake up we can make up for lost time."

"I can join you in the shower, honey."

"No thanks! I just want to wash up and then go to bed. We have plenty of time. Relax! Patience is the key. I'm going to shower now. What's for dinner? I'm starving."

I stared after his back. The bastard didn't want to make love to me. I let the tears fall as I went into the downstairs bathroom, and locked the door. I crumbled to the floor. I had lost Phil because I gained some weight. The bastard was going to pay. No one treated me this way and lived to tell about it. He didn't want to make love to me so I was going to ruin his life. He was mud.

I was sitting in the kitchen drinking my third cup of coffee when Phil walked into the room. He was dressed and his bags were sitting on the floor. I knew he was going back to his place. Our relationship was over and I didn't care. "Where are you going?"

"I need to go home and get some clothes, and check my mail, and plants."

"I did all of that for you, Phil. Let's get down to reality, here. You don't want me anymore because I gained some weight after always telling me that my breasts and ass were too small. Now I gained some weight in both, and you don't want to make love to me. How could you be so damn cold?"

"I'm sorry, Leann. I just need some time to rest and get over this. I do love you."

"Bullshit," I snapped. "If you did, we would have made love. I missed you for five years not once getting the chance to visit you. Did you meet someone else? Don't lie to me either."

"I didn't have time to meet women. I'm a doctor, Leann. Just give me some space."

"I think not! Get the hell out of my apartment and my life, Phil. I never want to see you again, you bastard! I spent ten years of my life with you, and this is the thanks I get for it. I thought you'd love me through thick and thin, but your words were lies. Men are dogs!"

"It's not about that. I'm just used to dating petite women. I've never dated anyone fat."

I was so angry I wanted to puke on him. "I'm not that fat. I'm still looking good for my age. How dare you be so cold to me, Phil? If you came back with a gut, and no hair, I'd still love you. It's about the person and not how they look on the outside. How many times did you tell me that? I hate you! Get the hell away from me! Where will you be working?"

"Why?" he snapped.

"So I won't visit the hospital," I snapped. I rolled my eyes at the dog.

"I don't know, Leann, and I'm seriously sorry."

"I don't need any apologizes from you. Just leave me the hell alone."

"I'm really am sorry," he said.

He picked up his bag and left. When I heard the slamming of the door I fell to the floor and wept like I had never wept in my entire life. I gave up ten years of my life for him. Men were coming after me constantly, but I said no because I was going to be faithful to my man in Paris. I could have found someone else, but did he give a damn about that? No! I changed my appearance so he didn't care anymore. Phil Thomas really didn't love me at all. The snake! He was going to pay in spades. I continued to weep hysterically.

Two days later I was sitting in my office working on a thousand-page manuscript. The $2000.00 I was charging kept me happy as I plodded along. The author wrote about relationships. I was learning a lot about what made a man tick. Men didn't like change, but who in the hell cared? Change was a part of life. I wanted to kick the author in his teeth, but I controlled the urge as I continued to type.

Beverly walked into my office a few minutes later without giving me the courtesy of knocking on the door. I looked up at her. "What's up?"

"I'm sorry I'm late but I had to recruit a new doctor. Since I'm the head nurse everything falls on my shoulders. Now I need to get to work and finish the document I was working on. I'll be in my office."

I stared at her. "Who is the new doctor?"

"A Phil Thomas," she said. "He's very handsome and had the nerve to flirt with me."

I saw red. "What?"

"He just broke up with someone because she got fat, but I was just his size. I couldn't believe the man. He was new on the job, and trying to pick me up. I turned him down, of course. I love Mel, and no other man is good enough for me."

I thought I was going to puke. The bastard was talking about me. How dare he? "Mel is a very lucky man," I said.

"Tell me about it. Phil Thomas is a dog, and he's climbing up the wrong tree."

"I feel sorry for the woman he's talking about."

"So do I. She gained too much weight for his taste, and then expected them to make love. He laughed about it. Phil turned me off fast."

"You should get to work."

"I should, and thanks."

I stared after her as I wiped my eyes. So the bastard was talking about me. I was glad no one knew that he was talking about me. Who in the hell did he think he was? Beverly worked at Ravenswood Hospital on the north side so let the games begin. In the meantime, I was going to go out with Bill who had been dying to date me because he didn't give a damn about my weight. Who did Phil think he was? I was going to make Phil's life a living hell. The bastard was going to pay. I smiled in with an evil frown.

I sat across from Bill in the restaurant. He was short and fat, forty-five and balding but still a nice, attractive man. I had no attraction to the man myself, but I needed him in my games. I took a sip of my drink. I was going to make myself drunk as a skunk because I had to sleep with him. Bill couldn't wait to get me in his bed.

"I can't believe you're finally going out with me, Leann. I've been trying to rain on your parade for the longest."

"I've been busy, Bill. It's not easy running a business, but I'm free now. I've gained some weight as you can see. Don't waste my time because of it."

"You'll always look good to me, Leann. I love you."

"I couldn't believe his words. "You don't even know me."

"I've known you since high school, so don't go there with me."

"I guess so. Thanks for being a great friend. Now let's eat and then we can go back to your place."

"You don't waste anytime. Is Phil out of the picture, and your life?"

"Of course because I've moved on," I shouted.

"He wasn't the man for you. I told you that over and over. I'm glad you finally got the message loud and clear. What would you like to eat?"

"A salad is fine," I said.

"Okay," Bill said.

An hour later, I was looking around his apartment. Bill was rich, having made major investments that paid off, and he didn't need to work. He did pro bono work at a law firm to keep himself busy.

He lived on Lake Shore Drive overlooking the beautiful water. I loved his place. Bill knew how to decorate an apartment, and his was to die for, completely done in all shades of green. I loved it. "Bill your place is to die for."

He smiled. "I'm dying to take off your clothes. Let's not waste any time, Leann. This has been a dream for me."

I smiled. "I'm not petite."

"There's more for me, Leann. Take off your clothes."

I stared into his eyes knowing he was being sincere as I slowly removed my clothes. Soon I was naked and from the way Bill was staring at me, I could tell that he was getting very hot. Phil would never look at my body but with disgust. I wanted Bill, pretending that he was Phil. "Come and get me."

Bill didn't waste anytime as he began kissing my breasts. I closed my eyes. I only saw Phil and he was giving my breasts pleasure. I didn't see Bill at all. I found myself on the floor. Bill was a mad man devouring my breasts as if he hadn't had sex in a long time.

I closed my eyes and pretended that Phil was making love to me. I was going to make love to Bill until I dropped. This was my fertile time of the month and pregnancy would be forthcoming. Phil was going to pay.

When Bill moved down to my soft area, I screamed out because I was on fire. I shouted my words of pleasure as he excited me until I collapsed. After I stopped rocking, Bill took out a condom, but I took it away from him. "I can't get pregnant because I'm on the shot. I want you inside of me with nothing between us."

Bill smiled and didn't hesitate when he entered me. I smiled as his seed exploded inside of me, knowing that my egg would be fertile. I was well aware of what I was doing. Phil, the bastard, was going to pay for hurting me. I smiled as Bill screamed out his orgasm. At least my body was finally getting some action, and the sex was fantastic.

A month later I was pregnant. I strolled into Ravenswood Hospital knowing exactly where Phil worked. Beverly was so full of information.

I left the elevator on the tenth floor and headed left, searching for Phil's office. He already had his name on the door. He was making a name for himself, the bastard, and some other woman was getting all the rewards. I knocked and walked in, not waiting for an invitation. Phil was sitting behind his desk with his eyes glued to a medical book. He was still so handsome. I cleared my throat to get his attention. "Hi."

He was surprised to see me. "What are you doing here, Leann?"

I frowned as I closed the door. What was I doing here? Did I have any pride? I was making a complete ass of myself over a man. Phillip wasn't worth it. He was because I invested a lot of time in this man, and no other woman was going to take my man. "I wanted to show you what you've been missing."

"I really don't have time for this."

"I love you," she cried.

Phil laughed. "It's not going to work. It's been five years and I am a different person now. I assumed you found another man, and that's okay by me. I didn't expect you to wait around for me. I'm getting engaged, so I don't want you coming to visit me anymore. Go somewhere else with your games."

The bastard!

"You make me sick," he declared. "Lose some weight and then maybe we can get together. I don't want to make love to a fat cow."

"You're going to pay, you bastard!"

"Don't come back here, Leann. We're over so get on with your life."

I ran to the elevator. What was wrong with me? I was so bent on revenge that I screwed up with no damn plan in mind. What in the hell was I going to do? He was engaged to another woman. I couldn't stand the pain. Something had to be done. Who was this woman? I was pregnant with Bill's child so I had to get rid of it. I didn't want any children, and especially a child from Bill. I wept all the way home.

Back at work I immediately went to Beverly's office. "Hi. What's up?"

"Are you okay? You look like shit."

"I need to get an abortion. Can you hook me up?"

Beverly was stunned.

I didn't need the look of shock on her face, but assistance. "Can you?"

"Take down this address. Can you go there tomorrow?"

"Let's just get this over with."

"Okay, I'm sorry."

"Don't be," I frowned. "I'm not equipped to become a mother. It's not in my genes."

"I know the feeling. I'll go with you."

I smiled. "Thanks. I appreciate your support."

"What are employees for?"

I smiled with her.

Three days later I wasn't pregnant any longer, and I didn't feel anything. Bill had been calling me, but I didn't want to talk to him because I felt so damn guilty. Besides I didn't know what to say to him. I had used him and I really didn't want to hurt him. If I saw Bill, I'll tell him exactly what I thought of him.

I found out that Phil was dating another nurse at the hospital, and after a few weeks he proposed to her. She was a size 2, and her name was Betty. I couldn't believe it. He didn't waste any time, the bastard! I couldn't let him get away with this. It was eating me up inside. I had given him ten years of my life, five of them waiting for him, and this was the thanks I got for it. Who did he think he was?

Finally I knew what I had to do. If I couldn't be with Phil then he wasn't going to be with anyone. I found myself sitting in the parking lot of Phil's apartment, waiting for him to leave for work. I had every intention of catching him before he got there. So far the coast was clear. I tapped my hand on the steering wheel as I waited patiently. In five minutes the bastard would be coming out. He'd never smile again, the snake! No one messed with Leann and got away with it. I was never going to be a size 6 again but Phil should have accepted me the way I am because he loved me. The cow was a liar. When he reached his car, I stepped out of my own, shutting the door. "Hi. Phil."

"What in the hell!" he shouted. "Are you stalking me, Leann? I'm going to get a restraining order."

I smiled. "I don't think so, you snake! Couldn't wait to move on to someone else, could you? How dare you talk about me behind my back? I hate you, you roach! I hope you burn in hell!"

"You're sick, Leann. Lose some weight and get a life. I'm not the man for you so just leave me alone."

"If I can't have you, Phil, then no one else will." I removed the small, black gun, and watched the shocked expression on his face.

"Are you crazy?" he shouted.

"No, you are," I pulled the trigger shooting him in the chest, making sure the silencer was on. I watched as he grabbed his chest, staring at me in shock before he fell to the ground. I smiled. No one used me, snake! I shot Phil five more times, and then I got into my car and pulled off, making sure I wasn't seen or heard. I smiled as I drove to Bill's house. I needed an alibi and some sex. I just killed a person and I couldn't believe it. I threw the gun in the river, and then headed for Bill's house. I was hoping he'd still talk to me. But Bill loved me, so I had sex when I wanted it. Bill would die for me.

"So you're finally here," Bill snapped. "I want you to leave, Leann. I love you, but I won't let women keep using me. I thought you were never coming back. We had sex, and you left. Why is that?"

I smiled. "I've been sick, Bill. I'm here now so let's talk later and get down to business, I want you."

"I don't think so. You used me."

"Bill, I'm in love with you. Let's get married."

He was stunned by my words. "Are you proposing to me? Where is Phil?"

"He's out of my life, Bill. I'm with you now. Let's make love." I began removing my clothes."

I smiled as Bill began kissing me. I grabbed his tongue and tasted it. I wanted sex badly and Bill would do for the moment. At least there was a man who loved me and being a size 16 didn't matter.

Bill was teasing my stomach and his finger was doing all the work in my private area. I closed my eyes seeing the shock on Phil's face as I shot him. I'd never forget the look on his face for as long as I lived. Revenge was so sweet. Men had to pay for hurting women. I'd have died for Phil, but he wouldn't have done the same thing for me. He was a loser and now he was a dead loser.

I felt an orgasm invading my body as I concentrated on the pleasure that Bill was giving me. I yelled out my excitement and smiled as Bill rolled on a condom and I didn't stop him. I definitely wasn't looking forward to getting pregnant again. Having an abortion wasn't any bed of roses so I wasn't about to go down that route again. I smiled at Bill. "I want you, baby, so come and get it."

He entered me and I held onto him as we rocked to the stars, getting our pleasures all over the place. Bill was a great lover and he knew how to make me come in a matter of seconds.

When we both lay spent we kissed, and my body went into madness for more pleasure. I was making love to Bill and not Phil. He was dead and buried, the bastard! I didn't feel sorry for this Betty person at all. I laughed to myself not wanting Bill to think I had lost my mind. I was beginning to think I had.

I shook as another orgasm hit me and we both shook in pleasure. It was the wee hours of the morning before I fell asleep, still seeing the shock on Phil's face. I was smiling as I slept.

Two days later I was working at my desk when Beverly burst into my office, tears streaming down her face. "Hi. What's wrong?"

"Phil's dead."

"What? I'm so sorry," I lied. "What happened?"

"A robbery gone badly," she cried. "They think Phil probably fought the thief before he was shot. The car was still there, but broken into. His wallet and keys were gone, though. He was in a coma for a day, but he lost the battle. He lost his life for material things. What a sad state of affairs. Betty is livid with rage."

I had to keep myself from smiling. "Is the case closed?"

"The police are still investigating the robbery, but they haven't found a suspect. It was if the suspect disappeared off the face of the earth. Phil was a very secretive man so they couldn't find out anything about him. He had so much potential as a doctor. What a waste!"

"I'm so sorry for you."

"Betty is the one suffering. She was going to marry him on Valentine's Day."

"But didn't he just meet her?"

"He's known her for years. She spent her vacations in Paris with him."

I had never been so stunned in my life as I stared at Beverly. "What? I thought they had just met?"

"Betty was Phil's one true love."

The snake! "I thought he was dating someone else?"

"Not that I know of," Beverly pointed out. "Betty was the only woman for him."

He used me, and I was skinny then. Why was Phil so damn cold to me? I did everything I could to keep the bastard happy. He was cheating on me the entire time. When I wanted to come to Paris to visit him he always had an excuse, and now I know why. I was glad the snake was dead. Good riddance! He didn't deserve to live.

"The funeral is on Friday. Are you going?"

I laughed to myself. "I didn't know the man."

"I want you to attend the funeral with me."

"I think not, Beverly. Funerals aren't my cup of tea."

"I was there for you, and I don't want to go alone."

"Okay, I'll go." Damn! How could I get out of this one?

I stared at Phil lying in the coffin. He looked like he was taking a nap. I smiled at him. I was alone in the room with him. "Thought you'd get away with using me, you bastard, but I had the last word. Now you're dead and gone," I smirked. "I hope you're burning in hell as your flesh is falling off, and you're screaming for mercy. You're probably a skeleton walking, you snake! No one messes with Leann and lives to tell about it."

"Who are you?"

I stared at the skinny black woman. She looked like she hadn't eaten anything in years. "I'm with Beverly, and I'm sorry for your loss."

"Thanks. I'm Betty. I can't believe he's dead. I'm still in shock."

"I know the feeling. Beverly told me you visited him in Paris."

"I spent all my vacations with him for the last five years and I took a leave of absence from my nursing job to go see him graduate," she cried. "This just can't be for real. Phil went to medical school for eight years, and now he can't even utilize his hard work. It's not fair," she cried.

"Did Phil talk about another woman in his life?"

"I was the only woman in Phil's life."

"I think not! I heard that he was dating other women when he was dating you. I don't know if it was rumored or not, but he was emailing someone, telling them how much he loved them and couldn't wait to marry them. I can let you meet the source." I smiled to myself.

"I don't think so. Phil told me that someone was stalking him because he didn't want her anymore. She had gained a lot of weight and didn't turn him on."

"That was cold," I snapped.

"I scolded him for it. If I got fat, Phil wouldn't give me the time of day. He assured me that he'd love me forever. I believed in him, but the other women were obsessed with him. At first I thought about her killing Phil. There are a lot of scorned women in prison for killing men."

I had to keep my cool because this bitch was getting on my last nerves. "I thought it was a robbery gone bad."

"It was, but the case is still open. I'm glad so the suspect can be caught and punished. Thanks for coming. The service is about to start."

I stared after her, and then I smiled at Phil. "You double bastard!" I hysterically laughed and then I screamed as he opened his eyes and put his hands around my neck. I fought for my life.

"What is going on with you?" Beverly asked, staring daggers at me.

I stared at her, and then at Phil's dead corpse. "I was just thinking about something."

"Let's take our seats."

I sat in the middle pew with Beverly. As I stared at Phil I felt his arms around my neck. He was staring at me, and then laughing. I was never going to be the same person again. Phil was going to make me pay in the grave, burning in hell. I let the tears fall as the service began. The bastard, Phil had the last laugh after all, and he was the one that betrayed me. I hysterically wept because I knew Phil was going to haunt me until my last breath! Damn!

"Carolyn is my name and I just turned 42. I work full-time and I live with a man."

"Everyone can call me Sky. I'm 42, and I'm dating a married man."

"Fantasia is my name. I'm a born again Christian."

"I guess everyone in this group is 42. I have cancer, and my name is Abby."

"I'm in an abusive relationship," Ebony cried. "If I leave my husband, I'm dead."

"Don't forget me. I'm India and I'm dating a younger man."

"What kind of cancer do you have?" Carolyn asked.

Abby looked at the pretty, but overweight woman. "I have breast cancer. It's being treated with chemotherapy to kill the cancer cells," Abby laughed. "I've been dealing with this for a year now. It's still kind of new to me."

"I'm very sorry," Sky said.

"I don't need the pity," Abby snapped. "I joined this group to forget about the issues going on with me. I need to dwell on the five of you. I'm single and having the time of my life."

"How did this happen to you?" Sky asked. "I don't mean to pressure you, but you have to know that we're going to ask questions. I do want to understand what you're going through."

Abby smiled at the pretty supermodel with the looks and the body to match. "I take the treatments twice a month for six months, maybe three to six months depending on how my body reacts. I never bothered getting a mammogram before. You need yearly mammogram checkups. She stared around the room. "I suggest anyone who hasn't taken the examination should think about making an appointment."

"This is so unreal," India said. "I have never known anyone with cancer."

Abby laughed. "Well, you do now."

"Why do you laugh about it?" Carolyn asked. "This is very serious and the leading cause of death for women."

"Thanks for the history lesson," Abby said. "Let's move on."

"She needs the laughter to get from day to day," Ebony said.

"Thank you, Ebony," Abby said.

"Well, I'm living with a man," Carolyn said, still staring at Abby. She felt so sorry for her. "I'm sinning in the eyes of God, but James has opened up so many doors for me. If he hadn't come into my life, I'd still be dragging along, depressed as hell. I'm a new woman because of James."

"How do you mean so?" Fantasia asked. "You're the caller of your own destiny."

"I've been taking care of myself for most of my life," Carolyn pointed out. "I just mean I've been out of town three times, out to different restaurants, movies, family gatherings, etc. I'm finally living my life and I have James to thank for it. Moving in with him is something that I'd never do. I've lived alone since my divorce in 1990, so this is so new to me. James gets on my nerves sometimes, but I like living with him. I'm in love with him, and that's the difference. He's ten years older than me, and thinks he knows everything. James is from another time I believe, but I can't imagine my life without him in it."

"You got it bad," India pointed out. "Men are dogs most of the time."

"So true," Carolyn agreed. "Maybe because I'm overweight I'm insecure. James likes me the way I am. He tells me I'm pretty and beautiful all the time. He also does many good things for me."

"Is he fat too?" Sky asked. "I don't mean to be offensive."

"I know," Carolyn said, staring at Sky. "He is, but he carries himself very well. James is so popular, and he loves himself. He thinks he's the king all the time. I believe God sent him to me."

"Then you should be married to him," Fantasia pointed out. "It's a sin to live with a man. I'm waiting for my Prince Charming and when God sends him to me, I'll know he's the man for me. I'm 45, and I haven't had sex in ten years. I don't miss it either."

"Wow," Ebony said. "How do you stand it?"

"I'm with God and he makes me pure. I'm into the Church."

"You're not getting any younger," Sky said. "It's time to settle down."

"That's the truth," Abby said. "My man couldn't deal with my breast cancer so he ran like a dog after a cat. So I decided to handle this crisis on my own. I believe there's a reason for this."

"That's so true," Fantasia said. "If you believe, then the cancer will magically disappear. You just have to believe that everything is going to work out all right. Maybe you're being tested for some reason. I'm sure you sinned most of your life. I did it a lot until I found Jesus."

"I made a lot of mistakes in my life," Abby cried, "but having cancer doesn't impress me. I couldn't have done anything awful enough to warrant chemotherapy. I'm vomiting most of the time, etc. it's not a pretty sight."

"I'm sorry," Carolyn said. "I can't imagine your pain."

"Let's move on," Abby said. "So you're in love with this man."

"I am," Carolyn cried. "I know he loves me, but it's difficult for me to understand that a man loves me. I've been so depressed lately, and so into my own world, I almost didn't see him coming."

"Maybe you just need to go on a diet," Fantasia said. "It's been known to work."

"I've been on plenty of diets," Carolyn snapped. "I'm going to be overweight for the rest of my life, and James understands this fact. I don't have to be petite to live in this tarnished world."

"So true," Abby said. "I have plenty of overweight friends with husbands. I'm the one that's single, thank you very much. It's really how you feel about yourself. Maybe James is in your life for a reason."

"I believe he's the one for me," Carolyn said.

"I thought the same thing with my husband," Ebony said. "Michael was the apple of my eye when I was in high school. I spotted him in the lunchroom and dreamed of him talking to me, and he did. We dated for four years and then got married right after high school... I couldn't be happier to be in love with Michael and he felt the same way about me. We had dreams; I was going to be an attorney, and he was going to be a doctor. Along the way our dreams didn't happen as quickly as we hoped they would. I'm an attorney, but when Michael flunked out of medical school he took his frustrations out on me. My man has turned into a monster."

"Do you have any children?" Abby asked.

"I have two children and they spend most of their time with my mother," Ebony cried. "I don't want them seeing their father abuse me day and night. They still love the bastard."

"I think you should tell them what's going on?" Sky said. "How old are the children?"

"Ten and sixteen," Ebony said. "I know they're old enough to understand that something is going on with their parents, but Michael will hurt them if I tell them anything. He's a nightmare waiting to happen. I even drew up papers to divorce him and he put me in the hospital for weeks. I couldn't press charges because again he threatened me and the kids."

"This is a nightmare," Fantasia said. "Something has to be done with him."

"I went to a shelter for a few days," Ebony said. "Of course Michael found me, and beat the hell out of me. I couldn't walk for days or show my face in public. I hate him!"

"Hate is a very strong word," Fantasia said. "Why did he flunk out of medical school?"

"I don't know," Ebony cried. "He didn't study or dedicate himself to it. His brothers and sisters are doctors, so he thought the medical degree was going to fall right into his lap."

"He's a sick bastard," India said. "He needs to be locked up before he kills you. I don't want anything happening to you. I just met you, and it'd be tragic."

"I dream of dying by his hands all the time," Ebony said. "I also see myself burning him in bed, or shooting him in the heart. I want to watch him die painfully by my hands."

"You need Jesus," Fantasia said. "Are you attending Church?"

"I do, sometimes," Ebony said. "I sometimes ask why this is happening to me?"

"It's not God's fault," Fantasia pointed out. "You're still alive and that's because of God. It's up to you to get yourself out of the situation because we have freedom of will."

"If only it was that simple," Ebony said. "I'm never getting married again."

"So you're just going to have sex in the meantime?" Fantasia asked.

"Right now I don't give a hell about men," Ebony shouted. "I want to start over being independent and just taking care of myself. I'm a damn good attorney and I need to get my life back."

"And you should," Carolyn said. "No man should put his hands on you. Sometimes James wants to slap me. I let him know right off the bat that if he puts his hands on me, he's going to prison. I'm going to press all the charges I can on the snake. We argue all the time because of his views."

"But you wouldn't give him up for the world," Sky said. "He's the soul mate for you."

Carolyn stared at Sky. "Are you being sarcastic with me?"

"I am in a good way," Sky said. "We complain, but the men we're talking about are still in our lives. I speak from experience because I'm dating a married man, and this has been going on for two years now. I told myself that I was going to give up on Luke, and move on. He's the center of my being, and I can't imagine my life without him in it."

Fantasia shook her head. "I'm with a group of sinful women. I think we need to bring Bibles so we can shake the Lord onto our lives. We can't survive with this sinning. If you two died today, and I'm speaking of Carolyn and Sky, then where do you think you both will be going?"

"I would hope Heaven," Carolyn said.

"I know to Heaven," Sky stated.

Fantasia shook her head. "Think again! Carolyn is living with a man without marriage; Sky is committing adultery with another woman's husband. I don't think so."

"So who made you the judge and jury," Sky snapped. "I'm going to Heaven."

"Read the Bible," Fantasia cried. "I've been there and done that. I'm a born again Christian."

"Are you in a relationship?" India asked.

"I was, but Benny didn't want to wait until we were married," Fantasia pointed out. "I told him to get lost."

"There aren't a lot of men out there for us," Carolyn said. "I can't wait around for someone to find me. James is the only man for me. I know he's the one for me because my life is so different. I used to be boring as sin. I have more confidence in myself."

"It's not going to work if you don't believe in yourself," Abby said. "You need to live for you."

"That's the truth," India said. "My man is 27 years old, and I'm 42."

Silence took over the room as everyone stared at India. She ignored the stares and walked over to the buffet table. "I'm going to get some pizza," she cried. "Why is everyone staring at me? I'm in love with Keith, and he feels the same way about me. Age is only a number."

"Is he mature for his age?" Carolyn asked. "James thinks I'm immature the way he talks to me. He's twelve years older and he thinks he can teach me things, and direct my path. The man doesn't have a clue."

"I don't use my age with Keith," India said. "I let him be the man he is and vice versa."

"Why did you date a younger man?" Fantasia asked. "There are plenty of men out there our age, and older. Carolyn is proof of that."

Carolyn rolled her eyes at Fantasia.

"So true, but I've dated men my own age, and much older," India said. "The men my age are looking for women under 25, and the older men are too set in their ways. With Keith, we compliment each other all over the place. It's a great relationship."

"How long have you been dating him?" Abby asked.

"Three years now," India said.

"And you two aren't married," Fantasia cried, shaking her head.

"Not at the moment," India said. "Keith is anxious to marry me, but I need to be sure. I do love this man, but I have to make sure that I want to spend the rest of my life with him. He doesn't want to move in with me because he has done that route before."

"He's a very sensible man," Fantasia said. "Living together will only make things worse."

"How so," Carolyn said. "James and I are having a great time."

"It won't last because it's wrong," Fantasia said. "Two wrongs don't make it right."

"Whatever!" Carolyn shouted. "James and I share a nice apartment, and we split the rent. There's no way I'm going to kick him out because I don't want to sin. Are you going to help me pay my bills? James is going to marry me when the time is right. He's talking about it all the time."

"We're not here to judge anyone," Ebony said. "I'm hurting all over the place."

"You need to leave that man," Fantasia said. "Why don't you come and live with me? I have a house my parents rent to me, and it's big. You and your children can live there for as long as you wish. I'll charge rent, of course, but it will be the solution for you. Your husband will never find you at my place."

Everyone stared at Fantasia.

"Are you serious?" Ebony asked. "I really don't want to get you involved."

"I have a lot of people at the church that can assist you," Fantasia said. "Your pain is over from your husband. He has to seek help before he kills you or someone else."

"Let me think about it," Ebony said. "Thank you."

"You also need to talk to your children," Sky said. "They need to know what's going on. I'm glad he doesn't abuse them."

"It's just me he can't stand," Ebony cried. "I've been there for my husband. I even encouraged him to study. I graded him on tests, etc. The man has no reason to be so abusive to me."

"He's a sick puppy dog," India cried. "I bet he wouldn't abuse a bunch of men."

"Of course not," Carolyn said. "I wish we could get together ten men and give Ebony's husband a taste of his own medicine. I bet after they got through with him, he wouldn't abuse his wife, or anyone for that matter."

"Vengeance is for the Lord," Fantasia said. "Ebony's husband will reap the benefits of his actions."

"Whatever," Carolyn said. "I just want him to get his a little earlier."

"I have to do something," Ebony cried. "The devil wants me to kill him."

"Don't let the devil win this round," Fantasia said. "We all need to bow our head and pray for Ebony and her sick husband."

"Let's hold hands," Carolyn said.

Everyone held hands and bowed their heads as Fantasia began praying. **"Lord we come here today for your guidance with Ebony and the rest of us. Ebony is more in need of your assistance. We need to pray for her husband and fix his mind so he can stop abusing his wife who loves him more than anything. We need to give Ebony the** *strength to walk away from the situation before she gets hurt. The six of us pray for Ebony's situation and our lives as well. Please forgive our sins, and bless the people who are less fortunate than we are. I accept these blessing from You in the name of the Father, the Son, and the Holy Ghost, in Jesus' Name. Amen!"*

"Amen," Ebony cried.

"Amen," Carolyn stated.

"Amen," Sky confessed.

"Amen," Abby whispered.

"Amen," India declared.

"Thank you all," Ebony cried. "I just might take you up on your offer, Fantasia. But I still need my privacy with my children. I can't have you telling me what to do, and looking down your nose at me."

"That's not going to happen," Fantasia snapped. "I resent your attitude about me. You and your family can move into the gatehouse, which are miles away from the house. It has five bedrooms, two bathrooms, etc. You're going to love it. I'm going to give you my information, and then you can call me when you're ready to take a look at it. Your husband will never find out. I live in the boondocks."

"It sounds like a blessing to me," Carolyn said. "I think God just answered your prayers with Fantasia."

"I agree," Abby said. "God is good. I feel so blessed right now."

"I will talk to my children and then take a look at your place," Ebony said.

"Okay," Fantasia said. "Call me when you're ready. I'll give you my cell phone number. I've been searching for someone to rent out the gatehouse. Now my dreams have just come true."

"For everyone," India said.

A week later the six women met again in the Hilton Hotel. Everyone grabbed a plate for a slice of pizza on this Friday evening.

"I just love pizza," Abby said. "How is everyone doing? I had an awful week with the chemo, but I feel very alive right now."

"Is that okay for you to eat?" Sky said.

Abby shook her head. "After throwing up all day, I'm hungry as hell."

"As sin," Fantasia corrected. "I want to read a few chapters of Psalms before we begin. Is that okay with everyone?"

"Do we have a choice?" India stated with an attitude.

"I don't think we do," Abby said. "Let's bow our heads and listen."

Fantasia started reading, sending up a prayer for India. The 27th chapter of Psalm was my favorite.

"Psalm 27: The lord is my light and my salvation who should I fear? The Lord is the strength of my life, of whom should I be afraid. When the wicked came against me to eat up my flesh, my enemies and foes, they stumbled and fell. Though an army this I will be confident. One thing I have desired of the Lord, that will I seek, that I may dwell in the house of the Lord all the days of my life, to behold the beauty of the Lord and to inquire in His temple. For in the time of trouble He shall hide me in His pavilion; in the secret place of His tabernacle. He shall hide me; He shall set me high upon a rock. And now my head shall be lifted up above my enemies all around me; therefore I will offer sacrifices of joy in His tabernacle; I will sing, yes I will sing praises to the Lord. Hear, O Lord, when I cry with my voice! Have mercy also upon me, and answer me. When You said, Seek My Face, my heart said to You, Your face, Lord, I will seek. Do not hide Your face from me; do not turn Your servant away in anger; You have been my help; do not leave me nor forsake me, O God of my salvation. When my father and my mother forsake me, then the Lord will take care of me. Teach me Your way, O Lord, and lead me in a smooth path because of my enemies. Do not deliver me to the will of my adversaries; for false witnesses have risen against me, and such as breathe out violence. I would have lost heart unless I had believed that I would see the goodness of the Lord in the land of the living. Wait on the Lord; be of good courage, and He shall strength your heart; wait, I say on the Lord!

"Amen," Fantasia cried.

"Amen," Carolyn praised.

"Amen," Sky said.

"Amen," Ebony confessed.

"Amen," Abby cried.

"Amen," India replied.

"I'm pleased to report that I'm now living in the gate house," Ebony cried. "I left my husband when he left the house for hours. I'm happy to be living in my own house."

"So am I," Fantasia said. "How are the children doing?"

"It's going to take some time for them to adjust," Ebony said. "They still love their father."

"I agree," India said. "They're children for heaven sakes."

"James wants to marry me," Carolyn cried. "We're going to search for rings very soon."

"I'm glad to hear that," Fantasia cried. "Is there any more good news?"

"I might marry my man too," India said. "Keith is begging me to marry him."

"This is wonderful news," Fantasia said. "I believe prayers work."

"Especially when more than one person prays," Carolyn pointed out. "I do want to marry James, but sometimes I think about his ways. He treats me like one of his sons, or something near it. The other day he said that I was disobedient to him."

"No he didn't," Abby cried. "How did you respond to that?"

"I looked at him as if he was crazy," Carolyn said. "I also told him that I was a grown woman. He had lost his demented mind. This is the reason why I don't want to marry him. I bought a sofa and table for the living room, and he didn't approve, of course. James doesn't care if we have any furniture in our living room for months. I couldn't stand sitting on the floor. I went against his wishes and he never let's me forget it."

"He's a character," Sky said. "I don't know if I'd want to marry someone like him."

"Everyone can't be perfect," Fantasia pointed out. "You have to dwell on the good things about James. What attracted you to the man? The fact that you love him and want to spend the duration of your life with him sounds like a plan to me. I don't see anything wrong with that."

"And you wouldn't" India pointed out. "Make sure you tie the knot because that's the only reason to date."

"Which is the right thing to do," Fantasia replied. "I do want to go to Heaven."

"Is there a Heaven?" Abby asked. "I wonder sometimes."

"Then you need to take your butt to church," Fantasia said. "There is a Heaven. I have plenty of books on the subject and I'm going to bring one to you. God is just waiting for the holy ones to join him."

"I do go to church," Abby replied defensively. "I just haven't had the energy lately."

"You look beautiful to me," Sky said.

Abby smiled. "Thank God for that. It has been a constant battle for me."

"Where is your family?" Sky asked.

"My parents and two siblings are always around," Abby confirmed. "They get on my nerves most of the time, believe me. I love them, but they think I'm going to die in my sleep. I need to be alone sometime. I'm okay right now. I'm going to have another slice of pizza."

"So will I," India said. "I'm hungry for some reason."

"I hope you're not pregnant," Fantasia said.

India rolled her eyes at Fantasia. "I don't think so because I'm on the patch. I'm not taking any chances on ruining my life with a baby. I admit that I'm over the hill. Keith and I just want to make our dreams come true, and live happily ever after. We don't have the time to worry about children."

"I agree," Carolyn said. "My daughter is grown, and so are James' children. He had the nerve the other day to inform me that he wanted to have a baby by me. I laughed so hard it wasn't funny. I'm not having any more children. My daughter was hell on wheels."

"I want to have my man's baby," Sky said.

"Now that would definitely complicate the triangle you're in," India said. "Is he going to leave his wife for you?"

"He loves the both of us," Sky said. "I do understand his point. I remember when I was in love with two men at the same time. Dale and John were the men of my dreams. I couldn't let either one of them go. When they found out about each other, they both left me."

"Torn between two lovers," Carolyn cried.

"Boy wasn't I torn," Sky laughed. "Dale was good in bed, and John paid all my bills for me. Why would I get rid of both of them because I had both worlds so to speak?"

"Who do you miss the most?" Abby asked.

Sky laughed. "I miss them both because I had good sex. I spent my money on me, and not my bills. I'd have played with the two of them for a very long time. I had no intention of ending my relationship with Dale or John. I think John was more in love with me which is why he paid all my bills."

"That would be nice," Carolyn said. "James doesn't do that much for me. If he does, I most certainly have to pay him back."

"Then why are you with him?" Ebony said.

"She doesn't have any confidence in herself?" India said. "She thinks because she's overweight she has to take the first man that comes along. She doesn't realize that she's a beautiful woman."

Carolyn frowned. "I think James is the man for me."

"How do we really know?" Abby asked. "I remember dating a lot of losers, and every one of them I believed was my mate in life."

"But you found out that they weren't," Fantasia said. "You found out that they aren't the ones for you. God will find a way, but you can't ignore His warnings, thank you very much. Sometimes the warning signs are so evident."

"So true," India said. "I think my younger lover is the stud for me."

"Have you met his friends, and family?" Abby asked.

"I met his father, and he's in love with me. His mother is going to take some work."

"I guess so," Ebony laughed. "You're practically his mother's age."

"Thanks a lot," India cried. "I just love him, and he loves me."

"And love makes the world go round," Carolyn said. "I didn't believe love was ever going to happen to me. I read romance novels, and listened to family and friends and the men in their lives. And then one day at work, along comes James. I can't believe he wants me."

"You need more confidence in yourself," Fantasia said. "Lose the weight if you're not happy, but if not, love yourself. Happiness isn't being skinny. I've never been married, and I'm a size 6."

"I second that motion," India said. "I think you should reassure this man, and be grateful. Men can't be perfect all the time, and we can't have everything. My man gets on my nerves at times. I sometimes forget that he's only 27. I have to stumble down to his level at times."

"The price you pay for love," Fantasia cried.

"But it's all worth it," India said.

"I agree," Carolyn said. "I've been lonely for a very long time. I had this one friend who was a good friend to me, but he wanted to be more than friends. I didn't have enough confidence in myself to believe that I could be with him. Jeff was white, and he needed a more glamorous woman on his arm. We're still good friends, but that's all. James understands me."

"I can't wait for the wedding," Abby said.

Carolyn smiled. "Me either. I think James and I will go to City Hall, and probably out to dinner with a few close friends and family. We're not going to make a big deal about it. I can't see myself walking down the aisle. I just can't picture it."

"Me either," India said. "I told Keith that if we jumped the broom, City Hall would be fine with me."

"I always wanted to get married in Las Vegas," Carolyn pointed out. "Now that would be nice."

"I agree," Fantasia said. "I just want it to happen. If he doesn't marry you, then it's time to move on. James wasn't the man for you, and you're wasting your time when your dreamboat is right around the corner."

"He's going to marry me," Carolyn snapped. "I'm not about to kick him to the curb. James has opened up wonderful doors for me. I love him, and I know he loves me."

"Then wait for your man, and pray," Fantasia said. "Marriage is the right step."

"I've done it before," Carolyn said. "I do know how I am. Have you, Fantasia?"

"No, but that doesn't mean I don't dream about it happening to me," Fantasia said. "I know when he comes to me I'm going to be ready for him."

"We're not having any sex," Carolyn pointed out. "This was James' idea, of course."

"He can't get it up," Abby said. "He probably needs Viagra."

Carolyn frowned at Abby. "He satisfies me in every way."

"I had this sixty year old man once," Abby said. "He had the nerve to proposition me. I gave him the time of day, and he proved me wrong. The man was so energized I got exhausted. He pumped me for days on end. I had to admire him for his stamina. He made me look like a damn fool. I found out later he used Viagra. He probably took six or seven of them. I can't tell you how many times he licked me."

"So gross," Fantasia cried. "The man had no shame."

"He wasn't dead," Abby laughed. "He gave me five or ten orgasms."

"You go girl," Sky cried.

"Right on," Ebony said. "Michael and I used to make perfect love, but after he left school, he just pounced on me until he got his, and then rolled off. I hadn't made love in a long time."

"It's not the end of the world," Fantasia said. "Just think about going to Heaven because you haven't sinned is a price to pay."

"We know," Abby said.

"I've spent a wonderful day with my man," Sky said. "I got a lovely manicure and pedicure and he joined me. Then we got something to eat, just talking about everything. I got to know more about my man than ever."

"Does he mention his wife and family?" Ebony asked.

"Just the fact that he's not getting along with his wife," Sky said.

"They all lie like that," Fantasia pointed out. "I bet he's having a grand time with his wife, and then with you because the mistress is always the most kinky, of course. Your man has his cake and eats it too, and it's frosty as sin."

"I know the game," Sky said. "How can I complain?"

"But you can have any man you want, Sky," Carolyn said. "I don't understand."

"Being skinny isn't the road to finding my soul mate," Sky said. "I've been dumped so many times, not to mention cheated on, that I've lost count. Men are dogs to everyone. I fell in love so many times, I lost count."

"So your relationship with the married man is safe," India said.

"I don't have to count on anything," Sky said. "I know my logic is probably stupid, but these are my actions. I can't fall hopelessly in love with him because he has a wife. I don't have to have his children because he has two. I just don't want the complications."

"I do understand your logic," Carolyn said. "Will you be okay if he ends the affair and stays with his wife?"

"I might be angry and hurt," Sky said. "I'm only human, but when I think about him making love to his wife, then I feel the anger. I'm going to move on, but the experience would have been worth it.

I'm not expecting anything to last forever. I'm in this relationship for as long as it lasts. If it lasts forever, then I'm blessed."

"Wrong word," Fantasia said. "You can't be blessed when you're committing adultery."

"I know," Sky said. "I want to be free, but he makes me feel so good. I'm sick of the dating game."

"I hear ya," Abby said. "I met someone the other day and he had the same line as most of them. You're the most beautiful woman in the world; where have you been all my life; I'm going to rock your world and then some. I laughed so hard I almost had an accident."

"That is so funny," Ebony said. "Men are so dense."

"All the time," Carolyn said. "James is not in that bunch, of course. All women are dense to him."

"He's a character," India said. "I'd like to meet him. What does he do for a living?"

"He's retired from CTA," Carolyn said. "But he's a hustler, meaning he doesn't sit around and do nothing. He's driving cabs, and on the selling wagon. My man knows how to make money. He makes more money than me and I have a job. He also used to be a playboy; he doesn't like rules, but to make his own. James is definitely a character."

"Is he a lot of fun?" Sky asked.

Carolyn smiled. "He is, very much so. We have so much fun together. He makes me smile. When I'm in the room with him, I smile all the time. Even when he comes into my presence, I smile. What does that mean?"

"You're in love," India said. "I do know the feeling, believe me."

"I do too," Sky said.

"Does he feel the same way about you?" Fantasia inquired.

"I think he does," Carolyn said. "He smiles at me, and does things for me. From time to time he will tell me that he loves me. I'm shocked when I hear the words. I never thought I'd hear those words ever again. The other day he told me that he liked living with me, and we should get married. I asked him where the ring was."

"He sounds like fun," Abby said. "He has two sons?"

"That I know of," Carolyn laughed. "James was the playboy stud in his time."

"Have you met his family?" Ebony said.

"I have," Carolyn said, "his neighbors, and etc."

"You might have found your mate," India said.

"You just need the ring and the marriage license," Fantasia said.

"Whatever!" Carolyn laughed. "I need some wine."

"How is everything going with you, Ebony?" Abby asked. "Is your husband searching for you?"

"I'm sure he is," Ebony said. "He doesn't like to lose, but he won't ever find me."

"That's for sure," Fantasia said. "I have bodyguards watching the gate house."

"You're a very important person," Abby said.

"I just know the right people," Fantasia said. "The bodyguards are ushers and deacons from the church."

"I'm in good hands," Ebony said. "My husband isn't aware of this club, so he won't be able to find me. I think I'm going to be okay."

"What about your work?" Carolyn asked.

"The police are aware of the situation," Ebony said. "If he shows up then he's going to be arrested. They have his picture all over the building. He's not going to ruin this for me."

"I'm glad I could assist," Fantasia said. "I knew this was going to be a great group"

"I agree," Abby said. "The five of you are so nice."

"I try," Sky said.

"This is going to be a great group," India said.

"I agree," Ebony said. "My life has changed for the better because of this group. My children and I are so grateful."

"We have to keep you around for a long time with us," Fantasia pointed out. "Let's all pray."

The group of six women bowed their heads in prayer.

Another Friday rolled around and the six women assembled for their group meeting at the Hilton Hotel.

"I just found out that it's going to take me a while to get married," Carolyn pointed out. "James is in the process of getting a divorce. I didn't know he was still married."

"My married man's wife came to see me," Sky said. "I had never been so frightened in my life. I didn't know she knew anything about us."

"I think I might have met my husband in church," Fantasia said. "I'm the head of my choir and I'm thinking about going to divinity school. I want to learn about the Bible, and preach throughout the world."

"I fell out the other day and I've been in the hospital for a week," Abby said. "My cancer is back."

"I think my husband is following me," Ebony cried. "I hope he hasn't found me because I'll be dead."

"My man has a baby by another woman," India said. "Now I have to deal with the baby momma's drama."

Silence took over the room as all six women prayed.

I tiptoed quietly because I didn't want the culprits to run. If he thought he was going to get away with this, he was losing his mind. What came out in the dark was going to come out in the light, the bastard!

I reached the office door and counted to ten as I listened to the moaning inside. Sethie swore to me that he was done with the bitch, but he was still banging the whore from hell. When was he going to leave her alone and concentrate on his loving marriage? I was sick and tired of having my marriage threatened by the likes of Gracie Jones. Obviously my husband couldn't get enough of her.

I quietly pushed opened the door, seeing the two of them lying on the desk, naked and pumping like the world was about to end and they wanted to get their last orgasm out of the way. I should have shot them both in the head, but going to prison for two sluts wasn't my idea of fun. I had been sleeping around lately to prove that I was still desirable to the opposite sex. Sethie wasn't the only one who could get his groove on.

I burst into the room, watching them spring apart. Little did they know that I had hidden cameras taping everything? I was going to have a field day in court as I cleaned out Sethie's pocketbook. I hoped this bitch was worth it.

"What in the hell are you doing here, Tanya?" Sethie snapped. "I moved out of the house, so I'm free to sleep with whoever I want to sleep with. I've been in love with Gracie for a very long time. I'm going to divorce you so fast you won't remember your own name."

I laughed at the two of them. The bitch was scared because she thought I had a gun in my purse. I decided to make the bitch suffer for sleeping with my husband. I reached into my purse. "I should kill the both of you in cold blood," I snapped. "This bitch has been a thorn in my side since the day I met you."

"Please don't kill me," Gracie cried. "I told Sethie I didn't want to do it in his office, but he wouldn't listen to me. I'm sorry for hurting you, and if you let me live, then I'll never bother Sethie again. You can have the man because I'm moving on with my life."

I laughed again. "Don't talk to me, bitch. I'm going to file for divorce and I'm going to take you for everything you got, you bastard! When I finish with your ass, you'll have nothing left, and Gracie will leave your ass. You're going to pay for hurting me."

I stared daggers at the two of them before I hurried out of the office. This time I had no tears. They were going to pay when I retrieved the evidence. I was sick and tired of men, and wished I liked women, but that was out of the question. I needed a man. I hurried to my car and drove off. It was time to take matters into my own hands.

A few days later I stared at my attorney, Heff Johnson. He was black, tall, and gorgeous, and I couldn't wait to get this over with. Lance had won all his cases, and I was ready to win. Sethie was going to wish he had never been born when I sucked up all of his money.

"Tanya, you know this evidence might not be admissible in court," Heff said. "I know this is a divorce case, so I might be able to let it slide. Your husband just decided that he doesn't want to divorce you. He thinks its better staying married to you for some reason."

I was flabbergasted. "The bastard doesn't want to divorce me because he knows I'm going to burn his ass in court. I can't believe this is happening to me. I want a divorce and he wants one too. Why is he deliberately trying to ruin my life? I hate the man."

"I tried getting him to sign, but he wouldn't come to any terms," Heff says. "I'm sure his attorney told him to do this. She's pretty good with divorces. He's probably sleeping with Brenda, so that would help if I can prove it in court."

I stared at him. "Sethie is a dog in heat, but every time I catch him sleeping around, he's with this Gracie bitch. Why can't he just leave the bitch alone? I'm so sick of her I wish I could shoot her in the heart and get away with it. If the bitch was dead, my life will be much better off."

"I'm afraid Gracie is three months pregnant with your husband's child, so she's going to be in his life for the duration. Sethie's attorney came up with an out of court settlement plan that will expedite a divorce. He wants the house, and the kids, and no alimony."

I stood up, almost knocking the chair down as I paced the office. "The bastard should be shot. He has cheated on me left and right, and he has the audacity to demand anything," I shouted. "I'm going to kill the bastard in cold blood, and then I'm going to get away with it."

"I can't hear those words as your attorney," Heff said. "I know there's an attorney-client privilege here, Tanya, but if I think you're threatening another human, then I have a duty to speak up, which is called exception to the rule. Please don't say these words to me."

"I'm sorry," I cried. "Does he actually think I'm going to give him my children?" I snapped. "I think Sethie has gone insane or something. There's no way I'm going to agree to his terms. Why is he so stupid? If he's free, then he can fuck whoever turns his head. I just want him out of my life and my house."

"Then we're going to court in two weeks because this is going to be a messy divorce. I want you to give me the names of anyone who can be a witness for you. I need someone who knows Sethie and can prove he's had affairs as well a few friends who can attest to your character."

I shook my head because that wasn't possible. I could use Miguel maybe, but I slept with him once. Vicky was my best friend, but no longer. What am I going to do? I need witnesses, but I don't have anyone to help me.

"This is bad," Lance said. "As I look at the witness list, Vicky is going to testify on her brother's behalf, and her testimony alone is going to be very damaging. Did you know she's pregnant with Miguel's child? I can't believe the web you've woven in your lives."

I shook my head again. "Get the tapes admitted into evidence because the judge will see that Sethie is a lying cheat, and then I can get my divorce. I just want to move on with my life. I have tapes to prove that he's sleeping around. Do you have any evidence on his attorney?"

"My paralegal is working on the dirt, but we really don't have a case without any witnesses. I was thinking about talking to Miguel. I know you slept with him only once, but in the state of mind that you were in, this could go in our favor. Miguel could also prove that you were very upset by Sethie's actions."

I smiled for the first time, and then sat down because I was getting dizzy with all the pacing back and forth. "I can't believe Vicky is pregnant by him, but if that's the case, then he has no choice but to be on Sethie's side. He's not going to ruin his relationship with Vicky."

"Then we're back to square one," Heff said. "Sethie is banking on not giving you anything. He wants you to walk away from this marriage with the clothes on your back. The man is certifiable, if you ask me. I can't stand the sight of men like him who does not believe that he should account for his actions."

I was in agreement. Sethie was acting like I was the bad penny, when he was the one sleeping around all over the place. This wasn't fair to me, thank you very much. I couldn't let him win. There was no way my children were going to live with him. They loved me.

"Heff, you're the best attorney in the world, and I know you can work this out for me. If I have to play dirty to win this case, then I'm going to do it. I know you can hire actors, who can pretend to have known me for a very long time, so let's do it. I read once that you played real dirty to win a case, but the prosecution could never prove it. I know your antics so use them for me."

"I don't play that way with divorce cases," Heff snapped. "Your husband just wants you to sign the papers and not clean him out of his money. You can get a nice settlement and never have to work again. As for the children, they want to live with you, so he has no say on that one. They're old enough to have an opinion."

"Thank God I don't have to fight him for the children, but I'm not signing any papers," I snapped. "Sethie is the one who abused our marriage, and he's not going to walk away free as a bird to live with his slut of a girlfriend, happily ever after. I'd have to begin all over again and there's something wrong with that picture. I want to win more than I want to eat."

"Then we're going to have to get dirty and nasty," Heff said. "I think I might have some moves up my sleeves. I'm going to have a conference with Brenda because she doesn't want us to go to court. She has a new agreement. I'm going to discuss it with her and then call you back."

"Don't let her win," I snapped. "I don't know this Brenda, but I've heard about her reputation, believe me. The two of you can be enemies in court, and I can't wait to watch, but I don't want to suffer in the process. My children are very upset that Sethie moved out of the house. This isn't easy for them."

"I'll get back with you in a few days, but I must get to court, Tanya. I have other cases to deal with, but yours is at the top of my list. Don't have any communication with Sethie, because he's taking notes. Let the kids meet him outside."

"If I set eyes on the snake, I'm going to lose my mind, thank you very much. I can't stand the sight of the man and don't know why I wanted to save my marriage. The man is a pain in my ass, and I can't believe he's turning this against me as if he caught me in bed. I confessed to being with Miguel because I was trying to save Vicky's life. Miguel is just someone passing through and I didn't want her getting hurt."

"Miguel is living in Chicago now and working at a restaurant to pay his way through law school so he's not going anywhere. I think the man is going to make something out of his life. I'm surprised by his moves, but he wants a steady career goal."

I was flabbergasted this time. Who would have thought that Miguel would turn his life around? Why in the world did he want to become an attorney? I smiled to myself for some reason. I always thought the man had more potential than working for Sethie's father. More power to him. "What restaurant?"

"The Loop, downtown on Michigan Avenue," Heff said. "He works the four to midnight shifts because he goes to school in the morning. He has really made a change in his life. He's going to be a father, so he has no choice in the matter. I don't think they're getting married."

I stood up. "I have another appointment. I hope you have some good news to give me after you talk to Brenda. Present the proposal to my husband again and get him to sign it. If he thinks I'm going to ruin his reputation, he might just sign the papers."

"Stay out of trouble, Tanya. I don't want you going anywhere near Sethie or Gracie. She's not going to disappear. She's pregnant with his child. We might wind up doing a DNA test if this goes to court. I can't bail you out of jail or anything worse."

I nodded, smiled, and left his office. So Miguel was getting on with his life. I was hungry all of a sudden, and I couldn't wait to eat. It was after four so Miguel should be at work. My attorney didn't tell me I couldn't go and get something to eat. I left the building with a smile on my face.

I walked into the restaurant searching for Miguel. Of course I found him. He was so appealing who could miss him. He was taking an order at and I hurried to grab an empty table near him. I hid behind the menu, staring at Miguel. He was still dark, tall, and very handsome. Although he was Hispanic, he still had a very nice tan. I concentrated on the menu, wondering why my heart was beating so fast.

"Can I take your order? The specials are rib tips and ribs. They're finger licking good. We also have a special wine that tastes wonderful with ribs."

I moved the menu and smiled at the handsome man. "Hi, Miguel. Fancy meeting you here." I smiled. "I have to say you haven't changed a bit, and you look handsome as ever. I think I'll have a salad and diet coke for now, and maybe some wine later on. Are you okay?"

"What are you doing here Tanya? I'm trying to move on with my life and get on with it. I'm sorry I even met you or Vicky for that matter. I'm in love with her and she doesn't give a damn about me. She's pregnant with my child, and lied and told me it was someone else's child. I know it's mine."

I shook my head. "Vicky has been known to sleep around, so you should have a test run to make sure. Why don't you sit down and talk to me? I can't believe you're going to law school. I think it's wonderful, Miguel. You're so good with your hands, and now you can use your mind. I still think about the one night stand we had, and my body still gets hot."

"Are you daring to flirt with me?" he snapped. "I think you and Sethie belong together because you both are mad as hell. Insanity comes to mind," he whispered. "I hope my baby isn't demented like Vicky and her brother. I think you're better off."

"You're causing a scene, Miguel, so please take a load off. I wouldn't want you getting fired because of me. I'm not insane at all. My husband sleeps around, and then he blames me for it. He has been sleeping around since I met him, and I did it once, and he's ready to ridicule me."

Miguel sat down. "The man has no scruples, and you should be glad to divorce him. Get it over with, and move on with your life. Tanya, you're a gorgeous woman and I loved making love to you. There's so much passion in you, and you need a man to bring it out."

"Would you like to take me home and have your way with me?" I asked hopefully. "I just want to feel your arms around me, and you inside of me, Miguel. I'm not going to hurt you, or make you testify at my divorce. I just want to make love to a handsome man. I need you."

"I'll meet you at midnight at my hotel," Miguel said. "I know I'm stupid for getting involved with you again, but I want you as much as you want me. Here's my key. Let me in when I knock. Be ready for me because I'm going to rock your world and then some."

I didn't think it was going to be this easy to seduce Miguel, but I was still hot, of course. I reached for the key as the electricity touched me, and I smiled. "Get me something fattening because I'm going to need all my energy to deal with the likes of such a handsome man."

He smiled and went toward the back. I smiled after him. I never thought that I'd be sleeping with Miguel again. I never stopped thinking about him and the way he made me feel when he made love to me. It was something very special, and Miguel was a pro. I couldn't wait to get him into bed.

At the hotel, I showered and then perfumed my body from head to toe. I smelled so good even I wanted me. The hotel was nice, but not expensive. Miguel was going to make lots of money one day, but he wasn't there yet. I had deep faith in him.

I got into bed in my naked glory and covered up for the time being. I needed a drink, but I couldn't find anything in the refrigerator. I couldn't wait for Miguel to walk in and get a glimpse of my naked body. He was going to get hard just looking at me. I couldn't wait. I had two hours to kill so I was going to take a nap. I was so stressed out with my problems, I needed the release.

Someone was kissing me, and at first, I thought I was in a dream or something. The kisses started at my neck, and then moved down to my breasts, exciting both of them before moving down to my stomach. He played with my belly button, and the kisses continued moving lower.

I smiled to myself as I moaned. The kisses were exciting me all over the place, and I wasn't about to open my eyes because I wanted the sensations to continue. I was about to explode with excitement. My nipples were at attention as he played with my left breast and moved to the right one. I screamed out when he bit one of my nipples, but it wasn't in pain, it was pleasure all over the place.

I opened my eyes to see a naked man. At first I couldn't focus on him, and then when he began kissing my lips, I knew he was the man for me. It was Miguel. I started to move, but he shook his head, and I stayed still. We kissed again and it was the most passionate kiss in the world.

My body was so hot; I thought I would die from the heat. I had never felt this hot before. Miguel stopped kissing my lips and moved onto my belly button again, playing with it for a while, and then he kept on kissing me until he reached my private area. I grasped because his hot tongue sent my privacy into a fire of electricity and then some.

Miguel guided his tongue right on my g-spot and I screamed out as my body spun out of control. His tongue sent chills of pleasure down my spine, not to mention a tickle feeling. I was about to have an orgasm, and it was just too fast for me.

It usually took me a long time to come, and sometimes I just faked it to make Sethie happy. This time I didn't have to fake anything because my body was just waiting to explode. I wanted this feeling of power to last, but the way Miguel's tongue was working on my g-spot, I knew it was only a matter of time before I climaxed.

I kept screaming until my body went into a sexual spasm. I yelled with passion as my body shook with thrills of sexual energy. Miguel kissed my lips, and the sensations continued. I was so suffo- cated with heat; I needed some water to cool me down.

Finally my body rocked. Miguel was so hot with all the pleas- ure that I was receiving that he instantly entered me. I can't remember if he put on a condom or not, but I didn't care because he was large, and the pain was perfect. He pumped, and I rocked with him, and it didn't take long for Miguel to burst his seed. He instantly spread his juices inside of me and I knew he wasn't wearing a condom. I let his pleasure continue as I rocked from another powerful orgasm. The two of us were magic together, and this time it was better than anything before. Miguel finally lay spent, staring into my hazel eyes as I stared into his gorgeous black eyes. We understood each other, without a word spoken, and then our lips met again. I was ready to make more love with Miguel for the rest of the night.

This time he had other ideas as he turned me over on my stom- ach and had his way with me again. This way of making love was very painful, but Miguel knew how to stop the pain by making sure I had multiple orgasms, so I rode with the program.

Why didn't I insist that we used a condom? I don't know what was messing with my mind at the time. I wanted to feel Miguel inside of me. Maybe deep down I wanted a baby by him. Did this have anything to do with Vicky? I was probably jealous of her being pregnant by Miguel. I knew it was his baby because he didn't sleep around. I made sure he was inside of me as we pumped for the rest of the night and then some. Something deep inside of me wanted to be pregnant, and if it happened, then my life was definitely going to change. After hours of lovemaking, we closed our eyes, wrapped in each other arms. This was the life.

The banging on the door woke me up from a peaceful dream. Denzel Washington was taking me into his arms, getting ready to propose to me. I knew I had died and gone to heaven as I looked into his eyes. I was going to be the next Mrs. Denzel Washington. The banging continued. I peeped at Miguel and he was snoring all over the place.

I searched for his shirt, and slipped into it as I walked to the door. "Who is it?" I didn't even know what time it was, but I couldn't believe that someone would be knocking on the door now. It had to be early in the morning because Miguel and I made love for the rest of the night. I felt my life was going out of control.

"Who is it?" I asked again. I knew it couldn't be the hotel staff because Miguel was living here on a permanent basis. I looked through the peephole and almost fell out. It was Vicky! What in the hell was she doing here? I couldn't believe this.

She continued to knock. I took a deep breath and opened the door. The shock on Vicky's face was priceless as she stared at me.

Vicky burst into the room. I hurriedly shut the door because I didn't want to start any trouble. We eyed each other warily. I could tell that Vicky was pregnant because she was sticking out, and her face was fatter. She was even putting on some weight, and Vicky was always skinny.

"What are you doing here?" Vicky snapped. "I came here to talk to my baby's father, and you're sleeping with him. I thought it was just a one-night stand, but I should have known you had the hots for my man. I can't believe you let a man ruin our friendship."

"You did that all by yourself, Vicky," I snapped. "Don't you dare turn this around on me? I was trying to make my marriage work, but you didn't give a damn about that. You kept telling Sethie that I wasn't the woman for him. Where were you when he was still sleeping with Gracie? I caught them together, and it made me sick. She's pregnant too."

"I told Sethie to leave that slut alone, but he couldn't. She had some kind of hold on him, and he just couldn't get rid of her. They were supposed to have gotten married, but he met you. They dated for five years, and Sethie should have married the woman he spent those five years with. I was very appalled at my brother's action."

"I'm sorry Vicky, but I wanted Miguel again. I stayed away from him to save my marriage, but that was a lie anyway. Miguel is the finest man that ever walked the earth and then some. He just made me feel good and wanted him. I never meant to hurt you. I won't sleep with him again."

Vicky laughed. "You can have the man. I just want him to take care of his baby with child support and spending time with him. I can't trust a man who will sleep with my best friend and then me. I hope you realize that Miguel is going to cheat on you."

"Of course, and I don't want him like that. I just want some pleasure. He's good in the lovemaking department. And he's going to law school and he's moving on with his life. I think he's a good person, but his looks will be the downfall of him. Women are throwing themselves at him."

"I need to sit down," Vicky said. "I admit I wanted a baby by Miguel because of his Hispanic looks. I'm positive my baby is going to be gorgeous with both of our good looks, and I'm not getting any younger, Tanya. Trying to find the right man is like waiting to win the lottery. I'm tired of waiting."

She was so right about that. I thought Sethie and I would be married for life, but I was so wrong about him. He couldn't stop thinking about his Gracie. Maybe the two of them belong together. Who was I to fault with love? Some people found their true loves often, and some never found them.

"I can't believe he's still sleeping," Vicky said. "Do you have something to drink in here? I'm so thirsty and hungry all the time. I can't believe I'm pregnant. It's taking its toll on me. I'm so tired all the time, and sometimes I don't want to get out of bed."

"So you and Miguel are on good terms about the baby?" I asked. "I'm surprised he didn't ask you to marry him. Miguel looked like the kind of man who'd take his responsibilities seriously. Anyway, he's a good man, so maybe he's going to make a good father."

"Maybe," Vicky said. "Can I get something to drink? I don't mean to use you as my slave, but I couldn't get up if I wanted to. I'm so exhausted, thank you very much. I think I'm too old to be pregnant. I just don't know what's going on? I do know I'm not going to do this again."

I stared at her for a moment before I walked over to the refrigerator and took out a bottle of water and handed it to her. "Here you are, Queen." I knew she was probably exhausted, but I couldn't resist the urge to play with her."

"Thanks Tanya," Vicky replied, opening the bottle of water, and taking a long drink. "This hits the spot," she cried. "So are you and Miguel dating now? I really don't care about the two of you. I just want Miguel to be responsible for his child. The two of you can live happily ever after."

"I'm not going to spend the rest of my life with Miguel," I snapped. "The only thing I'm going to do is sleep with men, and then move on. Falling in love is far from the pain I'm going to suffer again. I thought Sethie and I could work out our problems, but I was wrong about that. I'm never going to fall in love again. I know Miguel is just a plaything."

"Whatever," Vicky said. "Why don't you wake up the sleeping man? I can't believe he's still sleeping like tomorrow is never here. I want to make sure that Miguel and I are on the same page. You deal with him, and then you have to deal with our baby on the way. I'm sure Miguel is going to get joint custody, of course."

I walked over to Miguel and started to hit him, but I thought better. I got into the bed, and then kissed him right on the lips. I smiled as he returned the kiss before he even opened his eyes. He smiled at me. I removed my lips. "Your baby's momma is here," I said calmly.

Miguel jumped up and stared at Vicky. I guess he thought the two of us would be fighting over him, but that plan was long gone. I was never going to fight over another man again. I was just happy that Vicky and I were talking again. I really wanted to continue our friendship.

"Is everything okay here?" Miguel said, wiping the sleep out of his eyes. "Vicky, I told you that I'll support the baby, and everything was going to be fine. I'll go with you to your doctor's appointments, and I'll take the classes with you. I'm also in law school, and working, so I'm not going to have a lot of time. Why don't you let Tanya be your coach since the two of you seem to be okay with each other? I don't hear any glass breaking in here."

Vicky and I stared at each other, and then we laughed. We should give Miguel a show since he wanted a catfight, but it wasn't going to happen. I couldn't believe the turn of events, but I wasn't going to question them, either. "I'd love to be there for you and your baby, Vicky. I miss our friendship more than you know."

"I think its okay," Vicky said. "But let's get something straight because I'm not going to be in the middle of you and Sethie's fight. I love my brother, and my loyalties lie with him. I'll be there for you, but I won't testify for you or him. Leave me out of this domestic mess. Get a divorce and move on with your lives."

"That's what I'm trying to do," I snapped. "I want to let Sethie marry Gracie, since she's the woman for him. I can't believe I didn't shoot them when I had the chance. Men just move on with their lives, and we have to sit back and pick up the pieces."

"Don't talk about hurting my brother in front of me," Vicky snapped. "I told you not to marry him in the first place, because the two of you didn't need to be together. I told you that my brother cheated all the time. He doesn't know the meaning of being faithful to one woman. Any woman that thinks she can tame Sethie is a damn fool. I hate the way he treats women."

"I should have listened to you, Vicky, but I was in love with him. He knows how to con a woman, and I fell for his lines. I thought I was the one who could tame the man. It would be the biggest mistake of my life if I hadn't had my children. They mean the world to me."

"Then don't fight Sethie to get revenge on him," Vicky stated. "It's not worth it. Get as much as you can get out of him, and then let it be. Sethie is never going to change his ways, and you trying to stick him for everything will just make him a bitter man."

I stared at her, not sure what to do. I was so sick of men getting away with practically murder when they were the ones who were committing all the crimes. I tried saving my marriage, but Sethie was playing the victim. He cheated on me left and right, but when I decided to play his game, he didn't want any part of it. Men make me sick.

"I really need to get some rest," Miguel said. "I have homework I have to get done, and then I'll be back at work soon. I suggest you two leave and move on with your lives. I'm a busy man now, and rest is going to do it for me. I was up at the wee hours of the morning."

"And I can imagine what the two of you were doing?" Vicky stated. "I just need another minute to get my wind, and then I'll be moving on. I'll let Tanya take some of the load off because you're busy, Miguel, but I suggest you spend some time with me. I'm not going to be in this pregnancy alone, because I didn't start it alone."

"I know the drill," Miguel said, yawning. "It was nice ladies, but I really need to get some rest. Please leave and lock the door on the way out." He turned over and in the next five minutes he was snoring. I stared at him, and then shook my head. Sometimes men had it too damn good.

"Are you driving, Vicky? I'm here if you need anything. I can take you home, or we can go and buy some baby clothes. I think that'd be fun. We can spend some time together. I missed our times when we went out to dinner, and spent the day just talking."

"I'm famished for sure," Vicky said. "I think we can go and get something to eat, and then buy a few baby clothes. I'm having a boy so we can buy boy things, instead of trying to figure it out. I do miss our friendship. I was prepared to hate you for the duration of my life. You broke up my relationship with Miguel."

"I don't think so because you're pregnant by him, so I had nothing to do with anything," I snapped. "If two people are going to be together, then there's nothing another person can do to stop it, short of death, of course. I don't even think death will interfere."

"You and I used to be believe that all the time," Vicky said. She stood up. "Let's go. I'm getting tired again. I was thinking about stopping at the clinic so I can have a talk with my doctor. I'm feeling tired all the time and this can't be good for me or the baby."

I was concerned now. "Have you been spotting, Vicky?" If so, you should have taken care of seeing your doctor. I think you should just have bed rest until the danger zone is over. I think it's the first three months or something like that. It's been a long time since I had children."

"My clinic is right over there on 98th and Western. Why don't you drive me, and then we can come back here and pick up my car. I just want to go to sleep right now, but maybe Dr. Jones could give me some prenatal vitamins or something. I'm so tired all the time."

"Let's get this show on the road." I wanted Vicky to be okay, but I wasn't going to pressure her. I didn't want to get pregnant after all because I had my children, and it was time to focus on a career or

something.   Besides, Vicky would soon have a baby, and when I
wanted to baby-sit; I'd be able to keep him. I shook my head, not sure
what to do.

Two hours later, Vicky and I were sitting in McDonalds because Vicky had a taste for a Big Mac. I ordered the same thing, and we
sat in the back of the restaurant. I was staring at Vicky, because she
was eating like there was no more food left. I laughed at her. "Do you
want another Big Mac?"
    "I do," Vicky said. "Make sure they have plenty of lettuce on
this one. "My feet are hurting, and I need my strength, thank you very
much. Dr. Jones told me to eat first, and then take the vitamins she
gave me. I'm so glad my baby is going to survive. This is real now."
    "You're definitely going to have a baby," I said. "I think you're
going to make a great mother, Vicky. It's going to let you stay at home
and be with your children more. I love being a mother and my children
are good children. Of course, they are sad about our marriage, but they
will bounce back. Let me go and get you another Big Mac."
    "Thanks."   Vicky finished her fries and then she started on
mine. I smiled at her before I hurried to the counter. I think more
people ate out in the 21st century. I hurried back to the table five
minutes later, and watched as Vicky continued to feed her face. It was
fun having my friend back.

Two weeks later Heff and I, along with Sethie and his attorney,
sat in the courtroom before Judge James. I was glad it was a small
setting because Heff and Brenda were trying to work out an agreement.
I stared at Sethie. He thought he was all of that, but he didn't look like
shit to me. Why did I even fall in love with him?
    "Do the two of you want to save this marriage?" Judge James
asked.
    I looked at Heff and he nodded his head. "I want this divorce,"
I said. "Sethie and I hadn't been married for a long time because he
couldn't keep his pants up. I put up with his cheating on me to the point
that I had a one-night stand. Sethie had the nerve to get angry with me.
He's a snake."
    "Objection," Brenda said. "My client loved his wife, and when
he found out that she was sleeping around, he was devastated. He tried

to make their marriage work, but she was too busy cheating on him with her young boyfriends. She shouldn't get anything."

"Your Honor, we can show pictures of the defendant engaged in acts of sexual intercourse with numerous women other than his wife," Heff said. "He's the one that did all the cheating. My client had one affair."

Judge James read his folder, and then he motioned for the folder holding Exhibit A. He studied them before he reached for my demands. I wanted alimony, child support and the house. He could have joint custody because I wanted his two children to have quality time with their father. We were divorcing, not the children, so why should they have to suffer.

"Let's take a recess so I can study everything. I'll render my decision in thirty minutes." We all stood up as the judge grabbed the file folders and left. I had to wait thirty minutes until my marriage was over. I didn't like it, but I had no choice in the matter. The two attorneys left to make phone calls and I stared out the window.

"I see you and Vicky have resumed your friendship," Sethie snapped. "I don't want my sister involved with you, but she told me to get a life. I'm really sorry you couldn't accept me the way I am. I can never be faithful to one woman. Gracie is a part of my life forever."

I counted to ten. When I reached ten, I smiled at the snake from hell. "I'm never going to have a husband that cheats on me, you stupid bastard. You must think that you're all that hot, Sethie, but there are men that look way better than you do. I'm also a gorgeous woman, and there will be other fish in the sea. I'm going to find a man who's going to appreciate me."

Sethie laughed, and I counted to twenty this time. Who in the hell did he think he was? Men were trying to pick me up all the time. I was wondering if I was wearing a sign that said, JUST DIVORCED, because men were coming out of the woodwork and then some. I stood up because he wasn't worth talking to. I hurried to the ladies room before I exploded. If the judge didn't grant me my divorce, I was going to go off.

I stared at Judge James, hoping he had the decision I wanted to hear. I was faithful to my husband with one exception and I hoped he was not going to punish me for that. This was all about Sethie, and he had to pay for hurting me. I waited.

"I'm ready to render my verdict," Judge James stated. "I am very sad when a marriage can't survive, but in this instance, I blame the defendant for his actions. You have cheated on your wife from day one with this Gracie person. You should have married her instead of your wife and we wouldn't be here today. Gracie isn't worthy of being your wife, but she's good enough for you to keep as a mistress."

"I don't condone the plaintiff for her actions, either, but she put up with a lot from you before her one indiscretion. You have two children, and they're devastated about the divorce, but they love their parents. I'm going to grant the plaintiff sole custody of the children. You'll have visitation rights every other weekend, starting this week-end; the plaintiff gets alimony until she remarries, and the house where the children should remain until they're eighteen. You have two weeks to move out of the house, and if you threaten or hurt your wife again, then you're going to prison. This court is over."

I embraced Heff and laughed to myself at the shock on Sethie's face. He thought his bimbo girlfriend/attorney was going to win, but justice won after all. I smiled at him before Heff and I left the court-room. I wanted to celebrate with someone, but I didn't know who. I could call Vicky, but I didn't want her in the middle of this war with her brother. "Thank you so much, Heff. I got everything I wanted and then some. Justice is working this time."

"And you should," Heff said. "The defendant didn't have a leg to stand on. He's talking about appealing the case, but Judge James threatened to take away his parental rights, so he signed the divorce papers. In a few weeks you're going to be a free woman. How do you feel?"

I frowned at him. "I feel like a failure Heff. I just want to find things that make me happy, and raise my children so they can be strong and able to handle the demons in the world."

"What do you think about me taking you out to dinner? I know the perfect place and there are no stings attached, Tanya. I'm not blind, and you're a gorgeous woman, but I know it's going to take some time for you to think about men."

I stared at the handsome, black man. "Thanks, but I'm going to take my kids to a movie, and spend some time with them. I might call you for a rain check about dinner."

"You do that," Heff said. "You're a classy lady, and Sethie was a fool to ignore you, and treat you so badly. I have a feeling that you're going to be just fine. Give me a call if you just need to talk, and I'll be there for you. I have another divorce case I have to get to."

I embraced him, feeling the bouts of electricity enter my being. I then thought about Miguel and what he was doing. I shook my head as I left Heff's arms. I could get caught up in the ride, but this time I was going to take a break from men. I definitely needed one. "Bye Heff."

I hurried to my car and smiled to myself as I got in. Since I was going to get alimony for a very long time, I could do whatever the hell I wanted to do. Why should I work when Sethie was going to make sure that I never had to work? I laughed hysterically. It was so fun to win, and Sethie wasn't laughing now, and I was positive about that. His lies have finally caught up with him, and by association I have won. I continued to hysterically laugh.

I've dreamed of getting married and living happily ever after since I was ten years old. From the wedding ceremony all the way down to the wedding night with my man hopelessly in love with me. I was angry as hell when David Moore stood staring at me, asking me to marry him. What in the world did I think? I peered at the insensitive boor. He made me so angry.

"Are you going to accept my proposal, Dru?"

"And why should I David? You don't love me."

"That doesn't matter. We need to marry, and then our income will be set for life. I can quit my day job and began opening up my business. You can do the same thing. I've been dying for my own accounting firm. Now I can do it. My grandfather was specific in his will."

"I don't give a damn about Hal and his outrageous request. I'm not marrying anyone until I fall in love. I'm not in love with you."

"Love is just a feeling, Dru. We have to get down to the necessities of life. You can open your beauty shop. We'll have millions and I'm not willing to give that up. You're not a bad looking woman. I can stand to be married to you for a year. What's the big deal? Let's go to City Hall on Friday and make this official. We only have until then."

"Find someone else. I'm sure Kim is able and willing."

"My grandfather couldn't stand her. She's a gold digger."

I laughed. "And what are you?"

"A man looking out for his future," he stated. "Grandfather was taken with you for some reason. I can live with that. You'd make me the perfect wife. We'll both be busy getting our businesses going. It'll be fun. I have the perfect building right on Lake Shore Drive."

"I think not!"

"You can't be serious, Dru."

I was so in love with David, but he couldn't see the writing on the wall for the damn dollar signs coming out of his ears. What was he thinking? I did want to start my own beauty shop, though. Being married to David could still be a dream come true for me. I loved him, and if I became the perfect wife, he'd fall madly in love with me too. What in the world was Hal thinking when he specified this lunacy in his Will?"

"Are you changing your tune? It looks like you are by that pretty smile on your face."

I smiled despite the humiliation I felt. David could light up my world and didn't even know it. Was he dense or didn't want to see the roses in front of the vase. Kim didn't care about him, but he was falling all over her? She looked like a fashion model. If I had the patience I could have been a fashion model myself. I was still pretty, tall, and very petite, and lots of men were trying to get with me. I didn't have to settle for anyone like David. I was cutting myself short, but I was tired of working at the bank. I had been there for five years, and it was time to move on. I was only 39 and I wanted to begin my beauty shop before I was 40. Hal was giving me the opportunity of a lifetime, and I couldn't just give that up. I had to be reasonable here. Tiffany would think that I was stupid or something, but I'm going with the flow. David was a brilliant man, and Kim wanted to be with him. Make her sweat because she couldn't have him. Hal was like a grandfather to me. I couldn't believe he was gone. He died a year ago, and was still wrecking havoc in my life from the grave.

"Dru, what's going on in that pretty head of yours?"

David made me angry with his compliments. Didn't he see the effect his words had on me? He just didn't give a damn. Men were crazy as hell, believe me. I didn't care anymore. I've been waiting for my price charming to come and rescue me. I was almost forty. I wasn't going to keep waiting for it to happen. I should be glad that David wanted to marry me instead of being single for the duration of my life. I'll be an old maid.

"I'm dying here, Dru."

I focused on the desperate man. "Okay, we can get married, but you have to understand that I'm not going to be a wife to you in any way except in name."

"We have to be married in every way at least for a year before we can get the money, Dru. I'm not about to be married to a lovely woman and not spend any time with her, or have sex with her. Have you lost your demented mind?"

"You've lost yours. I'm not a prostitute for sale, David. How dare you ridicule me?"

"I'm sorry if I hurt your feelings."

"I'm not sleeping with you. I don't even love you, thank you very much."

"Of course not, but marriage means sleeping together and you need to understand the terms of our agreement."

"Whatever!"

"Then you have to fulfill my urges as my wife. What are you thinking?"

"I just don't know about this, David. I planned on being in love with my husband when I married him."

"What has taken you so long to get married, Dru? You're a beautiful woman and I'm sure the men are breaking down your door. What's the problem with you? Are you a lesbian?"

"I should slap your face for that comment," I snapped. "I don't sleep with women."

"I'm just wondering why you can't find the man of your dreams."

"Men are dense, stupid, and dumb where women are concerned. They can't be faithful to just one of them."

"I can. I'm not about to play on you. Why should I? You have everything I need and want."

"And Kim, the love of your life, at least she thinks she is. How is she going to feel about our marriage?"

"She'll have to learn to live with the decision I make. I was hopelessly in love with her at one point in my life. When I caught her in bed with two other men, I knew she could never be faithful to me. I'm not about to fall in love again and make the same mistake. I just don't need the emotions and then the heartbreak at the end. I've known you my entire life, so I know you won't cheat on me, Dru. We can make this marriage work."

"I need time to think about this, David. You're not asking me to go to a movie, but to change my whole life. I can't make such a quick decision."

"We don't have time, Dru. Friday is our wedding day and to-day is Wednesday."

"And why in tarnation are you just springing this news on me now, David?"

"I just received Hal's legal papers and met with his attorney. This is Hal's stipulation and it's not a death sentence for me. I'm not about to dishonor his wishes. Maybe he's doing something he thought was best for the both of us. I know Kim isn't the woman for me. Hal was aware of this fact when she tried seducing him."

I was stunned. "Hal was 90 years old."

"So true, but he had a mind of his own, believe me. He didn't look a day over sixty."

I smiled. "He was a very handsome man. I can't believe he's dead. Kim is a slut in heat to go after a man old enough to be her grandfather, and then some."

"Hal had money and that was the attraction for Kim. As for Hal, I can't believe he's gone either. I loved him so much."

"I miss him everyday."

"So do I. Are we going to make his dream come true?"

I loved Hal and I had to do this for him. I could stand being married to David because I loved him. I had been in love with him for a long time, but he'd never find that out. I didn't want or need his pity. "I'll marry you, but I don't know when I can perform my wifely duties."

"We can hire someone to take care of the house. I want you to focus on getting your business up and running. I have some ideas for you from my business administration classes. I can get us started at the same time. Let's go right now and check out the building I think would work for us. You're going to love it."

"Should we plan for the wedding?"

"I'll make all the arrangements and when you're ready to come to me, I'll be waiting. I'm not about to pressure you into doing anything you're not comfortable with. This will be a traditional wedding my friend."

If he uttered the word friend one more time, I was going to skin him alive. Instead I reached for my purse. "Let's go and find out what's going on? I need a lot of space for a beauty shop with a bathroom, and office space. I want to spend time taking care of the business side of the company."

"You need to hire an assistant too. We can't do it all."

"I know how to run a business, David. I've been dreaming and studying for a very long time."

"Two heads are much better than one, thank you very much."

"Whatever!"

Staring at the beautiful glass building on Lakeshore Drive, I had to admit that David had the eye and the business sense. The space on the tenth floor would be perfect for my beauty shop. I stared at the blueprints picturing everything in its place. "This will be perfect."

"I'm not so dumb after all," he stated.

"I guess not," I laughed. "Thanks for your assistance."

"I think so too, and more. We'll have plenty of money very soon."

"Is that the only thing on your brain?"

"At the moment it is, Dru. I have dreams and now I can fulfill them. I went to five banks in this city and no one wanted to take a chance on me...to most banks, I'm a black man and who would invest in me? I had no choice but to save money, but it's never enough. With Hal's generous offer, I don't have to depend on banks to make my dreams come true. I have enough to do it all myself. I love this feeling of self-worth. Hal made plenty of money, and why shouldn't I spend it?"

"I do understand," I stated. "It's been a dream of mine. I checked out two banks, and they turned me down flat. I was so disappointed because I banked at one of the banks that turned me down."

"I'm not surprised. Let's put a deposit down."

"We don't have Hal's money yet."

"No, but you saved some money and so did I. We have enough together for the down payment. What do you think?"

I smiled. "Let's do it."

On Friday David and I exchanged wedding vows in a beautiful ceremony. I wished I could have been in church with my family and friends sharing this wonderful day with me. But I wasn't getting married to a man who loved me. I had to be grateful for the small things."

"You look very lovely," David said.

I was pleased that he noticed the white long dress. It looked like a wedding gown with the veil, but I didn't wear it because I didn't want David to think I was marrying him for real. Of course this was for money only. "Thanks."

"Will you ignore me often?"

I smiled. "I'm sorry. What did you say?"

"Let's get something to eat. I'm famished."

"I'm not really hungry, David. I want to start preparing myself for the shop. I have so much to do in so little time. I need to call the contractors."

"Sam Contractors are the best. They're working for me and I have no complaints."

"Then my decision has been made for me," I laughed. "Thanks."

"We're going to have a nice dinner, Dru. I know this isn't the wedding you dreamed of, but we can at least have some fun. I want to take you to a lovely restaurant. We can celebrate our marriage in style."

"That sounds good, David. Let's get something to eat, and then I'm going to the shop."

"I hear the boss," he saluted.

I laughed at his antics.

I couldn't believe David had the sense to bring me to this restaurant. It was mainly couples here, and the soft music was perfect. I concentrated on my steak, which I ordered rare and was cooked to perfection. "Thanks for bringing me here. I came here a few times with Tiffany."

"How is Tiffany doing?" David asked.

"She's happy as ever, living her life to the fullest. She's more in love than ever."

"She's a very beautiful woman. Her husband is a lucky man."

I frowned because I found myself getting jealous of him complimenting another woman. Tiffany was classy and gorgeous, and men flocked to her like bees to honey. I wasn't a dog, thank you very much.

"But she's not as beautiful as my bride. You look radiant."

I smiled. "Thanks, but you don't have to compliment me, David. This is just another business deal."

"I wouldn't categorize our marriage as a business deal," he shouted.

I laughed. "Then what would you call this arrangement? You didn't propose marriage to me because you loved me, but to get Hal's money. It's a business deal so let's just deal with the ramifications of it."

"If you want too," he agreed. "I disagree, but I'm not about to spoil our day by arguing with you."

Silence overtook as I sipped my wine and concentrated on my dinner. Why did I sense that David was very angry with me? I told the truth so why did he care? I wasn't about to pretend that David was my Prince Charming on a white horse; and we'd live happily ever after with two children and a white picket fence. As long as I remember that this is a marriage of convenience, I can move on with my life.

"It's very warm today," David said.

I focused on my handsome husband. "I love the eighties in Chicago. Did you break the news to Kim? She's not going to be thrilled that you married me. I'm an ugly duckling in her eyes."

"Kim has been jealous of you even when we were just friends. She knows that she can never measure up to you. I'm going to break the news to her, and then move on with my life, Dru. I don't give a damn what Kim thinks. Our relationship was over a long time ago when I caught her in bed with not one man, but two, after she had declared how much she loved me the day before. I can't deal with a woman like her. I never will."

"She's not going to give up on you, David. She still loves you, and when Kim wants something she's going to move everything in her power, short of a mountain, to get it. I'll be watching my back."

"I'm sure you can handle, Kim. She has nothing on you."

I smiled at his faith in me. "Thanks. I'll put her in her place. When you feel the urge to cheat on me, with Kim or any woman, then be man enough to be honest with me. Our marriage is only for a year, and then your freedom will be earned."

"I'll inform you when it's going to happen, but don't hold your breath. Tomorrow begins my dreams."

"Mine too. I have interviews to hire a planning consultant. I don't really have the qualifications to start a beauty shop, but Irene Dalls is the best."

"She's very expensive, but she's worth it, Dru. We have a lot in common."

"Why?"

"I hired her too."

I laughed. "You have to be kidding me."

"I'm afraid not."

We did have something in common.

A month later I found myself sitting in my partially finished beauty shop with Irene, going over the initial plans. I liked what she was saying. She also spent time with David. My shop was becoming a reality. I couldn't wait for the process to begin. I didn't have time to think about making love to my husband. I wanted his body so badly; I didn't know what to think? We slept in the same bed, but I was hot as hell, and David was as cool as a cucumber. How could he stand being in the same bed with me? He said he wasn't going to pressure me, but I felt like attacking him. What would he think? He'd probably laugh and then reject me, and his rejection I couldn't handle.

"How many operators will be working for you?" Irene asked.

"Five in the beginning," I said. "We're going to start off small. I don't want to crowd the place, and then our clientele will grow. I'll have two receptionists and an assistant manager when I'm not available. David's firm will do my accountant work for me."

"You two are married and working on businesses together. I like the harmony."

If only she knew the facts. We were married in name only. Hal's Will and Testament will kick in soon, and we'd be able to make our dreams a reality. "It's working out."

"I admire the both of you. I think it's great. The two of you make the perfect couple."

"Thanks, Irene," I said.

We worked for the next hour, and then Irene was off to see David.

I watched her leave and then concentrated on my shop. I didn't have time to think about David. I was positive he wasn't thinking about me either.

Three months moved quickly and suddenly it was July, and summer was booming in Chicago. The beauty shop was still in the process, but David was ready to open up his accounting firm on Friday. I was very proud of him, and he was too excited to do anything but work on his business.

I was sitting in my shop when Kim walked in. I stared at the bitch from hell in a yellow sundress. The dress was so short I could see her black panties. I'm more surprised that she had any underwear on at all.

"Is David around? He's not in his office."

"You don't see him around here," I snapped. Did she have a clue?

"Don't you keep up with the whereabouts of your husband, Dru? He's a very handsome man, and we sisters are desperate women."

"I'm not about to follow him around like a robot, thank you very much. It's not my style or karma."

"Then you're going to lose him. Women are desperate I say again."

I stared her up and down. "I agree with that one."

"You bitch!"

"I don't have time for you, Kim. David is my husband now, so you need to get a life. There are other fish in the sea, and with that dress on, I'm sure you can meet more than enough to satisfy that wet appetite of yours."

"How dare you! You have the audacity to insult me, but since you got married, you got guts. It's been three months now. Have you two made love? I don't think so since your husband has been fulfilling his urges with me. David is a vital man, and he has needs."

"If so, then why are you here, Kim? Don't play these immature games with me."

"I have no intention of playing games. I'm just warning you that David will be mine very soon. You might be married to him, but a marriage license won't stop me from getting David in my bed."

"In your dreams, Kim," I snapped. "David is my husband now. I have no intention of divorcing him. Find your own man, and again, get a life."

"You heard my wife," David said, walking into the room. "Why are you here, Kim?"

"I thought we could make up for last night."

"I didn't see you last night, Kim so don't go there. I spent every waking moment in my new office. Get the hell out and stop bothering my wife."

"You dog!" she cried. "How dare you speak to me in that tone of voice?"

"You bitch!"

Kim smiled, and then she walked out of the room. I didn't like her smile, but I was more concerned about hearing what David had to say about her last statement. I hope he didn't hear me when I said there would be no divorce.

"I'm about to feed my face again. Why don't you join me?"

I was relieved he didn't hear my words. "I'm still busy here, David."

"Let's go out and celebrate, Dru. My doors will be opened to-morrow. You're the only person I want to share this day with."

I was so proud of him, so why argue. "Let's go."

This time we went to a famous restaurant in Chinatown. I tried eating with the chopsticks, but I got more food on me than in me. David was laughing at me. "I'm sorry."

"You look like a little girl, and I love it."

"Thanks a lot," I cried. I reached for my fork. "I'm an old-fashioned woman."

"And you look great in pink."

Why did he have to keep complimenting me?

"Did I offend you or upset you?"

"No," I lied.

"Don't lie to me, Dru. I can tell when you're upset."

"Why do you keep complimenting me? It makes me very un-comfortable."

"You're a beautiful woman, and I want you. "It's been hell try-ing to keep away from you, Dru. How can you stand being in the same bed with me and not feel the sexual vibes? I thought I was going to scream bloody murder last night. I spent almost thirty minutes in the bathroom taking a very cold shower."

I wondered what he was doing in the bathroom so long. I smiled at the thought.

"It's not funny at all," he snapped.

"I'm sorry, David. There are so many reasons why we shouldn't sleep together."

"And there are so many reasons why we should. We're man and wife."

"In name only," I pointed out.

"I have sexual feelings for you. Don't you want me? Level with me."

"Okay, you do turn me on, David." I couldn't lie if I wanted to.

"Then let's make love. I want you."

"Are you still sleeping with Kim? It's been three months."

"Don't ever bring her name up to me again. The bitch is out of my life for good."

"She told me something different."

"I don't give a shit," he interrupted. "I know this isn't the marriage of your dreams, but I won't cheat on you. I thought we agreed to caution the other person if we got the urge."

"I just don't want to make a mistake, David."

"It's not about to happen. I really care about you."

I loved him, and he cared about me so what was I waiting on? "Let's just play it by ear. Right now I could use another glass of wine."

"Your wish is my command."

I laughed.

Back at the house I had several more glasses of wine, and I was still sober. I kicked off my shoes as I flicked on the lights. I had a great time, and David was the perfect husband.

"Are you okay, Dru?"

"I'm not drunk, David. Let's go to the bedroom."

"Are you rejecting me?" I laughed.

"Why don't you take my hand and find out."

I did, and we ran upstairs. When we reached the bedroom I walked in, thinking about my actions. Did I really want to make love to my husband? It had been three months of pure hell. How did women that were single handle being celibate? I wanted David inside of me because I loved him. I reached out my arms, and he ran into them. I held him tight feeling the inside of me explode in heat. I was literally bursting with an inferno.

David was feeling the sexual vibes because he took my lips, taking them as if he was dying from thirst. I felt wonderful as his tongue connected to mine, and closed my eyes to let the pleasure take over.

When our kiss ended, our eyes met for a brief second, and then our hands tore off our clothes. I was naked, dreaming of this moment, and not believing it was a reality check. I was about to make love to the man of my dreams.

"Are you sure about this?"

I smiled at him. "With every beat of my heart," I cried. "Are you sure?"

He smiled. "More than life itself," he confessed.

He slowly eased me onto bed, and began kissing me all over. From my right breast, and then the left one, caressing my nipples to the beat of my heart. I smiled because I just couldn't believe it.

I screamed out my passion, and David wanted more as he moved down to the cove of my wetness, and then he manipulated his lips to give me the pleasure I had been missing for so many years. Tiffany loved making love with her husband, and finally I had something to compare it too. It was the most treasured feeling in the world when you were making love to the man you adored. "I love you," I cried.

Of course I didn't expect David to utter the same words, but the rejection did hurt as he continued to excite my cove. When I exploded inside, I let the magic take over my soul for the moment. The fact that he hadn't returned my feelings of love was a huge rejection. Why did I blurt out my love for him? Maybe he didn't hear me.

When my body was sated with pleasure, David reached for a condom and then entered my tight, but very wet cove. He excited every part of my soul, and then he pumped for his own release.

I dreamed how it'd feel having David inside of me, and my dreams were perfect. It felt healthy and very peaceful with David inside of me. I never wanted him to leave my sphere of pleasure. We could remain this way for the rest of our lives and I'd be contented.

My body was still on fire; I joined David in his pumping to reach the peak of his sexual madness. He was sweating and his eyes were closed as I watched the man I'd love forever. I could tell that he was about to reach that peak at the top of the mountain. I arched my hips to give him the pleasure that was due him.

David began moving slowly. "I want to savor every moment of this," he cried.

I smiled at his words. Why did he say them? I didn't give a damn but I knew the feeling, of course. When you were in the heat of the moment, and with the person you loved, you don't want to rush anything. I felt that I had all the time in the blessed world. I closed my eyes and let the comment linger as my body prepared for the splendor.

As we waited for the blast of sexual temptation to take over, I held onto David. I didn't want him to leave my sight, and run into the arms of Kim. Why did I think about her when I was about to shake with another orgasm? David was married to me. I had to be grateful for small favors. He didn't love me, and would probably always be in love with Kim. I was just glad he didn't see fit to marry Kim. Of course, I couldn't think about the fact that if he hadn't found her in bed with two other men, they'd be sharing his bed. I shook my head at the horrific thought.

"Are you okay?" he cried.

Was he staring at me? "I'm fine."

"It's time," he cried.

I let the magic evaporate as David screamed out my name. I exploded like a low airplane in the sky. We cried out together as we rocked each other's world. I knew my body would never forget this moment of sexual gratification ever.

Six months later I couldn't believe I was still married to the man of my dreams. David was so attentive to me that sometimes I thought he was falling in love with me, but he never uttered the words. I was so relieved he had not heard my confession. Luckily it was in the heat of the moment, so who'd pay any attention to words when you were about to explode with an orgasm.

David was in his office; his accounting firm was booming and we were both surprised by the hours he had to put in. Working for yourself, and being responsible for the jobs of other people, was a lot more work than we had realized. My shop would be open in December, and I couldn't wait. I was staring out the window at the bleak October day. It was cold and I hated winters in Chicago. I'd love to move to a warm climate, but that was impossible.

"Hi," the female voice replied.

I stared at Tiffany. "Hi. How long have you been standing there?"

"Long enough," she said. "How is married life? You look radiant. Are you pregnant?"

I laughed. "Are you crazy? Are you?"

"Not on your life. My husband and I don't want the headache."

"That's a shame because your children would have everything."

"Quit trying to change the subject. Are you pregnant, Dru?"

"No. Why do you keep asking me the same question?"

"Because I'm a nurse and I know these things. Let's take the test and find out."

"I'm not about to waste my time. I'm busy here."

"I want to invest in your beauty shop so don't reject me or I'll never speak to you again," she said as she handed me a check for five thousand dollars.

I was stunned. "This is too much, Tiffany."

"Think of it as a wise investment. I know my money will double the investment."

"I'm going to pay you back with interest."

"And I won't accept it. This is my gift to you. Let's go and take the test."

"Will you get off this, Tiffany? I'm not pregnant."

"Have you and David made love without protection?"

"A few times we didn't use anything in the heat of the moment."

"What do you have to lose?"

"I can't be pregnant, Tiffany. It's not the right time."

"And why not?" she snapped. "You and David are falling in love."

"I'm in love with him, but he doesn't return my feelings. Kim is the only woman for him."

"Kim has moved on, and so has David. He's a married man now."

"We have six more months, and then our contract is over."

"I think not, but let's go."

I stood up. "I'll do it if it will get you off my back. I'm not having a baby."

"How much do you want to bet on it?"

I shook my head at her. Tiffany wasn't an expert so I had nothing to fear.

Two hours later I was back at my desk, once again staring out the window. I was pregnant. How in the hell did Tiffany figure it out?

What was I going to do? I couldn't tell David because he didn't love me, and would think I was trapping him to stay in the marriage. I was only a month along, so I had the right to abort it. I shook my head. That wasn't an option for me. David and I had been making love constantly and he'd noticed that my stomach was expanding. The other day he told me that my breast was fuller. I told him I was eating too much and would go on a diet. He told me not to worry about it. He loved the excess weight. Why couldn't he just love me?

I couldn't have an abortion. What was I going to do? I didn't want David to blame me. This was a trick that Kim would pull to get her man. I'm not a woman who traps a man.

"Hi," David said.

I quickly wiped my eyes, reaching for a file folder. "Hi yourself," I exclaimed.

"Did I scare you?"

"A little," I said. "What's up?"

"I'm going to get something to eat. Why don't you join me?"

"I can't David. I have last minute details to attend too. My opening is very soon."

"I guess I can give you a break this time. I'm going to bring you something to drink."

"I need to go on a diet."

"I don't think so, baby. Some meat on your bones is good. Are you okay? You haven't been yourself lately."

I bent my face into the folder. "Just busy getting ready for the opening," I said. "How are you doing?"

"I just got another new client. Hal would be so proud of us."

I smiled. "Yes he would, and I'm sure he's aware of our success. I'm so proud of you."

"Thanks. That means a lot to me. I love you, Dru. I thought you should know the real truth. You've been my best friend, wife, and now lover. I wouldn't have married you if I didn't care money or no money. I told Hal that I was in love with you, and he made this agreement to get us together. I owe him my life."

I was stunned beyond words. "You love me."

"I heard your words the first time we made love, but I wanted to be absolutely sure. I didn't want to have a ghost of Kim still stalking me. I'm one hundred percent sure about my love for you. I couldn't marry Kim because I was in love with you. And you're the center of my world, and being, baby."

I let the tears fall this time. "I've been waiting for ages to hear you utter those words to me. I loved you forever, David. You're my universe."

"Why don't we take the rest of the day off and go home and please each other?"

"I'm pregnant, David. That's why I'm putting on weight."

"We can...you're what?"

I smiled at the joyous expression on his face. "I'm pregnant with your child."

"I was worried about the times we didn't use a condom. I wanted a child so much. I'm the happiest man in the world."

He opened his arms, and I fell into them, closing my eyes and letting the feelings of love embrace my soul. "Can we have a real wedding this time?"

"Make all the arrangements."

"How about Christmas Eve?" I asked.

"Sounds wonderful, but I have other plans on my agenda right now. I want your body."

I smiled. "Is that reason enough?"

"We have all the reasons in the world," he said as I took his hand and we headed home. I smiled because I had plenty of reasons for smiling.

I sat in my editor's office going over ways to give our magazine more of a reputation and pick up on sales. So far we had no great ideas, and that wasn't good.

"I'd hate to lose my magazine," Sue said. "It's my life."

"The stories are damn good," I replied. "Okay, you didn't make all the sales this month, but that doesn't mean it's going to be swallowed by the other major magazines. You're going to have some months when the sales are very low. Let's just make this month something to send the readers to the stores to buy a copy. We need a fresh celebrity who hasn't been interviewed a million times already."

"What do you have in mind since you seemed to know so much about magazines?"

I didn't like her sarcastic question at all. "Sue, I was merely trying to lend you some support. We have to keep the faith, especially in a business venture."

"Thanks. I'm just worried by the sales and profits for this month. I've been dying to interview Calvin James, but he doesn't give out any interviews. The man is a popular mystery writer, and five of his novels have been on screen and television. Now he'd be a great interviewer. I believe he has something mysterious to hide. What else is there?"

I smiled at her. "He's the black mystery writer. My sister knows him."

"You're kidding me."

"Rochelle used to go to high school with him. They write each other from time to time."

"This is very interesting. Do you think you can manage an interview with him?"

"I don't know. I tried once with Rochelle, but she said that he's not into interviews."

"But maybe you can persuade him with that delicious body of yours."

I was stunned at her request.

"Don't look so shocked Maddy. This is a very competitive game now, and people go after the things that they want by any means necessary. You and I need Calvin James to get our magazine back on the right track. I'm number 50 this year, and that's not a good standing. This is the first time that I've dropped out of the top 20 list since we opened."

"It has only been five years."

"You write, but you know nothing about the magazine empire. Just stick to your writing. I want you to seduce the man, Maddy. I'm not about to waste time beating around the bush. You're gorgeous. The man hasn't been married in years or is he? I just don't know anything about him. He writes good books and producer's line up for a chance to turn his books into movies. His movies have grossed more than a million dollars. We need him on the cover and we need ten pages of a mind-boggling interview."

"So I should sleep with the man?"

"And what's so wrong with that? Calvin James is very handsome. Why do you care? I don't see a man in your bed at the moment so this would be perfect for you?"

"Which is why I'm single and free," I snapped. "I'm not into games that men play."

"I don't give a shit about your personal life, Maddy. My magazine is the only thing I live and breathe. Get off your soapbox and let's get an interview. When will you see your sister again?"

"We're having lunch tomorrow," I snapped.

"Then get me some information on Calvin James. You're good at your job or you wouldn't be working for me. I want some results, and don't bother me until you have an exclusive interview with pictures. I'm sure you can persuade him. Men and women play games, so why not? It's not like he's ugly and fat, and you wouldn't be able to tolerate him. You might end up liking the man."

"Why don't you seduce him then?" I snapped again.

"My name and face are too public, girl. Mr. James wouldn't give me the time of day."

"Is this a direct order?" I asked.

"If you want to keep your job and that high salary I'm paying you, you'd better come back with the interview. I'd hate to have to fire you to keep the budget intact. Your salary could pay a lot of bills."

I stood up, disliking Sue immensely. "I have no choice, so I'll get right on it."

"I knew you and I had a lot in common, which is why I hired you in the first place. Thanks."

I walked back to my office feeling sick with rage for a minute, but understanding where Sue was coming from. She worked her entire life to make her magazine dream a reality, and now she was in a desperate state. Sue would to do whatever it took to keep her magazine on the stands, so who was I to judge her? If the shoe was on the other foot, I'd be moving heaven and earth to secure profits for my magazine. I could pull this off. Men played plenty of games, and I was the one sulking. But I was about to turn the tables. I smiled. This might just be fun after all.

"So what's going on with you this week?"

I looked at my sister. "The same old thing Rochelle. I love my job at the magazine."

"Your stories are inventive and very creative. I buy the magazine every week. I love it."

"Thanks, but the sales are low this week. How is your husband?"

"Bob is okay. He's out of town working on a movie. I'm going to join him this weekend. It's not easy being married to an actor with a hit television show that he writes, produces and stars in."

"But you wouldn't divorce him."

"Not on your life," she laughed. "I love him."

"I'm very thrilled for you."

"I'll be glad when you find the right man. I think men are crazy because you're gorgeous. I was always jealous of you. When I introduced you to Bob, I thought he was going to fall for you. "

"He's a very good man, and you're blessed."

"Bob has plenty of friends to fix you up with."

I nodded my head at her. "I think not! I just broke up with Denny who informed me about his wife after I fell in love with him. I'm taking a break from men." I took a bite of my lettuce. We were sitting in Wendy's, both dining on Taco Salads. I loved the chili the most. I needed to get down to some serious business, but I didn't know how to bring it up.

"I need a favor, Maddy."

I focused on Rochelle. "What do you need?"

"Calvin James is back in town and I promised to help him with a character he's working on for his book. She's going to be a psychiatrist this time, and since I'm the best, he wants me to educate him. I have everything written out, and books for references. I want to fly out to Los Angeles and be with Bob. Can you take the information to your place and educate Calvin?"

I stared at her. This couldn't be happening to me. The trap was falling right into my lap. "I don't know anything about shrinks."

"That's okay. I have all the information he needs on a disk and in books, so you won't really have to do anything."

"When?" I exclaimed.

"Tomorrow night. He's in town for a week, and then he's going back to New York. He's a very busy man. I can call him and let him know the change of plans. One look at you and he'll melt in his pants. I'm sure of it."

I laughed. "Don't be silly."

"I'm being very serious here, sister dear. You're a beautiful woman. Anyway, don't try interviewing him. Calvin is a very secretive man, and he intends to keep it that way. Just because he's famous now doesn't mean the media has to know his personal business. It's not fair or right to invade his privacy because he chose to write books. Bob is the exact same way. The media is always looking for skeletons in our closet and when they can't find them, they make them up. Can you just do this for me?"

"Our magazine caters to the rich and famous."

"Good. I need someone I can trust, and I trust you with my life."

"I'll be glad to help you out, Rochelle. You've been there for me on many occasions."

"What are sisters for? When are you going to start your own magazine? You've been with Sue long enough, and she's a barracuda. I don't like her. I wish you would get out from under her influence. I don't want you changing because of Sue."

"No one tells me what to do, Rochelle. You should know that."

"Then I'll give Calvin a call."

"Now let's eat and talk about something pleasant. I'm sick of business matters." I had to keep from smiling or laughing out loud. I was about to meet Calvin James. I couldn't wait for many reasons.

I was nervous as hell waiting for Calvin to come to my apartment. I was wearing a pair of jeans and a long blouse because I didn't want him to think that I was seducing him. I had to play my cards right for Calvin to be able to trust me, and then his secrets would fall right into my lap. He had to have something juicy for me. Anything scandalous could put our magazine right back in the top twenty. With the Calvin James interview, it might put us in the number one spot. He was a hit commodity at the moment.

The doorbell shrilled into the room and I jumped. What's wrong with me? I was usually in control. I took a deep breath, looked around my apartment, and then headed for the door. I opened the door, and froze. Calvin James was standing there with a smile on his face, wearing jeans and a shirt, looking more than handsome. The man was absolutely gorgeous.

"You must be Maddy," he said. "You and Rochelle have similar features. I'm Calvin James."

I was glad I found my voice, shaking his hand and feeling the vibrations throughout my body. "Hi." I dropped his hand because the electricity was too much. "I'm Maddy and it's a pleasure to meet you. We can go into the living room. Would you like something to eat or a drink?"

"I'd like both. I was hoping you would join me for dinner. I know a fabulous restaurant in the downtown area."

"What's the name of it?"

"Calvin's Place," he proudly announced.

I smiled. "I can order Chinese instead. I'm sure you won't have any peace. I'm very impressed."

"Chinese is fine. I like you already. I've known Rochelle for years, but I'd never forget a face like yours."

So he was flirting, which was a good thing for me. "Thanks for the compliment." I closed the door and we walked into the living room. "I'll place our order. What would you like?"

An hour later we were munching on Chinese and talking about everything under the sun. Calvin was very down to earth, and not stuck up at all. I really liked being in his company but I had to calm down. My body was on fire and I needed to be in control.

"Are you okay?"

"I'm fine. Why did you want to be a writer?"

"It's the usual story. I read mystery novels when I was young and when I became an adult I believed that I could write one. I was thirty before I finished my first one, and the rejection almost killed me. I took that one novel and revised it so many times. I thought I could recite the story backwards, but it finally sold, and the rest is history as they say. What is your line of work?"

"I used to model in New York, but I'm here searching for a career. I'm thinking about starting my own business, maybe dress making or doing hair. The beauty shop business is booming. I'm not sure right now."

"But you're not starving in the meantime."

"Exactly," I smiled. "How come you're not married?"

"I was married at twenty, but it was very painful. I'm single again. I told myself that I wouldn't fall in love. I'm forty now, so I'm sticking to my plan. I'm busy writing and then showcasing movies. I write the scripts for my movies. I just don't have the time for a social life."

"And what about sex?" I asked.

"Not too modest, are you? I get plenty of it because women are everywhere and some are desperate for a man."

"I see. Protection is the key for you, and all women aren't desperate."

"Definitely. I have to fulfill my urges without the commitment. Women have set me up by sleeping with me, and then a month later claiming to be pregnant. I've been to court five or six times in my life, but I've won all of my cases. I'm not interested in women, and the games they play. I might be changing my mind with the likes of you. Rochelle has been holding out on me. You're very lovely and my body is overreacting to your beauty."

I was flattered. Calvin James was playing right into my hands.

"Where is your husband, might I ask?"

"I feel the same way you do. Men play games, and I just fulfill my urges. Love and falling in love is just too painful for me. Who needs it?"

"My sentiments exactly," he said. "I like you."

I smiled. "I like you too." The game we weave out of deception.

We finished our meal and Calvin got down to business as he inserted the disk Rochelle left him. I was sitting on the sofa watching the man in action. Calvin James was a very interesting man, and it'd be a shame if I couldn't get to know the real man. So far, I've learned that he was married before. I needed to get on the Internet to find out his wife's name.

"I'll be finished in a few minutes, but I don't want to bore you."

"It's fascinating watching a master in action."

"Thanks," he smiled.

"Did your wife appreciate your writing skills?"

"Laura didn't at first, but when I started making money she came to her senses right away."

I smiled again. This was just too easy. His wife's name was Laura. "How long were you married?"

"Ten long years," he said.

"That's a very long time." I had to divert the subject. "I don't think I could stand being with the same person for more than a day." I laughed.

"I know the feeling, but when you truly love someone, you want to be around them all the time. I was twenty when I got married, and Laura was only eighteen. The two of us were young people trying to maintain a marriage. It was difficult work. And then we had interference from her family."

"I see. Family is the ruination of marriages."

"Absolutely! How about seeing a movie with me? It's been a while."

"You can't go out in public."

"I have a disguise. Sunglasses!"

"That's not going to work, but I'm curious. Let's go."

"Give me twenty more minutes, and you're mine."

"Should I change my clothes?"

"I don't think so. You're fine as hell."

I smiled at the way he was looking at me. I had to get this assignment done because I didn't want to find myself falling in love with Calvin James. I was on a mission, and that was the bottom line. Falling in love would be too damn complicated.

Calvin and I enjoyed the movie and he wasn't recognized. That was the beginning for us. Calvin decided to prolong his stay in Chicago. We spent a lot of time getting to know each other. I really liked being in his presence. Calvin wasn't only handsome and rich; he was intelligent holding both English and literature degrees. He was someone I could fall madly in love with. When he found out who I was, or what I was doing, then my game would be over.

We had just finished another movie, and Calvin was taking me home. It was a lovely spring day. I didn't want to go home. I had no choice in the matter because I had to get away from Calvin and start on my story. I was finally going to make a name for myself, and probably got a raise in the process.

"Do women daydream all the time?"

I focused on Calvin. "It's a habit with most of us."

"I see. What a lovely spring day. I love the summer months in Chicago."

"I know the feeling. The winters are hell."

"Especially the snow," he said.

We were almost to my place and I didn't want the evening to end. I knew I was barking up the wrong tree, only causing more pain to my being. I couldn't control myself. I was lusting after him. I wanted to wrap my legs around him and have him inside of me. I wanted Calvin James.

I also had a lot of information on his ex-wife. Her name was Laura Max James, and a friend of mine was digging up more dirt about her. I knew there was some dirt because Calvin didn't talk much about her. When I brought up the subject he became angry. Something tragic happened between the two of them, and it'd be a story for the magazine when I found out.

We reached my place. "Why don't you come in?"

"Are you sure? I want you?"

I took his lips because I couldn't control myself any longer. We kissed and then I released his lips. "Did I change your mind? We're just two people exercising our sexual urges and appetites.

"I get the picture loud and clear."

I smiled. "Then what are we waiting for?" We gladly exited the car and headed for my apartment.

Inside my bedroom our eyes met and then Calvin took my lips this time. I responded to his waiting tongue and we kissed again. My body was about to vibrate into an overdrive of sexual pleasures. I wanted him inside of me. I broke the kiss and removed my attire, standing naked. He devoured me with his eyes, and then removed his clothes.

We fell to the bed, and my senses were slowly losing control. I wanted to pull him on top of me, but he was the man. I didn't want to bruise his ego. I waited with patience I didn't have.

Both naked, Calvin slowly made love to my lips, and then he moved down to the center of my being and went to work on pleasuring me. I was stunned by his eagerness, but pleased as my body shot up to the ceiling with pleasure. I was burning with affection for Calvin James, and my body was appreciating his every lick. I closed my eyes, and with no time left over, I skyrocketed to the bed, bumping and yelling like a woman on fire.

Calvin didn't waste anytime entering me, adding the protection of safety, and then moving in a slow rhythm. I joined his bounce, and our rhythm intensified as we basked in the sensations that were liberating our sexual urges.

Calvin and I rocked each other's world for another hour, and then we stared into each other eyes as we snuggled up together. I was basking in the aftermath of our lovemaking. I wanted him again, but patience was the key, not to mention control.

"I feel great," Calvin replied. "With you I feel so different. This isn't just sex, Maddy. I want a relationship and it's scaring the hell out of me. I never thought I'd be uttering those words to another woman. After my ex-wife I never wanted to fall in love again."

"Why?"

"It's a long story. I'm not comfortable with talking about it now, or ever, Maddy. I hope my words won't ruin us. It's a part of my past. I've moved on, so why bring it up?"

I didn't like his words, but there wasn't a damn thing I could do about it now. "The past is the past. Let's concentrate on you moving down to the center of my being, and giving me more pleasure. I'm hot again, Calvin James."

"I like the way you're talking."

I smiled as he continued exciting my center of being.

Two weeks later I stared at my computer. "Are you sure about this, Beverly?"

"I don't appreciate your lack of my capabilities. I'm the best investigator in this city."

"But his wife is dead."

"She killed herself when she found out that Calvin was sleeping with her sister. Could you believe the two of them? How could her own sister do this to her, not to mention her husband?"

I was stunned beyond belief. "Where is the sister?"

"She's living in Paris or Greece. I don't know the gory details of her whereabouts. It was such a huge scandal in New York."

"Thanks for the information."

"It was a pleasure. I can't wait to read your story."

"Thanks." I stared at the closed door, thinking about the information that Beverly just gave me. This was unbelievable. But if I gave this to Sue, she'd make millions with the dirt on Calvin. I was attracted to him. I didn't want anything to destroy our relationship for the moment.

But the upside of the situation was that he didn't know the name of my magazine, and I still could write the story. Calvin would be angry, but he wouldn't know that I was the main source, or the culprit. Why not? I turned to my computer screen, clicking on my writing program, and began typing. I was definitely going to get a raise and more. I smiled at the thought.

Another week passed and I was nervous for various reasons. Calvin and I were still going strong as I sat in Wendy's with my sister, Rochelle. My story would be coming out next Friday. I got a raise too. Sue was wild with happiness. She was the very first magazine with the story on Calvin James. Not only was she going to make plenty of money, but also her reputation would be set for life. Sales would skyrocket and Sue didn't have to worry about her magazine making a profit. Well it was business, and Calvin just had to live with the fact that he was in the public eye, and your secrets couldn't be buried for long.

How did he feel about his wife committing suicide over him? Did he feel guilty? I was dying to ask these questions. I knew I had to keep my mouth zipped. Maybe he'd confess to me when the story came out.

"What's going on with you, Maddy? I'm so shocked that you and Calvin are dating. He's falling in love with you."

I was very pleased. "Thanks. You didn't tell him who I worked for?"

"I thought you took care of your business."

"I don't want him to know, Rochelle. He's livid with the media circus, and me working for a magazine isn't great for our relationship. Calvin and I are growing strong now. I don't want to do anything to ruin it. This is the first time I've been interested in a man who likes me."

"Just don't keep the secret too long because they have a way of backfiring on you. Calvin won't be pleased by the deceit."

I wanted to laugh because Calvin had a lot of damn nerves. His ex-wife was dead because of him.

"What's so funny?"

"I have to get back to work and then home to cook. I promised Calvin a home-cooked meal. He wants Mexican Scramble."

"It's been a while since I made that for Bob, but I still remember."

"Then write the instructions down for me."

"You're really falling for Calvin. Usually men are taking you out, and standing in a kitchen cooking isn't your idea of any fun. Men always cooked for you."

"Most of them did, but Calvin is different, Rochelle."

"I'm glad for the two of you. It's about time you settled down with someone."

I laughed again. "Calvin and I aren't getting married, thank you very much. Let's not go there."

"It's bound to happen in the near future because he's a family man."

"But he's not interested in marriage since his ex-wife."

"He told you about Laura?"

"Not that much, but it was a bitter marriage."

"It was. She killed herself."

"What?" I pretended.

"I can't tell you the details, Maddy, but let's just say it wasn't easy for Calvin. He was prostrate with guilt for a very long time. I'm glad he has finally gotten over the past, or you wouldn't be in his life. Don't ever hurt him, Maddy. Calvin is like a brother to me. I love him."

"I know the drill, and I'm not about to hurt anyone."

"I'm glad to hear that."

I stared at my sister. When she read the story she wouldn't speak to me again. I hated to lose my sister in the process, or my man, but this was pure business. I really had no choice in the matter.

"Why are you so silent?"

I smiled at Calvin. We were spending a quiet evening at my place. It was Thursday evening. I had to make love with him one last time. "Let's just make love. I want you inside of me."

I liked the smile lighting up his face. "Come and take me," he laughed.

I removed his shirt, watching the smile on his face. He was going to make me do all the work. When he was naked, I lightly ran my fingers all over his body. Tickling his manhood and giving him more pleasure was my goal. He was moaning out his satisfaction as I smiled. I continued my lovemaking techniques on the man I was truly falling in love with.

When he was filled with passion I removed my clothes, and continued my techniques on his body, bringing him to a boiling point of passion and utter nonsense of love. I prayed with the length of his inner thigh, hearing his moans of seduction, and loving the sound he was making in my ear, and to my sense of being. Calvin had his eyes closed, lost in his own passion.

When he was excited enough, I added protection and gently guided him inside of me. I moaned in excitement as he eased inside of me. I felt the sensations hit my being as we rotated with pleasure. I closed my eyes and gave into the wonderful ambiance as it rocked my universe.

Our thrusts of fury intensified as the bed shook. Our bodies gave in to the pleasure, and finally we rocked with bouts of it; letting the feelings enter and leave our body with sensational vibrations. We danced in passion and pleasure lighting up each other's world in more ways than we could possibly imagine.

Calvin bursting inside of me made me scream out and he yelled, matching each other with passion built to perfection.

My body was still shaking from the sensations; Calvin grabbed my lips, teasing me into another frenzy of passion.

My body baked again. We rode our passion until we lay spent from the evolution of orgasms. I had never felt this good after making love. Calvin was in my life for the duration. I had every intention of never getting caught. It'd be just too painful. I smiled as I hugged him tight. I was finally in love and it felt wonderful.

"Can you believe this?" Sue cried. "My magazine sold out in less than five minutes, and my printer is now getting more copies distributed. I've printed one thousand copies, and more are on the way. This is a dream come true, and I have Calvin James to thank for it. I should write him a thank you note."

"I love the raise in my paycheck."

"You did a great job, Maddy. How did you ever find out about his wife? I knew there was something sinister about Calvin James. I just couldn't put my finger on it. Why did he have to sleep with his wife's sister?"

"I don't know, but its news and everyone will know about it now."

"A job well-done. Why don't you take the rest of the day or week off? We need to come up with something to follow up this one. It has to be something newsworthy and more scandalous because the public is depending on us."

"Senator Greene comes to mind. I saw him the other day and he wasn't with his wife either. The man didn't have the brains to wear sunglasses or keep a low profile."

"Then after your week with pay, get on it."

"I will, and thanks Sue."

"I thank you, Maddy. It was a great day when I hired you."

I smiled.

Three days later I was so frustrated. I had been calling Calvin on his cell phone, leaving voice messages and waiting in anticipation. Calvin was angry at the story being spread all over my magazine, but he didn't know I did it, so why wasn't he connecting with me? I didn't want to call Rochelle because she was probably hit with the facts. Did she tell Calvin? My sister would never betray me. But if she's angry with me, she could do anything. Why in the hell was Calvin avoiding me?

I was working in my home office on the Senator Greene story for my next feature. He was cheating on his wife with three other women. I couldn't wait to run this story as it settled down with Calvin's story.

I had been typing away for an hour when I heard a knock on the door. I was only wearing a summer nightgown as I ran to the door, knowing it'd be Calvin. I was stunned to see my sister. She was angry as she burst into the room, shutting the door with a bang. She threw the magazine on the floor. "You double-crossing, bitch! How dare you ruin Calvin's future after sleeping with him, and hearing him declare his love for you? The media is having a field day with his past."

"I'm sorry Rochelle, but I had no choice in the matter. If I didn't save Sue's magazine then I'd have been fired. I needed my job."

"You should have walked away," she shouted. "This would have been the opportunity for you to start your own magazine."

"I'm sorry," I cried. "Maybe I can talk to Calvin and explain my actions. Why did you have to tell him?"

"He ran to me when he read the story," she stated. "He reads your magazine, believe it or not. He couldn't understand who could have found out about his past. When I told him that you wrote for the magazine, and that MD was your byline, he was broken with sadness. You betrayed him and me in the worse way possible. Calvin is out of the country until this mess blows over. Did you once think about the pain involved?"

"The man is a fraud," I snapped. "He slept with his wife's sister, and she killed herself over him. What kind of monster is he?"

"You don't know a damn thing about the situation, you fool! His sister-in-law wanted him and she took every opportunity of making all her dreams come true. When Calvin told her that he wanted nothing to do with her, she was a woman scorned and plotted against him. She made it look like Calvin was sleeping with her, and Laura fell right into her trap. He never slept with the bitch. Rosy was a very bitter woman, thank you very much. And the media twisted everything around, which they are noted for. How could you, Maddy?"

"I did what I had to do to keep my job. When you're in the public eye, then secrets are bound to get out. It's the name of the game."

"So you didn't give a damn about Calvin."

"I was falling for him. He's very good in bed."

"You bitch!"

I felt the slap, too stunned to move. "Are you sleeping with him too?"

Another slap erupted. "I have a husband who I love and adore."

"He's probably sleeping with his co-star. Slap me one more time, and you'll die."

"You're not worth it, you crazy bitch! Calvin is out of your life forever and so am I for that matter. If you dare to write a story on my husband, I'll spread all your secrets, especially when you carried on with our neighbor's husband. How does it feel when the shoe is on the other foot?"

I laughed. "You can't prove a damn thing."

"I have plenty of proof, you bitch! Try me. Then I'll make up stories in the process, ruining your damn impeccable reputation. Once your skeletons are out of the closet, Sue will fire you without batting her eyelashes. The woman doesn't give a hoot about you."

"I think you've said and done enough, Rochelle," I snapped. "It's time for you to leave my presence. I no longer have a sister."

"I don't know why you're so cold-blooded, but I hate you right now. Never speak to me again, Maddy, and remember, heed my warning. You won't like me when I get angry."

She slammed out the door, and I grabbed my aching cheek. The bitch didn't scare me at all. After I finished with Senator Greene, then Bob was next on my list. No one threatened me and got away with it.

Calvin was a damn coward anyway for not facing me like a man. He ran away instead. I wouldn't have cut myself where he's concerned because he's not worth it. No man is worth a grain of salt.

Ten minutes later I was back at work making sure my story on Senator Green was accurate and down to earth. It wasn't my fault that the senator was cheating on his wife with three other women, and expected to get away with it. Now who was the fool? He didn't have the grace to cheat with just one woman, but he had to be greedy and cheat with three.

Six months later when I was reading the newspaper, I was stunned to see Calvin's smiling face. He had just married an actress named Barbara Vain. I was muted as I stared at his laughing face. He most definitely had the last laugh on me. The tears fell!

Whatever!

It was a cool day on this early May. My birthday had just passed and I was still dwelling in the aftermath. I didn't do anything that special but had taken the day off, and that was a present to me.

I was now sitting on my blanket and staring at the water. It was so blue and I was celebrating in it. I loved the water, and although it was cool, I wasn't cold at all. I was truly feeling the serenity of my soul just peering at the water. It was my sanity.

I was now 45. I was thrilled to be alive to see a wonderful day, but I was still missing the love of my life. I was a romantic at heart; I wanted to fall in love, and live happily ever after. So far, my romantic dreams were on hold. What was happening to me? I dreamed so many times of falling in love, and finding my Prince Charming. So far, I was spending time with frogs.

I stared at the water for another ten minutes and then I opened the book I was reading, "As We Lay," by Darlene Johnson. Reading was my passion. When I was feeling blue and depressed, opening up a book always took the blues away. So far, this book was doing just that and more. I began reading as I took a sip of my bottled water.

I had been reading for an hour when I looked up, noticing that it was getting dark. I put my bookmarker into the page that I had left off, and closed the book. I didn't mean to stay out so late. I didn't have far to walk, but I was still a little nervous. I gathered up my blankets and other possessions. It was time to get home.

"So you like the essence of water too?" a voice asked.

I jumped at the sound of the voice, dropping my bundle at the same time. I stared at the black man a few feet away from me. "Excuse me?" I needed to get to my purse because I had a can of mace inside. I wasn't stupid venturing out alone. I stared down at my purse.

"I didn't mean to scare you," the deep voice replied.

"But you did," I snapped. "What do you want?"

"I was just making reference to the love of the water that you enjoy. I have the same emotion for the water. I had been staring at you for the longest, wondering why you didn't smile. I'm sure if you did your beauty would shine all over the place."

I laughed, despite the frightened state I was in. This man could be a rapist, and although my body wasn't petite, I still didn't want anyone violating my code of ethics. "Whatever!" I reached for my possessions, opening my purse, ready for an attack if this man moved. He was my height, older, and smiling all over himself. I stared at his hands, and I didn't see a weapon in them. I was miserable, and I had to get home. Why did I do such stupid things?

"Let me walk with you home. My name is Bruce Greene."

I shook my head. "That's not necessary, but thanks for the invitation. I don't live that far."

"Do you live in Prairie Shores?" he asked.

"Why?" He didn't look like a serial killer, but how could you really tell? They didn't have a sign on their face. I laughed at my own joke.

"I told you that smile would knock anyone out."

I hurried to the exit, anxious to get home. "Thanks, but I should be going."

"Please don't leave without giving me your telephone number. I still don't know your name."

"It's Olivia Hopkins."

"I knew your name would match that beautiful face of yours. It's a pleasure meeting you. I've seen you a couple of times. I just got the nerve to come over here and talk to you."

I didn't know what to make of the man. I moved toward the exit, and hoped he took the hint. His footsteps next to me were evidence that he was moving along. Was he going to be a stalker? That would be the first time for me. I laughed to myself again.

"What is so funny?" Bruce asked. "I'd like to laugh and smile with you."

"Are you following me? I do have a weapon on me."

He laughed. "Please don't use it on my helpless ass."

I laughed.

"You're beautiful, Olivia."

I knew I was beautiful in the face, but from the neck down I was a size 20. Was he blind, or was it just too dark for him. Of course he probably couldn't see anything.

"I live in Lake Meadows so we're probably neighbors. Did you just move over here?"

"I did last December 31."

"How do you like living here so far?"

"I love it," I smiled. "I also love staring at the water from my living room."

"I know the feeling. I've been here for ten years, and every year gets better."

I blushed, not knowing the reason why. We were on 30th Street. I was glad because I was almost home.

"Are you going to give me your phone number? Your cell phone is fine, and I'll give you mine. I wouldn't want to parade your home telephone number until we get to really know each other, and vice versa. I was thinking about a picnic on the beach where we met for our first day; on the second date, you can make that choice. How does that sound?"

I shook my head at the stranger not believing his nerve. Who did he think he was?

"Tomorrow sounds fine with me because it's going to be a lovely summer day."

I laughed. "Are you kidding me?"

"I think not! Why are you so negative?"

I look into his dark eyes. How did he know that I was negative? The man didn't know me.

"You stare at the ground, and you cover yourself with your purse and book; you wear long skirts when you're on the beach. I bet those pretty big legs of yours are dying for some air."

He was right about the big legs, which is why I hid them in long skirts. "Please don't analyze me, thank you very much. If you came earlier, you'd have seen all the half naked women."

"I did, and some of them were bigger than you, and had the nerve to show everything. I admire women like that. You should join the club sometimes."

I frowned. "Then you should be asking for their telephone numbers," I snapped. "Just leave me the hell alone!"

:"I wish I could, but there's something about you I just can't walk away from. Maybe you put a spell on me."

I laughed, despite the fact that I was angry as hell with him. Again, who did he think he was? "I'm not going to give you my digits, so leave."

"Then I'll keep coming around until you give in. I know you want to get to know me just like I want to get to know you. I think I'm going to like getting to know the real Olivia."

"Whatever!"

Finally I reached my gate, stopping in front of it. "This is it, so thanks for the walk home. I'm sorry to take you out of your way."

"Can I have your cell phone number, Olivia? I don't usually beg."

I stared at the man. Was he blind? "Are you blind, or you can't see in the dark?"

"My vision works in the light and dark. Are you dating someone or married? I don't see a ring on your finger. Maybe there's someone special in your life. If so, I do know how to take a hint."

I knew he wasn't going to leave me alone, so I reached into my purse and handed him my card.

"So you sell Mary Kay."

"I do, and we have some nice cologne for men."

"Then order me the best cologne. I will pay you when we have our date."

I stared at him. "Are you serious?"

"In a heartbeat," he said. "I trust you to pick out the best scent for me because my scent will be just for you, and only you."

I smiled. "I'll do my best."

"What time do you get off from work?"

"At six," I said.

"Then I'll see you at seven. Do you want to meet at the beach?"

"That's fine," I said.

"Put on something comfortable."

"I'll do my best," I smiled.

"I can't wait," he smiled.

"Whatever!"

I stared after him for a moment before I unlocked the gate, smiling to myself as I collected my mail and headed to the elevator. Bruce Green was probably full of shit. Right now I didn't have any faith in men. I'm sure Bruce was going to disappoint me too. I couldn't help but feel the vibes of happiness because I hadn't spoken to a man for two years, after breaking up with Johnnie. Was I still a glutton for punishment?

I was a very late and it was eight o'clock when I reached the beach. I didn't expect to see Bruce, but he was standing in the same spot, waiting for me. I smiled at him. 'I thought you left."

"And I thought you stood me up."

"I always keep my word."

"That's good to know because I keep mine too. The only way I don't would be if something happened to me. I'd do my best to get back to you, though. I'm not like those men who misused you. I do know my lesson. Now let's sit down on this blanket. I have beer or sodas."

"Do you have a diet soda?"

"I do. I just had this feeling," he laughed.

I sat down in my blue jean skirt.

"You're beautiful," he cried.

I laughed at him. "I bet you say that to all the women."

"Only to the ones that matter," he said. "There are some ugly sisters around," he laughed.

I laughed with him.

"I made tuna fish sandwiches. Is that okay with you?"

"It's fine," I said.

Bruce handed me a plate with tuna fish and potato chips, and my diet coke. I smiled at him. "Thanks."

"So what do you do for eight hours a day?"

I bit into my tuna sandwich, washing it down with the diet soda before wiping my mouth with a paper towel he handed me. "I'm a paralegal."

"How fascinating," he said.

"Thanks. What is your line of work?"

"I'm a website genius."

"Really! I'd never have guessed."

"I know. I do love my job."

"How come you're not married?"

He took a long sip of beer. "I just can't find the right woman. What about yourself?"

"I was supposed to have gotten married two years ago, but it didn't work out."

"So this is the reason why you don't like men. He was a damn fool. There's always someone out there. Do you ever think this man wasn't the mate for you, which is why you found out before you jumped the broom?"

"Maybe," I said.

"Did you love him?"

"I did for a while, but I was just desperate. We didn't have anything in common."

"Then it's for the best. Everything has a season, and a reason. I think marriage is highly rated. People marry for many reasons. I don't think love is the number one reason."

I was intrigued by his words. "So you don't believe in marriage."

"I do, but..."

I knew I'd never marry him. I wanted to get married, so we have nothing in common. I frowned.

"So you believe in happily ever after."

"I do, Bruce. I'm no spring chicken, but a romantic at heart who wants to enjoy the fruits of marriage."

"But you need to ask yourself why you are in your forties and have never been married? Marriage isn't for everyone."

"It's not because of me," I snapped. "Men are so superficial when it comes to women. If we're not petite, then forget about ever tying the knot. I'm never going to be petite."

"And there are men who want larger women."

"Whatever!"

"That's your favorite word, Olivia, and I'm sick of hearing it. You can't put one man in the same boat as the other ones. I don't like marrying someone, but that doesn't mean I can't fall in love and be happy. I believe there are two women for every man."

I almost choked on my soda. "So you have another woman in your life."

"I'm not saying that, Olivia, but how can we just love one woman for the rest of our lives?"

I shook my head. "I just want one man to love me the way a man loves a woman. I don't need two or three in my life. What's wrong with your thinking?"

"It's the way I am, Olivia. I hope I didn't scare you away."

"I just don't know what to think about you. I can see why you're not married." I stared at his ring finger to make sure. I didn't see any signs of him wearing a ring. I could understand why he didn't have anyone in his life because of his views on marriage. Every woman wants to find the man of her dreams and walk down the aisle of love. What was he on? I think the beer was clouding his judgment.

"Am I in the dog house now?"

I laughed. "Big time!"

"There's a lot I have to do to make it up to you. Are you busy tomorrow?"

"What did you have in mine?"

"We could venture to the other beaches downtown."

"That sounds nice."

"Can you get off early?"

"I'm off tomorrow."

"Me too, how about noon? We can make a day of it."

"Sounds like a plan to me."

"Good," he said, smiling.

Three days later I was sitting in Bennigan's having a dinner of salad and diet soda with my sister, Callie. I was trying to lose weight, but it was taking its sweet precious time.

"So why do you have a smile on your face, Olivia? You're usually frowning at our weekly dinners."

I stared at my older sister by two years. Callie was a famous photographer making plenty of money. She worked in New York and Los Angeles, but Chicago was her hometown and favorite place. "I met someone. I really don't want to jinx it."

"Do tell because I'm your sister and best friend."

"His name is Bruce and he likes me."

"I see. How long have you known him?"

"We've been out for two days, and he calls me. We talked for four hours too."

"That's a good sign, baby. What is his line of work?"

"He's a web designer."

"He's not poor. Where does he live?"

"In Lake Meadows," I said.

"Has he invited you over to his house?"

"No, but he hasn't been to mine either. What's your point?"

"I just don't want to see my sister hurt again. You almost lost your mind dealing with Johnny. Remember he's the one that called off the wedding. I actually tracked him down and beat the hell out of him."

I was stunned. "That was you."

"In disguise, of course," she said. "No one messes with my sister and lives to tell about it. I beat his natural ass, and had fun doing it. The snake didn't know what was coming when I put the karate moves on him. I should have murdered his ass, but he wasn't worth going to prison for."

"He had the nerve to call me, and threaten me, saying that I'm the one that had him beat up. I slammed the phone down in his face. Who did he think he was to mess with me?"

"My point exactly. I want you to be sure about this Bruce. Invite him over to dinner and let me and Harry get a glimpse of him. I want the best for my sister."

I loved Callie, but sometimes she could be a pain in my ass. "It hasn't been that long. I can't invite him to meet the family just yet. I'm taking one day at a time."

"When are you going to see him again?"

"Next week. He's busy the rest of this week."

"And what is he busy doing?"

"Why are you raining on my parade?"

"I'm the only one that loves you."

"I'm fat and men don't want me," I snapped. "I've heard it with Johnny."

"He's a loser, and can't conceive or know what women want. The woman he dumped you for has moved on."

"Good for her. I just want someone who loves me. I shouldn't have to be a size zero to make things happen. I thought there was someone out there for everyone, and size didn't matter."

"So true, but is this Bruce the one for you? Let me do some checking up on him."

I shook my head. "Just leave this alone, Callie."

"Harry is a good private investigator. This Bruce person won't know what hit him."

"No," I shouted. "Not yet."

"Let me know, and Harry is on it."

"Whatever! Can we just change the subject?"
"Sure. I just have my sister's back."
"And I love you for it."

A week passed and Bruce was a no show. We were supposed to meet at the beach, but he didn't make an appearance. I called his cell phone many times, but kept getting his voice mail. What was going on with him? We hadn't had sex, so that couldn't be the reason. The man picked me up, and practically begged for my telephone number. How could he be so shallow? I remembered back to our conversations. He did say that if he couldn't make a date because of something serious happening, then he'd let me know. I shook my head because I just don't know what to think.

I was sitting in my living room staring out the window. Something wasn't right. I didn't have his home telephone number or his address, but he had mine. What was wrong with this picture?

It was now three weeks when my cell phone rang. I was sitting in the law library at work. I hurriedly reached for it. "Hello."
"Hi. This is Bruce."
I was so stunned I almost dropped the phone. I had been sitting by the telephone waiting for him to call, and now he decides to do the honors. I was furious. "What do you want?"
"I've been out of town, Olivia. I'm so sorry."
"Just leave me the hell alone."
"Please let me come over so I can explain the situation to you."
I thought about something. "I can come over to your house."
"That's not a good idea because my brother Barry is entertaining his friends. Can we take a rain check on my place? I'm going to cook you dinner. I really need to see you."
I knew I was weak, but I didn't see my phone ringing with men wanting to see me. "You can come over. I'll be at home by eight."
"I'll see you at ten."
"Okay," I said.
"Thanks, and you won't regret this."
"Whatever!" I thought about making the biggest mistake of my life. I couldn't control the feelings that were invading my body parts, including the ache between my legs. I was a woman after all, and I did get horny. What was so wrong with that? Bruce would have an

explanation for his whereabouts, and then we were going to make love. I was ready and willing.

Bruce was on time and took me into his arms the minute I opened the door. He smelled like the Mary Kay cologne I ordered for him. My body was overreacting to his touch, but I was horny as hell. He felt very good in my arms.

"I missed you," he cried. "You feel so good."

So do you, I thought to myself. Not only did he smell good, but also he was perfect in my arms."

"I want to kiss you," he said.

I smiled. "You can kiss me." I looked into his eyes as our lips met and slowly closed my eyes. Bruce tasted like beer, but that was okay because his lips felt damn good touching mine. When he opened his mouth the beer was very evident. Our tongues met, and I opened my eyes to stare at the man who was highlighting my life at the moment. I let the kiss take its place.

Before I knew it I was on the floor and we were both naked. I don't even remember when I managed to take off my clothes. I was buck-naked and so was Bruce. I stared at his body seeing his rock-hard manhood standing straight out at attention. Bruce was big and eager to join me. His body was built like a basketball player, but he was stouter. I was very pleased.

Bruce was staring at me and I wanted to cover myself. I knew that wouldn't be appropriate so I just let him stare. My breasts were large. I had a booty on me, but wasn't that what men wanted? My stomach wasn't that flat, but it wasn't that big either. Let's just say I didn't look pregnant.

"You're so pretty," he said.

"Then take me," I cried. I reached for his manhood and began stroking it. I was surprised at my own aggressiveness, but I just couldn't control my actions. I wanted to feel all of him. I stroked him all over, and hearing his moans of pleasure excited the hell out of me. I was on fire.

Bruce shouted out, and then he pushed me to the floor and began devouring me with his tongue. His mouth went to work on my breasts. I closed and opened my eyes in ecstasy. I was about to boil over like boiled eggs, and I loved every minute of the sensations that were rolling around me.

Bruce excited my entire body with his tongue, and when he reached the center of my being, I cried out as his tongue went to work on locating my special button, getting into the groove of the moment. I held onto his arm because I was about to flow in a pool of water, never coming back to earth. I was on fire and my body rocked with thrills of sparks. I cried out so many times I lost count, repeating Bruce's name over and over. My body had never felt this way before. I knew Bruce was my soul mate because Johnny didn't make me ever feel this way. I was on cloud nine as my body began to shake.

When I finally came back down to earth, Bruce didn't hesitate in entering me. We didn't use a condom because we didn't have time and didn't want to break the moment. I wanted to continue to feel the magic my body was experiencing. Bruce yelled out his emotions and I joined in as we both christened the room with our passionate natures. I wanted to scream with happiness because Bruce felt so intoxicating inside of me. I rotated my body because I wanted to feel his spree entice me and it was working.

It was magic the two of us were sharing. Bruce kissed my lips, and we continued to spin our bodies to the music of our sexual feelings. I was still on fire as my body heated up for more pleasures. Was I going to have a heart attack because I was still receiving orgasms? Wow!

When Bruce exploded inside if me, I felt his juices enter me. I didn't once blink. I wanted his juices inside of me because I was falling in love with Bruce Greene. There was no doubt about that. He was my soul mate. I was going to live the rest of my life with this special man. I was now the happiest woman in the world. Bruce was my mate.

He began kissing my breasts and then playing with my nipples. I played in his black hair, and then massaged his wet and hot back. I never wanted this moment to end. Bruce was still inside of me, and after beguiling my nipples until they were spent, he began moving his body. I joined in the game with him because I wanted to make more magic with him.

My body was sizzling from the heat as we rocked until we couldn't move any longer. I exploded first and then Bruce shouted out his delight again. I thought I heard the floor moving because of the heat our bodies generated. Bruce was on top, and I was having the sexual time of my life. This was the verve. "I love you," I cried. "I love you so much, Bruce." I rocked with another orgasm, and Bruce entered me for the last time, and then we lay spent.

It took me a while to get myself together. Bruce stayed inside of me for a while and when he moved out, I felt so lonely. I wanted to declare my love for him again. I wanted him to do the same thing. Maybe he didn't hear me because of the temperature of passion. I got my breathing under control, and searched for my blouse, covering myself. I was still self-conscious about my body. I looked over at Bruce. He had his eyes closed. I didn't know if he was sleeping or not. "Hi." I said, breaking the silence.

He smiled. "Hi. That was out of this world."

"You could say that. Did you hear my confession?"

"I love you too, but we need to talk," he seriously replied.

I didn't want to hear his words. "Let's just not spoil the moment."

"I have to be honest with you. I'm married."

I was beyond words. "What did you just say to me?"

"I'm married, but that doesn't mean I can't see you. I love you, Olivia. I can still be in love with my wife too. I just love you both in different ways. Please don't end our relationship because of my confession. I love you, and we'll be together forever. It has nothing to do with my wife."

I jumped off the floor, running into my bedroom for my robe, before returning to the living room. "Get up, and get the hell out! I didn't see any sign of your wedding ring."

"I took it off, Olivia. My common sense told me not to get involved with you, but I had to talk to you."

"So now you had a booty call, and you can go back to your wife. I hate you, Bruce Green. How could you do this to me? You're just like Johnny."

"I'm nothing like him. I'm just in love with two women. I know you love me. We can work this out."

"How," I shouted. "I didn't see you for two weeks and now I know the reason why. You were spending time with your wife. Do you have children too?"

"I have two sons, fifteen and nine."

I wanted to be sick, and ran into the bathroom and threw up everything I had eaten that day. I was going to be sick for the rest of the day. I collapsed on the bathroom floor and wept. This wasn't the first time I wept because of a man, but this was definitely going to be the last time.

Bruce knocked on the bathroom door. "Honey, are you okay in there. I love you."

"Get the hell out," I cried. "I hate you for doing this to me. I hate you!"

"I know you love me, Olivia. Please just give this some time. I'm going to love you for the rest of my life. You and I belong together. I love you."

"You have a wife and two children," I snapped. "Is your wife slim or fat?"

"She's slim, but what does that have to do with anything?"

"You needed someone fat and skinny so you can have your cake and eat it too. I spit on you."

He jumped back, thinking I was going to actually spit on him. He made me sick. "I'm going to call the police if you don't leave."

"I'll be back, baby. I love you, and please call me. This isn't just a booty call."

When the front door closed, I wiped the tears from my eyes as I entered the living room, looking at the spot where we made love as I opened a window. The place reeked of sex as I sank to the floor, weeping. My life was over.

Two weeks later, while Callie and I were enjoying a spinach salad at Wendy's, Bruce called me again. How did he find all this time to call me when he had a wife and two sons? I sat the phone back down, determined to ignore it.

"So you found out that Bruce is married," Callie said.

I stopped eating, staring at her. "How did you find out?"

"I told you my husband is the best private investigator alive. I wanted you to find out on your own. How did you find out?"

"He told me after we had made passionate love."

"I give the bastard some credit for telling the truth. I'm sorry, though."

"Let's just change the subject. I had sex, and whatever!"

"I know you're hurting, Olivia. I've been there. Before I met Harry I was so in love with Brandon."

"I remember," I said. "I thought you were going to commit suicide over him."

"Never," she cried. "I almost lost Harry because of Brandon. We can move on and time heals all wounds. Harry is the man for you, and you're going to find yours too. Bruce isn't the one."

"How long has he been married?"

"Twenty years."

"That long, and they have young children."

"They got married right after high school because his wife was pregnant. She miscarried, and it took them this long to have another child. He married his wife out of duty instead of love. He was dating another girl at the time."

"The man is a snake."

"His wife trapped him into marrying her. She wanted Bruce, and whoever got in her way would suffer the consequences. Bruce is an honorable man, so he married her believing he was doing the right thing. I don't believe she was ever pregnant. If she was, it was probably by another man. She knew Bruce didn't love her."

"So mess around with me," I shouted. "He's a dog."

"I'm sure he didn't go out looking for you."

I stared at her. "Why are you defending him? He's married. I can't date a married man. It's a sin."

"I know, and he asked his wife for a divorce, but she's not giving him one."

"How do you know all of this?"

"My husband is the best, thank you very much. Sometimes, we can't help who we fall in love with."

"Can we move on? Bruce Green is out of my life for the duration. I never want to see him again."

"Do you still love him?"

"Maybe, but it had been two weeks."

"I'm sorry for your pain."

"Nothing a bottle of wine and a good book won't cure. I'm going to the beach tomorrow and let the water work its magic on me. I'm going to survive and that's the bottom line. I did when Johnny broke my heart, and I will again. I'm never going to talk to another man again. I promise you that much."

"We will see," she said.

I rolled my eyes at her as I finished my salad. Men would always be dogs!

At the beach on this Saturday afternoon, I closed my eyes as the water soothed my soul. I prayed that my body would heal from Bruce's lovemaking, and my heart would move on. God only gives you what you can handle, but I'm beginning to wonder about that. My heart is aching with pain. Why me?

I stared around the beach. Children were running wild, and couples were kissing, and dangling their feet in the water. The beach was crowded today, but no one said anything to me. I just wanted to be left alone to wallow in my self-pity. Why did this have to happen to me? I let the tears fall behind my dark glasses, and continued to peer at the water because it was my only friend. Five minutes later I opened my book, 'As We lay,' by Darlene Johnson, and finished reading.

"Hello. How are you?" he replied.

I looked up at Bruce for a moment before returning to my book. He had the nerve to sit down next to me. I searched for a security guard because I had nothing to say to this evil person.

"You look great, Olivia," Bruce declared. "I miss you so much."

I turned the page, ignoring him. I wondered if his wife knew where he was.

"I know I don't deserve your love, but I love you. I hope you can forgive me," Bruce said. "I love you."

I continued to read, but the tears were threatening to fall. Why did he care about me when he had a petite wife? The man had mental issues. I was glad he was out of my life.

"I want to tell you that I married Linda because she claimed to be pregnant with my child. Later she had a miscarriage, but I'm wondering if she was ever pregnant. I never loved her, but I made my bed so I had to lie in it. We tried for years to have another baby, and I finally found out she was taking birth control pills. When I asked her for a divorce, she got pregnant for real and I was trapped. Today if I ask for a divorce, she threatens to take my children away. I have to stay married to her. She knows I'm in love with someone else, and she doesn't care. The bitch is crazy."

I covered my ears with my hands. "I don't want to hear this."

"It's the truth, Olivia. I tried ignoring you, but the urge was just too great. You're the kind of woman I dreamed of falling in love with before I got caught up in Linda's trap. She's a spoiled bitch and went after me when I told her that I wasn't interested. I was dating her best friend, and that didn't stop her from trapping me with her games."

"So she put a gun to your head and made you sleep with her."

"It was just that one time when I was vulnerable and she took advantage of the situation. I don't know what to say, Olivia. I was a fool, but you're the woman I want to spend the rest of my life with. Are you so out of love with me?"

"I love you, Bruce, but the feelings will disappear very soon. All I have to do is keep telling myself that you're a married man with two little boys."

"I'm sorry," he said.

I stared at him. Maybe he was feeling the pain, but no man cried for me because I just wasn't worth it.

"The water is so powerful today. I can stare at it, and know the world will be a better place and my life will turn around. I'm going to continue to come here, and I hope we can be friends. I miss our long talks. We have so much in common. Do you need a website? I'll do one for free."

I stared at him. "I was thinking about doing some freelance paralegal work."

"Let me write up a proposal, and then you can approve it."

"It was just an idea."

"I know. It's a beginning."

I was so in love with this man, I had to spend time with him. "We can only be friends."

"I'll settle for that, Olivia. I just want you in my life. Can friends embrace?"

"Don't push it," I snapped.

He laughed. "Let's talk about your freelancing."

"Whatever!" I cried. Bruce smelled so good, and I wanted him inside of me. I was so glad we weren't in a private location because my morals would have tumbled out of the window.

A year later my sister and I sat in a Kentucky Fried Chicken on the south side of Chicago. "So you're still dating Bruce, the married man?"

I stared at her. "I am, but we're just friends."

"Have you slept with him again?"

I stared down at the floor.

"I see. You've gained more weight too. Are you pregnant?"

I stared at the floor again.

"Why Olivia? He's not going to divorce his wife to marry you. Are you insane?"

"I love him, and I'm proud to be carrying his child. I need him in my life. I don't have a lot of men calling me."

"But Bruce can't be your soul mate."

"He's the only man for me. I still maintain my independence when he's not around. He's already set up a savings account for our baby, and I'm fine with that. I just love him. I'll take him for as long as I can have him. I love him."

Callie shook her head. "I don't know what to say."

"Just be supportive, Callie. You're my sister, but you're my best friend too. I stood by you when you were dating a married man. I didn't once judge you. I need the same support from you."

"I'll be here when he breaks your heart."

"I'll survive. Right now I have to make sure I have this baby because I'm over forty years old."

"Is your health okay?"

"So far," I smiled. "I'm healthy as a horse. I just need to lose some weight."

"You're never going to be skinny."

"That's for sure," I laughed. "I just had three chicken legs, and KFC is the most fattening chicken in the universe."

"I agree, but I love my chicken."

"So how are you and Harry doing?"

"Okay, we're going to Paris for two weeks for a vacation."

"Do you need a babysitter?"

"No, but thanks anyway. Harry's mother is taking them to Disney World."

"They'll love that, of course."

"I'm hearing about this trip all the time."

"I can imagine. Bruce wants to take me there one day. He's so full of surprises."

"He seems very devoted to you."

"So you enjoyed the dinner I cooked."

"Harry was very impressed with the adultery."

I frowned at her. "You promised not to be mean."

"I'm sorry, but that just slipped. He's a good man to you."

"There has never been a man who looks at me the way he does. I know he loves me."

"Maybe so, but that doesn't make the situation right."

"I know, but I love him, Callie. I do love him so much. He's my world."

"Let's just change the subject," she snapped.

"Whatever!"

Back at the beach I leaned on Bruce's shoulder. "It's awfully warm considering it's almost midnight."

"Are you getting tired?"

"I like being here with you."

"Your face is glowing with love."

"I'm so happy to be with you, Bruce."

"How is our child doing?"

"The morning sickness is finally over. I'm two months, but it's different probably because of my age."

"Are you really okay?"

"I'm fine, baby. I love my website design."

"You need to be able to work at home since you're going to be a mother. We're no spring chickens."

"I know. You're going to have three children."

"I know this one is mine. I'm not sure about the other two."

"There are DNA tests."

"I know, but Linda refuses to let me have the boys tested. And really, what difference does it make now. I love them and no matter what, I'll always consider them my children. Plus, they're old enough to understand about DNA. I wouldn't put them through that."

"You're a wonderful father. I'm glad out baby will have you." Then, reverting to our discussion of Linda, I said, "She runs the show."

"Not for long. I'm going to rain on her parade very soon."

"What do you mean?"

"I'll tell you about it in time. Let's just say I have some pictures that might get me a divorce after all. Right now I just want to enjoy the love you and I have for each other, and our baby. I can't wait to see our son or daughter. Our baby is going to fulfill my every wish."

I smiled. "I feel exactly the same way." Our lips met.

Seven months later I was holding my lovely daughter in my arms. We named her Joy because she was definitely the joy of our lives. I was lying in the hospital after ten hours of labor. All I wanted to do was sleep.

"She's so gorgeous," Bruce cried. "She looks just like you. I bet she's going to have your pretty long hair."

"I'm just glad she's healthy."

"So am I. Do you need to sleep?"

"For hours," I cried. "Is that okay with you?"

"I'll feed our daughter."

The door burst opened and a petite black woman walked into the room, slamming the door behind her. She stared at Bruce and then me. "So you want to ruin our lives for this fat bitch. Are you drunk with issues?"

"How did you get in here?" Bruce shouted.

I reached for my baby. "Give her to me, Bruce. You can solve your problems outside this room."

"I'm going to make you pay in court," she shouted. "How dare you?"

"Linda, this is not the place for this kind of discussion. Let's go outside."

"You're crazy," Linda cried. "She's fat and ugly."

"I'm not going to discuss this now," Bruce said. "Let's go outside."

I stared at the woman with the short haircut. She was cute, but right now she was the ugliest thing on sight.

"You can't find a man of your own so you take mine," Linda snapped. "I can see why no other man wants your fat ass."

"We're going outside now," Bruce snapped.

I was relieved when he pushed the woman outside of the room. I kissed my sleeping baby, glad she didn't wake up to hear the screams of a mad woman.

Ten minutes later Bruce walked back into the room, and this time he closed and locked the door. "Is everything okay in here?"

"She's still sleeping. Why don't you lay her down?"

"Okay."

I looked at Bruce. Was he worth all of this madness and pain?

"She's sleeping like the beauty she is," Bruce said softly.

"What about Linda?" I snapped.

"She's not going to be a problem for us any longer."

"What do you mean?"

He got into bed with me and put his arms around me. I leaned onto his shoulders. "I want you to get some rest and not worry about Linda any more. I promise you, she won't be bothering us again."

"I have a right to know, Bruce. She scared the life out of me just barging into our hospital room. The woman is crazy."

"She's that, but I promise you that she won't hurt us again. Will you marry me as soon as the divorce goes through?"

I stared into his black eyes. "With bells on and more," I cried. "I don't want the baby mama drama, and the wife drama."

He laughed. "Did I tell you that I love you?"

"I haven't heard it today," I laughed.

"And I can say the same thing."

"I love you, Bruce Green. I want to spend the rest of my life with you."

"And I love you, Olivia, and I want to love you forever."

"And Joy and I want to love you in everlasting love."

"We make a great family, don't we?"

"We do," he agreed.

"And don't you forget it."

"Whatever!" I cried. Bruce kissed my lips, and I closed my eyes as I lay in his arms. I knew my future was all set. Bruce, Joy and I were going to live happily ever after. Whatever!

I decided to take a different route home this time because it was such a lovely day, and I wanted to enjoy the weather. I loved the summer months in Chicago because the flowers bloomed, the sun shone brightly, and the beaches and oceans were pure heaven.

Today was Friday and it was after six o'clock. I was just getting off from work after a long day. I loved Fridays because I had two days of freedom before it was time to go back to work. I didn't waste my weekends, believe me. I had every intention of spending them wisely. I planned on doing things that I couldn't normally do on the weekdays.

I lived in the Longwood area, called the historic district. Minorities are now living where they wanted to live, and I was glad we had the opportunity to move up in the world. I loved my house because it was mine, and I did it all by myself. I was 42, and proud of it.

I was lonely often, but I was waiting for God to send me that special person. At times I thought I was too old. I knew the men my age wanted a young woman on their arms, which was why I had been so lonely. I still believed that my mate was right around that corner. He was going to sneak up on me, and surprise the heck out of me. I just couldn't wait.

My favorite Psalm came into my head and I began reciting it: **The LORD is my light and my salvation-whom shall I fear? The LORD is the stronghold of my life—of whom shall I be afraid? 2 When evil men advance against me to devour my flesh, when my enemies and foes attack me, they stumble and fall. 3 Though an army besieges me, my heart will not fear; though war break out against me, even then will I be confident. 4 One thing I ask of the LORD, this is what I seek: That I may dwell in the house of the LORD all the days of my life, to gaze upon the beauty of the LORD and to seek Him in His temple. 5 For in the day of trouble He will keep me safe in His dwelling; He will hide me in the shelter of His tabernacle and set me high upon a rock. 6 Then my head will be**

exalted above the enemies who surround me; at His tabernacle will I sacrifice with shouts of joy; I will sing and make music to the LORD. 7 Hear my voice when I call, O LORD be merciful to me and answer me. 8 My heart says of you "Seek His face!" Your face, LORD, I will seek. 9 Do not hide your face from me, do not turn your servant away in anger; you have been my helper. Do not reject me or forsake me, O God my Savior. 10 Though my father and mother forsake me, the LORD will receive me. 11 Teach me Your way, O LORD lead me in a straight path because of my oppressors. 12 Do not turn me over to the desire of my foes, for false witnesses rise up against me, breathing out violence. 13 I am still confident of this: I will see the goodness of the LORD in the land of the living. 14 Wait for the LORD be strong and take heart and wait for the LORD.

I recited this prayer every day of my life. Lately I had been doing it more than normal because when the lonely blues took over, I had to keep reciting this prayer to quash the devil who was insistently trying to ruin my life. I felt his claws digging inside of me when he wanted me to take my own life because I wasn't worthy of living, and he'd give me everlasting life. I laughed to myself because damnation and hell was the only eternal life I was getting. I didn't treasure the thought of burning in hell.

In historic Longwood there was a long mountain like path that you could take. I was lucky because this path led me to the front of my home. I'd spend hours just staring at everything from my view point. I didn't have the grandest view, but the peace and serenity gave me some solitude. I had been living in Longwood for three years now. Most of my neighbors were white, and they didn't give me any problems. I was sure they didn't want me invading their turf, but when they saw that I wasn't a gangster, bent on disrupting their lives, they became friendly, at least most of them. I was a very quiet person, so I didn't need their attention. I had a best friend, and we spent a lot of our free time together, so I didn't need anything from my neighbors. I was just glad to be living in Longwood feeling that it had been a blessing for me.

I had turned the corner leading up to my house when I saw something near my porch. There were a lot of trees in historic Longwood, reminding me of Chicago State University which was nothing but trees. I never wanted to go to the University because of the mountain of trees and the fact that a few students had been raped in those trees.

I hurried to the object in the path, thinking it was nothing but a tree blown in front of my house. When the wind came over Chicago, everything in its path was in trouble. I reached the object, and stared in fright. It was a body. I covered my mouth in shock as I looked around. I had the only house on this side, and it'd take me a while to get to the next house. Was he dead? What was going on? Why was he in my neighborhood? We didn't have too much crime in this neck of the woods.

I had to do something. I reached for my cell phone as I moved closer, looking intently for any sign of movement. I didn't see any blood leaking and I knew I had to check for a pulse. I remember seeing something on television, and the first thing they did was see if the person had a pulse. Why was this happening to me? I had no adventure in my life.

I closed my eyes and prayed, reciting Psalm 27 three times before I heard a long groan. I jumped and then stared at the body. The man was moaning. I thought about running into my house, but I couldn't move. I walked over to him. I had to say something. "Are you okay? Can you hear me? I'm going to call an ambulance for you."

"Okay," the voice whispered. "Please don't leave me."

"What's wrong with you?"

"I was hit by a car."

I was stunned. "What?"

"They hit me and then they pulled off," he cried. "I can't feel anything."

"I'm going to call 911."

"Thank you," he whispered. "Can you stay with me?"

"Of course," I said as I called 911, giving the operator my address and answering a few questions before I bent down to the man lying on the walk. "Are you cold?"

"A little," he cried. "I know it's hot right now, but I can't feel anything. I'm just cold."

That was good because if he was numbed, he wouldn't be able to feel anything. "I'm going into the house to get you a blanket. I'll be right back."

"Please don't leave me."

"I'm going to get a blanket for you. I promise that I'll be back."

"Your voice is so sexy," he whispered.

I blushed and then smiled. "You're going to be okay."

I reached into my jean pocket for my keys and hurried into the house. It was imperative that I find a blanket so this man wouldn't die on me. I wasn't about to let that happen. He had a kind voice, and I knew he wasn't out to harm me in any way. I just had this feeling that he was a good man.

I grabbed a blanket and hurried back outside. He was still lying there where I left him. I ran over and covered him with the blanket. "The ambulance is coming sir. What is your name?"

"I don't know," he said.

I was stunned. "You don't know your name."

"No, but what is yours?" he whispered.

I stared down at the handsome face, his black eyes wide with pain and shock. I was sure his wife and children were missing him like crazy. "Are you in pain, sir?"

"No, I can't feel anything," he cried. "I hope I can walk."

"I'm sure you'll be fine, sir."

"You never told me your name. I'm trying to picture the name with that gorgeous and sexy voice of yours."

I blushed again. He was probably paralyzed but he was worried about me.

"Are you still there?"

"I am sir, but I don't know what to call you."

"I can't remember anything. Why don't you give me your name, and we can make up one for me?"

I laughed. "I can't make up a name for you."

"Why not?" he cried. "I'm sure when my memory comes back to me; I'll know who I am. In the meantime, we have to call me something when the ambulance and the police arrive."

He was right about that. "My name is Mimi."

"I knew it," he cried. "You're beautiful as your voice."

"Why are you flirting with me?"

"I don't know," he said. "I don't even know how long I've been lying out here."

"I'm so sorry," I cried. "Can I do anything else for you?"

"Just stay with me. Can you go with me to the hospital? What is the nearest one over here?"

"Chicago Memorial," I cried. "I don't know if I should go with you. I'm sure the nurse will call someone for you."

He tried laughing. "I don't know who I am"

"We can find that out by looking at your driver's license."

"I hope so," he cried."

I shook my head. "This is like a movie."

"I wished I was watching one now in the comfort of my living room, wherever that is," he said. "I'm so sorry to be bothering you. I'm sure your husband is wondering what's going on with his wife. You look like a domestic diva. I bet you have three children."

I laughed to myself because he didn't know me at all. "I'm not married nor do I have any children."

"I find that difficult to believe. Are you engaged, or divorced?"

"None of the above," I said, shaking my head. "Everyone in this life does not have to be married. I love the single life because I don't have to answer to anyone, but myself. Men want something from you, and most of them drain the heck out of you. Besides, I'm waiting for my soul mate, and I know he's right around the corner for me. I have to wait on the Lord."

"Psalm 27," he cried. "It's my favorite Psalm."

I stared at him in shock because I had never meant a man who was into the Bible.

"I do love reading, and the Bible is my favorite book," he said. "Are we going to name me?"

I knew I had no choice in the matter. I thought he had forgotten about the name. He looked like a what to me? I stared at his smooth and chocolate skin. He looked like a Denzel to me, but everyone couldn't be named Denzel, but I was going to name him. "Denzel," I cried.

He laughed. "Why do sisters love him so?"

"Because we just do," I cried.

"He's a family man."

"And he's devoted to his wife and four children. Paulette is the luckiest woman in the world."

"Maybe so, but there are women right here in Chicago who are very lucky. I think we both are lucky to be alive. I remember the car hitting me, and my life flashed before my eyes. It wasn't a pretty sight, believe me. I began reciting Psalm 27, and my other favorite Psalm 37: *1 do not fret because of evil men or be envious of those who do wrong; 2 for like the grass they will soon wither, like green plants they will soon die away. 3 Trust in the LORD and do good; dwell in the land and enjoy safe pasture. 4 Delight yourself in the LORD and He will give you the desires of your heart. 5 Commit your way to the LORD trust in Him and He will do this; 6 He will make your righteousness shine like the dawn, the justice of your cause like the noonday sun. 7 Be still before the LORD and wait patiently for Him; do not fret when men succeed in their ways, when they carry out their wicked schemes. 8 Refrain from anger and turn from wrath; do not fret—it leads only to evil. 9 for evil men will be cut off, but those who hope in the LORD will inherit the land. 10 A little while, and the wicked will be no more; though you look for them, they will not be found. 11 But the meek will inherit the land and enjoy great peace. 12 The wicked plot against the righteous and gnash their teeth at them; 13 But the LORD laughs at the wicked, for He knows their day is coming. 14 The wicked draw the sword and bend the bow to bring down the poor and needy, to slay those whose ways are upright. 15 but their swords will pierce their own hearts, and their bows will be broken. 16 Better the little that the righteous have than the wealth of many wicked; 17 for the power of the wicked will be broken, but the LORD upholds the righteous. 18 The days of the blameless are known to the LORD, and their inheritance will endure forever. 19 In times of disaster they will not wither; in days of famine they will enjoy plenty. 20 But the wicked will perish; the LORD's enemies will be like the beauty of the fields; they will vanish—vanish like smoke. 21 The wicked borrow and do not repay, but the righteous give generously; 22 those the LORD blesses will inherit the land, but those He curses will be cut off. 23 If the LORD delights in a man's way, He makes his steps firm; 24 though he stumbles, he will not fall, for the LORD upholds him with His hand. 25 I was young and now I am old, yet I have never seen the righteous forsaken or their children begging bread. 26 They are always generous and lend freely; their children will be blessed. 27 Turn from evil and do good; then you will dwell in the land forever. 28 For the LORD loves the just and will not forsake His faithful ones. They will be protected forever, but the offspring of the wicked will be cut off; 29 the righteous will inherit the land and dwell in it forever. 30 The month of the righteous man utters wisdom, and his tongue speaks what is just. 31 The law of his God is in his heart; his feet do not slip. 32 The wicked lie in wait for the righteous seeking their very lives; 33 but the LORD will not leave them in their power or let them be condemned when brought to trial. 34 Wait for the LORD and keep His way. He will exalt you to inherit the land; when the wicked are cut off, you will see it. 35 I have seen a wicked and ruthless man flourishing like a green tree in its native soil, 36 but he soon passed away and was no more; though I looked for him, he could not be found. 37 Consider the blameless, observe the upright; there is a future for the man of peace. 38 But all sinners will be destroyed; the future of the wicked will be cut off. 39 The salvation of the righteous comes from the LORD He is their stronghold in time of trouble. 50 The LORD helps them and delivers them; He delivers them from the wicked and saves them, because they take refuge in Him.*

I was speechless as he recited the entire Psalm 37 chapter. His memory wasn't that gone.

"Are you still there? Where is the ambulance?"

"I'm going to call them again. I can't believe they are this slow."

"You'd think this was the projects."

"Tell me about it." I opened my purse to find my cell phone.

"I hear the sirens now," he said. "I'm so cold."

"Let me sit close to you," I said.

"That'd be very nice. Your perfume smells good."

I blushed for the third time. What was wrong with me?" I moved closer to the stranger, cradling him in my arms.

"You do smell good," he whispered. "I'll be the luckiest man alive dying in your arms."

I blushed again. "You're not going to die. I think God has something else planned for you."

"I know He does by putting me right here with you."

"I don't see any blood."

"Thank God for that. I think the impact of the car threw me."

"You're a blessed man."

"I know God is working for me."

"He's working all the time."

The sirens came closer, and finally they were upon us. I stood up as the paramedics did their jobs. Denzel held onto my hand, so I knew I had to go to the hospital with him. I couldn't blame him for being afraid. He needed someone with him because he didn't know who he was. I was sure his family was worried sick about him. Finally we were on our way to the hospital.

I was pacing the hospital waiting room like a woman waiting for word on her husband. I knew I had no right, but Denzel had no other family for the moment. I should just walk away because he was going to get his memory back. I had no right to be here.

I headed for the exit of the hospital, and then I stopped. I had to know how he was doing, and I couldn't leave without acknowledging him. Besides he was dependent on me. I had to stick it out for just a few minutes, and then move on. So I sat back down to stick it out for the long wait.

It was an hour when a doctor walked toward me. I stood up. "How is Denzel doing?"

"He has two broken ribs, but he's going to make it. The man was in a lot of pain, but he didn't act like it. I say he has a lot of strength and he's not going anywhere. He kept asking me about you."

I was surprised. "What about me?"

"He wants you to come into his room. He needs another thirty minutes and then you can go in. The police want to question him about the hit and run driver. Denzel is lucky to be alive. Is this his real name? My name is Doctor Hayes by the way. The nurses couldn't find out any details, and he doesn't remember anything. He's going to have a loss of memory for a while, but it will come back in time. I'm going to take more tests before he's released. I'm sure he's going to be fine. Can he go home with you? He's worried about where he's going."

I stared at the doctor as if he had two horns sticking up from his head. There was no way I was going to let a stranger into my house. It was out of the question. "I don't know, doctor."

"Then he's going to be homeless. I don't have any insurance information on him."

"You can bill me, doctor."

"Are you sure?"

"Yes. I found him near my house."

"He's a very lucky man."

I stared at another handsome brother, and this one was a doctor. It made me proud.

Thirty minutes later I walked into Denzel's room. He was all bandaged up and had his eyes closed. I sat down in the chair next to the bed. I didn't want to wake him. He was such a brave man.

"Hi," he whispered. "What are you thinking about?"

"I didn't want to wake you."

"The doctor gave me some medicine for the pain so I'll be falling asleep soon. I'm sure I need to get some rest. The pain is almost gone, and now I can get the rest I need, and then worry about what I'm going to do with the rest of my life. I don't know anything about me. I had a life, but where is it? I don't even have a place to stay or money for that matter. This is so frustrating," he cried.

His monitor beeped a few times, and I jumped. "Denzel you need to calm down or the monitor is going to explode. Let me find your nurse so she can give you something else to calm you down."

"I'm sorry," he said. "I won't get upset. I just like you sitting next to me. Talk to me until I fall asleep. Tell me what you do for a living. I need to focus on someone else instead of me."

I smiled. "I'm a paralegal, and the top one so I don't really have to work, but I love my job. I do most of my work at home, and go into the office on Fridays for the meetings. I have my home office set up just like my work office so it works for me. I never wanted to go to work, so I made it happen."

"How so?" he seriously asked.

"I got my associate degree in paralegal science at Roosevelt University, and then I went back for my bachelor's degree. I also have a certificate and another associate degree on line in paralegal science. I'm so knowledgeable, I can work backwards."

"Wow," he said. "I'm impressed. I'd love to see your wall."

I blushed.

"I'm sorry. Please don't think you're obligated to me."

"It's okay if you stay at my house until your memory gets back. I'm sure your wife and children are frantic wondering if you're dead or alive. I wished you could go back to them."

"I don't think I'm married," he said. "I just don't feel it."

"You will in time, Denzel."

"I like the name."

"It's only temporary, of course." His eyes closed, so I knew the medicine was working, and that was the sign for me to leave. "I should go." I stood up.

"Will you be back?"

"I'll come by in the morning."

"Will you be working?"

"Yes, but at noon I'll be here."

"I can't wait to see you."

I smiled at him. "Me either."

Three months later Denzel was still living with me. He was a great cook and very handy around the house. He knew he had a job with his hands. I thought of him being a construction worker or something, but he might have plenty of money. We were sitting in the dining room, sharing a pizza for dinner.

"I can't believe I've been here for three months." Denzel said. "I hope I'm not getting on your nerves."

He didn't know the half of it. I was having the time of my life with a man in my house. "Its fine and you have earned your stay in this house. So much of my broken things have been fixed, and I owe you some money. Why don't you let me pay you? I also enjoyed the dinners, but I'm going to have to work out. I don't want to get fat."

"You look good to me, and I'm very attracted to you."

His words were music to my ears, "I know, but we shouldn't get involved. I'm sure your wife is searching for you."

"I'm not married," he said. "Why do you keep insisting that I am?"

"I think you are married with children. I can't fall in love with you and then you go back to your family. I'll be heartbroken. I've been waiting on the Lord for my soul mate. I don't think it's you, Denzel."

"And how do you know?"

"I just have this feeling so let's just keep this professional."

"You're the most beautiful woman in the world, Mimi. I've been hard as a rock since I met you. I'm aching all over and I want to make love to that gorgeous body of yours"

I wanted the same thing, but I didn't want to get hurt in the process. Denzel was going to remember his name, and his family, and then move on with his life. I was already in love with the man, and I wanted to spend the duration of my life with him. I prayed he was my soul mate, but he was a mystery to me.

"Let's just finish our pizza and maybe watch some movies."

"That's fine with me."

"I do want you, and that's never going to change."

"When you find out that you love your wife and kids, then everything will change."

"Maybe so, Mimi, but then again, I could be single. I have this feeling anyway; let's just have fun and take one day at a time. We can't be responsible for what happens next. I'm going to put my picture in the major newspapers hoping someone will recognize me. I can't wait for my memory to come back because it has been three months. I do want to get on with the rest of my life. I'm so good with my hands, and I love working with them."

"You do such a good job, Denzel."

"Thanks," he said.

Our eyes met and then I looked away taking another slice of my cheese and sausage pizza. It was time to move on.

I opened my eyes staring at Denzel an hour later. I was lying on his shoulder, and it felt good. He moved, and then our eyes met again, and then our lips took over. I couldn't control myself as the kiss was taking over me. I loved feeling his lips on mine, and our tongues' mating like teenagers. I wanted him more than anything, and I wasn't about to stop this sensational kiss. I was on fire.

Our kiss ended and we ran to the bedroom where we took off our clothes and stared at each other. His body was to live for and then some. I knew my body was great because I was at work on it twenty-four seven. "You're so cute," he cried.

I laughed. "Cute!"

"I didn't want to say the same thing everyone else was saying."

"I appreciate that."

He reached for me, and we met on the bed. Our kisses exploded with more fire as I closed my eyes and let our tongues do all the work. I was so wet between my legs I thought I was going to circle the room with my water. It was the sex juices eating me up alive and my pleasure of love wanted him inside of me.

Denzel began kissing me all over, making sure he was burning the fires all over my body. His wet tongue was doing the work because I was on fire again, and my body lit up with pleasure. I screamed out his name as he circled between my wetness. He fired inside and I screamed out his name this time. My body instantly exploded because it was ready.

I rocked as his tongue continued to frame my pleasure button. When my body couldn't go on any longer, Denzel entered me. We didn't have time to find a condom, and I prayed Denzel was safe. I didn't know anything about this man, and I was taking a large risk. It was to late now because it had been a long time since I had a man's penis inside of me. I closed and opened my eyes as the pleasure of him being inside of me ignited the fires inside of me.

I shouted more as he began rocking to his pleasures. We both rocked for a long time, and then we finally laid spent. I was still breathing heavily because my body had been unsatisfied for a long time. I was so happy. "I love you." I could kick myself as I stared at the shock on Denzel's face. I wanted him to utter the words to me, but he didn't say anything.

Five minutes passed. "I should get into the bathroom." I practically ran into the bathroom. What was I thinking? The man didn't know anything about me that much and I didn't know a damn thing about him either. I turned on the shower and cried because we slept together. Men were sleeping around all the time and they didn't run to the altar to marry anyone they slept with. I shook my head as the water cleansed my soul. I made love to a stranger, and I didn't use any protection. What was I thinking?

I couldn't stay in the bathroom forever, so I took a deep breath and walked back into the room. I thought Denzel would be asleep but he was watching television. "I was waiting until you got out of the bathroom. I love you too."

I was stunned.

"I do, and when you said it you just shocked me. I loved you the first moment I met you lying on the ground. I knew you didn't know anything about me, and trusted me enough to cradle me in your arms. You kept me warm, and alive, and I owe you my life."

"Which doesn't mean you have to love me," I snapped. "I'm sorry for blurting the words out, and we can move on. I'm going to reheat the pizza and watch a movie."

"Why don't we lie in bed and do it together?"

"I can't," I cried.

"Yes you can," he said. "We have to treasure the time we have together. Right now I'm happy, Mimi. I know my life will change when I find out who I am, but right now I'm not about to worry about it. I love you, and that will never change. I love you."

I flew into his arms. "I love you too." Our lips met again, and this time we made precious love like tomorrow was the last day for us. I had a feeling when his picture hit the newspaper his family, and possibly a wife will claim their man. I held him tight because I was going to enjoy all the memories we had.

Another three months later I was sitting in my office when the doorbell rang. I put down the brief I was working on for my attorney and hurried to the door. Denzel had gone shopping for food. He had planned on cooking all of my favorite foods. I opened the door, staring at the white woman. "Can I help you?"

"I believe you have my husband."

I stared at the woman. "Who is your husband?" I cried. I was going to puke and then some.

"Carey Coles. This is the address where I was told he could be reached."

I couldn't believe Denzel was married to a white woman. "Does he have children?"

"No, but we were working on that before he got lost. May I come in because it's cold out here? I know he's playing house with you, but the game is up. I came to take my husband home."

"How do I know you're his wife?"

"I brought the proof, and the marriage license, bitch!"

"How dare you?"

"And how dare you sleep with my husband."

"I love him."

"You're a slut stealing bitch!"

"It takes one to know one," I shouted.

"Where is my husband?"

"He's at the supermarket."

"We have maids for that," she snapped.

"Who are you?"

"Sheila Coles if you must know. Nice house."

"For a black woman, of course," I snapped. We can go into the living room and wait for Denzel."

The woman laughed. "You would, of course."

"I beg your pardon."

"You didn't know, but the games are over. I want my man back home with me."

I had a feeling that their marriage was on the rocks. The woman was desperate for some reason. "Would you like something to drink?"

"No thank you. Can you call my husband? I'm sure he has a cell phone, or you gave him one."

"He'll be home soon."

She laughed. "It kills me when sluts like you play house with another woman's husband."

"He was available for me to play house," I snapped. "I'm not a whore."

"You look like one to me."

"Why don't you come back when Denzel is home? I won't have you sitting in my home, and insulting me. Who in the hell do you think you are? Don't take out your frustrations on me."

"I've been searching for six months to find my husband," Sheila cried. "You don't know the pain I've suffered in the process. I thought my husband was dead and I was bent on finding the suspect who did this to him. I was going to make them pay for killing my husband. I never thought he'd be playing house with a slut. Can't you find your own man?"

"You should leave," I opened the door and Denzel was just walking up to it. "Baby, can you take one of these bags. I think I went overboard with spending today."

I grabbed the bag as he walked in and headed straight for the kitchen. "I spent over one hundred dollars, but we need every bit of it," he cried. "I missed you, baby."

"We have company," I cried.

"Who?" he asked.

"Your wife," I cried.

He stared at me in shock. "Where is she?"

"Sitting in the living room, but I was about to throw her out because her attitude stinks."

He hurried to the living room and I stared at the two of them. By the shock on Denzel's face, I knew he remembered his wife. It just took the sight of her to bring his memory back.

She milked it for all she could as she ran into his arms, and gave him a lingering kiss. I felt like I was going to puke. The fact that

Denzel didn't push her away made the tears fall, but I had no intention of letting them go any further. I wasn't going to give them the satisfaction. I knew my romance was over.

She kissed him for a long time to make a point with me, but why was Denzel letting her kiss him?

I cleared my throat, and then Denzel had the audacity to end the kiss.

Sheila smiled at me.

I couldn't see why Denzel would marry someone like her, and go out of his race to do it. I wasn't prejudiced, but Sheila was the most manipulative woman I've met.

"Honey let's go home," Sheila said. "I have so much to tell you. Your firm is surviving because your assistant is good, but you need to come back home."

"I remember everything," he shouted.

"Honey, let's not talk about that here. We have plenty of time to talk when we get home. I'm going to wash off that great body of yours, and make passionate love to you. I miss you so much, and I'm sorry for everything. Missing you for six months made me come to my senses, baby. I know we had a huge fight before you left and got lost, but I love you, and I want our marriage to work. Let's go home and talk about it."

Denzel stared at her, and then he looked at me. "I'll meet you in the car, Sheila."

She smiled at me, saying I have won. "I'll be waiting."

I waited for the door to slam, and then the tears fell. "You should be going."

"I need to see about my other life, but I will be back," Denzel said.

I turned away from him as my heart was breaking. "I think you should leave now."

"Mimi, my wife cheated on me with my assistant at work. I have my own construction firm."

I smiled. "You do have a way with your hands."

"I knew that wouldn't change. I'm going to straighten out my life with my wife."

"Why did you marry a white woman?"

"Sheila was attractive, and we had a great marriage, but I wasn't enough for her. My marriage is over."

"Get out," I cried. "I just want you to leave."

He stared at me for minutes, and then I heard the slamming of the door. I stared at the closed door for a very long time as the tears blinded me. I knew this day was coming, and when he put his picture in the paper, I knew my life was over. Denzel had a wife. Why did this have to happen to me? I recited Psalm 27 and 37 as I closed my eyes and the tears ran down my face. I remembered when Denzel taught me Psalm 37 and I knew it backwards now. But his name was Carey Coles, and Denzel was just a fairy tale.

Another month passed and my life was back on the right track. I mean my boring life was back on the right track. I had God in my life, so my life was far from jaded. I knew Denzel wasn't coming back so I had to move on. I thought about him day and night. I was never going to trust a man again. My best friend, Kim was out of town on business, and she warned me about getting involved with a man who lost his memory. I was so desperate I couldn't see the forest for the trees. I just wanted someone to love me, and make passionate love to me. What was so wrong with that? I was pregnant with Denzel's child at 42. This pregnancy wasn't going to be easy for me, so I had to get plenty of bed rest and visit my doctor weekly. I didn't want to have a child at this age, but I wanted something of Denzel in my life. I prayed we had a boy who looked just like him. I was going to be a good mother. I had Kim and her family, and my parents to welcome such a blessed baby. I knew this was my calling, and God wanted me to have this baby. I was going to, too.

It was Friday as I left the meeting and walked to my car. So far my job was on the right track. With a brief I done on some remarkable research we were able to win a civil suit, and get millions of dollars in the process. Everyone at the law firm was impressed with me, and I got a raise in the process. I loved my job; I didn't tell anyone about the baby yet, but I'd be showing soon. I was going to cross that bridge when I got to it.

"Hi," he said.

I reached my car staring at Denzel. He'd always be Denzel to me. He was smiling all over himself. "Hi."

"You are glowing for some reason."

I blushed. "What do you want?" I searched for my keys in my purse.

"I am in the process of getting a divorce from Sheila. She was caught in bed with another man. I tried working out my marriage because I thought it was the right thing to do, but I couldn't do it. I kept thinking about you and the way we made love. I love you, Mimi, and I didn't tell you that because I felt obligated. I love you."

I didn't know what to say.

"It's going to take some time for us to get back our relationship, but I spent the last month getting to know myself, and I know who I am, and what I want in my life. I love you."

"I don't know, Denzel."

"I've changed my name to Denzel."

I laughed at him. "What?"

"I'm Denzel Coles now," he proudly replied.

"You're crazy," I laughed.

"In love," he cried. "I not only want my name, but I want the love we shared and had. I need Denzel to make that happen. I love you so much, Mimi. Please say that you still love me too."

"Your wife isn't going to just give you a divorce."

"She has no choice because I have pictures, and if she wants a good settlement, she's going to cooperate with me. Why are you so full of a glow? Your face is full and different."

I laughed hysterically. "I'm carrying your child, Denzel."

"What?" he cried. "Are you pregnant?"

"I am."

"Were you ever going to tell me?" he snapped.

"No," I honestly replied. "I'm going to take care of our baby, alone."

"Is it safe?"

"No, but it has been done. I haven't been taking care of my body so I'm going to need a lot of medical care, and tender loving care. It's not going to be easy for me, but I'm determined to give you a healthy son."

He took me into his arms. "You're going to give me my first child."

"Your first son," I cried. "I love you so much." I smiled at him.

"And I will always love you, Mimi."

"My romance did end happily ever after."

"When do you want to get married because…"

"Not because I'm pregnant," I interrupted.

"We need to be legit when our baby comes into the world."

"Don't you have to get a divorce first?"

"I'm working on it," he said.

"Then when I see the divorce papers, we can run down to City Hall. Right now I think we have a lot of making up to do, I mean you do."

He kissed my lips. "I'm starting right now," he laughed.

Denzel Coles knew who he was after all.

I Am the Bomb!

My name is Macy Beth, and I'm all that and a bag of chips. I stared at Stanley who was getting so much pleasure I thought he was going to fall on his face or something. The man was sweating, pumping and screaming because he was getting his pleasure.

I was on top and I rocked and shook, getting my groove on. I knew I was coming in five more minutes because I was hot as a fire burning in the jungle. I closed my eyes as I speeded up my pump and circled the universe a few times. Finally, I screamed out, and Stanley joined me as we rode the curves of balls and then some. I opened my eyes staring at Stanley glancing at me with love. The man didn't have a clue. I removed myself from the brother, and hurried into the bathroom. I immediately turned on the shower and ran the hot and cold water. I wanted to cleanse my soul because I couldn't stand being nasty, dirty or smelly.

"Where are you going, baby? I'm ready for some more loving."

I ignored the sound and finished with my shower. Fifteen minutes later I turned the shower off, toweled myself dry, and then walked back into my bedroom. I put my hands on my hips and stared at the naked Stanley. He was 55 years old, bald, and old. "I think it's time for you to vacate my premises. I have things to do."

"I want to spend the night," he confessed.

I laughed at him. "And people in hell are screaming for cold water. Get your ass up and out of my house."

"You bitch!"

I stared at him. "Don't you ever call me a name again?"

"I just did," he stated.

"Get out Stanley."

"You make me, bitch! Get your ass over here and please me. I want some head."

I reached for the gun I kept under my pillow for protection. "You have five minutes to get your ass out of my bed, and out of my house. I might just give you enough time to get dressed, or kick your naked ass out right now. You little thang," I spitted. "Who do you think I am? I'm the bomb and then some."

He grabbed his clothes, not taking his eyes from the gun, and was dressed and out the door in five minutes. I waited a few minutes to be sure the coast was clear and returned the gun to its hiding place before rushing to the kitchen. Sex always made me hungry.

An hour later I was flipping the television trying to find something on cable. It was Friday night and I wanted to be alone. I didn't have to go out because it was Friday night. I was going to settle down with a good movie, diet soda, and microwave popcorn with plenty of butter added. They didn't put enough butter on microwave popcorn, so I was going to lend then a hand. I finally noticed Rocky V and put down the remote control. Now Sylvester Stallone was fine. Wouldn't I love to give him a ride down the gravy train of love? I laughed as I walked into the kitchen to get my snacks.

Twenty minutes into the movie my doorbell rang. I rolled my eyes before getting up to answer the door. Whoever had the nerve to bother me on my day of relaxation was going to get the tonguing of their lives, and then some. I was 43 and still going strong and I had the moves to prove it. I yanked opened the door, staring at May. "What the hell do you want? I told you not to bother me when I'm resting."

"How dare you sleep with my husband?" she snapped. "I should pull your weave out."

I shut the door, staring at the bitch. "Who do you think you are?"

"I thought we were best friends until I found out about you and my husband."

"Then you should be talking to your husband, bitch! I'm not the one, thank you very much."

"You slept with my husband, girl. What is the hell wrong with you?"

I laughed. "It was good too. Don't get angry with me because you're not pleasing your husband at home. I'm sick of you bitches getting angry with the other woman. I gave your husband plenty of head, and if you want to keep him out of my bed, then you need to brush up on your lovemaking techniques."

She hit me before I could react. The bitch! I touched my face and then I knocked her to the floor kicking her ass and screaming,

"Don't you ever touch me again, you whore! Who in the hell do you think you are coming over to my house and assaulting me? You have five minutes to leave before I have you arrested." I kicked the bitch a few more times and then waited for her to get up. At first I thought she wasn't going to move and I panicked, wondering if I had really hurt her. I had no intention of going to prison because of this tramp. If she wasn't so fat, she'd be able to keep her man at home. I warned her to lose some weight, but she kept eating like there was no tomorrow. Who did she think she was?

The bitch finally got up, and hurried to the door, jumping as I slammed it on her ass. I laughed to myself, and then went to look in the mirror to make sure I didn't have any marks or bruises on this pretty face of mine. I was okay! I smiled at myself and kissed the mirror. I was still the bomb and then some. I danced around the room before settling back down to watch Rocky's fine ass. I was on it!

I hated these Sunday family dinners, but unless I wanted to listen to a speech from my parents, I had no choice in the matter. I stared around the table at my younger brother and sisters. Connie was 42; Barbara was 39, Linc was 38 and Bina was 30. Then there were my parents, Lee and Mable Beth. My father still worked at the post office on a retired basis, and my mother was an interior decorator. I rolled my eyes at everyone.

"Everything looks good," Linc said. "I'm famished."

"We all know that," I replied. "When are you not famished?"

"Drop dead," Linc said. "I hate you."

"And I can't stand you either," I declared.

"Let's say a blessing," Mable said, rolling her eyes at me. I smiled at her, and bowed my head.

"We need to all hold hands," Mable said.

I was sitting next to Linc so I took his hand. I bowed my head again and listened to my mother.

"I'd like to thank you God for bringing this family together for another Sunday dinner. I look forward to these Sundays after church. Macy wasn't at church this Sunday or the last Sunday, so we're going to say a special prayer for her. Anyway, we thank you for this food we're about to eat, and ask that You continue to bless this family and everyone in this world. Amen!"

I opened my eyes as everyone said their amen's.

"Amen," I said to myself.

"Let's eat," Linc said.

"I hope everyone enjoys dinner," Mable said. "I thought I'd try a buffet this time, that's why I made chicken and fish both. Everyone can help themselves. It would be nice if you could bring your mates with you."

"I don't think so," Barbara said. "Macy was panting over my man."

"He was panting for me," Macy said. "It's not my fault that I'm the most gorgeous woman in the world. If you'd fix your fat ass up, then your man wouldn't be leaving the house."

"You bitch," Barbara said. "You used to be fat."

"A long time ago," I snapped. "I'm never going back to that life. I'm a size 6, and loving every minute of it."

"Someone is going to step on your toes for good." Connie said. "You're not all that. I know for a fact that you got more enemies than the war, so you need to watch your back."

I rolled my eyes at her. "Don't be jealous, Connie."

"You bitch," Connie said.

"I think you're talking about yourself," I said. "I'm the bomb."

"You're a whore," Connie said. "I can't keep track of the men you sleep with."

"She probably has AIDS" Barbara said. "Don't expect any sympathy from me when you're all alone and dying."

"I don't need any of you," I snapped. "If Mother didn't blackmail me, then I wouldn't be here. I do have my life to live, and I love every minute of it. Don't be jealous."

"When are you going to get a job?" Linc asked.

I bit into a pork chop, staring at the fool. "When are you going to stop living off our mother?"

"Fuck off," Linc said. "I'm looking for a job."

"Right," I shouted. "You've been searching for a job for three months now. Give me a break!"

"Can't we all get along?" Lee said.

"It's not our fault," Connie said. "Why does Macy have to be here?"

"Because I'm family," I snapped. "You don't have the right to comment at all."

"I think I do," Connie said. "I hate you."

I laughed at her. "Don't hate the messenger."

"Macy, why are you so mean to everyone?" my mother asked.

I peered at my mother. "Because I can, and I am. I took abuse when I was a size 26, and since I'm gorgeous you all can't stand my attitude. I took abuse by men who thought they were the bomb. Now payback is a bitch. No one will ever hurt me again."

"We love you," Lee said. "You're the eldest."

"She's no example for me," Connie said.

"I won't give you the money to start your own beauty shop. I think not."

"You have plenty of money," Mable said. "George left you a rich woman for the rest of your life. You'll never live long enough to spend all the money he left you. The man was totally in love with you, and you treated him like dirt. I can't understand him."

"Me either," Connie said. "We spoke all the time."

"And you slept with my man," I snapped. "George told me his moment of weakness."

Everyone stared at Connie.

"Way to go," Linc said. "Show the bitch whose boss."

"He loved me," Connie cried. "I should have been the one who married George."

"He was my husband, you whore," I snapped. "When he died who did he leave his money to?"

"I bet you had something to do with his death," Connie said. "I'm sure you're the one who tampered with his brakes. It can never be proven, but I bet my life that you killed George because you found out that he was totally in love with me. You snake! I hate you!"

I continued to eat, smiling to myself. I was glad George was dead, and I hope he was burning in hell. He had the nerve to sleep with my sister after declaring his love for me. Justice was served. "I'm not about to discuss my dead husband with you, trollop. Kiss my ass!"

Connie stood up. "I should beat your ass. It's time someone brought you down a peg or two. You have that size 6 body, but if you keep on playing your games, you're going to be alone."

"That's never going to happen," I laughed. "Men want this gorgeous woman, so sit your flat ass down."

"I want us to stop this madness," Mable snapped. "We're family."

"Just give me the rest of my money, Mother, and then you never have to deal with me again," I snapped. "I'll move away from Chicago and live my own life. I hate these family dinners."

"Sounds like a plan to me," Barbara said. "Did you know that George was gay?"

I stopped eating a piece of bread, staring at her. I thought I kept that secret to myself. How did Barbara find out? I came home early and found George in bed with a man. I almost choked the both of them, which was why George left me his entire fortune. He didn't want his secret to come out. How did this bitch know?

"The cat got your tongue," Barbara said. "I can ruin your reputation."

I counted to ten and then I laughed. "I'll tell the wife of the married man that you've been sleeping with for two years now. I'm sure Ruby Reynolds will love to kill your ass, and I'll give her the loaded gun. Don't play with me because I'm not the one."

"How do you know my business? Barbara asked.

"I know everything, you snake," I said. "Again, don't play with me."

"We all need church," Mable said. "I want silence at this table. Let's just eat."

I couldn't agree more. I was famished and I fed my face and pretended that I was the only one at the table. It was just fine with me.

Finally the dinner was over and I reached for my purse. Barbara was staring daggers at me, and I was staring right back at her. Who did she think she was? I slept with her married man. I walked over to her. "When is Randy going to get rid of the balloons on his right buttock? It looks damn good to me. I love it."

Barbara slapped me, and I slapped her back because I saw the punch coming. She'd be the last bitch who slapped me. We began swinging at each other, and then we fell to the floor tumbling all over each other. We threw punches for fifteen minutes until Linc grabbed me in a lock hold. "You two have lost your minds," he shouted. "Mother is weeping now."

I stared at Barbara who was heaving like a fat pig. "The bitch slapped me."

"I hope you rot in hell," Barbara cried.

"You're going to get there first," I snapped. "Let go of me, Linc."

"Get the hell out of here," Mable shouted. "I mean I want everyone to get out."

There was silence in the room as everyone stared at Mable. We were stunned by her crying words.

"Get the hell out of my house and don't come back until you all learn to love each other," Mable cried. "I mean now," she shouted again.

"You heard your mother," Lee said. "I want you all gone."

"It's been fun," I cried. I grabbed my possessions and hurried out the door. It was May, and the weather was very warm, so I didn't need a coat. I jumped behind the wheel of my car, relieved I didn't have to share dinner with the phonies of my family. I truly hated every one of them. I loved my mother and was sorry she was crying, but I had no intention of changing my rules. Learn how to take it, or get out of the kitchen. I hysterically laughed.

In the heart of Michigan Avenue in Chicago, Illinois I sat in my office. With George's money, I was able to start my own business. I owned the most famous and prestigious spa in this city. I didn't have to come in, but I mostly ventured in without anyone noticing it so I could catch someone not doing their job. At this moment, the bee got caught.

The knock sounded on the door, I smiled. "Come in."

I stared at Beyonce as she walked into the room. The girl thought she was the bomb, but she didn't have a clue. "Sit down, Beyonce. Can I get you something to drink?"

"I was about to do another massage," she cried. "What can I do for you?"

"I just have two words for you," I laughed. "You're fired."

"What?"

"Don't play me, girl. You got busted."

"I don't understand," she cried. "I'm like your assistant, and this is the thanks I get for my hard work. How could you do this to me?"

"You did it to yourself, bitch! No one steals from me. I should have you arrested."

"I don't know what you mean?"

I took out a file folder, and threw it at her. "Why don't you read it and weep?"

The folder fell to the floor, and Beyonce reached for it. She opened it and began reading. She was stunned. "I only took five thousand, but I've been paying it back in monthly installments. I only have one thousand dollars to go. I needed the money for my mother's operation, but you didn't give a damn," she cried. "You could have loaned me the money."

"So you steal from me," I laughed. "You're a stupid whore. You've been having sex with some of my men customers. This isn't a whore house, you dummy. I have a respectable reputation, and your whoring ass has ruined it. You have five minutes to get out."

"I'm sorry," Beyonce cried. "I need this job."

"You may think you're Beyonce the singer, but you're nothing like her. Get out of my sight or I will throw you out. If I see you at my spa again, your ass will be going to jail."

"You're going to die," Beyonce cried. "I wish you were dead."

"Whatever!" I slammed the door after her, and then settled back behind my desk. The bitch didn't have a clue. No one messed with me and lived to tell about it. I reached for my telephone and dialed a number. "Henry, please come to my office."

I hung up, smiling like a Cheshire cat as I waited.

Five minutes later I answered Henry's knock on my door. "Please come in," I said to the tall, good-looking man, locking the door behind him. "Have a seat."

He complied, staring at me. "Did I do something wrong?"

"Beyonce is fired. I want you to take over her duties."

"Excuse me?"

"Do you think you can handle the job?"

"I don't know…"

I laughed. "I'm going to give you a month to prove yourself, and a raise is in the works. When are you getting married?"

"In June," he cried.

"That's next month. Why don't you service me for now?" I removed my dress, showcasing my body for his eyes only. I didn't wear a bra or panties because I wanted to show off my body. "Come over here and give me some pleasure. I'm hot for you, Henry."

"You're gorgeous," Henry said, "but I love my fiancé. I can't cheat on her."

I laughed. "What she doesn't know won't hurt her?"

"I can't," he cried.

This sucker had the nerve to turn me down. "If you don't make love to me, Henry, you'll be fired, and you'll never work again. I'm going to skin you alive because no one turns me down. I'll make sure you never work in Chicago again," I snapped. "Get your ass over here." I went to lie down on the sofa, and spread my legs. "I'm hot, so let's get it on."

I waited, eyes closed, and in few minutes my body was lighting up with pleasure as his tongue did wonders for my private parts. I grabbed his hair and began playing in his head because I was about to come, and I didn't want to come too soon.

I tried holding on, but my body shook with the most gratifying and powerful orgasm. It was out of this world. After the sensations were spent, my body lit up with pleasure as his tongue continued to excite me. When I was spent for the final time, I grabbed Henry's lips, and make love to his lips, and then I removed his pants. He was inside of me because I was exploding with passion, and there was no condom in place. I wanted this toy boy inside of me, and no condom was going to work.

Henry continued to pleasure my body, and finally I was spent for the last time. I smiled at the boy. "You did well, and you still have a job. Next time when I say Simon says, you move, and when I say Simon says again, you continue to move. It's time for you to move into Beyonce's office, and began your duties. Keep your mouth shut, and your tongue and private parts working, and you and I will have a very long-lasting relationship. Now get out!"

I stared at the closed door, and then I hurried into the bathroom laughing hysterically.

The weekend was back again, and it was Sunday. I didn't have to go over to my mother's house, and that was fine with me. I heard through Father that she wasn't cooking, and was working diligently on a mansion she was decorating. It was no skin off my shoulders. I'd visit her next month so she could release some of my money. If George wasn't already dead, I'd shoot his brains off. Who did he think he was making my mother the trustee of my fortune? The man was demented which was why I was still alive and he was dead. I'd ordered something to eat and relax with my remote control. It was the best remedy for me at the moment. The doorbell shrilled into my silence. Damn!

I yanked opened the door as Connie burst into the room. I slammed the door. "What in the hell are you doing here? Where are the guards?"

"I'm your sister, and they didn't see the need to arrest me," she shouted. "I need to talk to you."

I walked into the living room and sat down. Connie was fine, and most of the men flocked to her. I was jealous of her, but I was the bomb, and didn't have to be jealous of anyone. "You have five minutes to get the hell out of my house."

"I need the money for my beauty shop," Connie cried. "I'll pay your ass back with interests. I have the perfect building for it, but the owner isn't going to hold it for much longer. I don't ask much of you, but I need this. Please don't turn me down this time."

"Are you begging?" I laughed. "Why don't you get down on your knees?"

"I don't think so," Connie said.

"Then this meeting is over," I cried. "I want to see you beg."

"You bitch!" Connie said.

"I'm the bitch that will loan you the money after you get down on your knees, and bark like a dog. I read this somewhere or saw a movie or something. I think it might have been a play. I don't give a damn, but you have five minutes, Connie."

I played with my fingers as I waited. Three seconds later Connie was on the floor, actually barking like a dog. I laughed at the bitch, and then I let her continue to humiliate herself for a few more minutes. I was truly having the time of my life. "Get up. I have forty percent of your business."

"I hate you," Connie cried.

"Don't make me angry or you'll be on the floor again. I'll get my checkbook and write you a check. Don't make me regret this venture, and if it doesn't profit in two years, then my money is out of it, and I'll demand repayment on the loan. Do you hear me? This is a business deal, not sisterly love. I want my money back with interest."

"I'll pay you back every red cent," she snapped.

"Whatever!" I grabbed my checkbook and wrote Connie a check for fifty thousand dollars. I stared at the zeros because I never thought this would happen to me. Most of it was George's money, but I've made good investments, and had my own money working for me. I was the richest woman in this city for sure and probably other cities. "Here."

Connie stared at the check in shock. "I wasn't expecting so much."

"I want an itemized list of everything you buy and spend. I want a report every week on the progress of your beauty shop. If you don't want me to be your shadow, you'll make sure that report is in my hand every Friday."

"Thank you," Connie said.

"Whatever," I cried. "Now get out."

Connie stared at me for the longest time trying to read into my soul. I was ice, and cold as sin, and that's the way I wanted it. Macy Beth was the bomb.

A few days later I was having lunch with Steven. He was 27 years old and another boy toy of mine. We were dining at a fancy restaurant on Michigan Avenue not too far from my spa. "How is school going?"

"It's fine, and thanks for the tuition."

"When are you going to start paying me back?" I snapped. "I'm not a friend where money is concerned."

"I'm still in law school, Macy. What's wrong with you?"

"I want my payments to begin next month, boy. Don't play with me."

"I'm still struggling?" he cried.

"I want one hundred dollars a month," I snapped. "This is no game."

"I don't have it," he cried. "I have rent to pay."

"Then I'm going to cancel the rest of your tuition."

"Why are you so mean to me? I'm in love with you and want to marry you."

I laughed. "Don't be infantile. I'll never marry anyone, including a boy toy."

"I love you."

"You love my money, and let's keep it that way. I've been married and I didn't like it."

"I love you."

"Boy, please," I cried. "Don't make me puke. This orange dress cost me one thousand dollars, and you're not worth it." I picked up my wine and took a long sip. "We can make love, but no one owns me ever again. Do you hear me?"

"Loud and clear," he shouted. "Why are you so mean?"

"If I was mean, you wouldn't be going to law school, you ass! Don't play me." He had the nerve to shake his head at me. I hysterically laughed.

Two hours later I screamed out my pleasure as my body rocked with a juicy and most satisfied orgasm. Steven was young, with plenty of energy and he pumped me for almost fifty minutes. I was having the ride of my life as I stared at his broad chest. Steven had it going on. When I was completely satisfied I hurried into the bathroom to clean myself, and Steven was out the door. I wanted to spend time with myself, and no one spent the night unless I wanted it. I hysterically laughed. I was still the bomb.

It was another month when I stared at the legal document. It was June, and the weather was booming with heat. I then looked at my attorney, James Knots. "What is wrong with Beyonce? She's going to sue me for wrongly firing her. The woman has no clue."

"She has a contract that you breached, Macy. Beyonce was hired for five years, and she has only worked four of the five years. We have to give her money damages, or she's going to take us to court, and probably win. What were you thinking?"

I threw the legal document across the room. "She stole from me," I shouted.

"Your word against hers," he pointed out. "The attorney she has hired is Irvin Jeans."

I was stunned as my eyes opened wide. "Are you sure?"

"It's right in front of your face," James said. "He has never lost a case."

"There's a first time for everything," I shouted. "What does the bitch want?"

"A million dollars," James said.

I laughed. "She's not going to get it. We have to find something on her where we can blackmail her. I need you to hire a private investigator to find the skeletons in her closet, and I'm sure she has plenty of them. We have thirty days before you need to file an answer to the complaint, so let's get a move on."

"She's clean so far."

"The bitch is guilty as hell about something. Find me something."

"Okay, I'll get right on it. Do you want to have sex?"

I stared at him. "I'm not in the mood but call me later."

I waited for James to leave and then I picked up my cell phone and dialed a number. No one messed with me and lived to tell about it.

Thirty days later I was sitting in my house, watching a movie on Lifetime. The telephone rang, and I reached for my cell phone. "Yes, James. What do you have for me?"

"Beyonce is gone," he called. "I can't find her, and the case has been dropped."

I smiled. "Maybe the bitch came to her senses."

"Did you do something to her?"

"Don't be stupid," I snapped. "I'm not that kind of woman. I'm sure she left town because she knew you were going to find something on her. It's not my fault she ran like a scared rabbit. The bitch is in the wrong league. Let's celebrate later on. I'm going to do a strip tease for you."

"I'll be over there later, Macy. I hope you had nothing done to her. It's as if she has disappeared off the face of the earth."

"I'm sure she'll resurface again. I'm missing my movie."

"I'll see you later."

I hung up the telephone and hysterically laughed. These people just didn't know who they were playing with. I was still the bomb.

A noise woke me. I turned off the snow screen television with the remote and stood up. I needed to go to bed in my bedroom.

I turned on the lights when I heard the noise again. Someone was in my house. I searched for my purse, but couldn't find it. I thought I left it on the sofa because my gun was in it. I silently waited, and then I heard the noise again. "Who is there?"

I waited, but no one answered me. I shook my head wondering if I was losing my mind. I lived alone, and no one was here but me. I walked out of the living room and headed for the stairs. My door banged opened, and I saw the shadow as I heard a loud noise. "Show your face, you coward!"

I stared at the shadow as it came toward me, and then I saw the gun. I covered my mouth in shock as the gun went off. I heard five shots, and then in slow motion I fell to the floor. I felt this awful pain, and then darkness took over my soul. I was dead. I opened my eyes staring at the nurse. I knew I was in a hospital. "What time is it?" I cried.

"Thanks for coming back to life," the nurse replied. "I thought you were going to die."

"The time," I snapped.

"It's September. Welcome back to life."

I ignored the nurse, and began wiggling my toes and moving my legs. I breathed a sigh of relief when I could, and I made sure my sight was working. The nurse left and then I closed my eyes and that awful night came back to haunt me. I didn't see the person who shot me, but I was going to find the culprit and make them pay for it. I was alive, and well, and still the bomb. "I need to get out of here."

The nurse walked back into the room. "In due time Macy," she said. "You used to be a nurse, so you know the rules. Your doctor will be in to examine you, and we will see. Is everything working?"

"So far," I cried. "Do they know who shot me?"

"I'm afraid not," the nurse said. "They have about twenty suspects. No one can stand you."

I smiled to myself. The bitch or bastard will pay. "I want my doctor, now."

"When he's available," the nurse said. "You don't run me or scare me. I call the shots here."

"Did anyone come to visit me?"

"Your parents came for a while, and your siblings, but they stopped coming. You've been alone for three months. I think they only came to make sure you died in your sleep. What did you do to your family and friends? They can't stand you."

"I need to talk to the detective on the case," I snapped. "The killer could still be out there."

The nurse smiled. "And it could be anyone."

I stared at her, and then I screamed.

The Root of All Evil

I focused on my best friend, Leslie Taylor as we sat in the, dining room of the Hilton Hotel. "What's on your mind?" Leslie asked. "Don't bother telling me nothing is wrong because I know you like the back of my hand. Tomorrow is your birthday and you should be thrilled."

I took a long sip of my Alizee as I stared at her. "I'm going to be 43 years old, and I'm miserable as hell. I know my husband doesn't love me, so it's time to suspend that part of my life. I'm not going to be 43 and married to the bastard of husbands."

"You had an arm load to tell me," Leslie laughed. "Dirk is very handsome, and the two of you have the perfect marriage. Where do you think it went wrong? I never thought he'd betray you with one of your friends from work. I can't stand the man, Racine, and I think you're better off."

"He married me for my money, and he has been very nice to me this last month. He knows when I turn 43 I'm going to be ten million dollars richer. Dirk wants half of my money for fifteen years of marriage. I thought he loved me, Leslie. This is so devastating to me. Why does money have to ruin lives?"

Leslie frowned. "You know money is the root of all evil, girl. Dirk has been cheating on you left and right. Of course he's not going to admit it, but you're not blind or stupid. You told me that he ignores you when he's home, and you haven't made love in years."

"Please don't throw my words in my face," I cried. I took another long sip of my drink. I wanted to get stoned so I wouldn't have to think about my marriage being over. I had already filed for divorce, and I was going to make sure Dirk got his papers very soon.

"Do you see that gorgeous black man over there?" Leslie pointed out. "He's a basketball star, and he's been staring over here for the last twenty minutes because I've been watching him. I know he's not staring at me, because I'm happily married to my white man and proud of it."

I stared at the handsome black man. I did recognize him as a basketball player for the Chicago Cats. I thought they were playing in Los Angeles or something. The man was surrounded by gorgeous woman, and having the time of his life. Why was he looking over here? "I'm not about to get involved with another black man. I think I'm going to search for someone white this time. I don't blame you for turning to another race, Leslie. I hated you for it, but I see that you're very happy, and you don't have a worry in the world."

Leslie laughed. "You're reading too many romance novels. Michael and I don't agree on a lot of things, but we made a pact to work out any issues before we go to bed at night. It's been fifteen years of ups and downs, and my marriage won't be in the book of world's records, believe me."

"I know, Leslie, but you're not filing for divorce. Two days ago I checked into the Hilton because I didn't want to go home. I just wanted to be alone, and I enjoyed it, Leslie. I'm never getting married again. I'm too rich and when a man finds out what I'm worth, then he's not going to love me for me. I think Dirk used me. I bought him a Mercedes, financed his legal career, and now he's a top attorney in his firm; bought the mansion we're living in, and set up a million dollars for Dirk in his own bank account. I'd think the man would be most grateful. I did all these things because I thought he loved me."

Leslie shook her head. "I'm sorry this happened to you, Racine. I know you want to be the happiest woman in the world, and have your marriage on the right track, but Dirk isn't your soul mate. I also know you don't want to hear this, but you're going to find the right man."

"Let's pig out and not discuss men," I cried. "I'm about to graduate as a registered nurse, and then I'll be working at the top hospital in Chicago. I know I don't have to work, but I want to give back to the world, and I want to help people. I had plenty of money when my parents died, and tomorrow I'll have more. Giving to the Chicago Public Schools is something I'm going to do because the schools in Chicago are in bad shape, thank you very much."

"File for divorce and move on with your life," Leslie suggested. "I want you to be happy and if that's being alone, then I'm all for it. Life is too short, and I don't want my best friend miserable. I think you've done enough for Dirk and he needs to visit the real world now as an independent man."

"Let's toast to that," I cried. I couldn't believe my marriage was going to end in a few days. I was going home and give Dirk the news. His days of using his wife was about to end and his meal ticket would be over. I hoped he had saved his money because I was done being his sugar woman.

I was about to pay the check when the handsome basketball player stopped at my table. I stared at the debonair man. He had all the curves in the right place. "Can I help you? I see your table of fans has left such an important man," I snapped.

"I'm sorry you don't like men, but I saw a gorgeous woman across the room, and I wanted to speak to her. My name is Evan Banks. May I sit down? I'm waiting for my take out, and I thought I could spend it with you. I believe that you are an unhappy woman."

I stared at him, and frowned. "I don't think you should sit down, and let me tell you that I hate men. I'm about to get a divorce, and then I'm signing off of men for the rest of my life. If you want a booty call, then I suggest you sleep with one of your fans."

He laughed at me, calling a lot of attention to himself, but he was already getting plenty of it. The man was on the news all the time so everyone knew who he was. He got more balls into a basket than Michael Jordan, and everyone was thrilled to have him on their team. "Will you just leave me the hell alone?"

"Not until you sit down and have a drink with me," he stated. "Your lovely friend is gone and it'd be a shame for such a gorgeous woman to be alone on her way home. It's almost three o'clock in the morning, thank you very much. Are you going to deny me a drink? I'll even let you pay for it."

I laughed as I sat back down. The waitress hurried over because she wanted to get an autograph from Evan. He complied and then our drinks were ordered. Evan wanted a beer and I ordered another glass of Alizee. Evan was very convincing, and I stared at the man with the gray eyes. He didn't look black at all. "So what do you want Mr. Banks?"

"Just to relax with someone that's not falling all over me," Evan said. "I love being a basketball player, but it's just a job to me, and nothing more or less. Right now I just want some down time and here come a lot of children. I love my children fans, so give me a minute."

I watched as Evan interacted with his young fans. There were over twenty of them and he gave everyone of them an autograph. The man had it going on and his girlfriend was the luckiest woman in the world. I frowned as I took another sip of my drink. I did hear on the news that he had just broken up with someone by the name of Sharon.

Finally Evan's screaming fans all left. I shook my head. "You have a way with the children," I stated. "I'm sure you have about five or six children running around Chicago." What made me utter such nasty words? "I'm sorry."

"It's okay," he laughed. "I don't have any children, thank you very much. I wanted to become a basketball player, and I made it happen. Do you mind taking this back to my hotel room? I just want some down time, and we're going to be interrupted with more fans."

I laughed. "You don't waste time, Mr. Banks, but I'm a married woman, thank you very much. I should go call a cab to go home. I'm sure there's something to do there. I'm not about to have sex with a complete stranger, but thanks for the offer, anyway."

He drained his glass and stood up. "I don't sleep with women I just met because rape is easily accessible to women. I don't trust women, and I've been celibate for a week now since I broke up with Sharon. I can't trust women just like you can't trust men."

I drained my glass, and I stood up. I was about to lose my mind, but there was nothing I could do about it because I wanted to spend more time with this hunk of a man. "Let's go to your hotel room, to talk only. I'm not in the mood for committing adultery."

He smiled, and his face lit up like a star in the sky, I thought to myself. Evan Banks wasn't just a basketball player, but a very happy and genuine man, who looked like he had a heart of gold. We hurried to the elevator before more fans bombarded us."

Of course Evan's suite was like a mansion, but I wasn't surprised about that. I took off my shoes because my feet were killing me. It was August, almost September, and the weather in Chicago was still hot. Since it was the morning, the weather outside was cool.

I sat in the lovely yellow room, getting comfortable on the sofa. Evan put some soft jazz music on the stereo and handed me a glass of red wine. I was probably drunk, but I'd take a cab home. My cheating husband was out of town so it didn't matter when I got home. "I like."

"It's where I stay when I'm in Chicago. I like the Oak Lawn area more than the Chicago area, and it has nothing to do with me being a basketball player. I need the silence more often than not. I saw you across the room and something just melted my heart. What is your name?"

"Racine," I said. "You do have a way with words, Mr. Banks. I thought a man of your caliber would be mixing and out partying until five in the morning. I'm sure the other ball players are mixing a lot of personal business, and having the time of their lives."

"I don't think so," Evan seriously replied. "Most of the players have their wives with them, and we can't sleep around with everyone because of ball players being a target for greedy women who are trying to get a lot of money from us. I'm sure you read about Justice Marks. A woman accused him of rape when he wouldn't give her a thousand dollars, and the bitch almost won her case. It's very dangerous for us, and we have to be careful."

"So you just picked me up, a perfect stranger, and now I'm sitting in your hotel room," I laughed. "I think you're breaking your own rules, Mr. Banks. I could be one of those women who are going to trap you into sleeping with me, and then make a video tape of it to blackmail you with."

He smiled. "I don't think so because my instincts have made me a lot of money. We both have money. I can tell by the way you dress, Racine, and also the way you carry yourself. We're going to talk, and then I'm going to call you a cab and make sure you get home because we don't need to drink and drive."

So far this man was a king. There had to be something wrong with him because I wasn't buying his kindness. Maybe he wanted something from me because all men were evil, and wanted me to make their lives a better place on this earth. My husband was proof of that.

"What is so wrong with your husband?" Evan asked. He loosened his tie, and unbuttoned his shirt. The man had a chest. I wanted to rub my hands all over his hairy chest, and make passionate love to the man. It had been a long time for me and I wasn't afraid to admit it, either. I was a woman starved for love, affection and sex. I yawned a few times.

"Why don't I give you a shirt to put on, and then you can take a nap, Racine. I'm not going to seduce you, or rape you thank you very much. I think we both are tired, and then we can have breakfast and talk in the morning. I have a feeling you're not eager to go home."

How did he know so much about me? I didn't want to go home because I knew Dirk was banging one of his whores, or two of them for that matter. I caught him in so many sexual positions I could sell the pictures to the newspaper and make money off the snake. I was hot, and I needed a bath, and his shirt would be great. I bet it'd smell just like him. "I need to take a bath, and you're on."

He smiled, and then hurried to his bedroom. Ten minutes later I was lavishing in a hot bath of scented water, feeling the aches and pains, not to mention the stress, leave my body. I closed my eyes and let the water work its magic on my neglected body parts.

A knock on the door sounded, and I opened my eyes. I had fallen asleep in the bathtub and now the water was cold as ice. I stood up, reaching for the towel. "I'm okay, Evan. I went to sleep, but I'm about to come out." I hurriedly dried myself off, and reached for the clean white shirt. I smelled his shirt, and then hurried into it. I then stared at myself in the mirror. I reached for my purse to refresh my makeup and then added more lipstick. I had a gorgeous short haircut, so all I had to do was pat it down, and I was good to go.

I opened the door and walked back into the living room. Even was wearing a yellow robe. Something told me that yellow was his favorite color. "I think I'm going to bed now, Evan. I can't thank you enough for being so nice to me. I can sleep on the sofa right here."

"I have two bedrooms, so you can have the green room," Evan said. "You look very good in that shirt, Racine, and your legs are skinny, but I think I like them. I hope the bath did wonders for you, because my shower enhanced my muscles if you know what I mean. Sleep tight."

I looked into his gray eyes. "Are you all black or mixed? I don't mean to pry into your personal life because I know you must get the media trying to find skeletons in your closet often. I don't want to be one of your groupies, but your eyes are mesmerizing. Are you wearing contacts?"

He smiled and his face flooded with light. He was more handsome when he smiled, of course. "I have gray eyes because my mother is pure Indian," he said. "I don't want this getting into the media hands. I kept my family private for a long time."

"I'd love to meet your mother," I cried. "I bet she's a beautiful woman to have raised a son like you. I never met anyone like you before Evan Banks. You're something else."

I walked toward the other bedroom. It was time for me to get some rest before I made love to Evan Banks right here on the hotel floor. I couldn't let this happen with a man I just met because I never wanted to trust another man again.

Ten minutes later I was curled up in bed staring at the ceiling. I thought sleep would instantly claim me, but that was out of the question. Another twenty minutes escaped me, and I was still staring at the ceiling. I kept smelling Evan's aftershave, and it was getting on my last nerves. I wanted him to make love to me like no man has ever tried.

I turned on my right side and closed my eyes. I had to go to sleep because my thoughts were tarnished, and all over the place. I had a stipulation in my contract for my millions, and I had no intentions of letting my husband find the evidence to fry me. It was out of the question.

It was six a.m. when I gave up trying to sleep and stood up. I was going to the kitchen to get a bottled water or something. I opened the bedroom door, listened for a second and when all was quiet, hurried into the kitchen. I bumped right into Evan. "I'm sorry."

"I couldn't sleep," he said.

"Me either." Our eyes met, and then we flew into each other arms. Evan took my lips, and the minute our lips touched, my moans began spilling out into the room. I was so sex starved, I couldn't control the emotions that were haunting me. Evan was a great kisser, and my entire body lit up with a volume of passion. My shirt fell to the floor, and Evan's robe joined the shirt and our bodies met on the floor. He captured my buds with his tongue, and I screamed out from the touch of his lips. He massaged both of my nipples, and then returned the favor with my breasts, giving my cups the attention they needed and then some.

I kept screaming out my pleasure, and prayed no one was in the next hotel room because I was giving myself away. Evan's moans followed mine and he eased himself inside of me because we both couldn't wait any longer. We pumped, and then we both exploded with screams of passion as our bodies collapsed into fits of vibrations.

After several moments, we both returned to normal and Evan went to work on the foul play area, exploring every inch of me with his tongue of pleasure. I yelled out this time when my spree of passion tingled with shooting stars. I couldn't stop the orgasms as they pounded my body and kept raising the pitch of sensations. I thought I was having a stroke as Evan bought me to the point of no return.

When my body couldn't take any more he entered me again, and this time a condom was our protection. Luckily the Hilton had plenty of them in their drawers. We rotated to the beat of our own sexual games, and Evan and I exploded on top of explosions, and we continued to ease our sexual burdens. Two hours later we fell asleep in each other arms wearing nothing but smiles. Right at this exact moment I was the happiest woman in the world, and I did believe in love at first sight. I was in love with Evan Banks. Miracles do come true, and so do my dreams.

I opened my eyes, immediately searching for Evan. He was staring out the window as I sat up in bed. "What time is it?"

"It's almost two in the afternoon," Evan replied. "I had to leave, I have practice and I hope the sex isn't going to ruin my game if you know what I mean. Anyway, when can I see you again, Racine? What we shared was so spectacular, and I want it again?"

I shook my head. "I need to go home and talk to my husband, Evan. It's my birthday today, and I'm filing for divorce. I just need some time and space. Give me your private number, and when the time is right I'll call you. I can't let my husband get anything on me."

"Don't wait too long, Racine because I believe I'm falling in love."

I flew into his arms, and we made love again. An hour later I was in a cab on the way home.

When I walked into the house, Dirk was sitting in the living room watching a game on television. I ignored him as I hurried to the bedroom and undressed before hopping into the shower. When I walked back into the living room in a pair of blue shorts, and a blue shirt. I walked straight over to Dirk. It was time. "Dirk, I want a divorce. The papers should be coming soon. Now you're free to be with your bimbos."

Dirk laughed before he focused back on the television. "Evan Banks is a good basketball player and a close friend of mine. He didn't once mind banging my wife so I could get it on videotape. Do you remember the stipulation in the Will, Racine? If I find evidence that you've been cheating on me, I get half of your ten million dollars. I want my five million right now, and then the divorce is fine with me."

I was stunned as I stared at my poor excuse for a husband. "Where is the tape, Dirk?"

"It's on its way by messenger. I never thought you had the guts to cheat on me."

"So you set me up," I cried.

He laughed again. "Of course I did bitch, because I want your money. Why in the hell do you think I married you? I found out about your Will, and the money you were born with. It's not fair that women like you have money, and I have to work my ass off to make something out of my life. You never worked a day in your life. I hate women like you. The gifts were mine because I deserved your cold frigid self."

"I wasn't frigid in bed with Evan," I cried. "Maybe you're the one that's impotent."

Dirk stood up ready to punch me when I pointed my knife at him. "Make me use it you, bastard, and I will cut you. Get the hell out of my house and take your things with you. I'll see your ass in court."

"It's been nice," he snapped.

I stared after the snake, and then I crumbled to the floor. I was played not only by my husband, but by Evan too. When was I going to stop letting men use me?

Three weeks later I stood up in court, staring at the judge. "I want this divorce on the grounds that my husband married me for my money only. I'm tired of his affairs, too."

"I also want a divorce," Dirk smiled. "I'm in love with a gorgeous woman. My wife owes me five million dollars, and I want this transaction approved and authorized in court."

"My attorney, Lacy, stood up. "Your honor, the Will clearly states that if no evidence of my client's adultery is proven, the husband forfeits the money. We have entered into evidence numerous exhibits of the affairs that Mr. Mills had with other women. "

"I grant both divorces," the Judge replied. "I also grant all specifications in the Will of ten million dollars to the plaintiff free and clear. Dirk Mills has no obligations to the Will because of his affairs which has been brought and approved as evidence. I also grant a restraining order against the defendant coming anywhere near the plaintiff, and it is the order of the court that the defendant must vacate Chicago, Illinois in thirty days. He's not allowed to live in this city again as long as the plaintiff resides here. If any rules of this judgment is forfeited, then the defendant will be arrested and spend five years in prison, with no possible chance of probation. I think you're a sorry excuse for a man to marry someone for money. You're evil as money. This is my ruling, and the court is dismissed."

I embraced my attorney and then hugged Leslie. I had won after all. Dirk was staring at me, his eyes shooting bullets, but he had made his bed, and now he had to lie in it. I did win after all.

A month later, back at the Hilton dining with Leslie, I couldn't stop thinking about Evan. I saw him win game after game on television. I still had feelings for him because he gave me the best sex ever, and that was the only reason. It had been a while for me.

"Are you going to be okay, Racine? If this place brings back memories we can go somewhere else. McDonalds is fine with me."

"My marriage is over and I have my life back," I cried. "I slept with Evan, Leslie, and I hate myself for doing it, but it was the best sex I ever had. I don't regret the sex. Evan talked about how he couldn't trust women and he was lying to me the whole time."

"I don't think he planned on sleeping with you, or falling for you," Leslie pointed out. "He tried calling you and me about fifty times before he finally gave up. He really wanted to apologize to you."

I shook my head as I sipped a glass of Alize. "I will never forgive Evan Banks."

"He's coming over here," Leslie cried.

I couldn't believe that the man would have the audacity to show his face. "What in the hell do you want? If you don't leave I'm going to cause a scandal," I cried. "I hate you Evan Banks. You had the nerve to video tape us making love for money. I'm sorry you didn't get paid because Dirk didn't get the money he planned on having. You might as well have stabbed me in the chest; or shot me with a gun."

"I'm sorry," Evan said.

"I should go to the ladies room," Leslie said. She abruptly left the table.

I stared after her. "Get out Eva!."

"I should never have slept with you, Racine. I just fell for you. I didn't give your husband the tape. He found one and had it fixed. I got rid of the tape I had and burned it in my fireplace. There are no extra copies. Your husband was bent on screwing you over so he used a woman who looked like you."

"How am I supposed to trust you ever again?" I cried.

"Can we go to my hotel and discuss this? We're causing a scene."

I laughed, and then I slapped him across the face so hard, he almost fell. "Stay out of my life or I'm going to take you to court for harassment. I wouldn't want to ruin your basketball career. I hate you! I hate you!" I began hitting him in the chest as the tears rolled down my face.

Evan let me hit him without stopping me.

I was exhausted as Leslie grabbed me and hurried me out of the hotel. We made a scene, and I was sure it was going to be the front headlines of the newspaper, but I didn't give a damn.

Four months later I received an even bigger shock. I was pregnant with Evan's child and too far along to have an abortion. Great! I was 43 and about to become a first-time mother. Leslie was thrilled for me, but I was so stressed out that I had to stay in bed for a week. I graduated from nursing school, but working in a hospital was put on hold until my baby was born. My blood pressure was sky high, and my doctor was threatening to put me in the hospital if I didn't get it down. I didn't want a baby.

I was showing a little, and every time I looked in the mirror the image of Evan making love to me was evident. I couldn't erase the images of our lovemaking from my mind. I had plenty of money, but no one to share my life with. My child wouldn't want for anything. I was thinking about giving up the child for adoption. I didn't want to be a mother, and a single mother at that. What was so wrong with my life? Where did I go wrong? I wished I never had any money. Money was truly the root of all evil.

The doorbell rang, and I slowly climbed out of bed and walked to the door. I opened it and then went to sit in the living room. I was exhausted with lying in bed. "I'm in the living room, Leslie. I can't lay down another minute so don't fuss with me. I'm going to stare out the window for a while, and when I get sleepy, I'm going back to bed."

I was shocked when Evan walked into my living room. "What are you doing here?"

"Leslie told me about the baby," he said. "Please don't be mad at her, but I have a right to know. I want to be a part of this child's life, and if you try and keep the baby from me, I'm going to take you to court. Please don't make me do that."

"It's not your child," I lied.

"We can prove it is with a DNA, Racine. I know I'm the father."

"Get out, Evan. I don't need anything from you. I have plenty of money or do you want some of that?"

"I think I have more than you," he said. "Would you like to see my bank statements?"

I smiled for some reason, and then I frowned. "Get out!"

"Money has been a curse for me, and you share the curse. I think we have a great deal in common. I have every right to be here and you're not going to get rid of me so easily. I'll spend the rest of my life making it up to you for the pain I caused, Racine. I love you, and you're the first person I let into my heart since Sharon. I love you."

I stared into those gray eyes of his as the tears blinded me. "I don't trust you."

"And I don't trust you," he confessed. "I believed you were just like all the other women I knew. Dirk talked about you so badly, I thought you deserved what was coming to you. I didn't work hard as a basketball player to have women accusing me of rape to get my money. Go out there, work your ass off, and make your own money. I'm not anyone's sugar daddy. I want to be loved for me, and not the basketball player. This is like a job to me, and only a job. When I go home, I leave my job behind. I want a wife and child to settle down with. I envy the other players with their wives. Some of these men met their wives when they were regular people. They can trust their wives, and wouldn't dream of doing anything to ruin their marriage."

"Men are dogs," I cried.

"And so are a lot of women," he declared. "Do you need anything?"

"I need for you to leave, Evan."

"Our child will have both parents. If you want to make this a nasty battle, then let's go to court. I was hoping you'd cooperate with me. Our child was conceived because of our lovemaking, and deserves our love."

"You can be in your child's life, but leave me the hell alone."

"That's fine with me. Leslie told me that your blood pressure is too high, and I know it's because of everything bad that's been happening to you, lately, but it's going to get better for us. If you ever forgive me I want us to get married. You can propose to me when you're ready."

I laughed again, and I could have kicked myself for it.

He smiled. "Let me run you a hot bath and wash your hair."

I laughed again. "Don't push your luck, Evan."

"You don't want me to wash your hair, massage and wash you up, and then lotion your entire body?"

My back was hurting for a reason, and I needed a massage. "Okay," I cried, "and then you can leave."

"Okay," he said.

I smiled to myself.

Five months later I gave birth to twins. Evan and I were shocked beyond words. We're raising our children together, but marriage isn't in the cards for me because I'd never trust another man again. Although Evan is still hoping, and he has truly made up for hurting me big time. In my eyes, money is still the root of all evil, and men were just as evil.

I woke up with this incredible feeling. I stared around the room, settling on the alarm clock. It was three o'clock in the morning. I reached for my telephone. I needed to hear Jasper's voice. I dialed his number, and prayed that he answered.

Jasper was out of town on business in New York City. I wanted to go with him, but being nine months pregnant nipped that in the bud. I listened to the phone ring. Jasper, please answer the phone.

"Hello," the voice whispered. "Honey, is everything okay? Are you in labor? I can get a flight out, baby. I'm so sorry I can't be there with you. This trial can be postponed. Why did you insist that I come? The senator can wait a few more days. He's not in jail for heaven sakes."

I smiled because I was so glad to hear Jasper's voice. He was okay. "Honey, I'm fine, and I just needed to hear your voice. I had this awful dream about you. I'm sorry for calling you so early in the morning. Go back to sleep. I love you so much."

"And I love you. How are you feeling? Is Trudy there with you? Honey, if she's not there, I'm on a plane in a second. There's no way you need to be alone, baby. Your pregnancy is a risk. I'm coming home now. After you give birth, then I can resume the trial. It's not easy being away from you. I miss you so much."

The tears fell because I missed Jasper so much. "Trudy is here, baby, sleeping like a baby as usual. I'm okay, Jasper. I love you to death, baby. We overcame so many obstacles to be together. I don't want anything to jeopardize our happiness in any form or fashion. I love you so much."

"Honey, please don't stress yourself out about our obstacles. We're married, and it's been almost six years. Our families disowned us because of our marriage, but we have each other and that's all we need. God is our source and He bought us together, forever. I love you."

"I know honey. I just thought my parents, or two siblings would be calling me by now. I'm about to give birth, and I'm forty. Why is color such an issue? I fell in love with a white man and my family hates me because of it. Trudy is my only friend."

"Baby, please don't stress yourself out. The baby is counting on you to stay calm. We went through sacrifices to be together and to have this baby because of the true and deep love we share. Have faith in God because He's our blessing."

I wiped my tears. "I should let you sleep, Jasper. Please be careful, and hurry home soon. I want you to be present when our baby is born. I want to look down in that tiny face and see your gorgeous green eyes. I'm so big and about to burst any minute. I love you."

"And I love you," he declared. "Our baby will have your gorgeous genes, hair and kindness. I remember when we met at the court house. I was running to get to court, and you were also running. We clashed right into each other and fell. It was so funny to me. I looked into your eyes and I just knew. I didn't see your color, but your beauty, inside and out."

I laughed. "You asked me out, and I rejected you so coldly, but you just persisted. When you showed up at my fashion show, I almost fell off the runway. I knew you were the one for me because I was on the runway, and I was a pro. When you unbalanced me, I knew I had finally found my soul mate," I cried.

"Vice versa," Jasper exclaimed. "I love hearing your sexy voice. Sometimes, I wake up and think this was all a dream. I prayed to God to give me a wife who loves me, and I love her. We both love each other unconditionally. I didn't specify color, of course. I didn't care."

"The same performance with me too," I cried. "I didn't ask my mate to be black. I just wanted someone who was my soul mate. I needed someone who treasured me in more ways than one. I understand your concept because I think I'm dreaming too."

"This is a definitely a reality check and remember faith will keep us alive and together. I'll always be with you, Catherine. Even when death overtakes me, I'll come back to you in spirit. I love you."

"I'll die with you," I cried. "Our baby is going to be very special, Jasper, always secure in the love of two parents. We'll have to be there for our child because of this still biased world. It's not going to be easy at all."

"God will guide us through on every level. Now you get some rest, and I'll be home very soon. Remember, I love you, and make sure Trudy takes care of you. Right now she's the only family we have."

"I'm sleepy now, baby. Thanks for everything, Jasper. I love you so much, and I'm so blessed to have had you in my life for five years. I look forward to the sixty more years with you.

"Me too," he cried. "I'm going to call you before court at ten. Promise me you're going to get some rest and be careful. I don't want anything happening to you. You're my solid rock, and without you, I'm nothing."

"Me either, baby." I hung up the phone as my tears blinded me to heaven. They were tears of joy all over the universe. I was the luckiest woman in the world to be with such a kind and loving man. Life was perfect.

Two days later I woke up with a sharp pain. I couldn't be in labor because I wanted my husband to be with me.

Trudy ran into the room. "What is it? I thought I was dreaming, but when I heard you cry out again, I knew this was reality in a nutshell. Where is your bag? I need to call your doctor. What am I going to do here? Where is your husband? What is going on here?"

I waited for the pain to ease, breathing a sigh of relief. "Will you get a grip," I snapped. "I'm not in labor, but you should call Dr. Hayes just in case. It was a few sharp pains, but they stopped. I just don't know."

"Where is your doctor's number?" Trudy replied. "I hope I don't have to deliver your baby because you're going to be in big trouble. I should call your husband. He needs to be here with you. Why would he go to New York City when his wife is nine months pregnant? Where is your mother?"

"Trudy, please shut up and call my doctor. I thought you were so in control. Snap out of it and give me some support. I'm just going through the final stages before the baby is ready to be born. Are you here with me?"

Trudy stared at me. "Let me take a few deep breaths and then I'll get myself together. I'm very strong and you can depend on me. I'll call your doctor, and we'll get his show on the road. I think we should call Jasper too. The two of you prepared for this moment, so now it's time for me to do the same thing. Whatever!"

The pain hit again and it was so awful I could scream, but I held it in. It was time for me to have my baby. "I think you should call Jasper so he can get a flight out, Trudy. I believe the baby is coming. I wanted to have our child together with Jasper, but things don't always work out the way we plan them, of course."

"I'll get right on it," Trudy said.

I watched her as she reached for her cell phone and then ran into the kitchen. The woman was a basket case, and you'd think she was having the baby instead of me. I prayed everything would be okay.

Trudy ran into the room with her cell phone. "Dr. Hayes is on the telephone. Can you talk to her Catherine? I don't know how to describe your pain and she keeps asking me all of these questions. I don't know what to do. This is madness, and I'll be glad when you have your baby. Please excuse me. I'm going to use the telephone to call your husband."

I smiled as she rose out of the room. I couldn't blame Trudy for being in a panic state. I was losing my mind, but I couldn't stress myself out. I put the cell phone to my ear. "Hi. Dr. Hayes. The pains are very sharp, about five minutes apart. I'll waiting for Jasper to get here before I give birth. It's like pain on the left and right side. It feels like two kicks or something. I don't think I'm in labor just yet, but it feels so strange. What do you think?"

"Let Trudy take you to the hospital so you can be monitored. I'm on my way. Catherine, I don't know if your husband is going to make it, so please don't prolong this blessing. It's not good for your health or the health of the baby."

I knew she was right, but I couldn't let it get to me. I wanted Jasper here and I was going to hold off for as long as I could. "I'll see you at the hospital, Dr. Hayes." I clicked off the phone as another kick happened to my right, and then to my left. This was truly a big baby. The pain ceased and I closed my eyes because I was relieved for the moment. Everything was going to be fine because I had the faith. I believed that God was truly going to take care of me.

"I left Jasper five messages," Trudy stated, walking back into the room. "I also paged him. What did the doctor suggest? I think you need to be in the hospital because you're forty years old and something could go wrong. I can't believe you'd have a baby this late in your life. Anyway, God is good."

"All the time," I cried. "Can you take me to the hospital or should we call a cab or ambulance? Dr. Hayes thinks its best that I am in the hospital so you're so right. Transfer the calls to your cell phone so you'll be able to talk to Jasper when he calls. I don't want you to miss his call. My bag is in the hall closet, ready to go. It's going to be okay, Trudy. I've been healthy my whole life. There's nothing preventing me from having this baby because it's the only one I'm going to have."

Trudy got her act together and drove me to the hospital. I was worried because usually Jasper would call me right back. A feeling came over me as I sat in the back of the car. "Trudy where is the cell phone? I need to call Jasper."

Trudy handed me her phone and I dialed Jasper's number. Another bout of pain hit, and I cried out. The phone kept ringing, and where was Jasper? I listened to five rings, and then his voice mail picked up. "Honey, it's me, please call me as soon as you get this message. I love you so much and I don't want you to worry. Trudy is taking me to the hospital because of the bouts of pain I'm having. I love you, and I'm so worried about you, Jasper. I just had this awful feeling. Please call me." I screamed as another bout of pain hit me. It was time.

"Breathe, the way we learned it," Trudy cried. "I love you so please just pant for me. Practice your breathing exercises. I love you so much, Catherine. Everything will be fine. Jasper is probably in the courtroom. He'll call you back."

I shook my head. "The pain is electrifying, Trudy. I think I'm in labor, and I wanted to save it for Jasper. Did you get the video tape camera? I want you to capture everything on camera for Jasper."

"I will Catherine, but right now you need to focus on giving birth. You're driving me crazy. I never want to give birth because the pain is just too much for me."

I laughed as the pain ceased for the moment. "Having a baby is the most precious gift in the world especially when two married people come together. I don't mean teen-agers having babies, of course. I love Jasper so much I want to give him everything and more. My heart is so full of love for Jasper."

"I know Catherine," Trudy said. "We're almost at the hospital. I never thought you'd find someone as loving as Jasper. I didn't approve at first but now I'm very happy for you. Jasper is loving, handsome, beautiful, special, and very romantic. The two of you are like a fairy tale in the making. I love it."

"Something is wrong with Jasper," I cried. "When I get to the hospital, please keep calling until you reach him. I just have this awful feeling that my husband is in deep trouble," I screamed as the pain continued to wrack me. "I need to push."

"No," Trudy cried. "It's not time." She pulled into the parking lot, and ran inside. Within minutes, two orderlies were assisting me into bed as the pain continued to destroy me. I panted as I prayed that Jasper would be okay. He was just fine.

Five hours later, I couldn't wait any longer. It was time for me to give birth. I stared at Dr. Hayes and Trudy who was stunned beyond words as she held the video camera. I was on my way to bringing a life into the world. Jasper hadn't called so the camera would have to capture this miracle for him. I was in a lot of pain, but Jasper was just fine. My husband would come home to me. Yes he will.

I pushed and pushed, screaming the whole time. A head was apparent as Trudy screamed, and then my crying baby came out. I was so relieved, but only for a moment, when I had to pant again. Another head came out, and I was speechless. Jasper and I had twins. My God I couldn't believe it. I heard the babies cry, so I knew this wasn't a dream. I was staring at my children, blinded by tears of joy. I had a son and a daughter.

I wept as my children stared at me. They were so light-skinned, looking just like their father. They both had black hair on their heads. They were the most beautiful babies in the world.

Trudy had fainted, but she was weeping with joy as she stared at the two babies. "They're so perfect," she cried. "I have two God babies. Did you know?"

"Of course not," I cried. "I think Dr. Hayes knew, but she kept it from us for a reason. I'd have been a basket case. Jasper and I chose Trinity for a girl and Matthew for a boy so meet Trinity and Matthew, Godmother."

"It's a pleasure," Trudy cried. "My cell phone is vibrating so let me go into the hall and take it. I'm hoping its Jasper. He's going to get the shock of his life. I'm still in shock myself, Trudy cried. "Now I have to go out and buy more things for the babies. I'm the happiest woman in the world.

I smiled at her, and then my children. Ten minutes later the babies were with the nurses, and I was calling Jasper. Why wasn't he answering my calls? I stared at the ceiling. "My husband is fine, God. I know you won't take him away from me. He has two children to meet. Please take care of him and bring him home to me and our children." I closed my eyes because I was so exhausted.

I opened my eyes and looked around the room. Trudy was on her cell phone. I smiled at her. "Is Jasper here? Where are the babies?" I stared at Trudy who had been weeping. "What's wrong? Are the babies okay? I didn't mean to sleep so much, but I'm still exhausted."

Trudy was weeping like a baby as she took my hand. "Catherine I need to tell you something. It's about Jasper and I just don't know where to begin?"

"Is he here?" I cried. "I'm sure he's so excited to see his babies and the shock on his face. Why didn't you wake me? I need to see my husband, Trudy. What were you thinking? We have Trinity and Matthew in our lives now. Are you insane?" I reached for the covers on the bed.

"Don't move because you're still weak," Trudy cried. "Just listen to me. Jasper hasn't returned any of our calls because he couldn't. He was in the courtroom when the defendant's friend bombed it. Jasper didn't make it, Catherine. I'm so sorry, but he didn't survive the explosion. I'm so sorry for you."

I stared at Trudy as if she had just lost her demented mind, and then I smiled at her. "Jasper is alive because I can feel it. We share this bond of love, so I know he's alive. Just get Trinity and Matthew so they won't think I don't love or want them. I need to spend time with my babies. I love you, Trudy and Jasper is alive. I know he is. Please get me my babies."

I stared after her and then I turned on the news. Every station was broadcasting the explosion in New York City. I watched the chaos feeling sorry for the hurt and dead. It wasn't me, so I had nothing to fear because it wasn't Jasper. He wasn't there. I smiled because Jasper would be home to his family soon.

I turned off the television as Nurse Helen and Trudy walked in with my children. They were so beautiful as I took them both in my arms. They smiled as I kissed them. "I'm your mommy and I love you both very much. Your daddy couldn't be here with you both, but he's on his way. He used to talk to you two all the time. Who knew we were having twins. I love you both, and your daddy loves you too. You two are in the midst of true love between two people. Our love is pure, spiritual, and true. I know Jasper will be coming home to us."

I reached for a bottle because I couldn't breast feed and began feeding Trinity. In tears, Trudy reached for Matthew, and began feeding him. He suckled hungrily. I smiled because they looked just like their father. He was going to be so proud of his children. I wept because I was just so happy. Trudy continued to weep.

The next day was a gorgeous sunny day. I stared out the window as my children slept. I was getting some of my strength back. Dr. Hayes wanted me to get out of bed to practice my walking and the normal things. I was still weak, but I was very blessed. God was so good to me and Jasper. I was very disappointed that my family or Jasper's didn't come to see the babies. Trudy called them both to give them the news, but so far it was just me and Trudy.

Some of my friends called, but God, Jasper and Trudy were my only friends. I really didn't need anyone else. I just wanted to hold my husband in my arms and give him a precious gift of twins. I was so happy.

The door opened and Trudy walked into the room. "I think we need to make funeral arrangements for Jasper, Catherine. I have his personal effects."

I motioned for her to join me outside the hospital room because I didn't want to wake the children. When the door closed I was livid with rage. "I will not make any kind of arrangements because my husband is alive," I snapped. "It's out of the question, and don't you dare tell anyone about this. I need you to keep the faith because it's all I have going for me. The most beautiful quality of Jasper was his faith in God. He believed and had no doubts. It was what attracted me to him. I knew with our faith in God, the two of us could move mountains together.

"It's difficult not sharing with my family, but they are missing out on my wonderful life. I have two beautiful children to present to my husband, and he'll move mountains to get here. Do you hear me?"

"I do understand, Catherine, but there was an explosion. Ten people are badly injured, and three lost their lives. Jasper was one of the three. I'm so sorry, but if you don't make any arrangements his family will, and excludes you. I love you so much and I had faith too. I believed God would save Daniel, but he died in my arms. My husband of fifteen years died. I prayed like I never prayed before. He died," she cried. "My husband is dead."

"I miss Daniel too, but there are some things we can't deal with or explain. Daniel had lung cancer because he smoked since he was fourteen years old. We tried getting him to stop and he did for two years, but his lungs were burned because of his smoking. He chose to smoke, so this isn't God's fault, Trudy. God lets us live our lives, with mistakes and all. He didn't put a cigarette in Daniel's mouth.

"I remember Daniel telling me just before he died to keep an eye on you, and help you find new love because you had so much passion inside of you. He said that it was his own fault for leaving you. Cigarettes were more important. He hoped that you'd forgive him because he was addicted, and he couldn't stop. He loved you more than anything, Trudy, and it was okay because God was calling him home and he was ready. He had seen the light, and it was the most beautiful light in the world. It was time for him to go through it, and he'll always be in your heart and soul. You can always talk to him because he'll be there. Daniel loved God, and he wanted you to love Him too."

Trudy crumbled to the floor and wept. I winced as I joined her on the floor, and took her into my arms. We wept together for Daniel who was only 45 and had his entire life ahead of him. It was such a tragic waste of a good man. He was so wonderful.

Trudy was so blessed to have had all those years with Daniel. I was just sorry for the two of them not being able to have children. It'd have been so wonderful to have a son or daughter looking like Daniel and Trudy.

I passed the next three hours by sleeping and feeding my children. I was exhausted and sleep was a pleasure to me. I opened my eyes and watched quietly as Jasper sat in the chair feeding his children with an innate flair. I wasn't really shocked because I knew my husband would come back to me.

Their little eyes stared up at him. I hoped they could see well enough to recognize their father. Jasper was weeping like a baby. I smiled as I slowly eased out of the bed. Jasper looked up and smiled at me. "You're a sleepy woman, but that's okay because you bought these two babies in my life. I didn't know we were having twins. I thought the nurse was playing with me. I'm so sorry I missed this blessed event. I love you so much," he cried. "I love you."

I kissed his lips. "What about the explosion, honey?" Our lips met in a very passionate kiss. I wept because I was so glad to see my husband. "Thank you God for bringing my husband home to me and our children."

"I signed the birth certificates," Jasper said. "I was in tears when I did it. The nurse said that Matthew was my shadow, and Trinity had my eyes. They're not green, but very light, like a light hazel or yellow. Honey, we have two children, a boy and a girl. Did you know?"

"I really didn't," I cried. "Dr. Hayes didn't want to hurt me by giving me the news for health reasons. I do understand where she's coming from. I'd have been a basket case. This was the best for us both. Now we have two healthy babies."

I reached for Matthew who smiled at me, and then closed his hazel light eyes. He was so precious. The tears fell as I watched him sleep. "He's so tiny," I cried, "and he's the first born by three minutes. They didn't wait to come out in this world. We have to protect them Jasper. I love you so much."

"I love you too," Jasper replied. "Should you be out of bed? I'm sure the birth couldn't have been that easy for you. Get back into bed so I can join you. The twins are sleeping now. I have to take care of my beautiful wife. No one has ever given me such a precious gift before. I'm going to treasure you for the rest of our lives. You're my gift, Catherine. I love you."

The tears were falling now as the children slept in their little bassinets and I got back into bed. I was still exhausted.

Jasper joined me in bed and we hugged and kissed each other. His lips were like firecrackers of love on my lips. The explosion of happiness and thrills were hot to my being, and we were only kissing. It was good to be in his arms, and kiss the love of my life.

Our kiss ended as our eyes met. I melted into his green eyes, and he melted into my hazel brown eyes. I loved his eyes. "What happened at the court house? Trudy was sure that you were dead and gone, but I never gave up hope. I believed you were still alive because of the feelings we shared. I'd know if you were dead."

Jasper touched my face, circling my nose and mouth with his hands. "You're so beautiful, Catherine. I love you so much. In the courtroom the defendant didn't believe he'd be acquitted, so he took matters into his own hands and bombed the place, escaping, but getting shot in the leg. I was thrown out the door, and was out cold for hours until someone found me in the debris. I was in the hospital for a few hours and then I left getting the next flight back to Chicago. I missed all of Trudy's messages because my phone was at the hotel. I'm so sorry I missed the birth."

"I'm just glad you're alive," I cried. "I couldn't imagine my life without you in it. I love you so much, baby. I knew you wouldn't leave me so soon. We have two beautiful children to raise, and they need two parents in love with each other. I'm so tired, but I'm so full of energy all over the place. I could run a marathon. Our lips met, and we snuggled up in each other arms and slept for the duration.

Faith was definitely a good thing. Jasper and I had each other and our children. That was the bottom line. We were a family and we didn't need anyone else. All we needed was God, and each other, not to mention FAITH.

www.ingramcontent.com/pod-product-compliance
Lightning Source LLC
Chambersburg PA
CBHW031958060726
47497CB00015B/307